W9-AGY-525

Also by Alexandra Joel

*The Paris Model*

# The Royal Correspondent

## ALEXANDRA JOEL

HARPER

*An Imprint of HarperCollinsPublishers*

Originally published in Australia in 2021 by HarperCollins Publishers Australia.

HarperCollins books may be purchased for educational, business, or sales promotional use. For information, please email the Special Markets Department at SPsales@harpercollins.com.

FIRST US EDITION

Library of Congress Cataloging-in-Publication Data has been applied for.

ISBN 978-0-06-311280-3 (pbk.)
ISBN 978-0-06-314304-3 (library edition)

21 22 23 24 25  LSC  10 9 8 7 6 5 4 3 2 1

*To my father,*
*the Hon. Sir Asher Joel, AO KBE*
*(1912–98)*

*An Enmore boy*

**Men don't like hard-case girl reporters.**
*The Journalist's Craft,*
Lindsay Revill and Colin Roderick (eds), 1965


**Act boldly.**
Dorothea Brande,
journalist, editor, and author, 1936

# PROLOGUE

## *London, May 4, 1960*

She gazed into the night from the limousine's window, her heart beating quickly. An immense gray stone wall loomed before her. At its center was the legendary balcony she'd viewed in countless newsreels featuring waving members of the world's most famous family. But this was real life, and she was about to breach Buckingham Palace, the official residence of Her Majesty, Elizabeth the Second, Queen of the United Kingdom and Her Realms and Territories.

Leaning forward, she saw a uniformed policeman check the official crested card propped on top of the dashboard, then wave the sleek car through a pair of open gates, their gold-tipped metal railings glistening like spears in the bright beam of a brace of lights. She wished she could stop time, or at least that the chauffeur would slow the limousine, for she wanted to savor every moment of this extraordinary evening. But the car purred on, past Grenadier Guards, still as waxwork models in their red coats and improbably tall black bearskin hats, then glided beneath an archway before drawing to a halt in a large inner courtyard.

With a quiver of excitement, she gathered the billowing skirts of her ice-blue chiffon ball gown as a footman wearing a scarlet and gold coat, black stockings, and knee breeches sprang forward and opened the car door. After following the directions of several other similarly attired attendants, she made her way toward a marble staircase adorned with a wide ribbon of rich ruby carpet. Pausing, she steadied herself, placed one white-gloved hand on the gilt balustrade and, with what she hoped might be taken for the poise of a princess, swept up the stairs.

Another liveried servant clad in eighteenth-century dress met her at the entrance to the ballroom. "Good evening," he said with a polite half bow. "Are you quite ready, ma'am?"

She straightened her bare, lightly tanned shoulders. "Ready as I'll ever be."

Having first glanced briefly at the embossed introduction card, the man announced her in a booming voice. "Miss Blaise Hill!"

Only then did her stomach begin to flutter. Who was Blaise Hill? An intruder, about to push her way into a place where she had no right to be. *Get a grip, Blaisey*, she told herself as she entered a room of astonishing grandeur.

Using the skills that were by now second nature, she began to methodically observe the details of the sumptuous decor and the appearance of the guests—after all, despite her crystal earrings and exquisite gown, she had not come to Buckingham Palace this evening to be entertained, but to work. Her eyes flickered up to the soaring gold and white ceiling from which hung six great chandeliers topped by shimmering cut-glass crowns. She noted the profusion of crimson roses spilling from classical urns, the velvet-draped triumphal arch framed by a pair of winged sphinxes, the gilded organ, the fluted columns, the ornate paneled walls.

Women in sparkling tiaras and jewel-colored ball gowns strolled by on the arms of debonair men sporting white bow ties and black tailcoats, their images multiplied by the mirrored doors. Some of the guests sipped champagne, others chatted together with the easy familiarity of old friends. The hum of their conversations mingled with the sound of lilting music; there was the occasional exuberant exclamation or peal of laughter.

Suddenly, Blaise's earlier discomfort returned. The glamorous people, the opulent surroundings—all were foreign, entirely beyond her own experience. What would Her Majesty's guests think if they knew who she really was: not merely an upstart colonial reporter but a girl with a dire secret buried in her past?

She took a deep breath. As if by magic, the advice she'd been given long before she left Australia floated into her head. *You've got to back yourself,* the man had said. Well then, if she wanted to make her mark in this glittering new world, she'd damn well have to do so.

# PART ONE

## Commoner

# CHAPTER ONE

## *Sydney, January 1957*

Blaise pushed open the faded yellow front door. The house at 68 Fotheringham Street, Enmore, was the last in a row of five dilapidated single-story terraces, each one beset by cracked window frames, peeling paint, and walls that listed at unintended angles.

Once inside she winced, unlaced her worn brown shoes, then pulled them off and rubbed her burning toes. "New shoes," she murmured, pursing her lips. "If only."

Carrying the offending footwear in one hand, Blaise shuffled down the side corridor in threadbare socks. To her right was a cramped space containing a blond wood-veneer lounge chair, slightly scratched. She'd always found it curious that her parents called this room the parlor. Surely such an old-fashioned term had no place in a world of fast cars, automatic washing machines, and television sets—not that the Hill family possessed any of those trophies of modern affluence. They didn't even have an indoor toilet.

As Blaise passed her parents' bedroom she glanced at the broken light fixture dangling precariously from a ceiling rose above the familiar patchwork quilt. She paused outside her own room— although it had never been hers alone. Until last year, she'd had to share it with her sister, Ivy. Blaise sighed. The younger girl's absence brought with it a pang of desolation. Though they'd once been a source of irritation, now she yearned for Ivy's chatter and even mourned her clutter. The jumble of rumpled clothes, hair ribbons, and stray socks, the stubby pencils and the drawings that lay about like scattered leaves had vanished, replaced by an unnatural, sterile order.

With a sudden surge of frustration she flung her shoes onto the bedroom floor where they landed with a clatter. "I'm home!" she shouted.

"Of course you are—who else would make such a racket?" Maude Hill poked her head around the kitchen door. "Come in and I'll make you a cuppa."

Maude and Blaise shared the same pert nose, heart-shaped face, and abundant chestnut hair, but there the resemblance ended. Unlike her petite, dark-eyed mother, Blaise was tall and had her father's blue eyes. Hers were as bright and clear as an Australian summer sky, although Harry's failing vision and hard life had by now leached most of the color from his eyes.

She noted her mother's blotchy, swollen face with dismay. "You've been crying again, Mum. Is it Ivy?" she asked gently.

Maude busied herself with the kettle.

"It's no good giving me the silent treatment. What's going on?"

Her mother struck a match and lit the gas. "She's coming home."

"But that's wonderful!"

"Have you forgotten what your sister's been through?"

Blaise felt her throat constrict. How could she ever forget the sight of Ivy encased in that iron lung, her small head with its newly cropped raven hair the sole part of her remaining visible? Blaise had thought Ivy would be trapped inside the metal coffin forever.

"Of course not," she protested. "But it's all behind us now—unless there's something you haven't told me."

Maude poured boiling water into the old brown china teapot. "It's the bad leg the polio has left Ivy with. She's going to need a lot of special exercise sessions." Her mother's bottom lip trembled. "Expensive ones."

"And if she doesn't get them?"

"The caliper they've given her will be useless. Her tendons will shorten and she . . . she might not be able to walk, even with those horrible metal bars strapped to her leg." Despite her unsteady hands, Maude managed to pour a cup of tea for Blaise and one for herself before setting the teapot down on the scarred wooden table.

"I don't know what we'll do," she said dolefully. "Even with the overtime your father's been putting in, we'll never be able to afford the physio . . . therapy." The hesitant way Maude sounded the word out made Blaise realize just how badly her mother was affected by this new calamity.

"Don't worry, Mum." She leaned across the table. "Once my Leaving Certificate results come out next week, I'll be after a good job. Then I can pay for Ivy's treatment myself."

The next morning, a Saturday, Blaise watched her father eat toast and drink a cup of tea, the mauve shadows beneath his eyes signaling his exhaustion. She'd heard the front door slam at midnight, followed by the sound of his feet plodding across the floorboards.

"Any plans today, Dad?" she asked casually.

"Let's take a walk, love."

"A walk . . . where to?" Blaise looked at him, her eyebrows raised. Harry was an orderly: after spending his days and half his nights pushing beds up and down hospital corridors, walking was the last activity he would normally suggest.

"Just round the neighborhood. Your mother thinks we need a talk about your future."

The two ambled down Fotheringham Street, smiling at Mrs. Gibson, who was sitting, as usual, in a lopsided armchair on number 62's tiny veranda, before passing the rusted bathtub old Artie Crawford from the boarding house on the corner had left on the uneven pavement weeks before. Discarded bits and pieces—collapsed tires, ragged carpet ends, broken prams, withered lengths of garden hose—seemed to accumulate in rickety cairns on the street's footpaths almost of their own accord. There they would lie, ignored for months until, once or twice a year, the entire decaying lot would be heaved onto a sanitation truck by the local garbage men and the same process would begin again.

"Well?" Harry asked when they reached the dusty tram yard. "What kind of job are you after? We only let you stay on the extra two years at school because after you won that essay prize your teacher—Miss Trent, wasn't it?—pestered us so much. She said you had potential, but . . ." He shrugged. "We're really struggling, Blaisey. Maybe it was a mistake."

They watched as several fawn-and-green-colored carriages were shunted onto a short track with a sharp metallic clang. "Your mum reckons you should go in for the same line as your Aunty Jean," Harry said.

Over Christmas, Jean Rollins, Maude's best friend, who was both Blaise's godmother and a secretary in the state Ministry for Health, had shown her how to memorize the keys on the Adler Universal typewriter she kept at home in her Stanmore flat.

"Jean said the pay's not much," Blaise said dismissively.

"She's got security." Harry folded his arms. "The public service is good like that."

Blaise rolled her eyes. "Only if you're a man—or stay single like Jean. She told me women hardly ever get promoted and, anyway, there's a rule. Once a girl gets married they chuck her out."

Blaise waited while a tram rattled by. "I want a job that will do more than pay for Ivy's treatment," she said earnestly. "I'm looking for something that will take me far, maybe to the very top. Then you and Mum and Ivy can live in a nice house, away from this . . . well, you've got to admit, people call it a slum."

"It's harder than you think to get a decent job, even tougher if you're a woman," Harry said. "I can't see as how you'll ever get what you want—unless of course you catch the eye of some rich chap."

Blaise threw up her hands. "I'll be making my own money, thanks."

Harry drew his sparse brows together. "Well, you know what they say around here. The only way a bloke from this part of town moves up in the world is by getting himself into one of the four Ps."

"I know, I know. Priest, pugilist, police, or press," Blaise huffed. "You've been telling me for long enough!"

"You're always so damned quick to fly off the handle," Harry protested. "You won't get anywhere if you don't learn to keep a lid on it."

"Sorry, Dad." Another tram clattered past. "I'm not exactly eligible to be a priest or a pro boxer."

"The police could be an option. Ted O'Rourke's a success— he's a superintendent now in Homicide, or is it Vice? One of them, anyhow."

Blaise groaned. "Are you kidding? I'd just be stuck telling schoolkids how to cross the road—I can't see them putting a woman in a decent squad."

Harry looked at his daughter, a speculative expression on his lined face. "I know you, Blaise Hill. It sounds to me like you've already got your eye on something."

Blaise broke into a grin. "I want to be a reporter. I reckon there's a lot of important stuff going on around here that never finds its way into the newspapers, so I bet it's the same in other places. I've been practicing by myself, trying to write stories about—"

"About what?" Harry looked surprised.

"I don't know, little things—anything from that break-in at the corner shop where I've been working, to what it's like for the new Greek family in the next street to make a home in Australia."

Harry rubbed his chin. "Blaisey, that's all very well, but do they even have women employed in the newspaper game?"

"Miss Trent said there's a few. Her brother, Tommy, is a re- porter at *The Clarion*. She thinks I should try my luck there. And guess what else she told me?" Blaise's eyes shone. "Journalism is the only profession where women aren't stuck with earning three-quarters of a man's wage—or less. There's a really old court ruling that makes the bosses pay everyone the same."

"And has Miss Trent said anything about *The Clarry* actually having a job for you?"

"Not exactly," Blaise admitted. "But she promised she'd ask her brother to put in a good word where it counted."

"I don't know, love." Harry frowned. "If you ask me, it sounds like a long shot."

# CHAPTER TWO

Despite a few half-open windows, a thick pall of tobacco smoke hung defiantly over the large room. It seemed as if everyone, from callow youths to grizzled older men, had a cigarette either clamped in their mouth or jammed between their fingers. On most of the crowded desks there was also a half-finished butt burning steadily in an overflowing ashtray.

"You all right?" asked the tow-headed boy who'd brought Blaise into the newsroom. "The name's Ned, by the way."

"Fine," she croaked. "It's just—does everyone always smoke this much?"

"You stop noticing it after a bit. Same as the noise."

The crash of hundreds of clattering keys, the strident chime the typewriters made when the end of a line was reached, the furious bang that erupted as their carriages were hurled back into place, the incessant ringing of telephones, and the clamor produced by dozens of simultaneous conversations created a wild cacophony.

"They're the reporters." Ned pointed toward the rows of desks behind which sat the men responsible for the din, some in shirtsleeves, others wearing loosened ties and rumpled jackets. "Those blokes are all hungry for just one thing: news, news, and more news. It's like a drug to them."

Suddenly, one of them cried, "Copy!" A boy ran up to him, took a pile of small typed pages in his hand, and darted out of the far door. Then another reporter yelled the same thing and a different boy appeared.

"It's getting close to deadline," Ned volunteered.

The ringing, the talking, the clattering, the shouting, the sheer unremitting sense of urgency that existed within that room made Blaise's pulse race. It was only then she became aware of how much had altered in the space of a few minutes. When Blaise had arrived at *The Clarion* she'd hoped that one day she might become a reporter. But ever since she'd entered that pungent, noisy room filled with taut-faced men, that hope had been transformed into a fierce determination. She *had* to join them.

Blaise watched with mounting excitement as her guide led her through the frenetic scene. When they reached a glass-fronted office in the far corner of the room, he stopped. "This is where I was told to leave you."

Through the glass, Blaise could see a small man with a bristling toothbrush moustache jabbing a pen at the front page of a newspaper. He was half buried behind a huge wooden desk littered with teacups, folders, phone books, and at least two full ashtrays. Blaise looked questioningly at Ned.

"That's the editor," he said.

Edgar McInerney didn't bother with a greeting. "So you want to come on board," was all he offered. "How old are you?"

"I'll be eighteen in June."

"Let's see your results then."

Blaise slid her diploma out of an envelope and silently handed it over, then watched nervously as McInerney put on a pair of horn-rimmed spectacles and scanned the piece of buff-colored paper.

"Your marks are excellent; you'll get no argument from me there," he growled, "and Mr. Trent said you were a good kid. But this is a tough business. From what I see in front of me," he glanced up dismissively, "I don't believe you've got what it takes."

McInerney handed back her certificate. "Sorry. Door's that way." He indicated the direction with a tilt of his graying head.

Blaise stood her ground. "You've got me all wrong, sir," she protested. "I'm keen and I'm smart. Plus, I come from Enmore, a place that makes you tough. I'll work twice as hard as anyone else. All I'm asking for is a chance."

"Girly—"

"The name's Miss Hill. Or Blaise."

"Miss Hill," McInerney said.

Blaise couldn't tell if the expression on his face was a grimace or if he was actually trying to smother a smile. Maybe he just couldn't believe that a girl like her, standing there in her laced-up school shoes, would dare to answer him back. She could hardly believe it herself.

"So you reckon you have what it takes to be a reporter, do you?" he said, scratching an ear. "You can't just waltz into a job like that, you know. There's a cadetship you've got to pass through first—takes years. And what happens if, after all the training we give you, all the time we spend showing you the ropes so that you finally have a vague idea of how to knock up a half-decent story, you go off with some bloke and get married, eh? What happens then?" McInerney banged his fist on the desk with such force that the teacups rattled. "It'll all go down the drain."

"No, it won't." Blaise's voice was firm. "Until my sister got sick with polio, my mother spent her time scrubbing other people's floors. All my life I've seen women like her struggling just to make ends meet. They have horrible jobs in factories or sweatshops because they're not educated, or can't speak English well enough. Sometimes it seems like it's just because they're women and no one will give them a break—pretty often, it's their own husbands holding them back."

"What, you don't believe a woman's place is in the home?" McInerney removed his spectacles from the bridge of his nose.

"Maybe, maybe not," she said. "But if what you're asking me is whether I'll let a man stand in my way, the answer's no. All I can tell you is what I'm set on doing, and that's to bring people the news—tell them what's really going on."

To her surprise, Blaise thought she heard the editor mumble something about getting soft in his old age.

"I hope you won't make me regret this," he said.

"You mean, I've got the job?"

"Not so fast. I'll try you out as a copy boy for a while."

"Only I'll be a copy girl, won't I?" Blaise said, beaming.

"There's no such thing around here," McInerney barked. "Take my advice, Miss Hill. If you want to get on in this place, you'd better try to fit in."

# CHAPTER THREE

Smiling broadly, Blaise presented herself to *The Clarion*'s middle-aged receptionist on Monday, January 21, her first day of work. "Hello there," she chirped. "I'm the new copy, uh, boy."

The woman arched one of her heavily penciled eyebrows. "Really?" She sniffed. "You'd better get yourself off to Kev Kennedy, then. He's the intake manager."

Her manner might have been abrupt, but Blaise didn't care. She was beginning a new, exciting life in a job that offered both advancement and, quite possibly, adventure. It was all she could do not to burst into song. Instead, she confined herself to humming Elvis Presley's "Hound Dog" while she tripped down a long corridor and turned into the newsroom.

Once more she was struck by its atmosphere: the noise, the clouds of cigarette smoke, the men at their desks pounding on typewriters, and the boys scooping up pages as soon as the reporters finished typing, then flying off and disappearing.

Where were the boys going? What happened to the pages when they arrived? Still puzzling over the answers to these questions, Blaise tore herself away. She hurried over to a corner office with "K. Kennedy" written in chipped gold letters on its door and an empty wooden bench outside, took a deep breath and knocked.

"Enter!" an angry voice yelled.

Gingerly, Blaise opened the door and walked in. The room was dim, save for a pool of harsh white light cast by a lamp that stood on the single desk. Behind it sat an alarming man possessed of a furious expression and a wandering, bloodshot left eye.

She didn't know where to look—it was impossible to meet the man's wild, lopsided gaze—so she settled for a spot slightly above his balding head. "Mr. Kennedy? I'm Blaise Hill," she said.

"Jesus Christ, I don't believe it!" Kennedy cried, slapping one veiny cheek in a theatrical show of horror. They've actually gone and landed me with a *female*. It's enough to drive a man to drink." Yanking open his drawer, he took out a half-empty bottle of Johnnie Walker whisky and downed two large gulps.

"What sort of a name is Blaise?" Kennedy asked. "I thought you'd be a bloke."

"I think my mother saw it in a magazine," she mumbled.

"Well, it looks as if I'm stuck with you now," her new boss said gloomily. "Which one of the boys brought you in when you did your interview with the editor?"

"It was Ned."

Kennedy leapt to his feet and stuck his head out of the doorway. "Williams!" he roared. "Get your lazy arse in here."

Blaise was relieved to see a familiar face, especially as Ned gave her a surreptitious wink.

"I gather you've already met Hill," Kennedy said. "Show her the lie of the land, will you?"

The boys Blaise had seen rushing about were now perched on the bench outside Kennedy's office. "Tim, Jacko, Fred—this is Blaise Hill," Ned said. Three quizzical faces looked up and muttered greetings.

Ned shoved his hands in his pockets. "All right, all right, I know she's a girl. But from now on she's an honorary bloke, got it?" The boys shrugged in agreement.

He turned to Blaise. "We sit out here while we're waiting to be called. It gives us somewhere we can practice our shorthand in between running around like scalded cats. We're all hoping to be cadets, but it's hard. There are only a couple of us who'll make it."

Blaise peered at the book Fred was balancing on his knees. "Is that shorthand?" she asked, pointing to a page of swirls and lines.

Ned ran one hand through his springy yellow hair. "Yeah, you have to learn it so you can write as fast as people speak. It's horrible, but everyone says eventually you get the hang of it."

"But will I get the hang of Mr. Kennedy?" Blaise said. "I mean, is he always so annoyed?"

A chorus of adolescent voices chimed, "Always."

"No, he's not," Ned chortled. "Sometimes he's worse!"

Blaise glanced over her shoulder. "I saw him take a couple of swigs of whisky."

"That's the reason he got moved over here," Ned said, lowering his voice. "Not that hitting the bottle is exactly unusual around this place. Pretty well all the reporters are big drinkers—goes with the job."

The newsroom buzzed like a frantic hive as Ned led Blaise up and down rows of wooden desks, pointing out one journalist after another. Some of the men nodded, but most were too engrossed in their work to pay her any attention. Miss Trent's brother, Tommy, was the exception. He smiled when they were introduced, saying, "Maureen told me you were starting soon."

Blaise would have liked to thank him for speaking to McInerney on her behalf, but his phone began ringing. "We'll catch up another time," he said, jamming the receiver to his ear.

"Trent is the newspaper's chief political roundsman," Ned explained. "I wouldn't be surprised if it was old Pig Iron Bob himself on the phone."

"You mean Mr. Menzies, the prime minister?" Blaise's eyes widened. "That's impressive."

"Yeah, well, it doesn't seem so special when you work here," Ned said airily. "Follow me—there's a lot more to see."

Blaise squinted in the glare cast by the neon lights in the next room. It was no wonder that most of the dour men who sat around the long oval table wore green or white eyeshades.

"What you see before you," Ned said with a flourish, "are what Mr. McInerney calls the paper's grammatical attack dogs."

"What are they scribbling away at with those blue pencils?" Blaise asked.

A man with thick glasses and a drooping moustache raised his balding head. "My dear, if there's so much as a misplaced comma we will find it. And don't get me started on adverbs," he said, thin-lipped.

Ned took her aside. "They're the subeditors. We shouldn't disturb them." Whispering, he quickly described the way the men corrected copy, cut text to fit the page, oversaw layouts, wrote headlines and worked with the picture editors.

"So this is where the boys bring the little bits of paper they collect from the journalists?" she asked.

"Yeah. Each page contains a single typed paragraph. If the deadline's on top of us we rush them over one at a time."

Blaise watched, intrigued, as the man who'd addressed her began placing some of the corrected pages in a small metal container he then inserted into the mouth of a pipe. With a weird sucking noise, the receptacle vanished from sight. "What on earth just happened?" she asked.

"He sent the copy downstairs to the compositors by pneumatic tube," Ned said. "Come on, I'll show you where it ends up."

Blaise heard the jingling, staccato sound well before she entered the room. Inside, the clamor was even more intense, a little like a hundred sewing machines, if a hundred sewing machines were stitching metal at full pelt.

"What are they doing?" she yelled above the racket. Lines of men were sitting at complicated desk-like contraptions, peering at pinned-up pages of copy, their fingers tapping steadily on giant keyboards.

"Setting type before it's cast."

"Can I pick some up and have a look?"

"Only if you want to start a strike," Ned warned. "There's a strict demarcation between the journos and the compositors. Operating a linotype machine is not an easy trade; the comps won't have a bar of anyone from editorial interfering with their slugs."

"Their *what*?"

"Slugs. That's what they call the lines of type."

Blaise glowed with pleasure. Most people had no idea what went into creating the newspapers they read every day. They simply sat at their kitchen table or on a train, turning the pages in complete ignorance. She, by contrast, was beginning her initiation into a world of arcane knowledge and complicated skills known only to a select few.

"What else is down here?" she asked.

Ned motioned for Blaise to follow him. Her mouth dropped open when she saw the enormous piece of machinery, crouching like a great silver beast in the middle of a cavernous lair. It was equipped with rollers, steel panels, trays, chutes, and long conveyor belts that looped up and down.

"That's the press. Just wait until you see it in action," Ned said. "It's an amazing sight. Oh, and one last tip," he added, pointing to the black-rimmed clock positioned prominently on one of the print-room walls. "We're ruled by the hands on that face. Four editions of *The Clarry* come out every day. The presses start up for the first one at ten o'clock the night before and they don't wait."

"So, no matter what, even if the story is really important, the printers can't delay?"

"Not unless the editor says so, and that only happens once in a blue moon."

As Blaise followed Ned past the inert machinery, she tried to imagine how it would look when it sprang into life. "Is there anything more you're going to show me?" she asked. "Only, it's so much to take in. I don't think I can remember half of what we've already seen."

"No one can. That's why all the journalists will tell you: don't trust your memory. You'll be in trouble if you leave any details out of a story, but it'll be a hell of a lot worse for you if you get them wrong." Ned scratched his head. "The two essential items a reporter always has with him are his notebook and a pencil. It sounds like we'd better get them."

Blaise glared back at the girls who worked in the stationery department, one a shapely brunette, the other a platinum blonde. They'd been looking at her as if she was an unwelcome insect.

The brunette took her time smoothing her tight angora sweater before pushing forward a single-lined notebook and a pencil. "And don't bother coming back until you've covered both sides of the paper and that pencil looks more like a stub," she said.

Blaise had barely left the room when she heard the same girl declare, in a jeering voice she suspected was meant to be overheard, "That one's only interested in *men's* work. Or maybe it's men full stop."

Then a second voice, presumably the blonde's, chipped in. "I wouldn't fancy her chances on either count." She sniggered.

"What's their problem?" Blaise said, scowling as she walked down the corridor.

Ned shrugged. "Those cows are just jealous you've scored a job in news."

"I've been meaning to ask you about that." She cocked her head to one side. "How come every woman I've seen so far does something clerical?"

"Hell, the union would have a fit if a girl tried to be a printer or a comp!"

Blaise stopped. "But Mr. Trent's sister told me there were some female reporters on the paper."

"Oh, you'll meet them," Ned assured her, "only they don't work in the newsroom."

"Where, then?"

"Upstairs, on the fifth floor. They're on the Women's Pages."

"I've never looked at that section much," Blaise said. "What's in it?"

"Let's see." Ned wrinkled his nose. "There's a lot on ladies' fashions, the social pictures of course—they're big—and stuff about visiting royals or movie stars, what they call celebrities."

"And that's all?"

"Pretty much. I don't know, sometimes there are stories about making a cake rise higher or how to match your curtains to your carpet . . ."

"Gawd." Blaise grimaced.

"That's what we all think," Ned said.

# CHAPTER FOUR

Blaise was striding across *The Clarion*'s grand, mahogany-lined foyer on her second day at work when she stopped abruptly, struck by the sight of the three extraordinarily smart women who had just sauntered past. Each wore an eye-catching outfit, immaculate gloves and a noteworthy hat—one had a sort of turban, another a wide-brimmed straw, and the third a tiny veiled confection. When Blaise saw all three were making for the lift she rushed forward and bounded in behind them. "Sorry," she panted, having nearly dislodged the straw hat from the head of a stylish Asian girl in a sophisticated black linen dress.

"No harm done," the girl said as she reached up to straighten the brim.

Blaise breathed in deeply, suddenly aware of a delicious fragrance. The combination of sweet and gently spicy scent was so heady that for a second or two she imagined she was in one of those exotic locations—Casablanca, perhaps—she'd only seen at the movies.

Blaise pushed the brass button marked "4." Then she saw an elegant, black-gloved finger extend and press the next shiny disk. Of course, she thought, as the doors slid smoothly shut. The glamorous strangers with whom she was sharing the newly perfumed elevator must be the ladies of the fifth floor.

"Tell me what they wore today, Blaisey." Even though a month had passed since Blaise started working at the paper, every night Ivy pleaded for another report.

It was late and the two girls were lying on their beds. Blaise rolled over wearily, propped herself up on one elbow and smiled at her sister. With her dark hair, now long again and flowing across the snowy whiteness of the pillow, her chocolate eyes and pale skin, the fifteen-year-old was destined to be a beauty.

Ever since Ivy was a little girl she'd spent her spare time either drawing and painting or else chattering away about her dream of becoming a dancer on stage at the famous Tivoli. Equipped with natural athleticism, good looks and a vivacious personality, she might have had a chance. But then the morning had arrived when she'd complained of a headache and a sore throat. They had all thought it was nothing—a cold, perhaps a touch of flu. Until that night, when the fever came.

Blaise had been woken by her sister's moans, seen the perspiration dripping from her brow. She remembered knocking frantically on her parents' bedroom door in the early hours of the morning. "Ivy's really sick!" she'd cried. Her mother and father had come running, their faces stricken as they heard their youngest daughter gasp for breath.

"Mum," Ivy had whispered hoarsely, "I can't breathe properly. And my legs won't move."

That had been the start of it. She'd been rushed to the nearby Children's Hospital, where Ivy's sentence was pronounced.

"Polio," the white-coated medical specialist had said gravely. "I'm so sorry; we'd all hoped there wouldn't be another epidemic. The disease attacks the central nervous system," he'd explained, "so the patient's muscles can't receive the right signals—that's why Ivy's paralyzed. Hopefully, she'll improve over time, but"—he'd held out his hands in a gesture of weary resignation—"considering how severely she's been affected, I don't believe it's possible for her to escape at least some permanent damage."

Blaise and her parents had wept.

The iron lung had kept Ivy breathing for weeks as her body slowly regained movement. That was a blessing, though she'd returned home six months later with the curse of a withered limb.

Blaise looked tenderly at her sister. With the sheet thrown over her no one would ever suspect that she bore the brutal evidence of her illness. Ivy was still perfect. But her childhood dream had been destroyed.

"Oof!" Blaise's head spun. Her sister had lobbed a pillow over the gap between their beds.

"I'm just making sure you don't go to sleep." Ivy giggled. "At least not until you've told me everything."

"All right, all right, I give in." Blaise held up her hands. "Now, let me see," she said, yawning. "The one with the shiny black hair had on a sleeveless green dress."

"Go on."

"I can't really remember the rest."

"You're supposed to be an eagle-eyed reporter, aren't you? Try harder!"

Blaise screwed up her face, concentrating. "I believe there was a cream suit and, oh that's right, a pink and white checked frock. There was a young blonde girl who wore blue with a wide belt and somebody else was in black—no, I think it might have been a darkish purple." She yawned again. "Sorry, it's been a long day."

"A tough one?" her sister asked.

"You don't want to know."

"But I *do*, Blaisey. When you talk about your work—well, it's as if you bring a whole fantastic world right inside this room."

Just thinking about what had transpired that day made Blaise's stomach churn. Yet sharing her life with Ivy was the least she could do. When she wasn't drawing or painting, Ivy spent most of her time helping round the house—Maude had decreed Ivy was still too fragile to be out and about. "Do you remember when I told you about that bad-tempered fat reporter?" Blaise asked.

"Not Mr. Sawyer?"

"That's the one. He insisted I go down to the compositors—who *never* welcome outsiders—and collect a can of compressed air for my boss." Blaise sighed. "Unfortunately, the only comp who wasn't on his linotype machine was busy banging down a row of slugs into their frame—you remember what they are, don't you?"

"Of course. I think I know just about as much about the paper as you do by now!"

Blaise picked up Ivy's pillow. "Take that, smarty pants," she said, sending it sailing back. "Anyway, when I interrupted this man he muttered"—she adopted a fierce tone—"'Christ, not that again.' I thought he was upset because they were all out of the stuff. You see, his precise words were, 'Bugger off and see if any of the other papers have some.'"

"And did you?"

"Oh yes." Blaise groaned. "I hared around the city for most of the day, but everywhere I went it was the same story."

"So the horrid Mr. Kennedy was angry with you when you came back empty-handed?"

"You could say that, only not for the reason that I thought he'd be." Flinching at the memory, Blaise continued. "First he glared at me. Then he sort of exploded, yelling, 'Bloody compressed air! I can't believe even you are so brainless you'd fall for that. They'll be laughing at you in every newspaper office in town.'"

"I don't get it," Ivy said, frowning. "Why?"

"Because there's no such thing. It was all a huge, ridiculous joke at my expense." Blaise heard a muffled titter. "Oh God, Ivy, not you, too!"

"Well, you have to admit," her sister managed to say between barely suppressed cackles. "It *is* pretty funny."

Blaise tried to look stern but couldn't stop her mouth from twitching. A moment later, both girls were laughing helplessly. Nevertheless, as Blaise drifted off to sleep later that night, she vowed that she would not fall into the same trap again.

Scanning the newsroom, she waited, poised to spring forward as soon as she heard someone call out "Boy!" With a further six weeks' experience behind her, Blaise had begun to feel, if not exactly smug, then at least fairly confident that she had acquired a good understanding of the way a newspaper functioned. When she heard a shout—"Sub needs you, Hill!"—she quickly ran over and presented herself.

"What is it, Mr. Travis?" The man had crinkly brown hair and was on the young side for a subeditor.

"I want you to go to *The Herald* and report to Mr. Halfpenny, their chief sub. Tell him that *The Clarion* requires a row of undotted i's as soon as possible."

Blaise scooted over to the rival paper. As the other copy boys had already filled her in on Halfpenny's fearsome reputation, by the time she reached the editorial floor she'd begun to feel unusually anxious. Telling herself to grow up, she stopped a reporter, who pointed out a thick-set man. Blaise squared her shoulders, marched across to the chief sub and stated her request.

There was a moment's silence, during which time Halfpenny's already florid color deepened to a shade of plum. "Do you mean to tell me," he shouted, "that *The Clarion*'s putting on kids these days who are so dimwitted they don't know when their legs are being pulled? Undotted i's, God help me!"

Twice was enough. Blaise decided she could no longer leave anything to chance. From now on she would keep her wits about her and her guard permanently up.

# CHAPTER FIVE

It was late, ten o'clock on an unusually cold autumn night, when Blaise finally emerged from Newtown station. Her head drooped as she took one tired step after another. Kev Kennedy wasn't pleasant to any of the copy boys, but he took particular delight in tormenting her. Often he assigned tedious extra work just before she was due to finish for the day.

Blaise's fingers still ached from that night's task. Kennedy had told her to "have a look at how the Circulation Department works," which in reality meant spending hours counting the mastheads that the city's newsagents had ripped from the front pages of unsold *Clarions* and returned to the paper. After that, she had to recount each one, hundreds and hundreds of them. Every newsagent who sent back these "overs" was due a refund, all of varying amounts. Kennedy would tear strips off her if she failed to get any of the sums right.

"More fool him," she muttered to herself as she began to make her way home from the station. "If he thinks that will put me off, he has another think coming." All the same, it had smarted on the morning after the first long night she'd spent in Circulation when Kennedy had sneered, "Hill, it doesn't matter how much you try to dazzle me, you're the last one I'd pick for a job here, see?" It was his favorite refrain.

A breeze sprang up, making the straggly gum growing hard against a fence begin to sway and several sheets of paper— newspaper at that—whip the backs of her bare legs. Their sting remained even as a fresh gust whipped the pages away.

Shivering, Blaise increased her pace. She nipped down one of the narrow lanes that ran behind a row of decrepit terrace houses, gripping her black satchel. Not that there was much inside of interest to a potential thief.

Since she'd started work, most of her modest wages had been spent on her sister's therapy. Twice a week Maude took Ivy to see a brisk woman who applied warm compresses, massaged her damaged leg, and demonstrated special exercises, although on a couple of rare days off Blaise had accompanied Ivy to the clinic. Her mother was convinced Ivy was improving, but whenever Blaise tried to help her sister repeat the exercises at home she had to hide her dismay at her painfully slow progress.

"Poor kid," she murmured. Nausea spiraled through her whenever she thought about her sister's affliction. Why had the polio attacked Ivy and not her? Where was the justice?

At least paying for her sister's treatment helped alleviate her sense of guilt. So far, the only money she'd spent on herself was for a new pair of stout lace-up shoes, although even this purchase served as a cruel reminder that, while she was free to run and jump, Ivy's stiff metal caliper and wasted leg meant she could manage little more than an ungainly lopsided walk.

Blaise kicked the empty Coca-Cola bottle lying in her path with a burst of frustration. Life wasn't fair. How satisfying it would be if she could lash out at Kev Kennedy and some of the other equally objectionable members of *The Clarion*'s staff.

She had turned into a deserted side street when she saw a gleaming, black and white finned Cadillac idling just ahead like a predatory shark. Blaise's breath quickened, for an expensive American car was a rarity in this neighborhood. She knew by now that good reporters always kept their eyes peeled for anything unusual—this could be an opportunity to pick up a story, one that might even make an impression on the irascible Kennedy.

Her fatigue forgotten, she stepped into the deep shadow cast by a crumbling wall. Almost immediately, the car's throaty hum fell silent, the door on the driver's side opened and a powerfully built man stepped out. He wore a double-breasted suit, tight around the shoulders, and put on a fedora, pulling its brim forward.

Blaise thought she heard the sound of footsteps, but although she peered into the gloom she couldn't see a soul. The man paused for a moment then gave a low whistle. To her surprise, Blaise recognized the boy who materialized. It was her childhood friend Joe Blackett. They'd been in the same gang of kids that had roamed the streets of the local neighborhood, kicking wizened soccer balls and racing each other down hills in their homemade billycarts. For an instant his red hair blazed, caught in the beam of a nearby street light.

There was just enough illumination to see Joe thrust his hand into the sports bag he had slung over his shoulder and begin passing over bundles of crumpled bank notes. The Cadillac's driver flicked his thumb quickly through each stack, checked that the rubber band securing it was in place, then threw the money into a carton propped up on the front seat of his limousine.

"Nice work, boyo. Here's your cut," he said, peeling off a few notes from the last bundle before tucking them inside Joe's sports bag. Next, he took a cotton sack out of the glove box and placed it in Joe's hand.

Blaise's eyes were wide. There'd been some talk in the newsroom lately about the amount of cocaine finding its way into the city's nightclubs via its grimy inner suburbs, but why on earth would Joe get himself mixed up in something like that?

She fought the urge to yell at Joe, to make him drop the bag and run away. The big man had a brutal look—anything she did was likely to make the situation worse.

Joe took a step back and held out the sack. "No, Mr. Ryan, not this time," he said. "It don't feel right."

Blaise stifled a gasp. She'd heard of the Ryans. They were notorious gangsters.

"I've done what I said I would," Joe continued. "I only agreed to deliver the drugs because you said you'd get off Dad's back.

Now, call off your standover men and let him run his tobacco shop in peace. I'm out."

"Not so fast, you little shit." The man slid one hand into his jacket. "Since when do you get to say what you will or won't be doing?"

"Since now." Joe's show of bravado was betrayed by the tremor in his voice. "Superintendent O'Rourke's from around here. If you don't leave us alone, I'll tell him what you've been up to."

The man's voice was filled with menace. "Now that's where you'd have a problem. Me and my brother have what you'd call a warm understanding with the super and his boys. All the same, don't go getting any dumb ideas. Your dad's business might not be able to carry on if he's hurt badly enough."

"You bastard!" Joe cried. The sack of cocaine dropped to the ground and the sports bag went flying as he swung at Ryan.

Blaise froze. She saw the glint of a gold watch on the big man's wrist as he thrust his arm forward, the gleam of the knife he gripped in his hand. Joe sprang sideways, but Ryan went for him. It took only seconds for the boy to be trapped in a headlock and shoved up against the car's polished duco. "Like to guess what I'm going to do with you?" Ryan said, his voice heavy with intimidation.

Joe howled and struggled wildly, his feet kicking out and his arms flailing. Somehow, he wrenched himself free, but Ryan wasn't giving up. With a roar, he launched himself at his prey.

Blaise glimpsed the desperate expression on Joe's face as he grabbed Ryan's wrist. Suddenly, Joe twisted to the left, the steel blade flashed and Ryan's fedora toppled from his head. The man slumped forward with a long, ragged sigh, before collapsing onto the pavement.

Blaise reeled back, breathing hard. She could see Joe, white-faced and motionless, standing over Ryan.

"Joe, it's Blaise," she called out from the shadows. Even after she'd emerged he barely noticed her but remained gazing in disbelief at the knife in his hand, then at the stream of blood trickling from Ryan's left side.

Blaise's mind was whirling. Perhaps the wound had not been deadly. Maybe the man could be saved. Yet when she forced herself to kneel down and look into his eyes she had no doubts. They stared straight ahead, glazed and empty.

"Listen to me," she said, clutching Joe's arm. "You've got to get away. Only, first, give me the knife."

He didn't move. She released her grip, took a handkerchief out of her bag and covered her hand with it. Next, she prised open Joe's fingers, removed the knife, wrapped it in her handkerchief and automatically shoved it into her satchel.

"Joe!" she said urgently. Once again, he failed to respond. She slapped his cheek hard.

"Jesus, Blaise—"

"Take your sports bag and that sack of coke and go home," she said. "When you get there, make sure you wash yourself right away and your clothes, too. And while you're at it, chuck the drugs down the toilet and give it an extra flush. If anyone asks where you've been, just say you walked me back from the station. Make out you're keen on me or something. Then, if the cops come around asking questions, I can back you up."

Joe looked confused.

"You idiot, don't you see?" she hissed. "I'm your alibi." She gave the boy a push. "Now go!"

# CHAPTER SIX

The next morning Blaise wondered if the garish images that appeared each time she shut her eyes during the long night had been just shocking dreams. Surely she hadn't really seen that criminal with Joe, or the bundles of crumpled bank notes? It was impossible to believe she'd watched a man die as a vivid pool of blood spread around him like a crimson cloak.

"You all right, Blaisey?" Ivy asked. "You look awfully pale."

"Just tired, that's all," she answered, attempting a smile.

Blaise steeled herself to maintain her usual routine. She couldn't stomach breakfast, but she washed her face, put on a skirt and took a fresh blouse from its hanger. Yet these simple acts did nothing to stem her growing horror. The nightmare was real. Even worse was her gut-wrenching realization that, although Ryan might have been an evil man, a life was still a life and she'd done nothing to stop the deadly fight.

Feeling numb, she mechanically cut up a tomato, buttered bread, found a slice of limp pink Devon in the wheezing refrigerator. Having wrapped her sandwich in greaseproof paper, she threw it into her satchel and, with her heart in her throat, started off for work.

Tension wound its way through her like a gyre as she headed for the copy boys' bench. She reminded herself that all was well; she simply needed to carry on as she normally did. The newsroom was roiling like the belly of a hungry wolf. There would be plenty to keep her occupied. A big car accident had occurred on the Hume Highway in the early hours of the morning and the federal budget was due to be announced in just three days. But the story every journalist seemed to be talking about was neither the accident nor the budget. As she scooped up copy from the busy reporters she was conscious only of feverish speculation about the identity of the murdered man who'd been discovered in Enmore the previous evening, who the killer was—and whether he'd had an accomplice.

Her heart beat furiously. She wondered if she was attracting more attention than was usual. Had Sawyer given her a knowing look? Had one or two of the journalists mentioned her by name? Was it possible a witness had emerged, that already news was leaking out that she'd been present at the scene?

Blaise fled to the ladies' washroom and stared at herself in the mirror. This was ludicrous. No one would ever suspect that a fresh-faced girl like her was connected to the death of a drug dealer. In any case, there was not a thing that linked her to the crime. She should settle down, get on with her job and stop imagining things.

Mercifully, she barely had time to draw breath until after two o'clock. Only then did she become aware of her urgent need to slow down and think, preferably somewhere quiet where she wouldn't be seen. She extricated her satchel from underneath the bench, slipped out of the newsroom and took the fire-escape stairs down to the second floor. That was the location of *The Clarion's* musty cuttings library—otherwise known as the morgue. Under the circumstances, the term had an unpleasant resonance.

Tiptoeing silently inside, she took a quick look around then settled into a threadbare armchair that had been abandoned behind a couple of filing cabinets. Suddenly ravenous, she remembered her sandwich. She plunged her hand inside her bag, but instead of finding a parcel wrapped in greaseproof paper, she felt her handkerchief—and something else inside. She took it out, then stared. The bit of stained cloth was wrapped around the bloody knife that had killed a man.

Hot, sour bile scalded her throat as she realized what had happened. While she'd been concentrating on getting Joe out of trouble, she'd failed to focus on her own actions.

Blaise let out an involuntary moan. The horror of Ryan's death must have affected her more than she'd thought. She'd obviously been so shocked and confused that she'd put the murder weapon into her satchel without thinking. The fact the knife had been sitting there all through the night, and that—even worse—she'd actually brought the ghastly thing to work, hadn't once entered her mind.

Blaise was appalled. She imagined policemen bursting into *The Clarion*, dragging her away in handcuffs. Ivy's future would be grim and the shame—it would kill her parents. Under normal circumstances, Joe could plead self-defense. At least he'd be able to explain about the threats against his father. But if Superintendent O'Rourke and his men were in the Ryans' back pocket, Joe was more than likely to be up for murder and she'd be facing an accessory charge.

After stuffing the incriminating evidence back into her satchel, she concentrated on steadying her nerves. The items must be made to disappear, but first she needed a good excuse for exiting *The Clarion*—preferably one that wouldn't get her fired.

As if on cue, Blaise heard Kennedy's voice. "D'you know if the copsh have identified that body they picked up in Enmore?" He'd clearly topped up his whisky overgenerously during lunch.

"Turns out it was Theo Ryan's little brother, Paddy." That was Mike Morton, the police roundsman; he and Kennedy were mates. "Looks like illegal gambling's not enough for the Ryan family these days. From what I hear, the murder was connected to a drug deal that went wrong."

"Christ!" Kennedy muttered. The news seemed to have had a sobering effect. "I never thought a vicious killer like Paddy would be bumped off. I wonder how they did it."

"Stabbed him," Morton said, "though Homicide haven't found the weapon."

"That's hardly a surprise. Have they identified the assailant?"

"Not yet. But the detectives tell me they're expecting to make an arrest any day—that's if Theo doesn't get to him first."

Blaise began to shake. She had to get rid of that knife.

When he wasn't hurling abuse, Kennedy spent the afternoon giving orders to the copy boys, Blaise included. With no opportunity to leave, she answered telephones, collected stories, fetched documents, pictures, typewriter ribbons and cups of tea, all the time feeling increasingly distraught. Worry gnawed at her constantly. It was impossible to concentrate.

"You away with the fairies today, Hill?" Kennedy shouted.

Blaise looked at him vacantly.

"You only forgot to tell the comps they shouldn't set that budget preview yet. The chief sub's furious—he told you himself the Treasury leak meant that copy had to be replaced."

She hung her head. This was a horrendous mistake.

"We got it sorted just in time, no thanks to you," Kennedy grumbled. He looked at her with a mixture of speculation and contempt. "I can see something's on your mind. Well, I only hope for your sake you haven't gone gaga over some fella. God only knows what anyone would see in you. You're a bloody disgrace!"

Blaise felt sick. As a rule, Kev Kennedy's belittlement didn't bother her. It had become like radio static: irritating but, due to its very ubiquity, without the power to penetrate. This time, though, his jibe hit home. She had to pull herself together. Now was not the time to attract unwanted attention, not after last night.

"Go down and find out if the report on the highway smash is underway. And for God's sake, keep your mind on the job," Kennedy instructed.

When Blaise reached the comps' room she had to dig her fingernails into the palms of her hands to stop them from shaking. Nobody who worked there ever did anything but make her life difficult. Mostly, they drew attention to the deficiencies of her figure, gleefully comparing her with the busty pin-ups stuck on the walls. As she walked toward the rows of men operating the linotype machines, she hoped today of all days would be different.

"Hey, Hill!" Ted, a greasy-haired printer in a knee-length, ink-spattered apron, called out from across the room. "Guess what one tiny tit said to the other?"

Jaw set, Blaise didn't break her stride.

"We'd better get some support before someone thinks we're nuts! Geddit? Nuts!"

There were hoots of laughter. Blaise knew the men were watching for her reaction from the corners of their eyes. "Knock it off, you guys," she said, forcing herself to appear unconcerned. Despite the familiar hot outrage that made her stomach churn, she could not afford to lose control.

It was nearing six o'clock before, tense and fearful, Blaise was finally free to leave. By a stroke of luck, Ned had been rostered on to count the newsagents' returns that night. She waved goodbye to him then quickly left the newsroom.

Hurrying out of *The Clarion* building, she headed down bustling Martin Place, passed the sepulchral bronze statues of the soldier and sailor that guarded the Cenotaph, and turned left in front of the GPO's wide colonnade. In George Street, office workers poured from marble and granite banks, insurance companies, law firms and accountants' offices, forming a rushing tide of anonymous humanity.

Blaise gladly joined the throng, reminding herself that she was just another inconspicuous commuter. Yet she couldn't banish her alarm. She had the impression that each person she passed looked in the direction of her satchel, their eyes like X-rays, so that, with a single glance, they could see the evidence of her guilt.

Blaise rubbed away the film of perspiration above her upper lip. She saw a rubbish bin, thrust her hand inside her bag, but checked herself. What was she thinking? She could burn the handkerchief in a back alley gutter, but the knife presented a greater challenge. Somewhere obscure was needed, where she could make the evil thing disappear forever—and where there was no chance she'd be seen.

As she approached the sandstone clock tower of the town hall a plan began to form. Joe was due to finish up his conductor's shift on the trams in thirty minutes. At this hour, catching the train would be faster than a tram. She'd be able to meet him at the Enmore terminus if she could run there from Newtown station fast enough. Then, once it was late, she'd make Joe go with her to some dark harborside spot, where they could safely throw the knife into the water. Considering the mess he'd got her into, it was the least he could do.

Blaise hurtled down the steps that led to Town Hall station, flashing her pass at the ticket collector as she pushed her way through the turnstiles. Then she sprinted along the platform and flung herself inside the last carriage as the train began to pull away.

# CHAPTER SEVEN

With her cardigan buttoned up against another cold night, Blaise scanned the darkening yard. She'd positioned herself at the same metal railing she and her father had leaned against when they'd discussed her future just a few months before. It felt like years ago. Finding a job had seemed like the most important thing in the world then. Now, all she wanted to do was to avoid a prison sentence.

She watched keenly as a group of drivers and conductors strolled out of the corrugated-iron sheds. The men slapped one another on the back and laughed, but she couldn't see Joe among them—he must have left for home. A chill ran through her. What if she was wrong? Someone might have seen something and tipped off O'Rourke. Joe had been in a bad way last night. He could well be with the detectives right now, confessing everything, including the part that she had played. The cops might be off to Fotheringham Street looking for her in no time.

A wave of relief swept through Blaise when she felt a hand grasping her shoulder.

"Joe, you're here!" she cried. "I thought you'd been picked up by—"

"The police?"

The voice was refined and had a cultivated English accent, nothing like the one she had expected.

Whirling around, she saw a tall, broad-shouldered man with thick black hair and eyes the color of silver shillings.

"Miss Hill, isn't it? I think you had better follow me."

"Why should I?" Fear made her brave; her temper flickered into life. "Who the hell are you?"

"Not the police, that's for sure." There was an unnerving hint of amusement in his voice. "Come on."

"Do I have a choice?"

"No."

"I could scream."

"With what I suspect you're hiding? I don't think so."

To Blaise's consternation, one of the tram drivers approached them. The fellow nodded briefly, opened a side gate then hurried on, although not before saying, "Number 2041, over by the fence, is free." The man's grip slid from her shoulder to her arm. He led her to the empty tram carriage, stepped inside, and pulled her in after him.

As the metal door clanged shut, Blaise's pulse began to race. What did he want? Girls were assaulted by men all the time; it was a fact of life. There'd been a report in *The Clarion* just this week about a kid from Redfern who'd been beaten and raped. Would she be the next victim? At least she had a weapon, Blaise thought grimly, but using it had to be the last resort—she was in enough trouble as it was.

"Well, who the hell are you?" Blaise demanded. Without waiting for an answer, she flew at the man, trying to claw at his face with her free hand, to stamp on his foot and wrench her trapped arm away.

"Don't even think about it," he said, deftly avoiding both her fingernails and her sturdy shoe while maintaining his grip. "Listen, I'm not going to hurt you. I'm close to Joe's family, really close, all right? He told me you might come here looking for him after work."

"Why should I believe you?"

"Because it would be in your own best interest." An edge of steel now inflected his cultured tones. "I know all about last night. Joe told me everything."

She stayed silent. Whatever he had in mind, she wasn't going to make it easy.

"I also know what you did for him," the man said, his voice softening. "The Blacketts are grateful—which means I am, too. You could say I'm in your debt.

"Joe thought you might still have the knife," the man continued. "He remembered you took it from him. If that's true, give it to me now, along with anything else that will tie you to the scene. Then I promise you won't have to worry about the police—or anyone else—coming after you. It's as easy as that."

He smiled for the first time, which made his striking face with its distinctive eyes appear more boyish. He was younger than she'd first thought—no more than twenty-six or twenty-seven.

"In any case, no one's ever going to believe that a couple of kids knocked off Theo Ryan's brother—especially Theo. I'll guarantee he's working up a plan to take out his revenge on a rival gang right now."

This mysterious boy-man in his well-cut gray suit was unlike anyone Blaise had ever met. It wasn't just that he was uncommonly good-looking, or his disarming confidence. She sensed that something reckless lay hidden beneath his polished self-assurance. Perhaps this was what drew her to him: she recognized the same quality in herself.

Blaise put her hand in her satchel, grasped the knife, still wrapped in the stained handkerchief, and placed it in his outstretched hand.

"That was wise," he said, regarding her intently with those silver-shilling eyes. "You won't hear from me again—at least, not for a while. But one day some useful information might come my way. That's when I'll repay you."

Two weeks had gone by since "the incident." This was the way Blaise referred to the events of that cold and bloody night, and then only to herself. She didn't want to dwell upon the man who'd approached her in the tram yard, yet his silken voice lingered in her ears. She could still feel the pressure of his fingers as he'd held her arm. Each time her thoughts wandered back to him she felt a disturbing thrill.

Blaise was even less inclined to ponder the circumstances that had brought him into her life, but every effort to cast them from her mind was stymied. At work there was still near-constant talk about the Enmore Killer, as the newspaper's headline writers had dubbed the unknown murderer. The reporters seized upon every available detail—the make of car, the most likely type of knife, the precise nature of the victim's fatal wound—yet still the identity of the crime's perpetrator remained a mystery.

"Looks like it was some hooligan from another mob of thugs," she overheard Morton say from her position on the bench outside Kennedy's office. The obscure lines and swirls on the pages of shorthand she was staring at dissolved into a meaningless hieroglyphic haze. "At least, that's what the cops are saying," the roundsman added.

Blaise was careful to keep her head down, though she strained to hear each word of the conversation.

"So, nice and neat and tidy, eh? An outcome all tied up with a bow, just the way O'Rourke would like it." This came from her boss.

"Yeah, but *I* don't like it," Morton complained. "One of my sources reckons there were bundles of cash found on the front seat of Ryan's Cadillac. I can't exactly see a crim leaving rolls of twenties behind. Course, I'll bet there were a fair fewer pound notes around once O'Rourke's boys ran their sticky fingers over the crime scene."

A mirthless laugh issued from Kennedy. "That'd be right."

The two men moved off, leaving Blaise disconcerted, her nerves jangling.

Hoping for distraction from her troubled thoughts, Blaise was disappointed when she failed to catch sight of a single member of the Women's Pages' chic staff in the foyer on the following morning. The only evidence of their presence was the faintest trace of perfume that, she fancied, still lingered within the close confines of the elevator. The world of fashion and smart society that they occupied might be an alien realm, yet her nightly exchanges with Ivy had at least helped her to appreciate the ladies' sleek elegance.

All thoughts of the glamorous trio vanished as soon as she encountered Kev Kennedy pacing up and down outside his office. "Here at last," he said. "Well, what are you waiting for?" He stabbed his finger toward a gesticulating reporter. "Don't leave Mr. Penfold like a shag on a rock. Hop to it!"

Hours later, Kennedy poked his head out the door. "I've been keeping an eye on you, Hill, and you're too damned slow." He rubbed his chin with disgruntled resignation. "I knew it would turn out like this."

Blaise pursed her mouth. Kennedy was a fiend.

"See if you can get this right, at least," he said. "Go down to dispatch right away. There's a delivery for up there." He jerked his head toward the ceiling.

Blaise felt a surge of anticipation. "You don't mean—"

"The fifth floor? Of course I do," Kennedy said witheringly. "What's *wrong* with you?"

Blaise handed the box of pink roses she'd collected to a pretty girl with blonde curly hair worn parted down the middle and pinned to each side by two carefully positioned tortoiseshell clips in the shape of bows.

"Aren't they lovely?" the girl said as she peered through the box's cellophane lid. "I'm Angela, by the way, the editor's secretary. Thanks so much." Then she disappeared around a corner, calling out, "Coming, Mrs. Hawthorn, coming!"

Blaise tried to hide her surprise. She had envisaged that, in distinct contrast to the newsroom, the space occupied by the Women's Pages would be clean and airy. She'd also guessed she would be inhaling that distinctive sweet and spicy fragrance that seemed to swirl around everyone who worked there. What she had not been expecting was the thrum of energy.

Up until now she'd had only a vague image of the way these women might pass their time. If pressed, she would have said that it was spent writing the odd caption—when they weren't busy attending to their nails. Now, she realized her assumptions had been completely wrong. One was typing furiously, another was focused on laying out a sheaf of photographs, and a third—the girl whose hat Blaise had nearly knocked to the ground—was answering a constantly ringing phone while sorting frantically through dozens of pairs of shoes.

"Honestly, Mrs. Hawthorn will be furious," the girl said to the persistent caller. "I specifically asked Mark Foy's to send around evening pumps for today's shots. I wouldn't say that tan suede brogues qualified, would you?"

Blaise tried to smooth her rumpled skirt. Normally, she gave little thought to the clothes she wore; her parents had never had enough money to allow for more than what was decent. This morning, just like every day this week, she'd washed her face, run a comb through her thick chestnut hair, and then looked for a bit of ribbon to tie it back. As for her choice of attire, that had been easy. The clothes she wore for work came from St. Vincent de Paul and amounted to just three plain white blouses and two pleated skirts. She'd worn the gray yesterday, so today she'd put on the blue.

Suddenly, she felt acutely self-conscious. Plenty of people might think she didn't belong in the newsroom, but at least down there everyone looked almost as scruffy as she did. Here on the fifth floor, among the expensive shoes, the scented air and the sort of girls who wore tortoiseshell clips in their hair, she would never have a hope of fitting in.

The same journalist who had sent her out on the idiotic "compressed air" errand had a job for Blaise that afternoon. "Go to the Premier's Department and ask for the press secretary, Matt Jones," he said. "He'll have a release for you." The chubby reporter drew his ginger eyebrows together. "Not that it will do me much good."

"What do you mean, Bill? What's the problem?"

"That's Mr. Sawyer to you," he said curtly. "The problem, since you've asked, is that the release will only say what the government wants us to know—as usual. We're waiting to find out who's won the big competition to design the Opera House they want to build at Bennelong Point, where the Fort Macquarie tram depot is now. I'm not expecting anything more than another boring statement about being down to the final thirty and the committee's still considering, but you might as well pick it up anyway."

It was a relief to be out of the office, away from the talk of the murder investigation. Blaise even hummed light-heartedly on her way to Bridge Street. She liked running errands; it gave her the opportunity to explore the bustling city. It was in this way that she learned where all the government offices and major banks, the courts, theaters, cinemas, and hotels were located. Having scrutinized *The Clarion* every day for the past two months she could now recognize most of the more prominent politicians and business leaders by sight. The society ladies whose pictures appeared in the Women's Pages presented a greater challenge—their images tended to merge into a blur of overly bright eyes and lipsticked smiles.

Recently she'd asked Tommy Trent how she would know when she was ready to write the kind of political reports he did.

"Say you are on your way to Parliament House and you see two blokes walking down the opposite side of Macquarie Street having a chat. If you're any good, you'll be able to work out who they are, what they're talking about, and who's about to have his feet cut out from underneath him."

Since then, each night before she went to sleep Blaise had focused on conjuring up the face of every person, whether important or not, she had seen that day. Then she repeated their name three times. She had no intention of forgetting anyone.

As she walked into the foyer of the grand colonial sandstone building that housed both the Treasury and the Premier's Department, Blaise hoped to spot someone who might be of interest. She paused, delighted, when she saw Joe Cahill himself, the former railway fitter turned state premier widely known as "Old Smoothie." The short, thickset Cahill was striding past while deep in conversation with a companion. This other, much taller man looked up and, for a split second, his eyes widened as they met hers. Blaise felt a fierce electric charge arc through her body. It was the silver-eyed young man.

An absence of new evidence meant that Ryan's death no longer featured prominently in *The Clarion*'s pages. But with the spotlight removed from this appalling incident, she found her thoughts increasingly returning to the handsome stranger from the tram yard. She wished they had met under different circumstances. He might have liked her, even . . . Blaise gave herself a shake. She was indulging in an absurd fantasy, as silly as the schoolgirl crush she used to have on Elvis Presley.

Still, she longed to know more about him. Who *was* he—a wealthy playboy, the son of a rich thug, some sort of behind-the-scenes political fixer? He was certainly an unlikely friend for the Blackett family to have, and she'd never heard any of them mention someone like him. She didn't recall ever seeing his picture in the paper, either, which was curious for someone so obviously well connected.

Blaise cursed her limitations—if Tommy Trent were here he'd be sure to know the fellow's identity, the nature of the discussion taking place and even the likely outcome. She could ask Joe Blackett for his name, of course, but something held her back.

Blaise shook her head. The less she had to do with anyone connected with Ryan's death the better. From now on, she'd banish the mystery man from her mind.

# CHAPTER EIGHT

The receptionist, a buck-toothed girl of around sixteen, was immersed in a copy of *The Australian Women's Weekly* when Blaise arrived at the entrance to the Premier's Department. "Take a right, then keep going and you'll see it," she said before returning to her magazine.

Blaise arrived at Jones's office but, with the press secretary nowhere in sight, decided to take a quick look inside. Just your standard government fit-out, she thought, with a trace of disappointment. There was the usual calendar featuring the flora of New South Wales hanging crookedly on one wall, a swivel chair, a cluttered desk, and wooden trays marked In and Out.

As Blaise turned to go—it wouldn't be exactly helpful if Jones caught her lurking in his room—her eye caught sight of a piece of paper resting next to the blotter. It bore the New South Wales government crest and, even more intriguing, someone had stamped "Strictly Confidential" across the top. By now Blaise was well aware that as far as every journalist was concerned, anything a mug left lying around in plain sight was fair game. After a quick look, she scribbled down a name in her notebook.

Blaise was back in the corridor, making a show of examining a framed map that detailed the state's principal waterways, when Jones appeared. "You from *The Clarry*?" he asked.

She nodded as the premier's press secretary handed over an envelope.

"Much as I expected. Nothing newsworthy here." Sawyer's double chin wobbled as he shook his head. "Now get lost."

"All right," Blaise said. "Unless you're interested in something I happened to see on the press secretary's desk."

"Like what?"

"Like a confidential memo from the premier. They've decided on the man who's going to design the Sydney Opera House."

"They've *what*?"

Blaise tried not to smirk. "He's got a weird sort of name. Hang on, I wrote it down." She showed the page to Sawyer.

"Jørn Utzon! He's that Danish architect who's come up with a design that looks like a lot of cracked eggs. Jesus wept, nobody in their right minds would've picked him." Sawyer whistled. "Well, unless you've got any more surprises for me, this time you'd better scram. I've got a story to write and it could just be a scoop."

Blaise stayed where she was.

"Yeah, all right," Sawyer said. "Thanks. You might not be as stupid as you look."

Blaise was returning from the mailroom when she nearly collided with Ned. "Watch it!" she cried. "What's the rush?"

"Sorry." He smiled sheepishly. "Kennedy's been asking for you. Better get back to his office and see what he wants."

When Blaise walked into her boss's room she saw him tipped back in his chair with his feet up on the desk. He looked at her sourly, his usual drinker's flush coloring his cheeks. "Time's up, Hill," he said.

"What, you mean I'm done for the day?" Her face lit up. She could get home early, maybe even spend an hour with Ivy before tea.

"Jesus, you're slow." Kennedy let his chair crash to the floor. "I mean done, kaput. After tomorrow, you won't be coming here."

Blaise was thunderstruck. She cursed herself for forgetting to tell the compositors about the budget piece. And then there were those stupid requests for nonexistent items she'd fallen for. On the other hand, she'd provided Sawyer with a scoop only that morning—even he'd admitted it. And it wasn't the first time that she had passed on useful scraps of information she'd seen or overheard to one of the reporters.

Her shoulders slumped. Kennedy had taken a set against her from the beginning. No matter how hard she'd tried, she'd never stood a chance.

So there it was. Sacked from her first job—what would her mother say? And what about her dad? She had ruined her opportunity to become a success in the single profession she was hell-bent on joining.

Blaise shivered as, unexpectedly, a picture of Ryan staring vacantly ahead appeared before her eyes. She thought she was done with those disturbing images but, with the extinguishment of every hope and dream she'd had, her defenses had vanished.

"Mr. Kennedy, what have I done?" she cried. "You can't mean what you said."

"But I do." He glared at her with his one good eye. "Anyway, it's too late now. The whole business is out of my hands."

Blaise stared at him dumbly.

"Oh, and McInerney wants you to look in before you leave. If I were you, I'd go there straightaway."

By the time she found herself standing outside the editor's office her initial shock had begun to dissipate. Instead, she felt her temper rise. Her father had warned her about flying off the handle and, so far, she'd been careful to keep herself in check. But what was the point? Kennedy simply wasn't fair.

Blaise gritted her teeth. She had a good mind to tell McInerney just what she thought of the man—and all the other loathsome individuals who'd shown such scant appreciation for her efforts while deriving so much pleasure from making her life hell.

She heard McInerney call "Enter." Good. She was ready for him. Blaise strode angrily into his office.

"Congratulations, Hill," he said with an agreeable smile. "Though I must say, I wasn't expecting you to look so out of sorts." A match flared as he lit a cigarette. "Do you always react to good news like this?"

She felt at a complete loss.

"Oh, Christ. You don't know, do you?"

"Er, know what, sir?"

"Why, as of now you are a fully fledged cadet journalist. Well done, Hill."

Blaise was stunned. "But I thought, I mean, Mr. Kennedy said—"

"I don't know what Kev said to you. I can only tell you what he told me." McInerney leaned forward. "And, by the way, all the other blokes—Morton, Trent, even Sawyer—agreed. Now, what were his exact words? Yes, that's right. He said that bloody Hill girl was the best copy boy he'd ever seen."

# CHAPTER NINE

Startled, Maude looked up from the stove. Ivy flung her arms into the air and shouted an exuberant "Hooray!"

"You've done it," Harry said, clapping his hands with glee. "Just think—my daughter, a reporter on *The Clarry*."

"Not quite. I'm a cadet."

"You're on your way." There was a light in Harry's weak eyes that Blaise had rarely seen. "That job is going to be your ticket to another world, mark my words."

Blaise glanced at her mother, who, so far, had said nothing.

"What do you think of our Blaisey, Mum?" Ivy chipped in. "Somehow she's managed to convince the people at the newspaper she's not a complete dill."

"Ha, ha," Blaise said.

"God knows, we can do with the extra money." As she spoke, Maude began to dole out greasy sausages and fried potatoes onto her family's dinner plates. "I'm proud of you, Blaise, I am," she said. "But it doesn't do to set your sights too high. That 'other world' your father's so keen on can be a lonely place. You should remember that."

"Don't be ridiculous, Maude," Harry said as he speared a sausage with his fork. "Blaise is going to have her name up in lights, or at least printed in the paper, which is almost the same."

Blaise took her sister's hand. "I know there's something special waiting for you, too," she whispered.

Ivy looked away.

Having downed a glass of beer, Harry declared, "I reckon this calls for a party. After all the troubles this family's had, at last we've got something to celebrate."

"Honestly," Maude retorted, "you can hardly swing a cat in here." There was a thump as she placed the bottle of tomato sauce on the kitchen table.

"Well, we'll just have us four, and the Marcellos from across the way. Then there's Jean, and what about your young friend Joe Blackett and his parents—we haven't seen Pete and Agnes for a while." He turned to Blaise. "Anyone else?"

"I'd like to invite Ned Williams, from the paper. He's been a good mate."

"Right then, that's the guests settled. They can come around after tea on Saturday. I'll buy some Streets ice cream and a few bottles of that Cottee's Passiona you like. Jean can do her lamingtons. What about you, dear?" he asked Maude.

"I suppose I'll bake something," she said wearily.

It was a fine evening. The day's heat had eased and a bright half moon hung in a soft black-velvet sky. Harry had borrowed some Christmas lights from a friend at work and strung them over the clothes line, so that the barren yard was transformed. Even the old choko plant that straggled across the back fence was rendered as verdant as the magical vines that grew in fairy tales.

Joe arrived first, bringing a bottle of sherry. "This is from Mum and Dad," he said. "They're sorry they can't come, but they had to go to a wedding."

Auntie Jean was next, bearing her lamingtons together with a box of chocolate liqueurs, still in their Christmas wrapping. "The under-secretary of the department gave them to me," she confided. "I've been saving them for a special occasion."

Jean was closely followed by Ned, carrying a flat brown paper bag in one hand and a bunch of purple dahlias in the other. "My gran grows them," he explained.

Last to appear were Gina Marcello, clutching identical two-year-old twin boys, and her husband, Tony, along with his recently acquired record player and a carton of discs. He set the turntable up outside on top of a greengrocer's box, while Gina excitedly showed off their new record collection.

A pleasant hour had passed, filled with laughter and conversation, Frank Sinatra's liquid vocals and Dean Martin's crooning, when Ivy turned to her sister. "Blaisey, if I hear 'That's Amore' one more time I'll go stark staring mad."

Ned put down the slice of Maude's jam roll he'd been cramming into his mouth and gave the girls a wink. "If you can convince the grown-ups to move inside, I've got a surprise that's guaranteed to sort that out."

Blaise had a word with Jean, which resulted in the adults decamping to the parlor along with the sherry and the chocolate liqueurs, the Marcello twins having long since fallen asleep in Maude and Harry's bed.

"Well?" Blaise prompted Ned.

The boy held up the paper bag he'd brought with him. Smiling slyly, he slid out an album cover depicting a gyrating figure.

"I can't believe it—the new Elvis LP!" she squealed. "How'd you get that?"

"From my sister. She's gone to the pictures with her boyfriend, so I sort of borrowed it." He grinned.

Within moments, smooth-as-silk ballads were replaced by pulsating rock and roll. Leaping to their feet, Joe and Blaise launched themselves into an energetic, whirling jive to the strains of "Blue Suede Shoes."

"Come on!" Ned said to Ivy.

"No," she protested, her eyes downcast. "I can't—"

"Dance? Course you can." He took her hands in his own, at first stepping carefully about the yard in time to the thumping beat. "Ready for a bit more action?" he asked. He hoisted the excited girl clear off the ground and spun her around.

As Blaise glimpsed her sister's dark eyes shining with pleasure, saw how for once Ivy was experiencing all the fun of being
a carefree teenager, she felt a spike of fear. If the exercises didn't
work or the caliper failed, how many more moments like this
would Ivy be able to enjoy in her life? She couldn't bear to think
of her ending up in a wheelchair.

*Dance while you can*, she thought. For this night at least, Blaise
didn't want anyone to suffer from a single problem. She turned
and twirled in the moonlight, giving herself over to Elvis Presley's throbbing voice and wild rhythms.

Only when she glanced over at Joe and saw him standing
hunched with his face drained of color, did she realize something
was wrong. "Are you okay?" she shouted over the music.

He pointed toward the house. "I'm going inside."

Blaise followed, pouring a glass of water and handing it to
him. "Hey," she said softly. "You're shaking. What's happened?"

Joe put his head in his hands. "It's been weeks now, but I can't
get what I did out of my head. Everything will be fine and then
suddenly, like just now when I was dancing, it all comes back to
me." He groaned. "That blood . . . I keep seeing it."

"Maybe you could try this." She made an effort to sound confident. "When I'm starting to get really anxious, I tell myself it
was either a bad dream or something I read in the paper that happened to someone else."

"Does it work?"

"A bit, maybe." Blaise paused. "Look, we both know it was
an accident. You didn't mean to kill Ryan, but he sure as hell had
it in for you."

Despite her best intentions, she was longing to question Joe
about the mystery man who'd turned up at the tram yard. This
was the perfect opportunity—she'd find out what she could and
be done with it.

"Actually, I want to ask you something about that night," she
said.

"Like what?" Joe sounded wary.

"I guess you know about the bloke who found me the next day—and what he took."

"Yeah."

"Who is he? He said he was close to your family."

Calmer now, Joe finished his glass of water with a gulp. "He came out from England and sort of appeared one day when I was still a kid—Mum knew him somehow. The guy's smooth all right, but you can tell he's tough. He always told me if I had a problem he'd try to help me out. I've not heard a word from the cops or anyone else, so it looks like he did."

"I spotted him talking to the state premier—he's on the young side to have those kind of connections. Don't you know anything else about him?"

Joe shrugged. "He hardly ever talks about himself. Anyway, he's mostly over in London. Usually we don't get any warning before he turns up, but you should see Mum when he does. She's always thrilled to bits."

"What sort of business is he in?"

"He invests in things." Joe ran a finger around the rim of his glass. "Dad says it's best not to ask questions, especially about his past."

"Well, at least tell me his name."

"Adam Rule." Joe frowned. "Blaise, you're right. I'm going to try imagining that night was just a bad dream. Let's not talk about it again."

Blaise scurried down the stairs to the cuttings library as soon as she arrived at work the following Monday morning. She flicked past endless files marked "R" before, disappointed at not finding what she was looking for, she sorted through them again. "Finally!" she exclaimed.

The folder that bore the name of Adam Rule was so slender it was little wonder that at first she'd missed it. Inside were only a few brief stories from the finance pages, dealing with Rule Investments' offshore activities, and a single photograph. This was more interesting. The picture showed Rule, apparently unaware of the camera, talking earnestly with an older man she didn't recognize. As she studied Rule's image, her cheeks grew warm. He was even more attractive than she remembered.

She was about to return the picture to the file when she read in the accompanying caption that it had been taken at the funeral of one of Sydney's most infamous nightclub owners, a gangster rumored to control an elite illegal casino patronized by, among others, some of the city's leading businessmen and even a smattering of senior politicians.

Blaise sat forward in her chair and stared at the photograph. "Who are you really?" she whispered.

Rule's life seemed to be composed of a series of contradictions. He lived in London but something tied him to Australia. He was wealthy and well connected but had a special relationship with the Blacketts, who were neither. Rule had access to the state's most senior politician, although it seemed he was also on intimate terms with at least one member of Sydney's underworld. Blaise allowed herself five more minutes of speculation before admitting defeat. However she looked at it, Adam Rule simply didn't add up.

Grasping a stack of bright pink hatboxes tied with black satin ribbons, Blaise tottered into the fifth floor's tastefully furnished reception. She peered over the teetering pile but could see only the top of Angela's curly blonde head. "Where do you want these?" she asked her.

"Right here." Angela stood up and pointed to a white table, bare save for a vase containing an elegant arrangement of tall frosted twigs hung with restrained Christmas baubles. "Thank goodness those hats have finally arrived," she said as Blaise set the boxes down. "I was getting desperate."

Although nearly nine months had gone by since making deliveries had been part of her job, Blaise had happily volunteered to carry out this errand, calculating it would provide her with a reason to visit the fifth floor and hopefully acquire a bit of gossip. Ivy continued to beg her for nightly updates about its glamorous inhabitants, but lately Blaise had been too busy training to become a real journalist to spend any time in the ladies' airy haunt.

"Why all the hurry?" she asked. "And how come you're so dressed up?" Angela was wearing a full-skirted black dress with a short white jacket over the top.

"Because the entire staff of the Women's Pages are going to an amazing fashion show at David Jones," Angela replied, a little breathlessly. "Mrs. Hawthorn says it's essential we look as stylish as possible, which means we'll all be wearing these fabulous new French hats." She untied the ribbon on the first box, lifted its lid, and reverently removed a boater trimmed with black velvet. "I have my eye on this one."

"It sounds like a lot of bother," Blaise said dubiously.

"Well it *is* a Christian Dior show." Angela beamed. "Every society woman in town has been clamoring for an invitation. Now there's none to be had no matter who you are."

Blaise shrugged.

"You have heard of Dior, haven't you?" Angela frowned slightly.

"Sure. My little sister is mad about fashion; she's always trying to fill me in. A couple of months ago I saw your editor's piece in the news section about his death—in Italy, wasn't it?"

Angela laid the boater on the table. "Blaise, Christian Dior has been the world's greatest couturier ever since he stunned everyone with his New Look ten years ago—those divine whooshy skirts made headlines around the globe. Do you realize how amazing it is that the first place his debut collection was shown after Paris was here in Sydney? And just think: today, we'll have the privilege of seeing his final creations. It's like alpha and omega," she said solemnly.

Blaise drew her eyebrows together. "Like what?"

"Greek, for the beginning and the end," Angela replied. "Mrs. Hawthorn is always on at us about learning new things."

"I can see that playing host to Dior's first and last shows has news value," Blaise said, "but is there anything else about this parade that's especially interesting?"

Angela's face lit up. "Only that seven of Dior's top mannequins have flown out from Paris by private jet to model the clothes. And, even better, one of them was originally a local girl from a property near Parkes, of all places. She was known as Grace Woods before she moved to France."

Angela paused while she smoothed back a stray curl. "Grace hardly ever models these days, but she's taking part as a special favor to the house and, of course, because of her Australian connection. Everyone says she has a unique personality."

She began restacking the boxes. "I'd better get these round to the others. The event starts at 1 pm sharp and Mrs. Hawthorn will have a fit if any of us are late."

As Blaise walked back down to the editorial floor she thought about how much Ivy would relish a firsthand account of the Christian Dior show. It was such a shame that every seat had already been allocated to those overeager socialites. Then she stopped. What sort of journalist was she if she couldn't brazen her way into a simple fashion parade?

Standing guard at the entrance to the grand David Jones ballroom was a reed-thin man sporting a white carnation in the lapel of his black suit jacket. Blaise couldn't miss the disapproving expression on his face as he looked her up and down. "Do you have an invitation, Madam?" he inquired with disdain.

She held up her press pass.

"I'm sorry. You don't appear on my list of media representatives." He brandished a piece of typed paper.

The man might be conducting himself with all the self-importance of a czarist count, but he wasn't about to keep her out. "Must be an oversight." Blaise folded her arms. "Which is a pity, as I'm sure you wouldn't want to risk any bad publicity. I mean, what with this being such a high-profile show." She glared at him with defiant eyes.

"I suppose you could stand at the back," he said grudgingly.

After positioning herself in an unobtrusive spot halfway behind a painted column, Blaise considered the department store's carefully groomed clients. The way they turned to each other, clucking and preening, reminded her of a flock of exotic birds. As the compere took her place by the microphone, the ladies settled themselves in their dainty gold chairs, making small fluttering noises while leafing through their programs.

The smoky vocals of Ella Fitzgerald purring "I Love Paris" set the mood for the first model's appearance. Blaise could see she was wearing an unfitted magenta dress, but as one haughty girl after another stalked by she started wondering how on earth she could possibly describe their vast number of outfits to Ivy. She tried to concentrate on a remote redhead and then two glacial blondes clad in spectacular evening gowns, but it was no good. The show had dissolved into a bewildering blur of colors and shapes.

Just as Blaise began questioning why she'd endured Count Carnation's withering looks, all for an inane activity that was a complete waste of time, the audience's coos of delight brought her attention back to the parade. Blaise watched with fascination as a stunning brunette, having first glided effortlessly forward in a scarlet cocktail dress, executed an expert twirl and made a languorous return. Then, just before disappearing behind a dove-gray satin curtain, the mannequin did what none of the others had dared to do. Pausing, she delivered a brilliant smile. "I bet that's the Aussie girl," Blaise murmured.

Finally, after one of the blondes drifted out in a frothy white bridal gown with a bouquet of lily-of-the-valley in her hands, the rest of the glamorous troupe joined her and swanned down the catwalk for the last time.

The guests' enthusiastic applause was still ringing in her ears

as Blaise quickly slipped away. She didn't care that she was wearing one of her tired pleated skirts, her usual white blouse and
lace-up shoes, but, all the same, she had no intention of making
herself the object of any more condescension just because she had
neither the means nor the interest to dress any differently.

She was waiting impatiently for the store's lift to arrive when
she caught the scent of a familiar perfume. Turning her head, she
realized with some alarm that the ladies from the fifth floor were
coming her way. There was the Asian girl with the shiny black hair
wearing a cream beret with a bow, Angela in her jaunty boater
and a couple of others she recognized. The group was led by a
beautifully attired woman in a tan and cream coin-spotted dress
and a fine straw hat in the shape of an upside-down flower-pot.
On anyone else it would have looked eccentric at best, but on her
this unlikely creation looked surprisingly chic.

Blaise nodded. The wearer had to be the editor of the Women's
Pages, Mrs. Marguerite Hawthorn herself. As she swept past,
Blaise felt chilled by her penetrating glance.

# CHAPTER TEN

## October 1958

Sitting squashed into a corner on the crowded train home, Blaise flipped open her notebook. Since becoming a cadet journalist she had passed from Kennedy's care—if you could call it that—into the hands of the chief of staff, a blond bear of a man by the name of Gordon "Gordo" Nott. During the past eighteen months, he'd made certain she rotated through shipping news, courts, police rounds, sport, finance, political and industrial, general news, and entertainment. She'd had so much to learn that her head whirled, which was why she'd made sure to record every bit of advice.

As her eye ran down the page, Blaise pictured each member of *The Clarion*'s team who'd had something significant to pass on.

"Don't bury the lead, start with what's most important," Eddie Tarrant, the tall, laconic fellow in charge of the City News Desk, had insisted.

"Remember who, what, where, when, why, and how—that's the bones of every story." That had come from the paper's rugged industrial reporter.

After returning from the pub one day in an unusually expansive mood, Sawyer had taken her aside. "Build your contacts," he'd advised. "Don't just stick to the obvious suspects. Cast your net wider. You never can tell who'll see something, have a bit of information or access to someone you're going to need."

The grizzled chief sub had growled, "Just make sure you spell everyone's name correctly."

"You might find someone's unusually gabby," Morton had observed. "That's when you have to wonder: why is that? What do they want you to know and what are they keeping back? Question everything!"

Even McInerney had involved himself in her education. Pulling Blaise into his office during a slower than usual morning, he'd said, "Imagine you're chasing a lead and you've rung every last person you can think of. You have just about gone through the phone book, you've pestered the other reporters, they've been no help and you still can't find someone who's prepared to go on the record, or at least confirm your story. The clock's ticking and you're practically on deadline. What do you do?"

Blaise's mind had been blank.

"You bloody ring someone else!" he'd roared. "What you *don't* do is give up."

There were two pieces of advice that every journalist had repeated, although it was Morton who'd expressed it most succinctly. He'd taken a minute to roll up his shirtsleeves, as if to signal this was serious business, "It's no good *thinking* you have the facts," he'd insisted. "When in doubt, leave it out." This was rapidly followed up by: "Protect your sources. Never reveal them, no matter what the police—or the courts for that matter—threaten you with."

Blaise snapped shut her notebook. These lessons were all very well, but after another frustrating day spent chasing sources who refused to comment, she'd come to the conclusion that she was laboring under a handicap these reporters had never experienced.

The problem was, real intelligence came from the sort of confidences, gossip, and whispered revelations that trickled down to journalists via private board rooms, government departments, unions, sporting associations, exclusive clubs and, most especially, the city's pubs—all places run by and for men—men with no intention, now or ever, of admitting a woman into their ranks.

Being female meant she couldn't drink in a public bar even when she reached the legal age of twenty-one. How the hell was she to pick up tips when she was deprived of access?

Blaise sighed. Like the lame jokes told at her expense, the situation was infuriating. *That's it*, she decided. She'd bail up Tommy Trent the next day and see what she could do about it.

"Is this actually coffee?" Blaise said, grimacing at her cup.

"Yeah, but as you're not exactly eligible for a schooner, you'll have to put up with it." Trent had suggested they go to Brown's, a run-down cafe around the corner from the newspaper.

He drew back hard on a cigarette then exhaled an acrid cloud of smoke. "My sister told me you were bright—turns out she was right," he said with a brief smile. "But I can guarantee you, among all the poetry and grammar that Maureen might have drummed into your head, she won't have told you this." He stubbed out his cigarette.

"First, you've obviously already worked out that no matter how good you are, you're going to be faced with plenty of brick walls for no other reason than because you're a girl. I say ignore them. Either batter those walls down, find a way round them or else slip through the cracks—if you don't, you won't get anywhere. You've got to back yourself, Blaise—nobody else will."

"So, easy stuff then," she said drily. "What else?"

"If you're any good at all, one day you will find out something that blokes—and they're always blokes—who are rich and powerful won't want you to disclose. They'll hold out inducements so you will turn a blind eye; most often it'll be cash. On the other hand, they might discover something—we all have our dark little secrets—and they'll threaten you with exposure."

Blaise's stomach lurched.

"Don't fall for it," Trent said as he stirred his coffee. "No matter how badly you want to get on, once you start looking the other way, you might as well give up the newspaper game. It's hard enough being a woman. Without integrity, you're nothing."

Blaise shifted uncomfortably in her chair. She was an accessory to a murder, a criminal act she'd been hiding for more than a year. What did that say about her principles? And, should her dark secret be discovered, how might it be used against her?

She pushed away the slice of fruitcake their waitress had just delivered to the table.

A fresh breeze whipped down Martin Place, forcing the city's office workers to bow their heads and grip their hats while they trudged up the hill to work. As Blaise hurried past a flower-seller huddled in a gaily striped booth, she noticed that even the golden petals of the daffodils he had set out in tin buckets were trembling.

At *The Clarion* there was little sign of the fresh spring day outside. The newsroom's fetid air reminded her that, in here, the climate never seemed to change.

"Hill!" The chief of staff waved her over. "Here are the stories I want you to look after. There's a new school opening this morning and a verdict on a robbery due to be handed down at the District Court. You know the drill—I don't want to see any flash Brenda Starr stuff. Just come back with the facts."

As Blaise set off on her first assignment, she considered what Nott had said. Ever since she'd become a cadet journalist, she had been careful not to step out of line. The trouble was, after her chat with Trent, she realized that playing safe would never get her anywhere.

Success would mean taking a dangerous risk. Despite the chief's explicit instructions, she'd have to do things differently—tear away smooth carapaces, pose far tougher questions, go out of her way to find unexpected angles—if she were to have any chance of being noticed.

As soon as she arrived at the new school she made a beeline for the most harassed-looking teacher she could see, who turned out to be the deputy headmistress. After Blaise had made sure to compliment her on the day's organization, she asked what the woman thought would be the school's greatest challenge. "I don't know how we'll manage all the pupils who've only ever spoken Greek or Italian," the worried deputy confessed.

It was just the tip Blaise needed. As soon as the official opening ceremony was over, she promptly marched up to the startled Minister for Education, demanding to know the steps he'd taken to deal with the situation.

That afternoon she hurried over to the District Court, where a youth accused of burglary received a guilty verdict. When she took his distraught mother for a cup of tea afterward, she learned there were four younger children at home, their father had "shot through like a Bondi tram" and the boy couldn't stand to see his little brothers and sisters eat yet another meal of cereal and milk.

Blaise tore back to the paper. The Minister for Education's bumbling response to her question provided an incendiary lead for the first story. The straitened circumstances of the convicted lad's family added a heart-wrenching human angle to the next. Blaise pushed her chair back from her desk and smiled. True, she'd blatantly ignored the chief's decree, but surely he'd have to be pleased with what she'd turned in.

Two days later, after a morning spent in the state parliament's press gallery, she met up for lunch with Ned on one of Martin Place's rare sunlit benches. The two of them had been the only ones out of the original five copy boys to be awarded a cadetship. "What's been happening in the newsroom?" she said.

"You've made a stir, is what," he told her, shooing away a marauding pigeon. "I've just heard that the Opposition's called for an inquiry into the education of migrant kids, and you know what else? The letters editor told me that a load of readers have already written in, insisting the Attorney-General review that robbery verdict. You've got an amazing knack for uncovering a good story."

"I just got lucky," she said modestly.

"Nah, you're a natural. I bet you'll be given a permanent as-signment soon." He started peeling a banana. "I reckon it could be courts, or you might even get to join Trent on political rounds."

"Not a chance," she said, although, as she bit into her cheese and pickle sandwich, she allowed herself to indulge in a moment of pleasant speculation. It seemed like her gamble had paid off. Perhaps now, with the ghastly Ryan incident well in the past and Ivy growing stronger all the time, a golden future might be fi-nally unfolding.

"You're joking!" she said hotly. The chief of staff had called her over as soon as she'd returned from lunch.

"It came straight from the boss's mouth." His expression was impassive.

"You mean from now on I'm meant to work for the *Women's Pages*?"

"There's something wrong with that?"

"They don't cover news, that's what's wrong—just ridiculous, unimportant stuff!" Tears of frustration pricked her eyes. An edi-torial backwater wasn't what she'd struggled for. "Is this some sort of punishment for stepping out of line?"

"Settle down, Hill," Nott warned. "I would have thought by now you'd have figured out that's where all female cadets end up."

Of course she had. She'd known it since her first day at the paper. But Blaise had felt sure that if she followed Trent's advice an exception would be made. "There must be something else I can do, there has to be," she begged.

Nott frowned. "It's settled."

Silently, she cursed the world's injustice.

"Unless . . . hang on a minute," the chief said, running his hand across the blond stubble on his chin. "Now I come to think of it, there *is* one position. Mike Morton could do with a part-time rounds ringer. There's a weekend bloke, but we need some-one on from Monday to Thursday, starting at seven p.m. and going until around eleven."

"What's involved, exactly?" Blaise brightened.

"It means calling around the police stations and picking up tips off the short-wave radio. If anything interesting comes up, you pass it on to Morton or, if he's not there, to the news editor."

He gave her a dubious look. "I admit that lately you've brought in some good reports, Hill. But you haven't shown much willingness to follow orders, so you'd better listen carefully. What you *don't* do in this job is write stories—ever. And if you take it, you'd still have to work on the Women's Pages during the day. There'd be more money in it, but the real question is: do you think you can hack the extra hours?"

Blaise felt like hugging the burly chief. "Just watch me."

# CHAPTER ELEVEN

Cerise lilies floated in a crystal bowl that sat upon the pristine desk. Their appearance was dramatic and yet elegant, with just a whisper of the exotic. The same could be said about the woman sitting opposite. Even Blaise, largely oblivious to matters of style, was aware that Marguerite Hawthorn, editor of *The Clarion*'s Women's Pages, was a legendary fashion plate.

Today her honey-blonde hair was arranged in a chignon. The dress she wore was violet and, without knowing how it had come about, Blaise could see that its narrow cut was perfect. Hawthorn's mouth was a slash of crimson. Between her fingers she balanced an ebony cigarette holder. Her age was impossible to determine.

"Well, what have we here?" she drawled.

"Blaise Hill. I've just been assigned."

"Yes, yes, I know that." Marguerite Hawthorn tilted her head to one side. "I was not asking who, my dear, but *what*. You are, how old, around nineteen?"

Blaise nodded.

"And you're still wearing the same clothes you had on when you started downstairs," Hawthorn observed.

As Blaise recalled the look Hawthorn had given her after the Dior parade, she blushed, then felt annoyed for doing so.

"I've had my eye on you for quite a while," Hawthorn said. "You must have grown another inch since you joined the paper and—turn around, will you?"

Blaise was so surprised by this instruction that she obeyed without demur.

"Mmm, starting to fill out."

This was too much. "Do you mind telling me," Blaise demanded, "what this inquisition has to do with my work here?"

The editor remained unperturbed. "Isn't it obvious? I can't send you out to cover a story if you turn up looking like"—she gestured dismissively with her cigarette holder—"that."

Blaise felt as if she was being examined with all the cool detachment with which someone else might assess a pork chop they were considering purchasing for their dinner.

"Remember, you will not only be representing *The Clarion*," Hawthorn said, "but also, and arguably even more important, me. A certain standard is expected." She returned to her scrutiny. "You know, the raw material is not bad. I'll ask Harriet to help sort you out. She'll know exactly what is needed—a few things that are smart, of course, but simple. Then, in time, we might attempt something a little more sophisticated."

She waved a manicured hand. "Report back to me tomorrow morning. Then I'll decide if you're ready for your first assignment."

Her cheeks still flushed, Blaise stumbled out of the editor's office. *I am a serious journalist*, she thought. "That Hawthorn woman is intolerable!"

"Ah, you've just come from Marguerite," remarked the same beautiful Asian girl with the shiny black hair Blaise had first spotted in *The Clarion*'s foyer. She had high cheekbones, a flawless complexion and looked to be a couple of years older than Blaise herself.

"Oops," Blaise said. "I didn't realize that I'd spoken out loud."

The girl laughed. "It doesn't matter. My name's Harriet Lawrence, by the way."

"So you're the one who's going to—"

"Sort you out?" She nodded. "I am. And you know what? I think you'll like it."

As Blaise walked through the entrance of Sydney's most fashionable emporium her forehead creased with dismay. She took in the great marble pillars and the elaborate wrought-iron lanterns; the silver-haired man who was playing a medley of show tunes on a gleaming grand piano; the poised, black-garbed staff wrapping bottles of perfume for customers sporting charming hats and expensive summer dresses.

People like her didn't shop in places like this. The store was a mecca for the wealthy who lived in suburbs, whether harborside or leafy, that were infinitely more salubrious than the one she came from. Blaise waited tensely for the touch of the uniformed concierge's gloved hand on her elbow, the disapproving shake of his head before he marched her swiftly to the door.

"I feel like a fish out of water," she said to Harriet.

The girl ignored her. "First stop, beauty parlor."

Blaise had never enjoyed the attention of a hairdresser; Maude had always done her best to tame her daughter's thick chestnut locks. The touch of unknown fingers kneading her head as her hair was shampooed was strange to her, as was the gossipy banter of the salon's Monsieur Leon. Feeling uncomfortable, she stared at the magazine on her lap as his scissors closed again and again upon her damp locks. She glanced up when he began selecting hanks of her hair, trying not to wince as he coiled each one tightly around a roller.

Next, Monsieur Leon steered her toward a hair dryer. She sat beneath its heavy, curved hood feeling hot and trapped as she listened to the gleaming machine's incessant whirr.

Still clutching the unread magazine, Blaise thought of her sister. Ivy would have loved every one of these new sensations. It was Ivy who deserved to be fussed over and indulged, not her own ungrateful self. The old familiar feeling of guilt lay heavily upon her. She had been the lucky child and, having miraculously escaped polio's dark shadow, she didn't deserve this excessive attention.

Harriet's voice interrupted her painful reflections. "You're in luck. As a special favor to the Women's Pages, Magda, the Revlon counter's most sought-after makeup artist, has agreed to look after you."

Another procedure? Blaise bit her lip as a curvaceous woman possessed of remarkably smooth, creamy skin and upswept black hair approached her.

"Do not worry, my dear," the woman commanded, speaking in a throaty European accent, the precise origin of which Blaise couldn't determine. "I promise I will apply just a little foundation, some eyebrow pencil, a sweep of mascara, the correct shade of lipstick, a touch of rouge and finish with some loose powder—hardly anything at all."

It sounded like a great deal of makeup to Blaise. As Magda stroked, blotted, penciled, and powdered, Blaise wished only to flee. All this fuss simply reminded her of the newspaper's belief that her future lay with the Women's Pages.

Once more Harriet broke into her thoughts. "I'm sorry, there's no time to linger." She looked at Magda with a smile. "Perfect," she said, then turned back to Blaise. "Clothes are next."

Their destination appeared at first to be a haven. Vases of white roses, shining racks of imported clothes, glass cases displaying glittering jewelry, silk scarves, and hat pins studded with gems floated before Blaise's eyes. Nobody spoke loudly. Indeed, everyone—from the elegant customers perusing these luxurious items to the immaculate staff—projected an aura of graceful calm.

"This," Harriet intoned, "is the famous home of Exclusive Fashions, where you will find treasures rich and rare."

She hustled Blaise into a changing room, but there all semblance of serenity vanished. A flock of sales assistants flew in and out, bearing a dizzying selection of dresses, suits, hats, handbags, gloves, and shoes. Bewildered, Blaise struggled into one frighteningly expensive outfit after the other while her companion played the role of tireless adjudicator.

"No, absolutely not," Harriet said about a severe black ensemble. "Far too old." She waved away a low-cut cocktail dress, observing, "I don't believe Miss Hill is quite ready for the sort of attention that would attract."

Blaise barely noticed which garments came and went. Time passed in a daze as she wrestled with yards of fabric, dozens of buttons and more millinery than she thought could possibly have been devised. Finally, she heard Harriet trill, "I think we have it. Wrap the navy blue suit with that striped sleeveless blouse, the one with the bow. Um, put in the white silk shirt as well, will you? Then there's the red skirt, the matching jacket—and don't forget the blue dress.

"Let's see." She proceeded to tick off items on her fingers. "Add the red pillbox hat, the navy straw, white gloves as well as black, and perhaps for now just the navy blue pumps and handbag—no, add the black suede, too, they're so useful in the evening."

Blaise jerked up her head. "Look, I can't possibly afford—"

But Harriet was already speaking to the sales women. "You darlings have been wonderful, quite wonderful," she exclaimed as they bore various garments away. "Now, what was it, Blaise?"

"Well, I—"

"Of course, you want to have a proper look at yourself. I quite agree. You can't see anything in here, the lighting's dreadful. Follow me—you need a nice, big, full-length mirror to appreciate the final result."

Blaise was thoroughly fed up. So many different people had poked and prodded her, smoothed bodices, buckled belts and done up zippers that she was exhausted. She had no intention of purchasing a single item, but as it seemed the only way she could escape was to do what Harriet wanted, she stumbled out of the changing room.

"Not so fast," Harriet insisted. "Hold my hand, close your eyes, and don't open them until I tell you to."

Blaise grimaced. She must look ridiculous.

"Now!" Harriet exclaimed.

An unfamiliar apparition appeared in the looking glass. The girl Blaise regarded was remarkably pretty, her chestnut hair falling in glorious soft waves, her pouting lips and sculpted cheeks a rosy pink, her cornflower-blue eyes sparkling. The dress she wore was exquisite: a full-skirted, tight-waisted style in shimmering sapphire that discreetly enhanced her lissom figure.

"Well?" the architect of this transformation asked with a smile. "What do you think?"

Blaise stared at herself, wide-eyed. "Crikey," she murmured.

The next morning, Blaise couldn't wait to show her family one of her new outfits—the red, she decided—and apply some makeup, although replicating Magda's efforts proved to be more of a challenge than she'd imagined. Peering into the bathroom mirror, she applied her lipstick twice before she was satisfied, and then had to deal with an unfortunate smudge of mascara that made her look as if she had a black eye. Now running late for work, she rushed into the kitchen, struck a pose and sang out, "Ta-da! Meet the new me."

Ivy squealed. Maude stopped stirring a bubbling pot of porridge. "What on earth have you done," she exclaimed, "robbed a bank or something?"

Blaise quickly assured her mother that her superior enjoyed a special understanding with a department store. "Honestly, the clothes and even the accessories cost practically nothing, and most of them were samples, so they were free. Besides, the editor, Mrs. Hawthorn, insists I dress like this for work. But I do wish I could bring home some things for you and Ivy."

"And where exactly would we wear swanky stuff like that?" Maude demanded.

Blaise's chin dropped. "It was just an idea."

"Well, I think you look amazing, like one of the fashion models you see in magazines," Ivy said, hugging her.

"And I agree," Harry added.

Maude turned back to the porridge, although not before Blaise heard her mutter, "I don't know where all this carry-on is going to lead."

At ten a.m. Blaise wandered into Mrs. Hawthorn's editorial conference with the breezy assumption that she would float, untroubled, through the ensuing hours until seven p.m., at which time her real work would commence. It took only five minutes for her to realize that this was unlikely to be the case.

"I had no idea there was so much to learn!" she confessed to Harriet after the team had spent a gruelling hour discussing the week's upcoming stories. "What's a bias cut? And how about a raglan sleeve? Who exactly is Balenciaga, and where are Prince's and Romano's?"

She sank into the chair behind her corner desk. "I know the names of every member of Cabinet, federal *and* state. I can tell you exactly how the court system works and, at a push, the hot favorite at Randwick Racecourse next Saturday, but I could barely follow what was being said in that meeting.

"I knew this wasn't for me," she continued glumly. "There I sat, all done up like Lady Muck, but the fact is, Mrs. Hawthorn and the rest of you might as well have been speaking Swahili."

Harriet held up her hands. "Stop!" She laughed. "Why don't you just shadow me for now? Pick up what you can, and tomorrow I'll start teaching you the language of fashion—and about the places this town's leading players head to when they want to see and be seen."

After a confusing day in which Blaise's mood swung between irritation and despair, it was with a sigh of relief that at seven o'clock she left the fifth floor behind her, keen to exchange its inhabitants' rarefied concerns for the grittier, more familiar preoccupations of the fourth. Yet, as she entered the newsroom, she became aware that the usual frenzied atmosphere had changed.

She checked her wristwatch. The first edition would start rolling off the presses in only a few hours, although, strangely, the normal buzz of activity was missing. Not only that, during her absence the editorial floor appeared to have undergone a mysterious elongation, for crossing it seemed to take an agonizingly long time. In the abnormal quiet Blaise was acutely conscious of the sharp click her high heels made every time one of them struck the floorboards.

She had almost reached the sanctuary of her desk when a wolf whistle cut through the silence. A moment later, there was a veritable chorus. Blaise blushed. She hadn't reckoned on the effect that her close-fitting red suit and styled hair, the mascara and the lipstick—and those black suede stilettos—might produce. What should she do? After no more than a split second's hesitation she decided on the execution of a pirouette, gave a brief wave and sat down at her desk.

There was applause. A craggy sports reporter called out, "Good one, Hill." She heard the sound of typewriter keys, a telephone ringing, someone shouting for a copy boy. The newsroom had recovered from its temporary distraction.

Blaise began shuffling through a pile of papers. She missed the protective anonymity provided by her former drab appearance. No way would she run that particular gauntlet again. In future, she'd bring her shabby old clothes to work and, once she had finished up on the fifth floor, execute a quick change in the ladies' washroom before clocking on down here. It would be just like playing Cinderella, only in reverse. The unwanted attention would disappear. Everything would be as it was.

Abruptly, she sat up a little straighter. "Like bloody hell," she muttered to herself. Why should she be intimidated by some idiotic men? From now on Blaise Hill, cadet reporter, was going to dress up to the nines whenever she wanted. The blokes in the newsroom were just going to have to get used to it.

# CHAPTER TWELVE

## *March 1959*

"Everything going well?" Harriet asked.

"Mmm. Why?" Blaise was checking some copy she had written concerning the items of clothing a woman simply had to pack when cruising on an ocean liner. She'd made sure there was nothing in it to suggest that actually embarking on a vessel other than a modest ferry designed to chug solely across the calm waters of Sydney Harbor lay completely outside her own experience.

"Well, I know you weren't exactly keen to join us up here. It's only been six months, but you seem to have really settled in."

Blaise leaned back and stretched. "I suppose I have. Don't get me wrong, being police rounds ringer is exciting, but I will admit I've found working on the Women's Pages is a lot more fun than I'd imagined."

"How are you managing that double shift?"

"It's a bit similar to having a split personality." Blaise smiled. "After a day spent on the fifth floor among fantasy and fragrance, I trip down to the smelly newsroom where I plunge into armed robberies and grievous bodily harm."

Although, thank God, she reflected, any talk about The Enmore Killer had ceased ages ago. Morton was sure that the Ryans' rivals, the Tomassi gang, were to blame, but with no evidence tying them or anyone else to the scene, the story had long since disappeared from *The Clarion*'s pages. The entire incident had assumed a dreamlike quality. Sometimes Blaise wondered if even her meeting with the silver-eyed Adam Rule had been real.

"Goodness," Harriet exclaimed. "Are you sure you can cope?"

Blaise didn't want to say that at least her peculiar life allowed her to spend time in the paper's beating heart, that it meant she wasn't confined to those subjects considered a journalistic dead end—even though she now realized that the all-male news-room's derisory opinion of the Women's Pages was undeserved. Why should men deem soccer more important than fashion? The Women's Pages were read by tens of thousands of devoted fans, attracted by the very topics she herself had once spurned.

"I'll manage somehow," she said. "Though, I have to say, these gorgeous new outfits are a help. My little sister, Ivy, is mad about clothes, and for the first time in my life I've begun to understand why." She laughed. "Boys have even started asking me out—not that I've much time for dates."

"You'll see," Harriet said. "In the end you'll fall in love with fashion just like me."

"But it's different for you. For one thing, you know so much about it," Blaise said.

"Only because my mother goes to the Paris collections twice a year. She made it her mission to tutor me." Harriet tossed back her shiny black hair.

"You've never really spoken about your parents."

"It's rather complicated. My mother's from a wealthy family in Hong Kong and she's obsessed with French couture."

"What about your father—is he Chinese, too?" Blaise asked.

"No, Dad's an Australian diplomat. He met my mother in Hong Kong—it was all very glamorous, until he was recalled home. I was born in Canberra, but she thought the nation's capital was the living end. They divorced soon afterward."

Blaise didn't know anyone with such exotic origins. "Where did you grow up?"

"Mostly in Hong Kong, though I used to visit Dad at different posts around the world. When I was eighteen Mother sent me to a finishing school in Switzerland, and after all that I was silly enough to believe I could follow in my father's footsteps. By then I could speak English, Cantonese, Mandarin, French—and my Italian wasn't bad. Dad tried to talk me out of it, went on about the White Australia Policy, but I ignored him."

"Don't tell me you actually applied?"

"Oh yes," Harriet said, making a face. "First, I discovered that I would have to leave the Department of Foreign Affairs once I married—"

"The public service is hopeless like that!"

"Exactly. Not that I *am* married—something my mother regularly reminds me about. Anyway," Harriet pursed her mouth, "even with my languages I soon found out Dad was right. When it came down to it, it turned out I was not only the wrong sex but also the wrong color."

"That must have been awful. But why didn't you listen to him?"

"I guess I just didn't want to face the fact that people like me aren't judged on their merits." She shrugged. "Mother had a word with Mrs. Hawthorn—they know each other from Paris—and I ended up here instead."

"It's lousy about Foreign Affairs, but I bet Marguerite is thrilled to have you on the staff—you're a fantastic stylist. And as for me," Blaise smiled warmly, "I'd be lost without you."

"Oh heavens, that reminds me," Harriet cried, tapping the side of her head. "Our marvelous Marguerite wants to see you about something."

The editor regarded Blaise with approval. "That spotted scarf looks chic," she said, drawing on her cigarette in its ebony holder. "Your work shows promise, too."

She moved her bowl of flowers—today they were blood-red tulips—a couple of inches to the left then straightened the papers on her desk. "In fact, you are coming on quite nicely. If only you didn't have this unfortunate attraction to crime. *Must* you continue that ringing around you do for Mr. Morton?" She exhaled a plume of white smoke. "It's not very seemly."

Blaise remained silent. The fact was, the incessant phone calls to police stations were becoming tiresome. Night after night she sat at her desk, passing on stories to the reporters while she remained trapped in the newsroom. The long hours had also started to take their toll. All she seemed to do during the week was work, sleep, and snatch hurried meals.

"So, I thought you should accompany me," Hawthorn finished saying.

"Uh, where was that?" Blaise stifled a yawn.

"For heaven's sake, pay attention." Hawthorn tapped her jade Montblanc pen on her desk. "Just remember," she said curtly, "this is a chance to view an important collection put together by the British Cotton Board. Plus, the queen's couturier, Hardy Amies himself, will be present."

Hawthorn consulted a slim black leather diary. "We will be attending the show in one week's time. Make sure you wear your navy suit with the matching straw Breton."

Blaise left Hawthorn's office with a wide smile and buoyant step. Where once she'd regarded attending an exclusive fashion parade as a duty performed only for Ivy's benefit, now she looked forward to it with a thrill of anticipation. There was definitely something about donning beautiful clothes that conferred a new assurance. She imagined it was like being an actress who, having first slipped into her costume, felt able to face any audience with confidence.

Ivy had remarked just that morning, "Blaisey, you seem to be standing up a lot straighter these days. And you're really, really pretty."

"Not as pretty as you."

"Yeah, well," Ivy had retorted with a cheeky smile. "You can't have everything, can you?"

The same thin man with the white carnation who had regarded Blaise with such distaste two years earlier gave no sign of recognition when she waved her invitation to the British fashion show beneath his long nose. Amused by his newly obsequious welcome, she took her place, no longer at the back of the room, half-hidden by a pillar, but right in the front row together with Mrs. Hawthorn, the city's other leading women's editors and the store's most important clients.

She'd decided that the event called for a pared-back elegance, so, bravely ignoring her superior's instructions, she'd jettisoned the Breton hat in favor of the more striking pillbox. To this she had attached an oversized scarlet peony made of French silk, which she'd borrowed from the fashion department. She might be an Enmore girl, but she was quite certain none of the well-off ladies around her would ever have guessed.

"I'm glad to see you forging your own style," Hawthorn observed with unexpected good will, "and that you have chosen precisely the right shade of lipstick and nail polish—Helena Rubinstein's Red Velvet, if I'm not mistaken. Well, well . . . our little sparrow is becoming quite the bird of paradise."

Blaise heard a rustle coming from the crowd of ladies behind her.

"The show is about to begin," Hawthorn said. "Look and learn, my dear. Look and learn."

"Some of Mr. Amies' frocks are very pretty, but they're not quite the same as Dior, are they?" Hawthorn said in a lowered voice as they made their way out of the department store. "To my way of thinking, he's more of a superior dressmaker than a true couturier. Nevertheless, I'm meeting Hardy for an interview over lunch. One can't ignore the man who outfits Her Majesty." She plunged one hand into her lizard-skin handbag and extracted a pair of gloves. "Why don't you wait with me at Prince's? When he arrives I'll introduce you, but I'm afraid you won't be able to stay."

Thanks to Harriet, Blaise knew that Prince's, a lavishly appointed subterranean venue located in Martin Place, was adored by both Sydney society and those with aspirations to join its ranks. Once she and Marguerite had been seated by a waiter at a salmon-pink upholstered banquette, she began to examine the scene before her with the interest of an anthropologist.

A tribe of women, dressed in the height of fashion, carefully lifted bite-sized morsels to their reddened mouths, intent on avoiding errant smudges; several men in dark suits and sober ties walked past discussing that day's fluctuations on the stock exchange; sommeliers poured wine and waiters flew about with platters of food that lay beneath shining silver domes. This unceasing activity was accompanied by the flash of cameras as the hawk-eyed social writers of the city's newspapers directed their photographers to take pictures. A blonde actress wearing an immense black feathered hat, a leading racehorse owner, and a formidable matron with bluish hair who led a prominent charity committee appeared to be the day's favorite subjects.

"Look at the way those socialites are posing," Blaise said, her mouth forming a moue of distaste.

"I hope you're not what one might call an inverted snob, my dear." Hawthorn gave her a steely smile. "Looks like it's time I put you on social rounds—you can start next week."

After noting the appalled expression on Blaise's face, she added, "Think of it as part of your education. To be successful, Blaise, you need to feel at home anywhere and be able to talk to every kind of person. You won't help yourself by being precious."

A moment later a waiter approached their table bearing a bottle of champagne. Blaise looked around and saw a dapper man with a red flower in his buttonhole bow in the editor's direction.

"That's J.C. Bendrodt, the owner," her boss said as she raised one hand in an elegant salute. "And there's no need to look so impressed—the Bollinger is simply recognition of all the helpful publicity this enterprise receives from the Women's Pages."

Blaise watched as Bendrodt made his way across the room then stopped to greet a man with thick, well-cut black hair who had his back to her. Something about the set of his broad shoulders seemed familiar. Suddenly he turned around and caught her staring at him. Blaise's stomach somersaulted. She took a sharp breath but held his intense, silvered gaze. Adam Rule inclined his head. Her pulse began racing when she realized he was striding toward their table.

"Hello, Mrs. Hawthorn." He shook the editor's hand. "You're looking very well."

"Why Adam," she said, "charming as ever. This is a pleasant surprise. May I introduce Miss Blaise Hill?"

Adam gave Blaise a guarded smile. "Actually, we've met before." He paused. "It's very good to see you again, Miss Hill."

Blaise found she could barely force her words out. An uninspired "It's nice to see you too" was the most she could manage. At least she wasn't dressed like a scruffy kid anymore. Blaise silently thanked Harriet for showing her how to look her most sophisticated best.

"I won't keep you," Adam said.

Blaise wondered if she was imagining the note of genuine reluctance in his voice.

"Although I'm sure your conversation would be far more diverting than the one I'm about to engage in with my banker. Goodbye, Mrs. Hawthorn." His gray eyes lingered on Blaise. "Miss Hill."

As soon as Adam had left them, Hawthorn turned her perfectly made-up face toward her. "Well, well," she said, narrowing her eyes. "How on earth do you know Adam Rule? From the look he gave you, I'd say you have an admirer."

Blaise couldn't decide if her pounding heart was due to Adam's unexpected appearance, or the way he reminded her of the awful deed that had brought them together. "Oh, I ran into him somewhere or other," she said, hoping her breezy tone would disguise her tumultuous feelings.

"Hmmm. I wonder where that might have been." Hawthorn smoothed the starched napkin on her lap. "Well, I can't blame a girl for being interested. He's an extremely good-looking young man. However, just in case you're considering some sort of romantic interlude, I have one piece of advice. Don't."

"Of course I'm not," Blaise protested, although it had taken only this fleeting encounter for her to realize she was still as drawn to Adam as she'd been on the day she'd first seen him at the tram yard. And that look he'd given her . . . had it really meant anything?

Blaise quickly collected herself. "I must admit, though, now you've made me curious," she said. "Why warn me off?"

"Because he's a man with secrets," Hawthorn answered. "Oh, I know he went to boarding school in England. He's a financier, lives in tremendous style, and has impeccable connections in London as well as in Australia. But his origins are all mist and shadows—nobody really knows him. That tells me"—she glanced at Blaise, frowning—"that Adam Rule is a man with something to hide."

# CHAPTER THIRTEEN

Angela dumped a weighty book on Blaise's desk the next afternoon. "Mrs. Hawthorn wants you to study this—she says it's part of the job."

The title on the cover read *Paintings from the Louvre Museum*. Blaise began to flick through the pages but soon found herself lingering over the glossy plates. The pictures were a revelation.

Having just arrived at a striking circular depiction of sinuous nude women taking their leisure in the privacy of a Turkish bath, it was with the greatest reluctance that Blaise forced herself to close the book and put it to one side. She wrote herself a brief note—*Ask Harriet how to pronounce "Ingres"*—marked the page, then returned grudgingly to the story she'd been writing about the correct way for the mother of the bride to dress for her daughter's wedding reception.

That night, Blaise was already halfway down the stairs to the newsroom when she turned around. Perhaps she'd have enough time to sneak a quick look at the paintings between following up on a recent spate of assaults in seedy Darlinghurst. She ran back to the fifth floor, tucked the book under her arm and set off once more, smiling to herself at the bizarre duality of her working life.

A few days later, *Treasures from Great Britain's National Gallery* arrived on Blaise's desk. She picked it up and this time thought immediately of her sister. She couldn't imagine why she hadn't done so before, as Ivy was drawing more than ever. Blaise had recently bought her a set of watercolors and, to Blaise's admittedly untutored eye, the pictures she produced were excellent. If anyone were to appreciate these art books, Ivy would.

That weekend, the two girls snuggled up together in Blaise's bed.

"Who do you like best out of Degas and Renoir?" Ivy asked in a tone of reverence. "Or"—she opened the second volume—"how about Turner and Constable?"

"I can't tell," Blaise said. "They're all so beautiful."

"Gosh, Blaisey," the younger girl sighed. "If only we could go to London or Paris and see the pictures in real life. Then we'd know."

Over time, other tomes materialized on Blaise's desk. There was *The Royal Families of Europe and the United Kingdom*, *The World's Palaces*, and *Majestic Gardens*; books containing the photographs of Cecil Beaton; about Chanel and Schiaparelli, Cartier and Tiffany; Princess Margaret, and the recently ennobled former film star Grace Kelly. The short stories of Guy de Maupassant and Somerset Maugham soon followed, together with works on etiquette and the principles of French cuisine.

One day, Blaise was examining a small volume that set out the correct manner of addressing a range of dignitaries when she saw Angela approaching.

"Morning," the girl sang out. "What are you up to?"

Blaise adopted an arch expression. "Acquiring knowledge." She tapped the book with her forefinger. "Thanks to this, should I run into either an ambassador or a peer of the realm when I'm on the train home tonight, I'll know exactly how to address them."

"Well, that's a relief," Angela said cheerily, her curls bobbing. "I'm sure Mrs. Hawthorn will be delighted. By the way, she wants you to join her for lunch in her office tomorrow."

"Do you know why?"

"She said something about assessing your progress."

The following morning Blaise chose her clothes with particular care. Yet just as she was about to leave for *The Clarion*, she took another look at herself in the narrow bedroom mirror and realized the combination of her new black pencil skirt and crisp white shirt appeared dull and uninspired. Something was missing.

She rummaged through a pile of odds and ends Ivy had left heaped on her bed, found a wide black satin ribbon, and quickly tied it in an artful bow around her neck. With her hair brushed back into a ponytail, the application of Madame Rubinstein's Red Velvet lipstick, and the addition of a black patent leather belt to match her pumps, the young woman she'd considered insipid only moments before was rendered miraculously smart.

Blaise gave a nod of satisfaction. If there was one thing she had learned from working on the fifth floor, it was that the clothes you wore had the power to communicate—or, for that matter, disguise—who you were, long before a word was spoken.

"Help yourself to smoked salmon," Hawthorn said, pointing to a pale green plate edged with a thin band of gold. "I also have a little duck pâté." She spread a dainty sliver on a triangle of toast and handed the unfamiliar delicacy to Blaise.

The two women were sitting side by side on the cream linen sofa that, together with a black lacquer coffee table and the crystal bowl of ever-changing fresh flowers, was a feature of the editor's office. "Now," she said coolly, "I am interested in hearing your views."

Without further preamble she straightened her collarless black and white tweed jacket and inquired, "Why exactly do you think that Coco Chanel is enjoying such a successful comeback?"

Blaise barely had time to respond before Marguerite followed up with, "What was the real reason Princess Margaret didn't marry Group Captain Peter Townsend?" And so it continued.

For the next twenty minutes she peppered Blaise with questions. Was Yves Saint Laurent the right choice to replace Christian Dior? How appropriate was it for MGM studios to dress Princess Grace for her marriage to the Prince of Monaco? In what manner should an Australian home be decorated—with Danish Modern or antique English furniture?

The interrogation was unrelenting yet, to Blaise's surprise, she found she had opinions on all these subjects. Even more unexpectedly, she realized that she'd actually enjoyed engaging with the matters the editor had raised.

"You've impressed me," Marguerite said, folding her unblemished damask napkin.

Blaise beamed with pleasure. Compliments did not fall easily from her boss's crimson lips.

"I'm aware you have not previously been interested in such things," Marguerite added, "but one must be realistic. It is only in these realms that a female journalist can make her mark."

She couldn't have extinguished Blaise's jubilation any more effectively than if she had doused her with the water from that week's arrangement of tangerine roses. Blaise felt a cold fury well up inside her.

Why should an understanding of a particular couturier's work or the merits of a film star's wedding dress rule out a woman from covering an armed robbery or a political crisis? Marguerite was wrong. One day Blaise would demonstrate to her and everyone else that it was possible for a woman to report on anything—even one who'd grown accustomed to wearing high heels and lipstick. All she needed was the opportunity.

It was with an effort that she replied, "Thank you, Mrs. Hawthorn. I will remember your advice."

Blaise sipped her drink. "Ooh, that's delicious, Harriet. What a way to fill another gap in my knowledge."

It was a Saturday night and the pair—Harriet in a belted chartreuse sheath, Blaise wearing a white silk one-shouldered dress despite the cool July weather—had descended the famous staircase at Romano's so that Blaise could sample one of the nightclub's trademark champagne cocktails. Harriet had allayed Blaise's concerns about being a year underage by assuring her that, thanks to her sophisticated frock, she'd easily pass for twenty-one.

"I hope you won't mind." Harriet smiled. "But I've invited a couple of sweet guys I know to join us. It seems to me with all the hours you work, you don't have nearly enough fun. Wouldn't you like to have a boyfriend?"

"I haven't really considered it."

The secret fantasies she entertained about Adam Rule surely didn't count, although his handsome face with its straight brows above those wonderful eyes still regularly floated unbidden into her mind. Her crush, or whatever it was, remained as intense as ever. In fact, just thinking about their last encounter was enough to induce a rush of longing. She drank a little of her cocktail. "I've never felt serious about any of the boys I've been out with," she said.

Blaise took another sip. "As for the physical side, I'm what Mum would call a 'good girl.' It's not on principle, though," she insisted. "I don't believe in double standards for men and women, not in a job or anything else."

"Maybe you're just waiting for someone special."

"I suppose I am."

Harriet lifted her glass. "Well then, if we can't drink to romance, what should we toast?"

"Self-improvement?"

"Perfect." Harriet giggled as they touched glasses. "While we're on the subject, how are you finding Marguerite's special brand of finishing school?"

"Let's say it's a touch overwhelming." Blaise laughed. "Not that I'm complaining—I've learned a huge amount, and thanks to the social rounds I'm clocking up some amazing experiences. The Royal Ballet's production of *Swan Lake* at the Empire Theater was so beautiful I nearly cried."

She'd been startled when she'd caught sight of Adam Rule at the intermission, just as she'd lined up a trio of bejeweled ladies for a press photo. Though he'd been with a group of people, Rule had smiled spontaneously when he'd seen her. Blaise's chest tightened as she remembered the way his eyes had then swept over her with the same stirring look Marguerite had commented on when they were at Prince's. Sadly, as she'd been working, there was no opportunity to exchange more than a few words with him.

"How did you like last week's Debutante's Ball?" Harriet asked.

"I'm prepared to admit even that had its moments," Blaise said with a smile, "although the idea of 'coming out into society' in this day and age seems pretty outdated. But . . ."

"But what?"

"I'm not sure I'll ever acquire the polish Marguerite seems to think is so essential. On the other hand," Blaise sighed, "I've made no headway at all in the newsroom."

Harriet nodded. "So whenever you're at work you're betwixt and between?"

"It's worse than that," Blaise said. "When I'm at home, my mother makes it pretty clear that she disapproves of the way I've changed. Mum says I'm aiming too high, dressing and speaking differently. She thinks I'm getting above myself." Blaise shook her head. "To tell you the truth, these days I'm beginning to feel I don't belong anywhere."

"If there's anyone who knows what it's like not to fit in, it's me," Harriet replied, her dark eyes flashing. "I've one foot in the East and the other in the West, and both treat me like an outsider."

"Harriet, I'm sorry. I never thought of that."

She shrugged. "The way I look at it, people like us have an advantage over everyone else. Outsiders see the world more clearly—and it can give you an edge, make you try harder."

"So being a square peg in a round hole is not as bad as it seems."

"I suppose we'll see, won't we? In the meantime, what you need is a really great night out." Harriet looked up. "Ah, I can see the boys now. You never know," she winked, "you might be about to meet the one you've been waiting for."

As Blaise eyed the bland young men sauntering toward them she doubted that would be a likely outcome.

# CHAPTER FOURTEEN

## *August*

Blaise drummed her fingers on her desk. She was always fed up by Thursday, the last day of the week she undertook her double shift. She'd spent nearly a year as police rounds ringer, but there wasn't much satisfaction to be had when you were working for hours in a smoke-filled room, making endless phone calls and had no opportunity to write a single word about the stories your own lonely efforts had unearthed.

So far that night she'd contacted the suburban, the city, and the water police, followed by a call to CIB and then an extra one to the Kings Cross station because that was invariably the busiest. Shaking her head, she wondered what more she could do, since she'd also pestered the Vice, Fraud and Major Crimes squads, the central fire brigade, and the main ambulance depots. Having already made her way through the list twice, she wasn't looking forward to starting all over again.

Usually, stories poured in; there was no lack of crime in a city like Sydney. But tonight was painfully slow. It was already nine o'clock and the only events that were even remotely interesting were a fire at a small factory in Mascot and an assault outside a Kings Cross nightclub, apparently initiated by one of the new Top 40 disc jockeys. That had sounded like a promising lead, until her police source rang back a minute later, saying an eyewitness had been overly excited and the DJ was not, in fact, the culprit.

Blaise stared at the hands on the newsroom clock. Nine-ten. Nine-fifteen. Every criminal in the city must be tucked up in bed. When the phone rang she felt a twinge of anticipation, but it was only the reporter who'd been sent to Mascot saying that with the fire now under control he was heading back. Nine-twenty. Nine-twenty-five. As the time crept slowly by, Blaise felt her eyelids begin to droop.

The phone rang again. If this was another case of mistaken identity, she thought she might throw something.

"Hello, Hill," Constable Moore said. "Not out with your fella?"

For some time now, Blaise had been cultivating Richard Moore, an officer who worked nights at Bondi Beach police station. She'd bantered with him, might even have given the impression that, were it not for a jealous boyfriend, there would be nothing she'd rather do than join him on a date.

Blaise suspected that Moore was aware of exactly what she was up to, and that he also knew she knew, but didn't care. They were both working night shifts and the odd flirtatious remark helped pass the time.

She'd become skilled at matching her conversation to the person on the other end of the line, and her strategy had worked a treat. Despite Blaise's frustration at being barred from writing, she was delighted that when it came to covering crime, *The Clarion* was trouncing its rivals. Not that there'd be anything of interest in the paper tomorrow, because tonight nothing was happening. But maybe her copper mate had something. "Nah," she replied. "Need a break from all the attention. What's up, Richie?"

"I've a strange one for you. There's a body on the beach."

"So, a drowning?" asked Blaise, grabbing her notebook and pencil.

"That's just it. There's not a drop of water on him. Some blokes who were night fishing found him over by the rocks. Can't tell you who he is, though. The detectives won't release the name yet."

"Can you at least describe him?"

"Sure. Well dressed, but like a hood, if you get my drift. Suit a bit too shiny, shoes a bit too pointed, and from the look of his bent nose and cauliflower ears I'd say he's been in a fair few fights."

At this stage, Blaise would normally have handed the story over to Mike Morton, but something held her back. "How tall is he?" she said. "What color is his hair? Anything else? . . . Okay, okay." She took the answers down in the shorthand she had by now perfected. "Do you know how he died?"

"It's murder, all right—done with a knife. I reckon it must have been carried out somewhere else, though, because there's barely any blood on the sand."

"Thanks a million. I'll get someone onto it."

Blaise put the telephone down, biting her lip. It was time to alert Morton. But, as she rose out of her chair, her phone rang once more. Good old Richie, she thought. Maybe he'd come through with the victim's name.

"Blaise Hill speaking."

"Good evening." Her pulse quickened. She knew that honeyed voice, she heard it in her dreams. "It's Adam Rule."

"This is unexpected," she said, trying to slow her breathing.

"Is it?" He paused. "You might recall I told you some time ago I'd be in touch one day."

"Yes." She gripped the telephone so tightly that her knuckles turned white.

"The police are keeping back certain facts about the body that's been found on Bondi Beach."

Blaise took a sharp breath. She'd only just heard about the murder, yet Adam Rule sounded as if he might know more than she did. "You're well informed."

Rule ignored her remark. "The victim is a man called Donny Artelli," he continued. "He's one of the gang boss Frank Tomassi's enforcers. Tomassi's had a long and bloody war with Theo Ryan."

Blaise wondered about exactly what sort of connections Adam Rule had.

"When Frank wants someone taken care of, Donny's the man who does it."

"I see."

"There's more. Donny Artelli was found wearing a gold watch."

"Yes?"

"It's inscribed with Paddy Ryan's name. Says: 'From your loving brother, Theo.' "

"Really." Despite her best efforts to remain calm, Blaise's heart was pounding. It wasn't just that Adam Rule was on the line, though that was enough in itself. The information was stunning—and she still couldn't understand how Adam had the details.

"They're convinced the watch proves that Donny was responsible for killing Paddy Ryan. Apparently, his boss didn't like the way Theo was trying to muscle in on the cocaine market. The police are sure Donny's murder was a straightforward case of revenge. Theo Ryan's been biding his time ever since Paddy died, but he's had plenty of trouble making inroads on Tomassi's turf. Once that watch turned up on Donny, he decided to strike."

The pencil slipped from Blaise's hand, landing on her desk with a clatter. Another man had died—an evil man, but one who was innocent of Ryan's murder. And how had he come by the watch?

She sat back in her chair. At least the news meant she and Joe were finally off the hook. The scenario Adam had just set out in his cultivated tones sounded so convincing even she half believed it had happened in just the way he'd described.

"And you're absolutely certain of these details?" she asked. "I mean, if someone were to write it up exactly as you've described it, it would all check out?"

"It would."

"And where would a reporter have obtained a story like that?"

"From an impeccable source."

Blaise heard a click as Rule put his phone down.

She immediately called Richard Moore. If he confirmed what Rule had said, the story was in the bag.

"Jeez, Blaise, you've got bloody good contacts," Moore said. "I won't deny it, but just remember, you didn't get it from me."

She scanned the newsroom. Morton was nowhere to be seen. Although her next step should have been to inform Eddie Tarrant, the news editor, she decided that could wait for a few minutes. This was a major story, one in which Morton had taken a special interest. He would not be happy if he was sidestepped.

Blaise frowned. It was highly unusual to have no idea of a reporter's whereabouts. The newsroom had an ironclad rule that if one of their blokes went out he had to leave a contact number or at least a location with someone—and, in Morton's case, that someone was her. She rang the most likely squads and police stations, but still couldn't find him. Next she called a few of his more out of the way haunts, but again she drew a blank. Blaise racked her brains. When was the last time she'd seen Morton?

"Oh no," she said under her breath. She had glimpsed him leaving with Kev Kennedy hours ago. At the time she'd thought he was attending to some minor matter and would return in minutes. Now it struck her that the pair must have gone out drinking. Although she'd never seen Morton in the state of inebriation Kennedy habitually exhibited, it was rumored that on occasion the police roundsman could go on a blinding bender.

Blaise checked the clock. It was nearing ten p.m., close to when the first edition would be going to print. What should she do? Morton was a fine journalist. He'd taught her a lot and never given her a hard time. She didn't want him to get into trouble. Then an idea struck.

It was ten minutes to ten when she ran over to the news editor, brandishing her copy.

"What's this?" Tarrant frowned.

"Morton has phoned in a real cracker," Blaise said, panting. "I've just finished typing it up."

Tarrant had a quick look. "Strewth! It's a cracker, all right. Take it to the subs right away." His weather-beaten face was split by a grin. "I'm calling McInerney. For breaking news like this, I reckon he'll want the first edition to wait."

Blaise left her copy with the subeditors then raced toward the lift. She had only just rushed into the print room when she heard the foreman yell, "Hold the press!"

For a moment, she was shocked by what she'd done. Having sneaked a story of her own past the news editor, she was now responsible for the newspaper's most serious, once in a blue moon break with procedure. Thank God she'd remembered to put Morton's name on the copy.

She imagined a sub's blue pencil flying over her report, then a compositor hurrying to set the type and lock it down. But, with her excitement building by the minute, she was determined not to leave the press until she saw the final product.

When the printers clamped the new plates in place the foreman shouted, "Okay to go, boys?"

"Yes, boss," came the reply.

As soon as he pushed a large green button, the great silver beast shuddered and roared into life. So fierce was its thumping pulse Blaise could feel her legs, her belly, and the floor beneath her feet vibrate. She was sure that if she touched the walls she'd find that they, too, would be shaking.

Newspapers began flying from the churning press and were immediately tied into bundles. Blaise stared, captivated, as they were heaved onto dozens of trolleys and wheeled into the loading dock. There, strapping men hurled the bundles of papers onto a fleet of black trucks bearing the *Clarion* masthead emblazoned in gold paint. Within moments the vehicles sped into the night.

Charged with excitement, she skipped back to the newsroom. Each one of the papers that had just been driven away carried a front-page story she had written. The piece might be appearing under Mike Morton's byline, but she had the immense satisfaction of knowing that Blaise Hill, cadet reporter, was its real author.

# CHAPTER FIFTEEN

Almost as soon as the adrenaline rush of seeing her story in the paper had subsided, Blaise felt the first stirrings of disquiet. She gnawed at her bottom lip—a caper like that could get her fired.

Her stomach was in knots the next morning. Though she filled the hours with as many tasks as she could think of before finally resorting to proofreading every single recipe scheduled to appear in the Women's Pages during the next three months, time passed at a glacial pace. Finally, at midday she received the editor's summons.

It took only a glance at the crocodile smile on McInerney's face to know that her worst fears were likely to be realized.

"Take a seat, Hill," he said. "I think it's time you and I had a little chat."

Blaise perched nervously on the edge of a straight-backed chair.

"Morton certainly wrote a good piece about The Enmore Killer." The editor smoothed his moustache. "A real corker, don't you think?"

"Yes, sir."

"But the funny thing was"—he paused and leaned forward—"when the bugger crawled in to see me earlier today, he didn't seem to know anything about it."

McInerney adopted an expression of exaggerated surprise. "I was just about to congratulate the man on delivering a magnificent scoop when he launched into a groveling apology for being on the turps last night. Can you imagine that?"

"Ah, no, sir. I mean, yes, it is difficult to imagine," Blaise stammered.

Abandoning his show of geniality, McInerney grabbed a rolled-up newspaper and gave his desk a furious whack. "Oh, I think you can, Hill. You wrote it, didn't you?" he demanded, jabbing his finger in her direction.

Blaise nodded, her heart sinking.

"So you admit it. That was a grave contravention of news-room protocol. You know perfectly well that if you couldn't find Morton you should have brought what you'd learned to the news editor."

"Yes, but—"

"But what?"

"I didn't want Mr. Morton to get into trouble."

"Well, that's some sort of an excuse, I suppose." A moment of strained silence was broken by an unexpected chuckle. "Hill, you had a bloody cheek," McInerney said. "All the same, you did a damn good job. Who'd you get the information from? Don't tell me it was that mug constable Morton tells me you've been cozying up to."

"I can't say." Blaise hoped that protecting both Adam and Richie wasn't going to make everything worse.

"Really. Then it's lucky for you every detail checked out— and that *The Clarry* well and truly got the jump on all the other papers." He scratched his ear. "Which puts me in a quandary."

"Sir?"

"I'm not sure whether I should promote you—or throw you out the door."

Blaise woke with a start the next morning. During the night she'd been beset by lurid dreams in which a dead body with a bloody knife in its chest rose from a sandy beach. Then somehow she was back in that dark Enmore side street, and the dead man was pointing an accusing finger and speaking her name. She felt sick to her stomach.

"Thank heavens you're awake," Ivy said. "You've been thrashing about like mad."

"After a week stuck at work I'm probably just short of fresh air," Blaise muttered.

She felt a surge of anxiety. McInerney's final remark had left some room for hope, but if the worst was to occur, she'd prefer to know as soon as possible. Now the weekend stretched out before her, with nothing to occupy her thoughts but if and when the editor's axe would fall.

"I know what you need!" Ivy declared. "Let's go to Nielsen Park."

This secluded beach, nestled in a gentle scallop of Sydney Harbor, had been one of their favorite places to swim before Ivy had fallen ill. "Do you really think you'd like that?" Blaise asked tentatively.

"With Mum wanting to keep me wrapped up in cotton wool all the time, what do you think?"

Blaise hesitated. The experience would not be as Ivy remembered. There'd be no carefree running on the sand, no frolicking in the water.

"Please, Blaisey," Ivy begged. "I'm dying to do something we used to do before . . . you know."

Blaise lay back on her pillow. Perhaps a trip to the beach wasn't such a bad idea. Although it was still winter, lately the weather had been very mild. She pictured a benevolent sun shining from a pellucid blue sky, the two of them setting off on a small adventure. "It's a deal," she replied.

Having placated her mother with promises of vigilance, she made careful preparations. Sandwiches were concocted from corned beef and mustard, oranges were found, a thermos filled with lemon cordial. Sheer force of habit prompted Blaise to put on her swimsuit underneath her clothes, though she acknowledged this was foolish—it wouldn't be fair to leave Ivy by herself while she dived into the water. At the last minute, she grabbed a couple of towels and stuffed them into an old canvas haversack.

Somehow their inclusion made it feel more like a real visit to the beach.

Every part of the trip turned out to be difficult. The walk to the tram stop, with Ivy hauling her heavy leg forward, each step making her grunt with effort. Then entering the carriage, a feat achieved only by Blaise half dragging her sister on board before bundling her into a seat. Next there was the struggle to step down onto the pavement when they reached the city, followed by a bus ride and a similarly problematic entry and exit.

Ivy never complained, not when the thin-lipped woman on the tram stared at her, shaking her head, or when some children laughed as she strained to keep her balance on the crowded bus, and not even when she overheard the conductor mutter, "Jesus, I hope she's not contagious."

Blaise felt wretched. As she walked down the path that led from the bus stop to the beach with Ivy limping beside her, she was conscious of the pain and humiliation her sister had already endured on a day she'd hoped would bring her pleasure.

As if she knew what Blaise was thinking, Ivy put a hand on her sister's arm. "All those people that stare and carry on . . ." She shrugged. "You know what? I couldn't give a flying fig about them."

Blaise hoped this was true. When they reached the concrete promenade that divided the narrow stretch of sand from the leafy park behind, she looked for somewhere they could rest. Stopping at the first wooden bench that had a bit of shade, she said, "This is the perfect spot."

Both girls collapsed onto the seat. "I wish I could paint this view every day," Ivy pronounced after catching her breath. "I'd never, ever grow tired of it."

Water with the pale green hue of ancient glass lapped the sand; further out in the harbor, the shade became an intense jade mixed with shimmering patches of aquamarine. Rocky sandstone head-lands marked by hollows and striations stood on each side of the beach. Across the harbor, to the north, was a swath of dense native forest. Sturdy ferries ploughed past and sailing boats skimmed by, their colored spinnakers billowing in the faint breeze. Seagulls shrieked; a pelican with bright yellow rings around its sharp eyes paused briefly on top of a crumbling wooden post before soaring away on powerful wings. Small children with buckets and spades built teetering sandcastles while a couple of leathery old men perched on the steps that led down to the beach, playing chess with a seriousness belied by their near-naked appearance.

It had been a good idea of Ivy's, after all, Blaise thought. A peaceful haven was just what they needed. Smiling lazily, she stretched out her arms. "This is wonderful."

"I know what would make it even better," Ivy said. "Let's go swimming!"

Blaise frowned. Her sister's damaged leg was held in place by bars and straps; without them she would fall. "We could give it a go, I suppose," she said doubtfully, "only you don't have a swimsuit."

"I do!" Ivy giggled. "I wiggled into my old one just after my bath this morning. If you can help me get to the water and sort of hold me a bit when we're in, I know I can manage."

"I guess we could try." After all, they'd come all this way.

Once the girls had moved down to the beach, they took off their shoes and their light dresses. Ivy bent down and undid the buckles on the leather straps that held her caliper in place.

"Ready?" Blaise still felt uncertain.

"You bet."

Ivy leaned heavily on her sister while she hopped forward with her good leg. Because the fine sand slid away with each step, a journey that would once have taken a few seconds required ten difficult minutes to negotiate.

When the first cool ripples lapped their toes, Ivy exclaimed delightedly, "We've made it!"

Blaise helped her to sit down with her back to the water. Then she hooked her hands beneath her sister's armpits and gently drew her away from the shore until she could no longer touch the sandy floor of the bay. With her long, dark hair drifting on the gentle swell, Ivy reminded Blaise of a mermaid.

"Blaisey, this is amazing," she said. "It's as if there's not a thing wrong with me. See, I can float perfectly well. Let go, just for a little bit."

Blaise, her own mood lifted by her sister's euphoria, agreed. "But only for a minute. And I'll be floating right next to you."

She took her hands away from Ivy, rolled onto her back and let her body go limp. The tension in her head and neck began to ebb as she gazed up at the azure sky. High above her, a tiny silver airplane appeared and disappeared behind wisps of cloud. She wondered what it would be like to fly through that vast blue haze.

Abruptly, there was no sky and no airplane, only a green blur as a swirl of water engulfed her. She came up for air, coughing. In the distance, she saw the departing speedboat whose wild white wake had sent an errant wave crashing across the tranquil bay. Blaise reached out for Ivy, but felt nothing but air.

"Ivy!" she called out anxiously, swiveling around. Blaise plunged beneath the water and opened her eyes wide. It was no good. There was so much turbulence she could see only shadows and swirling particles of sand.

She kicked her way up until she broke through the surface, once more screaming out her sister's name. She must have been insane—just a moment ago she'd been imagining Ivy was some kind of mythic sea creature, when the truth was her vulnerability was far greater than that of an everyday mortal. Fear clutched at her throat.

From behind her came a strangled gasp. "Ivy!" she cried, swinging around. "Thank God." She seized hold of her sister and towed her back to shore.

Blaise fought back her tears. "I'm so, so sorry," she said, wrapping her arms around the spluttering girl. "I should never have brought you here." She'd wanted to give Ivy a treat. Instead she, the lucky, reckless sister, had been the cause of a near tragedy.

"I don't care, Blaisey," Ivy wheezed. "It was all worth it, every bit. Just to be free for a few minutes, to remember what it was like to be me."

⁓

When Blaise woke on Monday morning it was to the sound of rain beating upon the tin roof. Yawning, she wandered into the kitchen.

"Not again," she groaned.

Maude was hurrying to place her stock of pots and pans beneath several small torrents. "That damned landlord!" she said. "I've been asking him for months to fix these leaks."

"I wish I could help us move to something better," Blaise said, although as she stood on the sodden linoleum, contemplating the disaster that might well lie in store for her at work, the fulfilment of this ambition seemed absurdly far-fetched.

This somber mood accompanied Blaise all the way to *The Clarion*. When she arrived at her desk at the Women's Pages, damp and disheveled, she put her head in her hands. It was only a matter of time before McInerney pronounced his verdict.

At least the day promised distraction. With Harriet away in Hong Kong for a short visit home, Blaise had been made responsible for working with one of the photographers on a story titled "Surprising Spring Accessories." Mrs. Hawthorn had instructed Blaise to create several compositions to illustrate the shoes, hats, handbags, and gloves that would best complement each other. "But don't make it too predictable," she'd added.

Blaise worked steadily, even humming on occasion. For one shot she added a witty brooch in the shape of a giraffe; a second benefited from a boldly striped scarf; in a third picture she included a pair of oversized black sunglasses.

"Looks great, kiddo," the photographer declared after he'd taken his last picture. "Mrs. H should be happy."

Blaise had just finished tidying up the studio when she looked at her watch. She'd been so absorbed in her work that she'd nearly forgotten just how precarious her position at the newspaper was. It was nearly seven p.m. and still there'd been no word from McInerney.

She had put on her jacket and was gathering her bag, pencils, and notebook when she heard the distinctive sound of high heels tapping down the corridor. To her surprise, a moment later, the women's editor appeared at the studio door. She looked extraordinarily stylish, even for her, in a severe black gabardine suit with a narrow belt.

"I'm so sorry," Blaise said in a rush, "but I can't help you with anything right now. I'm due at the newsroom in a minute."

Hawthorn tapped her way across the echoing studio. "Not anymore," she said, folding her arms. "Mr. McInerney has decided your services are no longer required downstairs. That chapter has ended."

Blaise felt faint.

"I'm not suggesting that your work isn't good," Hawthorn said. She'd propped herself up against the edge of the layout table, somehow managing to appear impossibly elegant in this uninspiring room with its jumble of lights and miscellaneous props.

"The story you had no business writing—it was outstanding. And that is why you still have a job, although from now on you will be working only on the Women's Pages. You will be pleased to know that, as it's a permanent assignment, you shall be regarded as a graded journalist and paid accordingly."

Blaise gulped. It was impossible to celebrate either her promotion or her extra income. All she could see was a future yawning before her, year after year of belts and bags and gloves, of an endless parade of vacuous nonentities all clamoring to have their picture taken at fashionable nightclubs and lunching spots.

"By the look on your face, you don't find the prospect wholly appealing," Hawthorn said. "Listen," she added in a gentler tone, "why don't you sit down? You're positively reeling."

Blaise slumped into a rickety armchair.

"I suppose you understand that your little escapade could well have had quite a different outcome."

"Yes, I do." Blaise had concluded that abject contrition was her only option. "Believe me, I'm very grateful to you and Mr. McInerney."

"So you should be," Hawthorn said, arching one eyebrow. "And now that we have that matter sorted out, I'm delighted to inform you that as the Board of Management is so pleased with the revenue our section has been generating, both the size and the scope of the Women's Pages is to increase. From now on, we will be running not only more interviews but also a range of short pieces examining a variety of women's issues."

"What sort of issues?" Blaise hoped she didn't sound as sceptical as she felt.

"Despite what you might think, I am not referring to the height of one's hemline or whether the women in Paris are wearing shocking pink this season—though, of course, fashion will always remain of singular importance. However, I only have to look at a young woman like yourself to realize that times are changing. It is my belief that the Women's Pages must change with them."

Blaise felt a faint glimmer of hope. Perhaps there was a chance—slim, but a chance nevertheless—that she would still be able to make her mark.

Marguerite smoothed the nonexistent wrinkles in her ensemble. "As a matter of fact, I already have an important assignment for you."

Blaise looked up.

"You are no doubt aware that Princess Alexandra will begin her royal tour of Australia on the seventeenth of this month. I want you to cover the Sydney leg of her trip, starting in September. Naturally, we need stories about what the princess wears, who she meets and so on. But, in view of your reputation for producing the unexpected—keep your eyes open."

# CHAPTER SIXTEEN

## *April 1960*

At the sound of a faint cough Blaise glanced up from the column she was writing. The subject had been sparked by the headline "Do Women Want Equal Pay?" *What dopes, of course they do,* Blaise had thought when she first saw it in a rival newspaper, but since immersing herself in the story she'd had one interruption after another and now her copy was running late.

"Yes?" she asked, a little more brusquely than she had intended.

A freckle-faced girl was standing in front of her. "I'm the new copy boy."

"Good to know there's another female on board," Blaise said in a warmer voice. "And you're here because . . . ?"

"I have a message from Mr. McInerney. He wants to see you in his office right away."

As the girl scurried off, all thoughts of the vexed column disappeared. Blaise hadn't heard anything from the editor since her exile to the fifth floor had begun months ago. What did his summons mean? She'd had a far better time working for the Women's Pages than she had ever thought possible, and had discovered that the world of fashion could be fascinating. She'd leapt at the chance to practice the art of interviewing and even written the occasional, substantial article. But she'd still give her eye teeth—hell, she'd throw in every pair of her new Italian stilettos—to be given a crack at covering crime or politics.

Maybe now she'd served out what McInerney had deemed an appropriate sentence, he had at last set aside her lapse in judgment. With every stair she skipped down she felt increasingly optimistic. She would be cast out no longer. A position in the newsroom must have come up and, finally, she was being invited to fill it.

"Take a seat," McInerney said when she appeared at his door. "I'm about to have a cup of tea. Do you want one, Hill?"

It wasn't the most gracious invitation, but still Blaise was thrilled. This was an unusual level of courtesy from a man who had never been accused of excessive charm.

"Thank you, I would, sir," she said. "Black, please."

McInerney buzzed his secretary. "Jen? The usual for me and a black tea for Miss Hill." Then he settled back in his chair.

"I might have something for you," he said, looking over his spectacles.

"You mean, in the newsroom? Whatever it is, I'll do it." Blaise beamed.

"Not there, no. You will not be coming back to level four."

Blaise was shocked. He must have some sort of clerical role in mind—it might even be in the wretched circulation department. But what could possibly make him think that, after spending three tough years devoted to reporting, she'd be remotely interested? She fought back the urge to seize one of McInerney's overflowing ashtrays and smash it against the nearest wall.

"I'm sorry," she said heatedly, "but if I'm not going to work here in news, I'm not interested." Blaise was so annoyed that she barely noticed Jen coming in with the tea.

The editor took a sip. "That's a shame," he muttered. "I was wondering if you'd like to go to London."

Blaise was certain she'd heard incorrectly. "Did you say *London?*"

"That's right." McInerney put his cup down with a rattle. "You know who Roger Croft is, don't you?"

"Sure."

Roger the Dodger had been *The Clarion's* royal correspondent for years. His stories also ran in *The Advocate*, the London-based paper owned by *The Clarry's* aging proprietor, Sir Ernest Greene. Blaise had never spotted the venerable Sir Ernest, and the only time she'd met Croft was on one of his rare visits to Sydney. He'd struck her as more English than the English—even though one of the reporters had subsequently told her that he'd been born and bred out west, in Broken Hill. Although Croft occasionally filed a story on other topics of interest to Australian readers, he was renowned for the unalloyed enthusiasm with which he covered the activities of the queen and her extended family.

"Well," McInerney said, "it seems that yesterday the plummy fool was tackling a downhill run at St. Moritz—probably showing off to his toffee-nosed mates—when he went A over T. To cut a long story short, his left leg is fractured in three places. A cable came in this morning."

Blaise's pulse began to race. If McInerney was thinking what she thought he was thinking, then Croft's misfortune was her lucky break.

"Gee, that's terrible," she said. "Poor old Rog." Blaise waited a beat before, with the best poker face she could muster, asking casually, "Who's going to cover Princess Margaret's wedding at Westminster Abbey next month then?"

"Haven't a clue." McInerney was equally expressionless. "Until you turned it down, I was hoping it might be you."

Blaise abandoned her show of indifference. "You know I'd kill for a chance like that."

"Thought you might," McInerney responded with a sly smile. "You did an excellent job during the Princess Alexandra tour last year. I don't know how you persuaded her lady-in-waiting to do that interview, but our readers lapped it up. Then you capped the whole thing off with the piece about the cop. How did you beat the others to that?"

"Kept my eyes peeled, sir." The policeman had played the hero by throwing himself on a rogue firework during the schoolkids' pageant at the Sydney Showground, right next to the royal enclosure. "Guess I must have learned more from Mr. Kennedy than I thought."

The editor took a last gulp of tea. "Of course, it would have been a better story if the bloody rocket had gone off *in* the royal enclosure, but you can't have everything."

The firework report might have been a matter of her own sharp observation, but she had Adam Rule to thank for the interview. Since he'd rung her last August about the Bondi murder he'd continued to call from time to time, passing on useful tips about various well-known personalities. Although these exchanges always left her with a hammering heart, his manner was invariably brisk and business-like. They had met only once more, during Alexandra's tour, after he'd told her to hurry over to the Hotel Australia where he'd been waiting for her with an "old friend."

When he'd revealed who the woman was, she'd blurted out, "Why are you helping me?"

"Because I think you're remarkable," he'd said, then rung off.

Stunned and delighted, she had sped over to the hotel, but spent only a few minutes with Rule before he'd left her alone with the princess's aide. Still, it had been long enough for her to know that the man still had an intense effect upon her. She'd been sure she'd detected more than a hint of interest in his eyes, although nothing had ever eventuated—unless you counted those occasional, tantalizingly brief phone calls.

Blaise's thoughts snapped back to the present. "Thank you very much for the opportunity, Mr. McInerney," she said soberly, attempting not to show her wild excitement. London! She'd never dreamt an assignment like this was possible.

"My secretary has all the details you'll need," McInerney said, taking off his glasses. "The paper will help rush through a passport—I'm guessing you don't have one?"

Blaise shook her head.

"Didn't think so. Jen will organize a seat on a plane—it's too late to go by ship. She'll also give you the schedules for the functions and press briefings you'll be attending, enough pounds sterling to see you through, and the details regarding your accreditation."

McInerney shuffled through some sheets of paper. "Oh, and here's a first. As every hotel room and driver in London has already been booked, Sir Ernest has agreed to make his own Cadogan Square flat in Knightsbridge available. There's also a chauffeur he uses when he's in the UK; Jen will tee him up for your engagements. Much as our proprietor would like to be visiting London for the festivities, he's not well enough to travel at the moment."

McInerney looked up at Blaise. "Is there anything else you need me to tell you?"

"No, sir. I'm on top of it," she replied, although her mind was filled with nothing but questions.

As Blaise sat next to Harriet beneath one of Hyde Park's weeping figs she thought back to the previous evening, when she'd broken the news to her family. Her father had danced a jig around the kitchen table and begun singing "Land of Hope and Glory." Maude's hand had flown to her mouth. "Bloody hell," she'd said. "Our daughter, going to a royal wedding." Ivy had tapped her arm. "Just keep your eyes peeled for passing dukes, Blaisey. Maybe one of them will take a fancy to you and we can all move into his castle—as long as it's got decent plumbing and a roof that doesn't leak."

Blaise picked up her sandwich. "Just as well Marguerite gave me all those books on palaces and etiquette. Who would have thought they'd come in so handy? Still, there's heaps I don't know. I didn't want to look like a goose, though, and ask McInerney— do you think you could help me out?"

"No problem," Harriet replied. "I've grown up surrounded by protocol."

"You're a godsend." Blaise took a bite. "I learned a bit about it during Princess Alexandra's tour, but a royal wedding—and in London—that's in a different league."

"Of course, you'll need to know how to curtsy," Harriet advised.

"Crumbs. That wasn't on the curriculum at my high school."

"It's not hard. Just copy me." Harriet stood on the grass and adopted a dignified air.

Blaise jumped off the bench. "Like this?" she asked, pulling herself up to her full height.

"That's fine. Now, with your arms relaxed and curved slightly inward, keep the left leg straight and cross your bent right leg behind you. Next, while maintaining your upright posture, bend your left leg, lower yourself, and then rise."

Still grasping her sandwich in one hand, Blaise was making a wobbly attempt to execute this maneuver when she heard loud guffawing. She whipped her head round and saw a pair of gnarled, khaki-clad gardeners leaning on their rakes as they shook with laughter.

"Where do you think you're going, love," one of the men called out from across the lawn, "off to the Palace to see the queen?"

"I'll give Her Majesty your regards, shall I?" Blaise shouted back at him with a grin.

# CHAPTER SEVENTEEN

Hawthorn recapped her Montblanc pen. "So, that's it for this week's pages. Just as well," she said, glancing at her slim Cartier watch, "it's already after seven o'clock. There are only a couple of other matters."

She looked down at her notes. "Angela, bring me the file on the freelancers I like. We have our subs and at a pinch they can produce stories, but I may still need an extra pair of hands while Blaise is in London. And Harriet, given the public are in the throes of wedding fever, what about putting some pictures together for a feature on royal brides of the past?"

"A fashion spread on ball gowns might work well."

"Could be overdoing it." Hawthorn frowned. "Remember, we want to inspire our readers, not intimidate them.

"Now, last of all," she turned toward Blaise, "the very best of luck. Actually, I thought you might like a little something to remind you of us."

With a smile, she produced a small flask of the distinctive scent favored by the ladies of the fifth floor: Shalimar by Guerlain. "Vanilla, rose, and jasmine," she pronounced. "Said to have been inspired by the lustrous beauty in whose honor the Taj Mahal was created."

"Thank you, I'm very touched." Blaise swallowed, temporarily overcome by this unexpected gesture. "I would never have been able to take on this assignment without your support. I can't thank you enough for everything you've taught me."

"I'm sure you will make the most of it," Hawthorn said.

"There's no telling where a clever young woman who's willing to work hard will end up."

On their way out of the editor's office, Harriet took Blaise aside. "I've been meaning to tell you. I know a girl from my ridiculous Swiss finishing school—we lost touch for ages but she dropped me a line last week to say she's in London and is working at *The Advocate*, of all places. I've written back and told her to look out for you. Her name is Pandora Fraser-Barclay-Hughes."

"God, what a mouthful, I'm not likely to forget that in a hurry," Blaise said. Her friend meant well, but it was impossible to imagine hitting it off with a painful English debutante.

Harriet tilted her head to one side. "Want to go to Romano's for a farewell cocktail after work?"

"Sorry," Blaise said. "There's something I need to sort out."

One by one, Blaise waved goodbye to each of the ladies of the fifth floor as they left for the night. The past fortnight had gone by in a blur but at least now, thanks to Marguerite and Harriet, she had a near-encyclopedic knowledge of Princess Margaret's tumultuous past love life, a passing familiarity with Court etiquette, and a number of fabulous begged and borrowed additions to her wardrobe.

She placed her press accreditation, brand-new passport, airplane tickets, and a bundle of crisp English pounds on her desk. Everything was in order—she had even bought herself a small Kodak camera, for although *The Clarion* would use the work of professional news photographers, she'd promised Ivy she would take as many pictures as she could. "Especially of what everyone's wearing," her sister had insisted, "and any passing dukes."

Although her trip to England would last only a few weeks, Blaise had been engaged in a busy round of farewells. She'd eaten a lamington with Auntie Jean, had a cup of Mr. and Mrs. Marcello's bitter coffee, and drunk Coca-Cola with Ned at Brown's cafe. Finally, she'd sipped a milkshake in Newtown with Joe Blackett, the two of them sticking uncomfortably to the Paragon's red vinyl seats, while both ignored the one subject that was uppermost in their minds.

Blaise had always kept in touch with Joe, worried for his sake as well as her own that one day his nerves might get the better of him, but even after Donny Artelli's murder had put them both in the clear Joe had refused to talk about anything to do with Ryan. It wasn't until he'd finished his double-scoop caramel malted milkshake that he mentioned Adam Rule was back in town.

Still puzzled about the way Rule came by the Bondi murder details, Blaise had made a few discreet inquiries about him back in September. Having failed to turn anything up she didn't already know, she'd chosen not to pursue the matter. What was the point? The truth was, though, the frisson of danger that surrounded the man only added to his appeal.

On an impulse, she'd leaned across the Paragon's Formica table and told Joe one of the reporters was chasing Rule for a story, adding, "It would really put me in editorial's good books if you gave me his number." She'd taken out her notebook and pencil, then placed them both in front of Joe with a firmness that did not allow for opposition.

Joe had reluctantly scribbled the details down. "For Christ's sake, don't tell Adam where you got this." He handed the notebook back to her. "I'm only giving it to you because, uh, you know . . ." His voice trailed off. "I *owe* you. But you're wasting your time—publicity is the last thing he's after."

"You never know," Blaise had replied, "maybe he'll make an exception."

Now, as she sat at her desk in the empty office, staring out the window at the glimmering lights of the city, Blaise wondered whether to pick up the phone. At the very least, she should thank Adam for all his help—an expression of her appreciation was long overdue. He'd made the incriminating knife and handkerchief disappear, and provided the information that had resulted in her scoop. Then there were the tips he'd passed on and the interview with Princess Alexandra's lady-in-waiting he'd set up. Without him she might not be sitting here, free as a bird. Certainly, she'd never have been invited to go to London.

Blaise chewed the end of her pencil. *Admit it, Hill,* she told herself. The action she was contemplating was not motivated by good manners. Adam still fascinated her. It wasn't just that she was intrigued by his mysterious life, or even that ever since he'd said she was remarkable she'd nurtured the vague hope that perhaps she had made an impression on him. The truth was, she'd never forgotten the touch of this silver-eyed man. She wanted to feel it again.

She dialed the number Joe had scrawled in her notebook. Yet when Adam answered, in his unmistakeable, mellow voice, she hesitated. For a second she was on the verge of replacing the handset. "It's Blaise Hill," she said instead. "I'm leaving for London the day after tomorrow."

Although she had never rung him before, Adam didn't sound surprised. He merely suggested that she might like to go for a drive.

Blaise sat beside Adam in his Alfa Romeo as it sped away from the city beneath dark skies heavy with bruised and swollen clouds. Glancing across at him, she was taken by his evident ease. Adam's refined features were relaxed, his hands rested lightly on the steering wheel. By contrast, she felt keyed up, and a thrum of excitement coursed through her belly and limbs.

They had crossed the great gunmetal span of the Harbor Bridge and then traversed a sprawl of red-roofed suburban homes before a salty fragrance began to waft in through the car's open windows, closely followed by a glimpse of foaming surf. Still they drove, and as one beach followed another, Adam recited their names. "Newport, Bilgola, Avalon," he said, the words made graceful by his cultivated tones.

Having lived in Sydney all her life, Blaise had heard of these places yet never visited any of them. As she traveled through this new terrain, observed its palms and twisted trees, still thick with creamy frangipani, it seemed to her she had left behind not just the tough, urban streets and lanes she knew, but something of herself as well. In this more physical domain of primeval vegetation, sea and sky, the old rules no longer applied.

They talked, not a great deal, but easily. Adam spoke of London. She told him about her work at the newspaper. She didn't mention the circumstances that had brought them together. Nor did she ask how it was that he knew so much about the Tomassis and the Ryans, even though she was curious. That didn't mean he was tied up in anything illegal—or did it? She stole a look at his handsome profile. Now was not the time to start playing reporter.

Not until the car glided to a halt did she feel a faint ripple of nerves. "We're at Palm Beach," Adam said, loosening the knot of his plush tie. "There's a place along the sand I think you'll like." He didn't wait for her to answer, merely opened his car door and stepped outside. Blaise did the same.

Neither moon nor stars lit the night. The sole source of illumination was the blinking beam of a lighthouse rearing from the crest of a nearby cliff. The night would have been quiet, too, were it not for the waves. As Blaise stood beneath the inky sky, she felt enveloped by their pounding, rushing roar.

Adam's fingertips brushed her cheek. It was nothing more than the briefest caress, yet the effect of his touch was as powerful as his grip had been on the day they'd met. "I've thought about you a lot," he said.

It was exactly the sort of romantic encounter she'd imagined in her daydreams, yet suddenly she felt ill at ease. Here she was, miles from home, on a beach with a near stranger—she wondered at her mad impulsiveness. Then Adam smiled, a smile that contained an unexpected vulnerability, and her misgivings floated away on the breeze.

After they'd deposited their shoes, his socks, and her stockings in the car's boot, Adam brought out a blanket and a bottle of brandy. "It's this way." He motioned ahead.

She began to walk with him along the beach, the sand cool

and damp beneath her feet. To her right were the shadowed out-lines of bungalows, flowering hibiscus and palm trees; on her left were the breakers. She and Adam neither spoke nor touched, yet Blaise was acutely conscious of the taut thread of attraction that connected them.

"Here it is," Adam said a few minutes later. He unlocked the side door of a weathered wooden boathouse then followed her inside.

"Wait there," he cautioned, "until we have some light." She heard a match being struck and an oil lamp spluttered into life, revealing dark polished floorboards and rows of shelves hold-ing fishing tackle, books, and files. There was a desk, a chair, a corduroy-covered couch in one corner and, beside it, a wooden table. He put down the brandy and the blanket, then opened a window. A swirl of fresh sea air gusted into the room.

"I know it doesn't look like much," he said. "There's an old cottage behind this place I bought last year but it's run-down and needs work. I like to come here when I need to think."

Blaise knew that was not the reason he had come to the boat-house on this dark night. She also knew why she had rung him, why she'd agreed to the drive, why she was with him at this very minute. It wasn't just Adam's looks, appealing as they were, or the edge of danger she discerned beneath the surface of his smooth demeanor. She sensed something even deeper, a hidden tenderness.

"What do you think of my boathouse?" he asked.

"It's the perfect place to hide away."

"That's exactly why I like it." He looked at her with a trace of the same defenseless quality she'd noticed earlier. "I've never brought anyone here before."

Adam took off his jacket and hung it on a hook. "Would you like to sit down?" he asked, his beautiful voice a little huskier than usual.

They sank into the couch's soft upholstery.

It amused Blaise to see the way Adam had adopted the role of polite host, even in this humble place. Perhaps his manner was a shield; perhaps he was less confident than he appeared.

"A drink?" He picked up the brandy from the table. "I'm afraid I don't have any glasses."

"All right." She swallowed a mouthful of the fiery liquid, then he followed suit.

"I'm not surprised you've been assigned to cover the royal wedding," he said. "You're an excellent reporter."

Blaise raised her eyebrows. "Don't tell me you read the Women's Pages."

"I read every story you write." Adam looked almost shy.

"I'm surprised."

"What can I say?" He smiled. "Right from the start, you beguiled me."

"Is that so?" Blaise said with a quick laugh. "I was sure if you thought of me at all, it was as a scruffy kid with a temper."

Adam became serious. "Before I'd even set eyes on you, I already admired the way you stood by Joe. He said he was a mess after Ryan was killed, that his mate Blaise Hill was the one who kept it all together and told him exactly what to do. Then, at the tram yard—"

"When I launched myself at you like a wild thing," Blaise broke in.

"But that's just it." He swallowed more brandy. "You didn't hesitate to take me on. That was brave."

"And completely crazy."

"That too. But it made an impression." Blaise's breath caught as Adam took her hand. "All the same, it was only later, when I saw you that day at Prince's, that I realized you were most definitely not a scruffy kid—at least, not anymore. You had become this magnificent woman."

He searched her face, as if seeking permission, before pulling her toward him and kissing her gently. Blaise felt a warm flame flicker deep inside. In two days' time she would travel to a foreign land, yet this was where a more precious journey would begin—beside the ocean, with this man.

Adam grazed her willing mouth with slow, brandy-laced kisses for a long time before he unbuttoned her pale pink silk blouse and slipped it from her shoulders. Stroking her hair, he clasped her to him so closely she could feel his heart beating.

"I couldn't forget you," he said, "but I was convinced—considering how we met—that it was best if we didn't see each other. I'd say I'm delighted you called, except that would be a huge understatement."

His mouth sought hers once more. Then their tongues were exploring, tasting each other, acquiring new, private knowledge. It was as if they were not just kissing, but exchanging secrets in their own unique language. As they separated briefly, Adam whispered, "I've been hoping this would happen for a long time."

So had she. It seemed to Blaise that ever since this unusual man had stepped into her life she had been waiting for this moment to unfold.

She felt his hands reach behind her, unfasten her plain white strapless bra and let it fall. Her pulse quickened as he lightly traced the outline of her breasts with one finger.

"I always thought there was something arresting about you," he said. "But it's only now that I can see how beautiful you really are." Then he paused, a hint of uncertainty on his face. "This is your first time?"

Blaise nodded.

"I can stop if you want."

"No."

Before she went to England, the girl she was would be transformed. Blaise rose to her feet, undid her black skirt and stepped out, leaving on only a pair of simple cotton briefs. Strangely, despite her near nakedness, the nerves she'd had earlier had not returned. Even after Adam stood up and removed his tie and shirt, revealing the bands of muscles on his torso and chest, she felt no qualms, only a yearning to meld her body with his. When Adam folded her in his arms, the feeling of his bared chest pressed hard against her skin was as intoxicating as the brandy had been.

"You have no idea how desirable you are," he said, before leading her back to the couch. As she lay down, the way he looked at her with his pale eyes made the heat in her belly start to burn. She was conscious of the sound of his breath, the shadows playing across his strong face, the lock of his dark hair that fell forward when he embraced her. She reached up and stroked his shoulders, his broad chest. He kissed her lips and her neck, the delicate tips of her breasts.

Blaise shivered with pleasure. She wished these new, delicious sensations, this night, her time with Adam, would never end. Yet, abruptly, she sensed the atmosphere shift. Adam pulled away, his muscles tense.

With a sigh he leaned forward until, just for one fragile moment, his forehead gently touched hers. Then he stood up, shaking his head.

"What is it?" she asked, feeling self-conscious for the first time.

"I know what you think you want and, God knows, I'd like nothing more than to make love to you." He groaned. "But not now, not like this. You're young."

"I'm nearly twenty-one, Adam. You're not so much older."

"What I'm trying to say is you'd have regrets—and I've more than enough on my conscience as it is." He collected Blaise's clothes and handed them to her. "I'm sorry. I should never have taken you to this place."

Blaise flushed, angry with herself as much as with Adam. How could this have happened? To be rebuffed, treated as if she was a precocious child, was unbearable. Had she done something wrong? Despite what he'd said, perhaps she was lacking in some way. Was she insufficiently attractive, not well bred enough?

After they had dressed in uncomfortable silence, Adam led Blaise back along the beach to the car. She tried to pull away when he took her hand, but he drew her toward him, meeting her gaze.

"You deserve a better man than me," he said above the noise of the sea.

During their quiet return to the city, Blaise wondered miserably why Adam would have expressed such a questionable, glib sentiment. It was glaringly obvious that the disparity between their lives lay in his favor: he was wealthy, moved in an infinitely more elevated stratum of society than she did. On the other hand, she was sure their attraction had been mutual. Blaise felt it still, hovering in the space between them. She couldn't understand what had gone wrong. She had longed to give herself to Adam, to join him in an intimate realm she had never experienced. Why had he spoiled something so special?

When they reached the corner of Fotheringham Street she asked him to stop the car. She let herself out, determined that he wouldn't see how much his rejection had hurt her, but as she stepped onto the footpath she heard his door open. A moment later he grasped her by the shoulders and turned her around so she was forced to look at him. "I'd like to see you again, keep in contact at least," he said.

His touch reignited all the yearning she'd felt when he'd taken her in his arms in the boathouse. She found it hard to speak.

"Well, perhaps we'll run into each other in London," he said, releasing her from his grip.

"It's a big city," she replied at last.

"Not as big as you might think." He ducked his head and kissed her cheek.

Blaise left him then. She walked down the street, pushed open the door of number 68 and closed it quietly behind her.

PART TWO

Courtier

# CHAPTER EIGHTEEN

## *London, May 4, 1960*

It was the storm that made the memory of that disturbing night so vivid, hearing the boom of thunder and then the long, rolling bass notes that followed, over and over, like the sound of the ocean.

As Blaise gazed through the curve of the bow window at the rain beating down on the sodden gardens of Cadogan Square, she tried to fathom Adam Rule's behavior. He'd dropped his guard, revealed his feelings, shown how much he wanted her—only to pull away, claiming he'd made a mistake. What had made him change?

As for herself, she'd been naive, reckless—she could see it now—and all it had brought her was humiliation. Her face burned as she remembered Adam's rejection. True, he'd said he wanted to see her again, but why would she allow him the opportunity to toy with her once more? It would be excruciating.

A glance at the ornate ormolu clock on the mantelpiece jolted her back to the present. If she didn't get a move on, she'd be late, and no one can be late for Her Majesty the queen. Blaise dashed into the luxurious flat's dove-gray marble bathroom and turned on the bath taps, marveling at the hot water that immediately gushed into the vast tub—it was nothing like the tepid trickle she was used to back in Fotheringham Street.

It took only a moment to slip out of her clothes—a fitted sweater and slim ankle-length trousers—followed by her underwear. Each item was black: she'd decided to adopt the "art student" look, at least for casual situations, after no less an authority than British *Vogue* had deemed it the latest fashion. Today a bearded man in Foyles bookshop had told her she'd look just like the film star Audrey Hepburn, "if Audrey had your coloring—and your figure." Then he'd winked in a suggestive manner. Once she would have blushed, but after dealing with the print-room blokes at *The Clarion*, it took more than a flirtatious remark to unsettle her.

Blaise took a moment to observe herself in the bathroom's mirrored walls, trying as she did so to imagine she was seeing herself through the eyes of just one man. Amid the clouds of steam, the multiple images of naked breasts and limbs reminded her of the painting by Ingres she'd found in Marguerite's art book, the one picturing the sensuous women of the seraglio. That was all very well, she thought moodily, but she'd clearly lacked sufficient appeal.

Sighing, she sprinkled the water with rose oil and lowered herself into the tub. She'd allocated just ten minutes of indulgence, but the temptation to remain languorously immersed while she continued musing was near irresistible. She could not forget the feeling of Adam's bare chest against her skin, the intensity of his gaze.

Blaise reached for the cold tap, flinching as the icy water splashed her face. At least that should help bring her to her senses. Trying to work out Adam Rule, let alone comprehend what had or had not happened between them, was a waste of time.

Instead, she reminded herself of the distinguished individuals who'd be attending tonight's royal ball at Buckingham Palace. Two thousand guests, representing the titled, the wealthy and the talented, drawn from around the globe, would be there, together with—and this was the astonishing part—her. Once she arrived, she couldn't let anything or anyone distract her from her job. She'd struggled through so many peaks and troughs during her short career that now this amazing opportunity had turned up, she had no intention of failing.

A sudden tremor ran through her, causing tiny ripples to fan out across the surface of the rapidly cooling water. It was the first time she'd succumbed to her misgivings about the daunting task that lay ahead. But now was not the time for doubt. Tonight, at the Palace, she would have to be fearless.

Blaise emerged from the bath, dried herself and applied a few drops of Shalimar behind her ears and on the inside of each wrist and elbow. If anything was going to help make her feel invincible, it was this enticing scent. Putting on her gown was next. Made of ice-blue silk chiffon, it tapered to a tiny waist then floated out over clouds of tulle. In a dress like this, any girl—even one from Enmore—could be taken for a princess.

Earlier that day, a spray of white orchids had arrived, although, much to her disappointment, there'd been no accompanying note. Blaise assumed the corsage had been organized by her friends from the Women's Pages, but she couldn't help wondering, with a small, shivery thrill, if it was at all possible they'd been sent by the frustrating man she ought to forget. At least she was sure of one thing. Those gorgeous blooms would add the perfect finishing touch to her ball gown's strapless bodice.

She couldn't help but smile. Only by working on the Women's Pages had she'd learned that, at least in one aspect, the art of superb dressing was surprisingly like journalism. In both cases, the addition of just the right detail made all the difference between the ordinary and the outstanding.

Blaise drifted out of Sir Ernest's flat, gathered her billowing skirts in her white-gloved hands, and stepped into the lift. Taking several deep breaths, she told herself: *You've got this, Blaise Hill. You're simply off to a royal ball held by Her Majesty the Queen in honor of the imminent marriage of her little sister, Princess Margaret. Piece of cake. Nothing to it.* Somehow, the words had a hollow ring.

As soon as Blaise arrived in the wood-paneled foyer she spied a uniformed man smiling at her.

"Miss Hill, is it?" he said in an unfamiliar, sing-song accent.

"My name's Andy—I'll be your driver for the next couple of weeks while you're on assignment."

"It's good to meet you, Andy, only do call me Blaise."

"Please come this way, *Miss* Hill," he said with a hint of emphasis. Obviously, he preferred to keep things formal—or perhaps this was the way he'd been instructed to address everyone he drove. As she'd never come across a chauffeur before, she couldn't be sure.

Although she'd been in England for only a couple of days, Blaise had already noticed that differences in status were conveyed in a way she'd never witnessed in Australia. The men she passed in the streets of Knightsbridge all wore bowler hats and, most peculiar of all, no matter whether rain threatened or not, every one of them carried a furled umbrella, like a secret sign that silently telegraphed their impeccable respectability. She'd also seen several nannies in crisp fawn uniforms issuing instructions to their well-presented small charges when she'd taken a stroll that afternoon in Cadogan Square's exclusive gardens. It had reminded her just how far she had traveled from the rough streets she used to tear around with Joe and the rest of their gang of grubby kids.

The chauffeur looked to be in his late fifties. He was of medium height, had graying hair and wore a black tie, white shirt, trim black suit, and black peaked hat, a uniform that might have given him a sinister appearance, were it not for his cheerful manner. He opened the building's front door, indicated the midnight-blue Jaguar parked on the street and helped Blaise inside.

"We'll be driving down Constitution Hill, Miss," he said.

"Not the famous Mall?"

"No, Miss. The Mall's right out of our way, but you'll still see its color when we turn in front of the Victoria Memorial. The city authorities started painting it with iron oxide around six years ago so that it looks like a big red carpet, rolling all the way down to Buckingham Palace." He paused. "By the way, Miss, if you don't mind me saying so, Mall isn't pronounced the way you said it. It's meant to rhyme with pal, not ball."

Blaise had made the hurried purchase of a guidebook before she left Sydney, but this brief exchange was enough for her to realize she'd need the help of a real Londoner if she wanted to avoid making a complete fool of herself.

"Thanks for setting me straight," she said as the Jaguar purred forward, "I can tell you're a mine of information."

"Oh, you'd be surprised, Miss." She heard a low chuckle. "When I'm not needed by Sir Ernest, I'm free to drive all sorts of people. Only I'm a bit like a doctor or a priest—I never repeat a word I hear."

"Well, perhaps you can tell me something that's not controversial."

"Right you are." Andy pointed straight ahead. "See that big chunk of sculpture up ahead? It's the memorial I just mentioned, over eighty feet high and made of solid marble."

As they joined the crush of limousines circling the monument, Blaise looked up in awe at the towering statue of an enthroned Queen Victoria and, soaring above her, a winged, gilded figure. "She's called Victory," Andy said.

Blaise smiled. "I'll make her my inspiration."

# CHAPTER NINETEEN

Blaise stood alone in Buckingham Palace's sumptuous ballroom, clutching a shallow glass of champagne while puzzling over what on earth she should do next, when to her relief a slightly foppish, middle-aged gentleman with a pair of twinkling eyes peeled off from a group and approached her.

"You look very charming, my dear, which does make it rather a shame that you're all by yourself," the man said. "Do let me remedy the situation." He performed a theatrical half bow. "Cecil Beaton, at your service."

Blaise didn't try to hide her excitement. "How do you do, Mr. Beaton," she said, enthusiastically shaking his hand. "Blaise Hill—I'm a great fan. Those dresses you designed for *Gigi* were so beautiful I went to see it at my local cinema three times."

"You're very kind."

"No, honestly," Blaise insisted. "I love your photographs, too—especially the one you took of Princess Margaret wearing that fairy-tale Christian Dior gown on her twenty-first birthday." Blaise blessed Marguerite. She would never have heard of Cecil Beaton, let alone seen that famous picture, if it hadn't been for her.

"Thank you, Miss Hill, although, after all these years, I'm afraid the bride-to-be's fiancé has quite superseded me as her favorite photographer." His lips thinned. "I should have known something was going on between the two of them when Armstrong-Jones was invited to take the official pictures for her latest birthday—instead of me!" He adjusted his bow tie. "At least

Her Royal Highness had the good grace to confess she'd been unfaithful to me before the wretched photographs were published. But what's a chap to do? Times change." He sighed. "Well, enough of that. No doubt I've said too much already, but you know, you have an unusually sympathetic presence."

Blaise found herself wondering whether the loose-lipped Mr. Beaton might have consoled himself by over-indulging in the liberal quantities of champagne being dispensed by a small army of obliging waiters.

"Let us return to the more pleasant subject of gowns," Beaton said. "I knew you were a girl with wonderful taste as soon as I set eyes on you. That dress you're wearing is superb—Givenchy, if I'm not mistaken?"

"Let's say it was inspired by him." Blaise smiled. She wasn't about to reveal that she'd borrowed it from a local dressmaker by the name of Miss Louise.

After Blaise told him that she was covering the ball for a Sydney newspaper, Beaton launched into a description of an assignment he'd undertaken for *Tatler* magazine with a tipsy debutante. "And then," he continued with an exasperated expression, "after I'd finally steered this impossible, hiccupping girl into position, she promptly passed out in the floral arrangement I'd been using as a prop. The thing was ruined, and it was frightfully expensive." They were both laughing when Blaise felt a sudden bump, immediately followed by the unpleasant sensation of cold liquid trickling down her bare back.

She spun around. A man with a crop of blond hair and an expression of horror in his tawny brown eyes was pointing to an empty glass as if it, rather than he, was responsible for drenching her. "Oh, God," he said with a rueful smile. "That was unforgivable."

A waiter discreetly glided over and passed the man a large damask napkin.

"I think you should hand that to me, Charlie," said Beaton waspishly. "Clearly, you can't be trusted."

"I couldn't agree more," Blaise said, struggling to keep her temper. She must look a complete sight and, worst of all, if the dress was ruined, she'd have to pay for it.

Beaton carefully blotted her back and her gown. "There, no harm done," he declared. "That will dry out nicely. You should see what those Hollywood stars do to my dresses when they are on set—they're even worse than the debs."

"They can't be worse than me," the blond man said remorsefully.

"Probably not." Beaton peered at him. "Although I do wonder whether this little mishap hasn't been an elaborate way of persuading me to introduce you to my charming new friend. I can't say I'd put it past you." He turned toward Blaise. "My dear, it seems this is my cue to present the conveniently clumsy Honorable Charles Ashton. Charlie, this lovely young lady whose dress you very nearly destroyed is Miss Blaise Hill, from Sydney, Australia."

"How do you do," Ashton said with a warm smile. "Now we have been formally introduced, I wonder if you could bring yourself to join me for the first dance? I promise I'll try not to make a fool of myself again, though I can't guarantee the odd toe won't come to grief."

Her anger fading, Blaise found his charming remorse difficult to resist. "Thank you, Mr. Ashton," she said. "I will take the risk."

Then the band struck up a stirring version of "God Save the Queen"—and there was Her Majesty, no longer the mythical monarch in the golden wattle dress whose image Blaise had seen hanging on countless schoolroom walls, but a living, breathing young woman. Blaise felt herself being pressed back as the crowds parted. She peered between two women wearing sparkling diadems as Elizabeth II walked into the room, just a little ahead of her husband, Prince Philip.

"How irksome it must be for him to trail two steps behind his wife wherever they go," Blaise whispered to Charles.

"Probably," he whispered back. "But you see it's all about

deference—rather an old-fashioned quality, I know, but it's still very much the thing over here."

One of the women standing in front of them bent over to say something to her companion, which allowed Blaise a far better view of the royal party. Whatever the queen might be thinking about her twenty-nine-year-old sister's surprising choice of husband, her serene countenance remained unreadable. Princess Margaret, by contrast, was far more animated. With her sapphire-blue eyes shining, she passed through the ballroom smiling gaily and nodding at various friends. Blaise wondered what her relationship with her sister was really like—the two seemed to possess such different personalities.

Following Margaret was the slim, rather dashing Antony Armstrong-Jones, his unusually white teeth gleaming as he flashed an occasional grin. Blaise detected the slight limp she'd read was a legacy from the polio he'd contracted at sixteen. With a pang she thought of Ivy. How she would have adored to go to a ball like this. Sisters—they were bound to each other, no matter what paths they followed.

"Tony looks just like the cat that ate the cream, doesn't he?" Charles murmured in her ear, although Blaise wasn't so sure. There was a hint of strain around the man's mouth that made her wonder if Armstrong-Jones might be having second thoughts.

As she gazed across the room at the opulent display of imperial grandeur, the great mirrors and lavish gilding, the glittering chandeliers and, below them, the diamond tiaras of the royal ladies, it amused her to wonder if the statue of Queen Victoria she'd just seen came magically to life, how that formidable old sovereign would regard the scene in her splendid ballroom. No doubt it would be much to her liking, for it seemed that the modern world had barely penetrated the Palace. In fact, had Blaise herself not known better, she would have sworn the sun had never set upon the Empire.

# CHAPTER TWENTY

"Shall we?"

Having waited until the royal couples had taken to the dance floor, Charles Ashton swept Blaise away. As he did so, she silently thanked Aunty Jean, who'd been a keen participant in the ballroom dancing competitions held at the local Returned Services League's hall. In between teaching Blaise how to type during her school holidays, she'd spent many happy hours demonstrating the finer points of the quickstep, the waltz, and the foxtrot to her goddaughter.

Jean would have approved of Charles Ashton, Blaise thought, for despite that unfortunate collision—which was seeming less accidental by the minute—he was proving to be a very good dancer indeed, expertly guiding her around the ballroom to the strains of "The Blue Danube." She was determined not to be impressed by the man, even if he had an "Honorable" before his name. Probably he occupied himself with an undemanding job in an auction house or private bank when he wasn't fox hunting on an ancient estate. He was certainly looking at her in an appreciative manner, but although he was not unattractive, she couldn't imagine the two of them would have a great deal in common.

Ashton held her a little closer. "Lucky me," he said, "literally running into the prettiest girl in Buckingham Palace. If you don't mind sitting out the next dance, I'd like to get to know you better."

After Blaise nodded in agreement, he led her toward an uncrowded corner then took two glasses of Bollinger from a waiter carrying a silver tray. "So, Miss Hill," he said as he passed one to her, "are you a friend of the bride or the groom?"

"Neither, and by the way, I'd be much happier if you called me Blaise. I'm actually the acting royal correspondent for an Australian newspaper called *The Clarion*, but my stories will also appear here in *The Advocate*. It doesn't look like it, I know," she gestured toward her ball gown with a smile, "but I'm working tonight."

"I see. Well, you must call me Charlie. I know your paper's owner, Sir Ernest Greene. The old boy spent a weekend at Beech Hall, my father's Cotswolds place, not long ago. We did a little pheasant shooting," Ashton said. "Ernest is something of a Palace favorite, but then, as he provides the royals with such consistently favorable coverage, I suppose that's hardly surprising. As far as British dailies go, *The Advocate*'s seen better days, but it still holds its own among those that count in this land."

Charlie Ashton was proving to be more interesting than Blaise had first imagined. "You seem to know a great deal about the newspaper industry," she said.

"I make it my business to do so." He smiled. "After all, I am a politician."

"You must think I'm an idiot. I . . . . I didn't realize," she stammered.

"No reason why you should have," Charlie responded breezily, waving her embarrassment away. "There are hundreds of us MPs toiling away in the Commons. Lately, I've been working closely with that chap over there."

Blaise saw a dapper man with a receding hairline dancing with a glamorous redhead. "That's John Profumo, the Minister of State for Foreign Affairs, with his wife."

"Attractive, isn't she?" Blaise said.

"Valerie Hobson had an enormous hit on the London stage in *The King and I*, but she gave it all up for Jack."

"I'm surprised. Lots of actresses keep on working after they marry."

Charlie laughed. "I don't know how things are done in Australia, but it would be unthinkable for a senior British politician to wed a woman who continued to perform in public. It would ruin his career."

Blaise said nothing, though she wondered how difficult walking away from well-deserved stardom had been for Profumo's wife. It seemed wretchedly unfair that, no matter how successful a woman might be in her own right, her husband's profession inevitably came first.

"I've actually just been made Profumo's parliamentary secretary," Charlie said with a note of pride. "I think Jack could go right to the top."

"What's he like?" Blaise asked. "It's an unusual name."

"He has it all: talent, wealth, and buckets of charm. His family were some sort of Italian nobility, but they settled in Britain in the 1800s—made a fortune in insurance while they were at it. Profumo's a decent chap, with a distinguished war record. The ladies like him, too," he added.

"Is that a prerequisite for a successful political career in this country?" she said pointedly.

"It doesn't hurt." Charlie winked. "My father's always quoting what he claims was Prime Minister Disraeli's advice, though I suspect Father made it up himself. According to him, Dizzy said the best way to make your way in the world is to be master of the subject of the day—and to get on well with women. Who knows, perhaps the old roué really did say it. He certainly won over Queen Victoria."

Blaise smiled uncertainly. Neither Marguerite's nor Harriet's tutelage had encompassed nineteenth-century British politics.

"Tell me," Charlie went on, seeming not to notice her discomfort. "What happened to that silly man Sir Ernest usually has reporting on occasions like this?"

"Oh, you mean Roger Croft." Blaise handed her empty champagne glass to a passing waiter. "From what I can gather, he had a skiing accident. It seems he was halfway down a mountain in Switzerland when—"

All at once she fell silent. Every muscle in her body felt rigid.

Adam was the last person she would have expected to see in the ballroom. He hadn't said a word to her about attending any royal functions when they'd talked about London. It seemed he was intent on keeping her permanently off balance, so that she never knew where he'd turn up or what he'd do next. The man was infuriating, yet it had taken only a quick glance at the line of his square jaw, his generous mouth and straight brows for her to yearn to be in his arms instead of the svelte brunette he was currently dancing with.

"Is something the matter?"

"I . . . no," she said, willing herself to remain composed, even though her heart was pounding. "I think I caught sight of someone I met in Australia, that's all."

Charles followed her gaze. "Not Adam Rule, by any chance?"

"Why, do you know him?"

"Practically grew up together," Charlie said, "before we went our separate ways. He's a distant relation with a poverty-stricken, rackety background. He received an English education only because of my sainted father's excessive sense of duty. Rule's terribly wealthy now, of course, although . . ."

"Yes?" At last she was learning a little more about this secretive man.

"Quite frankly, we don't see eye to eye. Between you and me," Charlie dropped his voice, "he's not to be trusted."

"Really?" Blaise was taken aback by Charlie's vehement reaction. "Just how bad can his character be if he's received an invitation to Buckingham Palace?"

"Oh, I wouldn't read too much into that," Charlie said dismissively. "Armstrong-Jones has all sorts of louche friends—he and Rule chummed up at boarding school. But a sweet girl like you would do well to stay clear of him."

Two people had warned Blaise away from Adam: first Marguerite Hawthorn, and now Charlie Ashton. Yet with her Adam had played the part of an honorable man—if anything, too honorable. These contradictions should have been enough to put her off, but instead they only made him more intriguing.

Aware that Charlie was asking her something, she forced herself to pay attention. "Sorry, must be the time difference between Sydney and London getting the better of me. Every now and then I drift off. What were you saying?"

"I was inviting you to have dinner with me the day after tomorrow—if you can stay awake." He gave her a warm smile.

Blaise drew her brows together. "Thank you, that sounds lovely, but I'm afraid I can't. As it is, in between attending functions and press briefings, I don't know how I'm going to write all the stories I need to file."

"It seems a great pity to come such a long way and not have a little fun. You know the old saying: all work and no play makes Blaise a dull girl," he teased.

Blaise thought how easy the path through life must be if, like Charlie, you had a father with a "place in the Cotswolds" and were in possession of impeccable social credentials. He might be a member of parliament, but he didn't seem overly burdened by his responsibilities.

"I'll have to see. If you call *The Advocate*'s editorial secretary, she'll know where to reach me. I'll just find the number—"

Blaise was fumbling in her purse for a card when she felt the touch of a hand on her shoulder. She looked up sharply.

"My apologies for startling you, Miss Hill. I hope I'm not interrupting anything." It was Adam, looking more striking than ever in his white wing collar and severe black tailcoat. He stood very close to her, ignoring Charlie.

Blaise struggled to maintain her composure. "Hello, Mr. Rule," she said coolly, although she had to clasp her hands together to stop them trembling.

"Well, well, if it isn't you, Adam," Charlie said. "Astonishing, the people who turn up at the Palace these days."

"Charles." Adam gave a curt nod of acknowledgment then

turned his attention back to Blaise. "Miss Hill, I was wondering if you'd care to join me for the next dance."

Blaise hesitated. She still felt Adam's rejection keenly; any further involvement with him was out of the question. But she was damned if she'd let Adam see how much his dismissal mattered to her.

"Excuse me," Blaise remarked to her disgruntled partner. Then she smiled at Adam with an airy insouciance she knew to be entirely artificial. "Why not, Mr. Rule?"

Her breath caught as she felt him place his arm around her waist and hold her right hand in his left. She was almost painfully conscious of his nearness, of the pressure of his fingers against hers and the way he never took his gray eyes away from her face. His thick dark hair was brushed back, his shirt front with its row of onyx studs was formal and stiff, yet she kept remembering how he'd looked at the boathouse: the stray lock of hair falling forward, his bare chest.

"You're breathtaking." His expression was controlled, although she could tell from the slight hoarseness in his voice that it came at a cost. "Those orchids suit you very well." Perhaps he had sent her the corsage after all.

As a flush of heat rose to her cheeks, Blaise wished she could be equally self-contained. She found herself longing for him to kiss her, which was crazy—the man was obviously nothing but trouble.

She became conscious that although the last notes of the waltz had died away, Adam hadn't moved. He still held her in his arms, his eyes searching her face.

Blaise jumped when she heard a voice chirrup beside her, "I can see you have no shortage of dance partners, my dear, although I'm hardly surprised." She hadn't noticed that Cecil Beaton had wandered over.

Blaise seized the opportunity to smoothly extricate herself from Adam's grasp.

"As you're far from home, I thought you might need a guide

to this evening's festivities," Beaton remarked. "There are some interesting people you really should see." He looked at Adam. "I hope you don't mind if I take—"

Blaise quickly interrupted. "Cecil, that's very kind." She had to escape, break Adam's hold over her. He would only cause her more pain.

Turning toward him, she said, "Unfortunately, I need to file a report about the ball first thing in the morning and I haven't nearly enough material." She strived to sound merely polite and professional. "Thank you for the dance, though. It was . . ." Suddenly she found herself uttering words she had definitely not intended to say. "I hope I'll see you again."

Blaise turned away so abruptly it was impossible to gauge Adam's reaction. Yet, as she left the dance floor, she could feel his pale eyes watching her.

"Good lord, Joe Loss and his band are actually playing that vulgar tune 'Fings Ain't Wot They Used T'Be,'" Cecil Beaton exclaimed, shaking his head. "Well, at least the lyrics are apt. Just look at all those doubtful types the princess mixes with these days—did you know Armstrong-Jones had to find a different best man at the last moment?"

Blaise shook her head. "What happened to the first one?"

"It was meant to be that inventor chap, Jeremy Fry—comes from a terribly rich family, made their money out of chocolate bars. But he pleaded a bout of jaundice, of all things." Beaton lowered his voice to a whisper. "The real reason is less savory. A Palace flunky discovered that Mr. Fry had been convicted for what the police call 'importuning for immoral purposes.' Well, we all know what that means."

He rolled his eyes. "Not that one should assume it's Jeremy's fondness for attractive young men that's the problem, so much as his being silly enough to be caught making overtures at absolutely the wrong time and in quite the wrong place. Of course, his wife, Camilla, has a roving eye herself, although she confines her own taste strictly to the opposite sex. Between you and me, I believe they're *both* extremely fond of Tony," he said with a sly look. "But then, there are plenty of members of Margaret's set who are equally erratic. Just look at her, dancing the cha-cha with Colin Tennant, Lord Glenconner's mad son. Tony absolutely loathes him."

"What's behind that?" Blaise prompted. How extraordinary it was to be propelled into a high-flying world of secrets and scandals, and how fortunate that Cecil was so magnificently indiscreet.

He lowered his voice once more. "When Armstrong-Jones was employed to take the pictures at Tennant's wedding to that nice Lady Anne, the Earl of Leicester's daughter, he was made to eat in the kitchen with the servants." Cecil gave a delighted smile. "Tony will never forgive him for the indignity."

"Well, at least Princess Margaret is happy," Blaise observed mildly.

"She might be now, but Tony's never been known to curb his physical appetites. I very much doubt the princess has any idea what she's in for."

Cecil's torrent of gossip may have been diverting, but even if she wanted to, she'd never be able to include his scurrilous observations in *The Clarion*. Instead, she looked around the room for someone she *could* write about.

"I'm trying to find some of the European royals," Blaise said. "There don't seem to be many here."

"Oh, dear me, no—they don't approve of the match, you see. Queen Ingrid of Denmark is the only one to have put in an appearance, and as she's Margaret's godmother, she could hardly decline, could she? There's none of the Swedes or the Norwegians or even the democratic Dutch, just a handful of minor, former royals over from Germany, all of whom are related to Prince Philip," he sniffed.

Blaise smiled blandly, though privately she noted the delight with which her companion had remarked upon the absence of crowned heads of state. Being supplanted by Antony

Armstrong-Jones in the royal family's affections clearly rankled even more than she'd thought.

As Cecil led her around the room, Blaise tried to focus on his acerbic commentary. He'd soon identified—and slandered—enough lords, ladies, and cabinet ministers, as well as the dashing young men about town who made up the so-called Margaret Set, for her head to spin. But she didn't see Charles Ashton again, or Adam Rule. Both men had vanished.

Whether it was due to the incessant chatter, too much Bollinger, or her unexpected encounter with Adam, Blaise wasn't sure, but, whatever the reason, she was very definitely beginning to sway. "My apologies, Cecil," she said, clutching his arm. "Riveted as I am by your commentary, my jet lag is well and truly getting the better of me. I don't think I'll be able to stay much longer without passing out."

Beaton nodded. "Not to worry, my dear. Now that Her Majesty has retired for the evening, you can safely slip away. I'll keep an eye out for anything interesting."

When Blaise left the ballroom, retraced her steps through the long gallery, and descended the grand staircase, she found herself reverting to an old habit. Yet, as she tried to recall the names and the features of every new person she'd seen during this extraordinary evening, one handsome face she knew only too well kept on returning.

# CHAPTER TWENTY-ONE

Walking into *The Advocate*'s newsroom on the day after the ball was the oddest sensation, a case of full-blown déjà vu. For a moment, Blaise could have sworn she'd never left Australia. The number of journalists pounding away on their typewriters might have been greater, but the atmosphere was identical to the churning hive at *The Clarion*. There was the same fug of smoke and sound of urgent conversations, the same constantly ringing phones—and the same absence of female faces. The chief of staff, Johnny Norton, showed her to Roger Croft's desk, which was cluttered with used notebooks, snapshots of royals at various events, an empty gin bottle, a cracked ashtray, and a small, wilted pot plant.

Norton was an overweight man with piercing black eyes and a gravelly voice that suggested a lifetime of long days and nights spent in close company with alcohol and cigarettes. "I must say," he remarked as he took his time looking Blaise up and down, "you're easier on the eye than Dodgy Rog."

"Yeah, well, that wouldn't be hard," Blaise said. *Same old lines, too,* she thought as she slung her bag onto the floor and sat down.

"I'll leave you to it, then," Norton rasped, straightening a tie that seemed to bear the traces of that morning's egg. "Anything you need, just give one of the copy boys a yell. Oh, and if you haven't got something better to do, you might like to join me for lunch. Unfortunately, El Vino's doesn't see fit to serve women at the bar—even if they look like you—so if you'd rather rub shoulders with the lads, we could go to the Clock, or maybe meet some of the *Mirror* chaps over at the Stab. Then there's—"

"Sorry, but did you just say the Stab?"

"Otherwise known as the White Hart," Norton said with a yellow-toothed smile. "No one's ever agreed on where the name came from—some say it's short for 'stab in the back,' due to its patrons' habit of indulging in murky office politics. But a stab is also what the print boys over here call a line of type that's been established, so it might be that. Personally, I'd go for the first interpretation, Miss Hill. Fleet Street is filled with dark deeds perpetrated by madmen, gossips, unprincipled eavesdroppers, and plotters, otherwise known as the gentlemen of the press."

Blaise nodded her head. "So, just like the Sydney newspaper scene, then. By the way," she added, "call me Blaise or, if you prefer, just Hill is fine by me. If you've ever come across any Aussies before, you'll know we're not nearly as formal as you Brits."

"Hill, then. And you can drop the Mister—Norton will do. As a matter of fact, I know your editor, McInerney, pretty well, and a bloke called Kev Kennedy, too. They've both done stints over here in the past. Jesus wept, when it came to drinking, that mad-eyed Kennedy could give anyone a run for his money." He emitted a wheezy cackle. "Lately, the only Australian who's been working out of *The Advocate* is old Rog, and the less said about him the better. Personally," he shrugged, "I'd be happy if the bloody man never came back." With a disdainful expression, Norton picked up Croft's sad-looking pot plant and deposited it in a nearby rubbish bin.

Blaise was anxious to wrap up her story, but it seemed Norton hadn't finished yet.

"The thing that makes Fleet Street what it is," he said, "is that Great Britain's eight national dailies and ten Sundays are located right here, or near enough, along with the London offices of most of the major regionals—that makes for thousands of newsmen in this one small place. You'll soon find that the Street of Shame is really more like a village. It's got its own little ways, of course."

"What sort of ways?" Blaise asked. Since Norton was determined to hold her up, she might as well find out what she could.

"For one thing, where a bloke works more or less dictates where he drinks," he explained. "If you want to find a chap from *The Telegraph*, you wouldn't go anywhere other than The King & Keys. If it's someone from the *Daily Mail* you're after, then it's straight to the Harrow in Hanging Sword Alley. That is, of course, unless the bugger's holed up at the Mucky Duck, more formally known as the White Swan. Once you're across all that, it makes it easy to find who you're after—or, for that matter, how best to stay out of a bloke's way."

Blaise was dumbfounded.

"Don't worry your pretty little head about it. If you come for lunch I'll fill you in on the lot."

She gritted her teeth. The way Norton carried on was odious and she still needed to get some research out of the way. On the other hand, when would she have another opportunity to mix with real Fleet Street journalists?

Because of the time difference between London and Sydney, she'd need to have her copy filed by eleven o'clock that morning, but there wasn't much on afterward, other than a press briefing at five in the afternoon. She had to make time to go down to Westminster Abbey, as the next day's huge crowds would make it impossible to take in any details of its Gothic architecture or the decorations in the surrounding streets. Then she'd planned to take a proper look at the Mall—Andy had promised that he'd finally drive her down this grand boulevard. She wanted to see the white banners bearing red Tudor roses that had been installed all the way from Admiralty Arch to Buckingham Palace.

Blaise made a quick calculation. If she could bash out her story fast enough, she should still have time to grab a bite to eat with Norton at the—what was it? The Stab. "All right, sounds good," she said. "Is midday too early?"

"Are you joking? The editor opens his drinks cabinet at eleven o'clock. By noon the newsroom's practically deserted."

"What, you mean every single reporter will be in the pub? How long do they stay?"

"I really couldn't say." Norton's tone was breezy. "Journalism is thirsty work."

Blaise settled down to write. It was fairly standard stuff—a description of the Palace's ballroom, its flowers, and the refreshments on offer; who was there and what they wore; Margaret's happiness, her diamond necklace, earrings, bracelets, and tiara; the queen's own tiara, satin Hartnell gown, and so on. Despite Cecil's tales, she couldn't think of a single detail that would give her story a little extra sparkle—at least, nothing that wasn't so libelous as to be unprintable. She racked her brains. If the usual details about frocks and floral arrangements were all she wrote about, she'd hardly be returning to Australia in a blaze of glory.

Blaise frowned. By now, she was largely immune to the sound of telephones, but her train of thought had been broken by one that seemed to be ringing far louder than the others. It took her a few seconds to realize it was Roger Croft's—someone who wasn't aware he was out of action must be after him. True, Charlie had said he'd call her, but after last night's vanishing act she doubted she'd hear from him. A tingle ran down her spine. The only other person it could be was Adam.

Blaise seized the phone. "Yes?"

"It's Cecil, Cecil Beaton." She felt curiously let down.

"I'm sorry, you've caught me at a bad time." Blaise glanced at her watch. "I'm just about to file my copy, although I can't say it's very lively. Unfortunately, my editor would have a fit if I included any of the stories you told me."

"Oh dear, was I terribly naughty? Just as well I rang now, then." There was the sound of a delighted trill at the other end of the line. "As it happens, I've a splendid little tale you might like to include." He paused. "It seems that the Duchess of Buccleuch arrived at last night's ball wearing her famous emerald and diamond brooch, one of the family's heirlooms."

"I remember that brooch. It was impossible to miss."

"Well, the duchess is certainly missing it now. Right at the end of the evening she discovered that her favorite jewel was no longer pinned to her ball gown. Apparently, the Palace staff were up half the night frantically searching." He laughed. "In the end, bits of furniture and some of the heaters were dismantled. Eventually, they even started taking up the floorboards."

"You're kidding!" Blaise was noting down everything Cecil said in rapid shorthand. "And did they find it?"

"Not a trace, which means someone must have taken it. Personally, I wouldn't put it past one of Tony's friends."

Blaise smiled. There was nothing like a whiff of scandal to enliven an innocuous royal story.

# CHAPTER TWENTY-TWO

Johnny Norton showed Blaise to a small table at the back of a shadowy room then left her to buy some drinks. As he wandered over to the long, pitted bar, she peered through the gloom. The Stab was nearly as smoky as the newsroom, though, in addition, it was imbued with the distinctive yeasty smell of beer, overlaid with the malodorous scent left behind by decades of boozy journalists.

Conscious of heads turning in her direction, she realized just how out of place a girl like her must seem. There were only a couple of older women among the Stab's patrons, but they looked hard-faced and tough; no doubt they needed to be to survive working on Fleet Street. She tried her best to appear at ease, even though, because of Australia's absurd rules and regulations, she'd never actually been inside a pub before—not that she was about to take Johnny Norton into her confidence.

He soon reappeared with a greasy-looking tray on which stood two foaming beers and a couple of packets of crisps. It seemed that lunch was to be of the largely liquid variety.

"These public houses don't merely provide the hard-working hack with refreshment." He glanced around with affection. "They're a combination of oasis, intensive care unit, bureau de change, job center, and Arabian souk. Hang around the pubs for long enough and though you'll hear countless rumors, tall tales, and blatant lies; you might just come across a tip that could change the course of history."

He handed Blaise a drink. "I appreciate you filling me in on Fleet Street," she said, "but I'm only in London for another week, which doesn't give me much time to pick up anything else." She took a tentative sip from her glass of ale. "I mean, what would you say is the mood of the country? Right now, everyone seems swept up in the royal marriage."

"That won't last long," Norton said sullenly.

"What, the people's high spirits, or the happy couple's wedded bliss?"

"Both."

"How's that?"

"Let's take the 'happy couple,' as you call them. They're both just as pretty, spoiled, and headstrong as each other. And you know what they say about the amorous Armstrong-Jones, don't you?"

"I don't, actually."

"If it moves, he'll have it." Norton guffawed. "Believe you me—that marriage will be a disaster."

"Well, what about the country, then. Are you any more optimistic on that score?"

"As it happens, I am." Norton wiped a dribble of beer away from his mouth with the back of his hand. "There are big changes about to happen in Great Britain. I predict the establishment will be on the receiving end of a smacking long before Margaret and Tony's marriage collapses."

"The establishment?" It wasn't a term she was used to hearing in Australia.

"The ruling class. The royals, of course, anyone with a title, plus the landed gentry. The people who head up the civil service and the Foreign Office, or else the church. The big bankers and industrialists. Men who've been to posh schools like Eton or Harrow, or went to university at Oxford and Cambridge. The lot of them mix in overlapping circles and make sure to help one another out, whether it's access to a plum job or anything else. The establishment locks out anyone they think is the wrong type. By God, though"—he tore open his packet of crisps with sudden ferocity—"if there's trouble brewing, they protect their pals' backs."

The words of her mother flashed vividly into Blaise's mind. Maude had certainly never moved in an elite strata, but she'd still warned her daughter that when times were tough the "well-to-dos" didn't hesitate to close ranks. Blaise had thought her mother was just sounding off, but now she wondered if she'd had personal experience.

Norton crunched his way through a mouthful of crisps. "From the look of you," he said as he picked crumbs from his teeth, "you're not old enough to have heard of Burgess and Maclean. They were upper-class chaps, went to Cambridge, and were in top jobs at the Foreign Office—before someone gave them the nod and they bolted for Mother Russia."

"You mean, they'd been spying for the Soviets?"

"No doubt about it. Course, they should have been uncovered years before, only, seeing as they'd attended the right schools and universities, no one in power believed that men from the same bloody rarefied background as themselves could possibly be traitors. If you ask me"—he tapped his bulbous nose—"I'm certain there are more of them out there right now, spilling the United Kingdom's secrets to the Russkies."

Still on her first drink, Blaise waited while Norton returned with two more beers. He glanced at her barely touched glass and, without a word, set them both in front of himself. "Not so long ago," he continued, "our current Prime Minister stood up in the House of Commons and defended another ex-Cambridge, ex–Foreign Office type by the name of Kim Philby. I'll bet you anything you like he'll be the next one who'll do a midnight flit to Moscow."

Blaise was beginning to wonder if Norton, with his wild conspiracy theories about Soviet spies, wasn't a little mad. Surely this sort of widespread treachery didn't happen in Britain.

"The problem," he said, "is Macmillan's still living in the past.

I don't think he has any idea what's going on, and even if he does suspect something, he'll do whatever it takes to cover his backside. As for his ministers, they think they're born to rule, that they can get away with anything."

He leaned in so close to her that Blaise could smell the beery fumes on his breath. "I'm after a political scandal, though there are a few other papers who are counting on catching someone in the Palace making up to a certain lady with whom he shouldn't be seen.

"In the end, it won't matter which paper lands the story, or whether it's about spies in high places, nefarious political goings-on, or a member of the royal family with a wandering eye. All that's important is that, when the news breaks, the gloves will well and truly come off." Norton smiled with glee. "Then we'll see who's been born to rule, won't we?"

The day of the wedding dawned bright and sunny with clear blue skies. Just as well, Blaise thought as she looked out of the Jaguar's window on the way to the abbey, for she saw a host of rumpled people surrounded by rugs and picnic baskets who'd obviously spent the previous night camping out on the pavements lining the route.

"They tell me there's half a million well-wishers expected in London today," Andy remarked from behind the wheel.

"I'm lucky to be one of them," Blaise said excitedly as they passed bright baskets of spring flowers hanging from lamp posts and buildings festooned with garlands of pink and blue hydrangeas. "Look how many people are crammed into the grandstands across from the abbey!" she exclaimed as Andy slowed the limousine to a crawl.

"Each of those seats has been sold for twenty-five quid." He shook his head. "Well, I suppose it's better than standing on your plates."

"Your . . . what?"

Andy chuckled. "Apologies, Miss—that just slipped out. It's

the way we Cockneys talk, in rhyming slang. 'Plates of meat' means 'feet'—there's a load of expressions like that. You might greet a friend saying, 'Hello, me old china.' 'China plate' stands for 'mate,' d'you see?"

"I do. But what exactly is a Cockney?"

"Anyone born close enough to hear the church bells of Mary-le-bow," he said. "It's in the East End, where the working class live."

"Sounds a bit like the place where I come from," Blaise said.

"What, you, Miss? I'm surprised to hear that."

"I didn't always wear fancy clothes like these," she said. "Thanks for the lesson, though I can't imagine I'll be coming across any rhyming slang inside Westminster Abbey."

"You never know," Andy said. "I did hear the groom's invited his cleaning lady." He stopped the car and helped her out. "Enjoy the wedding, Miss."

It was impossible not to be swept up in the mood of keen anticipation that fizzed about the animated queue Blaise joined in front of the abbey's great west door. She wished Harriet was with her—apart from the sheer fun of sharing this experience, she would have loved to hear her expert friend's thoughts on the extraordinary outfits worn by some of the ladies.

From what she could observe, it seemed as if the very best of fashion had passed away with the great Christian Dior. Without either a clear direction or a single towering authority to inspire them, the ladies had either stayed loyal to the designs of the past, which now looked outdated, or had created a chaotic effect by adding every imaginable embellishment to their ensembles.

Thank heavens Harriet had lent her the classic dusky-pink, three-quarter-length silk dress and matching coat she'd put on that morning, or she may well have found herself in the same fix. Gray suede gloves, matching shoes, and a handbag had completed the outfit. She'd twisted her chestnut hair into a chignon, on top of which she'd perched a pillbox hat trimmed at the front with two deep-pink carnations.

Blaise smiled to herself. What a long way she'd come from the girl who owned two skirts and had no interest in fashion. She was sure Maude would not have approved of her borrowing such an extravagant outfit, but if Marguerite Hawthorn had been there, she at least would have been proud of her protégé's appearance.

As she took her seat in an elevated section that had been specially constructed to accommodate the hundreds of extra guests packed inside the abbey, Blaise noted the discreetly placed television cameras—the attempts that had been made to camouflage them with an abundance of greenery having been only partially successful. This would be the first royal wedding ever televised. How strange it would be to have one of the most intensely personal moments of one's life beamed around the world to hundreds of millions of anonymous people. Margaret had been in the public eye ever since she was born, so perhaps it didn't seem intrusive to her, but how did Tony Armstrong-Jones feel about it?

He cut a fine if diminutive figure and certainly looked relaxed enough as he chatted to his best man. At the last minute, Dr. Roger Gilliatt, a neurologist of impeccable reputation and the son of the queen's gynecologist, had replaced the unsuitable Mr. Fry.

So remarkable was the scene in the soaring, flower-filled abbey's interior and so unlikely was her presence among the select company that Blaise felt almost as if she were in front of a television set herself, or at least viewing a Movietone newsreel. But, of course, instead of being in dreary black and white, the glorious spectacle unfolding before her was in vivid technicolor—and she was experiencing it at first hand.

Gazing down, she saw the unmistakable symbol of wartime Britain, Sir Winston Churchill himself, making his way along the aisle. She realized he had to be well into his eighties by now. Having been brought up by her parents to revere this doughty hero, she'd always thought of him as indestructible. But the frail old man she observed leaned heavily on his walking stick as he shuffled down the deep blue carpet at the center of the diamond-patterned floor.

The Duchess of Kent appeared positively cross when she took her seat, in contrast to the smiling Queen Mother, a vision in pale gold lamé and a hat swathed in mink. "For reasons I cannot fathom," Cecil had confided at the ball, "the old queen is a huge fan of Tony's." The groom's mother, the Countess of Rosse, set off her beautiful face with an odd tulle headpiece shaped rather like a busby, while the queen, entering last, looked stern and wore a long turquoise silk and lace ensemble with a matching cocktail hat.

Blaise told herself it was time to stop acting like a gawking tourist. She was a journalist with a job to do. First, she focused on the rows of the great, the good and the well-connected who sat along the timber pews, eagerly waiting for the proceedings to begin. While it was easy to identify the more famous faces, she didn't have a clue who most of the others were. Fortunately, the Palace press office had supplied her with a list, together with a plan that showed where the most notable people were seated and various details concerning the ceremony. She slid it out of her handbag and took a surreptitious look.

Using the notes to guide her, Blaise identified the poet John Betjeman next to his paramour, Lady Elizabeth Cavendish (Harriet had informed her that it was Her Ladyship who'd brought Tony and Margaret together), dear Cecil Beaton, the French poet Jean Cocteau and, nearby, the urbane playwright and performer Noël Coward. She was also able to pick out two former British prime ministers, bald Clement Attlee and Macmillan's predecessor, the unfortunate Anthony Eden, whose brief tenure had been marred by the controversial Suez Crisis.

It was easy to spot Australia's current leader. Robert Menzies was regarding the queen with an expression of undiluted adoration from beneath his bushy black eyebrows. The Dukes of Marlborough, Richmond, Northumberland and Buccleuch were present as well, although Ivy would be disappointed to learn that they had been accompanied by a quartet of duchesses.

Her eyes continued to move along the rows, then stopped at Lord Mountbatten. He was living up to his reputation for vanity, for he'd ignored the sober morning suit dress code and was instead conspicuously attired in the gold-braided formal uniform of an Admiral of the Fleet, complete with a celestial array of stars and medals.

Charles Ashton, his blond hair catching the light, was sitting halfway down the abbey, in close conversation with a vital-looking, gray-haired man her list informed her was his father, Lord Bennington. Blaise worked her way carefully down the left-hand side of the nave and had nearly finished examining the right, only to be disappointed. Among all the famous faces, one—by choice, very much less well known—had proved elusive. Her heart skipped a beat when finally, toward the rear, she spotted Adam's strongly delineated features, half obscured by shadow.

As she observed his composed expression, she pondered why it was he never looked either impressed or intimidated. He seemed to have the gift of appearing at ease wherever he was, be it a Sydney tram yard or Westminster Abbey. Perhaps it was because he'd known poverty as well as wealth.

She couldn't understand why Charlie disliked him. But then, hadn't she had doubts about Adam herself? Maybe she shouldn't have been so quick to dismiss them. Of course, it could be that Charlie simply resented his father's generosity; she imagined a good English education was frighteningly expensive. Or was the cause of their animosity something else entirely?

That was the problem with Adam Rule. While there was no end of questions, answers were maddeningly elusive.

She only had herself to blame for their assignation ending so disastrously. She'd rushed everything, tried to start their relationship with what should have been its culmination, when it had hardly even had a beginning. Maybe if she came to know Adam, developed a friendship, then one day he would explain what he'd meant when he'd said she deserved a better man than him. Blaise sighed. Mere friendship had never been what she'd wanted.

A sudden, blaring fanfare of trumpets brought her back abruptly to the unfolding spectacle. There was a brief moment of absolute silence, before a swelling chord sounded and the abbey's organist launched into a robust version of "Christ is Made the Sure Foundation." Blaise watched intently while a swan-like Princess Margaret, on the arm of her brother-in-law, Prince Philip, began to glide down the aisle.

As the princess approached the high altar, Blaise was struck by the enchanting design of her pure white silk organza gown. There was none of the usual elaborate embroidery seen on royal wedding dresses, no beading or appliqué to distract from its elegant lines. The voluminous skirt swooped into a semicircular train, while behind her floated a long, diaphanous veil edged with narrow silk piping. The simplicity of the princess's dress only heightened the impact of the spectacular, recently purchased Poltimore tiara that she wore on her bouffant hairstyle. With its dazzling diamond scrolls and flowers, the tall circlet flashed and glittered beneath the glare of the television lights.

There was no way around it. Although when it came to brides the word "radiant" was sorely overused, Blaise knew she'd be hard-pressed to find a more apt description of Her Royal Highness, the Princess Margaret, on her wedding day.

Led by the queen's only daughter, the nine-year-old, fair-haired Princess Anne, the eight little bridesmaids, looking terribly serious in their puff-sleeved dresses, lined up in twos behind the bride. Prince Philip retired to his seat, Tony stood by Margaret's right-hand side and the Archbishop of Canterbury, attired in a magnificent embroidered cope and pointed mitre, began the service. Blaise jotted down her impressions of everything, from the heady atmosphere and the white-robed choir's heavenly voices to the pristine beauty of the bride's attire.

All proceeded smoothly until it was time for the wedding vows. There was the faintest rustle among the congregation when first, Princess Margaret failed to repeat Archbishop Fisher's line "From this day forward." Then she beat him to the next line by blurting "For better or for worse" before he'd had a chance to get the words out.

Blaise decided these little slip-ups were hardly surprising. Poor Margaret had been forced to wait long enough to be married. She could hardly be blamed for being in a hurry.

The hot television lights began to make Blaise feel faint, but she couldn't wait around. Time was moving on and she had to file her report. "Excuse me, excuse me," she said as she pushed through the crush of wedding guests lingering outside the abbey. Dodging sideways, she was congratulating herself on avoiding a collision with a stout dowager draped in lime green satin when she felt the slender heel of one of her shoes give way.

As Blaise staggered forward, her head swimming, she realized with horror that she was about to fall flat on her face in front of the entire crowd. Then a firm hand grasped her elbow and, to her relief, she was hoisted back onto her feet. "Good heavens," she heard Charlie Ashton say, "we do meet under dramatic circumstances. At least I'm here to rescue you this time, instead of drown you in champagne."

She glanced at the livid bruise high on his right cheek. "You know how accident prone I am." He smiled sheepishly. "Had a bit of a collision with a door the other night." With barely a pause he added, "I wonder if you'd take pity on a poor bumbler and accept that dinner invitation of mine for this evening? I thought we might go to Rules—it's London's oldest restaurant, been in Covent Garden for well over a century. What do you think?"

Of course the restaurant *would* be called Rules. It seemed she couldn't escape Adam, even while another man was beseeching her for a date. "First things first," she said. "I'm afraid I'll have to lean on you, Charlie, until I've hobbled over to my driver's car."

Charlie smiled broadly. "My right arm is yours to command."

There was something about Charlie that was definitely winning: for one thing, his obvious admiration of her. After being rebuffed by Adam Rule, it was gratifying to be the object of such straightforward appreciation. "I think I can now safely declare that you have redeemed yourself," she said as the Jaguar cruised into view.

A night out would mean she wouldn't have time to write up the honeymooners' departure for the Caribbean on the Royal Yacht *Britannia* or the street parties and celebrations that were taking place afterward but, at a pinch, she could do it if she started early enough the following morning.

"So that's a yes?" he asked with an appealing enthusiasm.

Blaise smiled. Perhaps Charlie was right: it would be a waste of a once-in-a-lifetime opportunity if she didn't at least sample London's delights. And the man was not just sweet; he was definitely good-looking. He might even provide the antidote to her hopeless infatuation with Adam.

"Now that I think about it, a historic restaurant in Covent Garden could be a good subject for a color piece in the newspaper," she said, not wishing to sound overly eager. "Why not pick me up at eight o'clock?"

# CHAPTER TWENTY-THREE

Blaise was surprised when the restaurant's head waiter greeted Charlie with the affection of an old friend. He seemed to have a knack for—what was it? *Pleasantness*, she thought, a cheerful cordiality that immediately made people warm to him.

They were shown to a small, dimly lit corner table from where she had an excellent view of the drawings and photographs that covered the saffron walls. Charlie suggested they order roast venison. "It's one of the specialities of the house," he said expansively, "and I'll order a good red to go with it."

While they waited for their meal he amused her with tales of boyhood mischief, including a description of the time he'd placed a small gray mouse in the drawer of his nanny's bedside table. Then he moved on to some hilarious anecdotes about his political cronies.

Blaise was still laughing when the venison arrived. She took a bite of the rich, seasoned meat before pronouncing it "absolutely delicious" and adding, "I've never tasted anything like it. As for the wine—it's wonderful."

"Excellent." Charlie grinned. "Just wait until you see what I've planned for the rest of the evening."

He really was wonderful company, Blaise thought, and charmingly transparent. What you saw with Charlie Ashton was what you got, unlike . . . well, Adam. As she finished her second glass of claret it occurred to her that this was the perfect opportunity to discover more about his past, if only she could find a way to work his name into the conversation. But Charlie surprised her.

"Look, about Rule," he said. "When I saw you dancing with him I wondered—sorry if I'm speaking out of turn—I wondered if there was something going on between the two of you."

"I can't imagine what gave you that idea," she said quickly. "I barely know the man." She bit back the questions she'd been on the verge of asking. Probing further would betray her interest and, anyway, Charlie had already made his own views perfectly clear. She would only spoil what was turning out to be a fabulous evening.

They left the restaurant and walked over to the Jaguar. Charlie had become acquainted with Andy after Blaise's near fall at the abbey. Having learned Sir Ernest would have no use for the chauffeur for some time, he'd suggested that, other than when Andy was driving Blaise to royal events, he retain the man's services for his own private engagements.

"The 400 Club," Charlie instructed him, "Leicester Square." Then he turned to Blaise. "The club claims to cater for the upper classes."

"And does it?"

"Its patrons like to think so," he said, laughing.

When they arrived he told Andy, "Don't bother waiting for us. That will be all for tonight." As the car glided away, Charlie took her hand before escorting her inside.

A group of back-slapping men who all sounded like Charlie and seemed to have either been to school with each other, attended the same Oxbridge colleges, or served in the same Guards regiment quickly surrounded them. While she found the men cheerful and welcoming, their wives and girlfriends were, by contrast, decidedly cool toward her. Maybe it was because she came from Australia—one of them had actually thought it amusing to mimic her accent—or else she wasn't sufficiently "upper class" for their liking. On second thoughts, considering how their eyes lit up at the sight of Charlie and the way their laughter tinkled each time he made a witty remark, perhaps they were more concerned she would remove such a desirable single man from their midst. Well, they had nothing to worry about on that front. She'd be back in Sydney in a little over a week and the eligible Charles Ashton would be all theirs again.

"We should be dancing," he said to Blaise, squeezing her hand. "Then I'll have the pleasure of attracting even more envy from my chums. Not only are you by far the most interesting woman here, you look gorgeous."

Blaise's eyes sparkled. She'd splashed out on a form-fitting little black dress, and it had been worth every penny she'd spent.

Then, suddenly, it was midnight, they'd said goodbye to his friends and were out in the street. He hailed a cab, but instead of giving the driver the address of the Knightsbridge flat, he said, "Take us to The Flamingo."

"Wardour Street, guv?" the cabbie asked.

"That's the one."

Blaise settled back, enveloped by a warm buzz. The wine over dinner and more drinks at the 400 Club had already made her tipsy. "Charlie," she mumbled, "about that early start tomorrow . . ."

"The night is young!"

"All right, you win," she said, giving in immediately. The truth was, she was having more fun than she'd ever had in her life.

Soon they were passing through Soho, which reminded Blaise of Sydney's sleazy Kings Cross. Every street was lined with gaudy neon signs, gentlemen's clubs, bars, cheap restaurants, and the odd pawn shop. She peered out the window at the lurid scene, thinking how appalled her parents would be if they knew this was the sort of place she was spending her time in London.

"You should see your face." Charlie smiled.

"Well, there are rather a lot of shady types hanging about." She giggled, pointing to a man dressed in a ghastly green suit who was hawking the delights of the "Lovely ladies, lovely ladies" on view inside.

"What do these lovely ladies *do* exactly?" she asked.

"Oh, he's talking about the showgirls. They stand around as still as Grenadier Guards, only they haven't a stitch on from the waist up."

"So they don't move at all?"

"Not a fraction. If they did, the Lord Chamberlain's men would close the place down." He squeezed her hand. "Come on, why not broaden your horizons?"

The Flamingo Club was a great deal wilder than the 400, but Charlie was right—if she wanted to see a cross-section of London life, this was the place for it. Tattooed thugs rubbed shoulders with socialites while off-duty showgirls shared their tables with men dressed in pinstripe suits. There were boys dancing with boys, girls with girls, and black faces among white. Within the Flamingo's four walls, the outside world's usual rules about sex, race, and class had been joyfully abandoned.

Charlie pointed out a few identities: Oliver Reed, an up-and-coming film star, looking rather drunk, a couple of heavy-set men he said were notorious criminals called the Kray twins, and even a fellow Conservative politician.

"Why don't you go over and say hello?" Blaise suggested.

"Because the attractive young lady he's with is most definitely not his wife," Charlie said. "There's a form a chap follows when dealing with a friend's private indiscretions, which is to behave as if one were deaf, dumb, and blind. It's by far the wisest course. Now, come on—there's a famous English cocktail I insist you try."

She smiled woozily. "I suppose I could always put it down to research."

Blaise groaned. The newsroom's formerly unobtrusive overhead lighting now seemed blinding, while the usual din had become unbearable. The previous night had passed in a fantastic whirl. She dimly remembered a group of musicians performing a set of electrifying hot jazz while a couple of girls jived on top of a table. It was just possible she had been one of them. She had no idea what time she'd finally arrived home, waved Charlie a blurry goodbye with a kiss on the cheek and, finally, collapsed onto her bed.

Her sole regret was that he had introduced her to a Black Velvet, a cocktail made from champagne and Guinness that he'd told her was a London speciality. Now she was feeling its gruesome effects. Blaise massaged her temples. She hadn't written a word, nothing about the rapturous crowds down at the docks, or the princess's yellow chiffon going-away ensemble.

God, though, she'd had a great night. The problem was, if she kept up this excess of drinking, dining, and dancing, she'd never get anything done. Vowing to mend her ways, Blaise inserted half a dozen small sheets of paper and carbons into her typewriter and made a start on the opening paragraph. She'd barely progressed any further when she heard a voice with a refined, cut-glass accent coming from somewhere behind her left shoulder.

"Oh, I see you've led with a description of that perfectly hideous toque Princess Margaret wore. Didn't you think it was incredibly—well, there's no other way to put it really, is there?" She tittered. "Incredibly old hat?"

Blaise turned around, which made her head thump more intensely than ever. "And you would be . . . ?" she said weakly then caught her breath. Blaise had never seen a frock like the one on the very pretty girl standing in front of her. It bore no resemblance to the fashions the couturiers were producing in Paris, or the classic suits and dresses that Marguerite and Harriet had encouraged Blaise to adopt. Nor was it like the matronly clothes donned by so many women, both at home and in London, which tended to make even the flightiest teenagers look middle-aged.

In contrast to her own sedate cream blouse and slim navy skirt, this girl was wearing a daringly short, gray and black striped flannel pinafore over a tight black turtleneck sweater. Her long legs were clad in sheer black stockings and she'd teamed them with flat suede shoes. As for her hair, rather than having been set with rollers in a Monsieur Leon–approved style or else pinned up in a neat French roll like her own, she wore her thick blonde tresses loose to her shoulders and flicked up at the ends. Between the little striped dress and the casual hairdo, she looked young, fresh, and strikingly original.

"You're Blaise Hill, aren't you?" the girl said, smiling. Without waiting for a response she announced, "I'm Dora Hughes, and I can see you're staring at my dress. I hope that means you like it."

"I do! But it's so . . . so different!"

"Isn't it just?" Dora performed a quick twirl. "And if I want to wear it at night, I just take off the sweater and put on some heels. There's this incredible boutique in the King's Road called Bazaar. You simply must go there. Mary Quant has fantastic stuff and there are new things coming in all the time. Her gear is brilliant, really cutting edge, and it's not expensive. There's nobody else in London like her." With barely a pause Dora announced, "I know, I'll take you! I'm doing an interview with her this afternoon."

"Whoa, Dora, slow down."

"Sorry! I know, I'm always rattling on at a mile a minute—everyone says that, including our mutual friend, Harriet Lawrence. How is Harriet, anyway? The last time I saw her we were both mooning over our yummy French ski instructor. I always thought she wanted to be a diplomat, but she's just written to tell me she's in Sydney working on the Women's Pages at *The Clarion*."

"Wait a minute," Blaise said. "You mean to say *you're* Pandora Fraser-Barclay-Hughes? Crikey, with a name like that I thought you'd be dressed in florals and be spending your time at hunt balls or something. How come you call yourself Dora Hughes?"

"I think you've just answered that." The other girl laughed good-naturedly. "If I didn't, everyone would assume I was simply a spoiled debutante. I'm serious about my job."

Blaise thought back to Mrs. Hawthorn's comments when they'd been waiting for Hardy Amies at Prince's restaurant. Her boss had virtually accused her of being an inverted snob and, although she'd brushed it off at the time, she now realized, with a pang of guilt, that Marguerite had been close to the mark.

"I'm terribly sorry, I seem to have fallen into the same trap," Blaise apologized. "I'd really love to meet whoever's designed your frock—just looking at you makes me feel like a frump. Only, I had a pretty late date with a guy last night." She winced. "To tell you the truth, I'm suffering from my first ever hangover, and it's a shocker. I also have to finish this story right away. But maybe we could meet up later? I've nothing more planned, except I have been invited out to dinner again."

"You have a lot of invitations for a girl who's just arrived in London," Dora said. "Not that I'm surprised—you're awfully nice-looking, although, now I can see you properly"—she extracted a pair of owl-shaped black glasses from her pocket and perched them on her nose—"those big blue eyes of yours do look rather bloodshot. So," she said, removing her glasses, "who was last night's lucky man?"

"Just a bloke called Charles Ashton."

"Not the Honorable Charlie, rising political star and heir to Lord Bennington's estate?"

"That's the one. Anyway, I met Charlie when I was working—covering the royal ball two nights ago—and one thing led to another."

Dora fell silent.

"Oh, I don't mean *that*." Blaise laughed. "He's not that fast a worker!"

"But he *is* quite the charmer, isn't he?" Dora said. "All the debs are after him—except for me. He's not my type. Charlie's far too conservative for my liking. I'd rather be with someone different, like an artist or a musician or—"

"A photographer? They seem to be all the rage these days."

"Exactly." Dora giggled. "But, you know, Tony Armstrong-Jones is really talented. Every top fashion magazine is after him. Unlike those studio poses with pillars and bunches of roses that good old Cecil Beaton goes in for, he likes to shoot models knocking over glasses or leaping about in the street."

"Oh heavens, you weren't the girl who collapsed into Cecil's floral arrangement, were you?"

"Guilty as charged," Dora said, laughing. "Goodness only knows, I can't see Tony giving up his job, or his girlfriends, for that matter. Still, he's great fun and—oh, there I go, running on again." She smiled. "Look, I'm not due to see Mary until two o'clock, so you've plenty of time to sort yourself out. Then you absolutely must come with me to Bazaar—it's by far London's most original boutique."

Blaise's head felt worse than ever. "I'd love to," she said, "but I just remembered that I half promised Johnny Norton I'd have lunch with him. We went to the Stab yesterday, and he insisted on showing me some of Fleet Street's other watering holes to-day. The man seems to think they're an essential sight, a sort of journalist's equivalent to the British Museum or the Tower of London." She groaned again. "The very last thing I need at the moment is a pub crawl." Running one hand through her rich chestnut hair, she added, "I thought Australian journalists were fond of a drink, but from what I've seen so far, the British pack would leave them for dead."

"Just tell Johnny-boy you have to go out on an assignment," Dora said.

"But I don't."

"Really? As you've probably guessed, I work for what this newspaper quaintly terms the Women's Section. I've decided it's time ye olde *Advocate* was shaken up—don't you want to do the same thing at *The Clarion*? From what Harriet tells me, its Women's Pages are still pretty safe."

Marguerite Hawthorn had introduced changes, but maybe the injection of something really different—even shocking—was just what was needed.

"I think I'll sit in on that interview after all," Blaise said.

"You won't be sorry." Dora's tone had become earnest. "Mary Quant is going to start a fashion revolution."

# CHAPTER TWENTY-FOUR

The teleprinter operators seemed to have vanished. There were six unattended machines inside their room, all rattling away at top speed while they automatically spewed out rolls of paper displaying breaking news from international wire agencies and *The Advocate*'s own foreign correspondents. Copy boys rushed in, tore off reports from New York, Moscow, Rome, and a dozen other cities, then raced out again, but there was still no sign of a single operator. Blaise pursed her lips. If her copy didn't go off in the next ten minutes, she'd miss *The Clarion*'s deadline. McInerney would be ropeable.

"I wouldn't wait around, love, if I were you. They're all at a union meeting," a passing subeditor called out when he saw her hovering by the door.

"Do you know when they'll be back?" She tried not to roll her eyes when she caught the man staring unashamedly at her legs.

"No idea." He shrugged. "After their meeting is over they'll be sure to go for a drink."

Considering all the time *The Advocate*'s staff spent in pubs and wine bars, Blaise found it difficult to comprehend how they produced a newspaper at all. She hung around for another five minutes, although, just as the sub had warned her, there was no sign of anyone returning. That was it: she had no choice but to do the job herself. She'd watched how stories were input often enough—unlike the compositors, *The Clarry*'s teleprinter operators had never been fussy about who touched their machines. In appearance, these resembled a typewriter, but instead of producing rows of printed type, they created electrical impulses that could be transmitted to another destination—even one as far away as Sydney. Once the text was received, it could easily be edited, set, and turned into a printed page.

Blaise slipped inside the empty room and began to type. Unfortunately, her headache hadn't improved one bit. In fact, her head seemed to throb more each time she pressed down on a key. *That will teach you,* she admonished herself, *not to go out carousing.* Seasoned drinkers like Johnny Norton might have hollow legs, but she clearly didn't have the same capacity.

As soon as she'd finished, Blaise took herself off to the reporters' tea room in search of a couple of aspirins and a tall glass of water. She was on her way back to her desk when she heard someone calling, "Miss Hill?"

"Mmm?" she muttered, as a lad of around sixteen scampered over. "Who are you?"

"I'm Colin, one of the copy boys." He grinned. He was pale and thin, with a snub nose and a recalcitrant cowlick with which his comb had obviously long since lost its battle. "Mr. Gifford wants to see you right away."

*Now what?* Blaise thought. She seemed to have spent half her working life being hauled into editors' offices. And in her experience the outcome tended to be unpredictable. Racking her brains, she tried to think what Max Gifford would want.

Blaise had been introduced to the tall, spindly man as soon as she had arrived at the newspaper. She'd been surprised to see that, unlike the ordinary business shirt and lounge suit that McInerney wore in Sydney, *The Advocate*'s helmsman sported a starched, blindingly white collar and cuffs, a conservative dark tie, a carefully tailored black jacket, and dark gray pinstripe trousers. Indeed, every one of the senior men, with the exception of Norton, including the chief sub and all the section editors, dressed in the same way. When she'd first seen them working behind the windows of their various offices, she'd felt as if she had stumbled into a firm of

Edwardian stockbrokers instead of the premises of a great publication that was churning out newspapers in the second half of the twentieth century.

With her headache still grinding away, she knocked on Gifford's door. *What does he want?* Blaise wondered wearily. Then it occurred to her that, most likely, the teleprinters' union had different rules over here about who touched its machines. Hell, perhaps she'd inadvertently set off a strike. That would lead to a tremendous fuss as well as a permanent black mark against her name. She felt a sudden wave of panic.

"Come in, come in," Gifford said pleasantly enough. She'd not noticed it when she'd first met him, but now she could see that the man looked worn out. His narrow shoulders drooped beneath his dark jacket, while his starched collar was as limp as the hand that waved her inside.

"I have a telegram for you from your editor, Mr. McInerney," Gifford said weakly. "I suggest you read it, and then we can discuss what he has written." He handed her the unsealed envelope. "Miss Hill, you might want to sit down."

Her legs weak, Blaise slumped into a chair. This summons had nothing to do with the teleprinter. It could only mean one thing—they'd found out what she and Joe had done. After Adam's assurances that the Tomassi gang had been blamed for Paddy Ryan's death, she'd assumed her problems were over. But she must have been mistaken—why else would she be receiving an urgent cable?

Unless her sister had taken a turn for the worse. Blaise felt her chest tighten. *Please don't let it be bad news about Ivy*, she prayed silently.

"Miss Hill, you are going to read it, aren't you?" Gifford prompted.

Blaise's stomach lurched as she reluctantly opened the envelope and scanned the brief telegram.

Shocked, she looked quickly at Gifford, then back at the single page.

*LYING CROFT SACKED STOP FOUND PORTO-*
*FINO DANCING RUMBA WITH COUNT X STOP*
*JOB YOURS STOP MCINERNEY*

Blaise was speechless.

"Well?" Gifford asked. "Croft has been on thin ice for quite a while. Now, it seems the damned fool has been stupid enough to be caught in a compromising situation, and, as you can see, I'm not merely referring to his specious claims of a so-called skiing accident." He dabbed at his thin mouth with a handkerchief. "I never cared for the man. Croft always seemed so terribly"—he cast around for the right word—"inauthentic."

At that, Gifford succumbed to a violent coughing fit, which had the single benefit of allowing Blaise a moment or two to collect her thoughts.

"I'm dreadfully sorry," he said after a final clearing of his throat. "I don't know what's the matter with me these days. Must be an early summer cold. Anyway, I realize that the offer is rather sudden; I myself received a cable from Edgar McInerney only this morning. This Croft business has put us in rather a tight spot."

Gifford sighed. "You do seem on the young side. Nevertheless, our Mr. Norton assured me you were unlikely to get yourself into any trouble. That's what's needed in a royal correspondent, someone who's level-headed, with an unblemished past."

He smiled. "I can't imagine a girl like you would have had either the time or the inclination to acquire any skeletons to rattle away in her proverbial closet, so I suppose you could say that, in this regard, your youth is in your favor."

Blaise didn't utter a word. All she could think was that if Gifford knew about her role in the backstreet death of a gangster, she'd be marched out of *The Advocate* quicker than he could say "Princess Margaret."

He cleared his throat. "Well then, that's that. There'll be a pay rise commensurate with your new duties. Now, remind me, when are you due to fly back to Australia?"

"In just over a week," she managed to say.

"Then canceling won't be a problem. You might as well telegram your acceptance straightaway."

It seemed not to have occurred to Gifford—or McInerney—that she might need time to think over such a momentous step. Both of them obviously assumed that she'd jump at the chance to be based in the great newspaper city of London. But was she really ready?

She didn't even know how to pronounce the names of the streets, let alone comprehend the vast intricacies of Palace protocol. For the first time in her life she'd be completely alone. Save for Dora—whom she'd only just met—and the wretched Norton, her brief acquaintance with Cecil Beaton and Charlie Ashton, plus whatever it was she shared with the problematic Adam Rule, she didn't know a soul.

"I'd like to think about it overnight, if that's all right, sir," she said. "It's a great honor, of course, but I . . . well, when I left Australia I wasn't planning to stay on."

"I'll see you tomorrow morning then," Gifford said. "As you are no doubt aware, our proprietor is very particular about his newspapers' coverage of the royal family. If you prove suitable, who knows? We could well find that your talents might be of use to us here at *The Advocate* on other stories."

Blaise rose unsteadily to her feet. If she'd understood Gifford correctly, he was dangling before her the chance to be not just a royal correspondent but a real news reporter on a major Fleet Street paper.

"Thank you very much, sir," she said. "I'll be sure to bear that in mind."

As Blaise sat down at her desk she knew she should be delighted by the astonishing opportunity that had unexpectedly come her way. Instead, she felt completely overwhelmed. Her headache might have disappeared, but that didn't make her decision any easier.

Staying on in London would be a huge step, one that, in her most fervid imaginings, she'd never contemplated. It would mean leaving all her family and friends behind—and she was hardly an experienced journalist.

She looked across the newsroom at the rows of reporters scribbling in notebooks, busy on telephones or crouched over typewriters. Every one of them had been required to serve five years on a provincial daily before clawing their way onto this great Fleet Street newspaper. Joining their ranks was a spectacular opportunity, so why was she hesitating?

With a sudden swipe of her arm, she cast Croft's piles of rubbish into the same bin where Norton had dumped the man's deceased pot plant. That at least helped her to focus.

Maybe she should discuss the matter with Dora. Sometimes it was easier to talk over an issue with a person you barely knew. Plus, Dora could provide her with a female perspective on Fleet Street. It was difficult enough for a woman to occupy a desk in a Sydney newsroom. Working in London might well prove to be brutal.

# CHAPTER TWENTY-FIVE

"Psst. Are you awake?"

Blaise felt someone prod her shoulder. "Course I am," she mumbled groggily as she lifted her head. "Who wants me?"

"There's a girl at the front desk," Colin announced. "Says she has a big story, only I can't find any free reporters."

"Well, why haven't you dragged one of them out of the pub?" Blaise said testily. "You know I'm only in London for another week, and that's strictly to write about the wedding and a few other bits and pieces."

Back at *The Clarion* there were always strangers coming in off the street, claiming to have an amazing tale that was certain to make the front page. Apparently, it was no different in London. Ninety-nine times out of a hundred either a grudge had led these so-called sources to make baseless allegations about someone who'd rubbed them up the wrong way, or all they had to offer were a few details about a local dispute of decidedly limited interest—unless they were simply delusional, which accounted for most of them.

On the other hand, what if this girl, whoever she was, had come across something important? Blaise supposed she should at least listen to what she had to say. If it sounded like it might lead to something, she could always let Norton know about it.

"I'm due to meet another reporter at two o'clock," she said, "so this is the best I can do. You find the chief of staff and tell him I'm sorry, I can't make lunch because an assignment's come up. I'll nip down to the front desk and have a word with this girl."

"Yes, Miss." Colin scooted off.

The girl was sitting, smoking, on one of a pair of cracked leather sofas in the small anteroom that served as the editorial department's reception area. Not a classic beauty, she was nonetheless striking, with a lithe, shapely figure, high cheekbones, and a cloud of dark hair. She rose to her feet when she saw Blaise coming toward her.

There was something feline about her face and the way she moved, an artless sensuality that Blaise thought most men would find extremely seductive.

"Hello, I'm Blaise Hill. I believe you're after a reporter?" She shook the girl's hand.

"That's right," she said. "I've a story for you, a good one."

"Well, why don't we both sit down and you tell me what it's all about."

The girl blew out a cloud of smoke. "It's hard to know where to start, really."

"What's the gist of it, then?"

"The what?"

"The main bit." Blaise wished she'd hurry up.

"I've got some information about a member of the royal family that's shocked even me," she said in a flat little voice, "and in my line of work, that takes some doing."

"What line is that?" Blaise asked.

"I'm a model," the girl said. "Started in Soho when I was fifteen."

Blaise could imagine what that meant. A good-looking kid with little education, she had probably been forced to become one of the topless showgirls Charlie had told her about. She couldn't be more than eighteen now and already seemed jaded. "I'm sorry," Blaise said, "but how would I know if what you have to tell me is true?"

The girl dropped her cigarette butt on the tiled floor then ground it out with the tip of one of her black stilettos. "Guess you'll just have to trust me."

"Go on then."

"One night, a few months ago, I joined some friends at a sort of studio, right on the river. It was his place, the royal I mean," she said. "We all had a lot of wine, I passed around a reefer of pot—it's easy to get in Soho if you know who to ask. Anyway, he ended up sitting on the floor with his head in my lap. Don't get me wrong, nothing happened between us."

She lit up again. "Not that I would have minded. I thought he was lovely, but I was with someone else. Anyway, I think he'd had too much to drink or smoke or something, because that's when he told me about it." She inhaled quickly. "He said he'd been having an affair with a married woman. She was going to have a baby—and he knew it was his. Then he laughed and said there'd be the most god-awful ruckus if it ever came out, because the baby was due only three weeks after the most important day of his life."

"Who was this mystery royal?"

"I'm not that silly," the girl said with a knowing smile. "How much for an exclusive?"

"I beg your pardon?"

"Oh, I get it. You want me to tell you the price. Say . . . two hundred quid?" The girl's expression was curiously blank, as if she'd grown accustomed to being handed money for favors.

Blaise blinked. Sometimes, back in Australia, reporters had been known to slip a source a pound or two; perhaps for a really good tip a fiver might change hands. But she had never heard of anyone being paid such an outrageous sum.

It appeared the girl might belong in the delusional category. Otherwise, she probably depended for money on whatever boyfriend she had at the moment and struggled to get by the rest of the time. Perhaps this was one of those times, and she'd concocted the story out of sheer desperation.

"Look, I'm not in a position to negotiate with you," Blaise said kindly. "But I'll pass on what you've told me—and your request—to our chief of staff. How can he contact you?"

"I'm staying with a friend. Does the name Stephen Ward mean anything to you?"

Blaise shook her head.

"I'm surprised—Stephen's very well known," the girl said, a little self-importantly. "He's a medical man, sorts out backs and frozen shoulders, that kind of thing. Anyway, you can reach me there."

Blaise took the number down in her notebook.

The girl frowned. "We're just friends. It's not as if he, you know, looks after me. I still need to buy my own clothes and food, then there's cigarettes and having my hair done—and helping out my mum. I want some pictures taken, too, good ones, so I can be a real model. The money will help set me up. I wouldn't be asking"—she shrugged—"but there's no other way unless, well, you know."

Blaise did. "If this story does come to anything, would the newspaper be able to quote you as a source?"

"Sure."

"Well then, you'd better tell me your name."

"Christine Keeler." The girl smiled for the first time. "I wouldn't mind having my picture in the paper."

# CHAPTER TWENTY-SIX

A chaotic scene greeted Blaise when she and Dora emerged from the Tube station. Black cabs trundled past, red double-decker buses lurched toward their stops, cars tooted, and pedestrians streamed along the footpath.

"We're in Sloane Square," Dora said, raising her voice so it could be heard above the noise of the traffic. "It's the heart of Chelsea, my favorite place to live in London. Chelsea's arty, not snooty like Knightsbridge and Belgravia. The flats are lovely and there are some beautiful houses on Cheyne Walk, right opposite the river. As a matter of fact, I live just around the corner from here in a super old red-brick building in Sloane Gardens. It's a shame you're not staying longer, because I'm having a party for my flatmate next week. You'd meet some interesting people."

"Actually, I might be here for a while," Blaise said.

"Why, what do you mean?"

She explained about Roger Croft's sudden exit from the newspaper and McInerney's offer.

Peals of laughter greeted her. "Oh, that's hilarious," Dora said. "Roger Croft, finally caught out lying—and in the arms of his Italian count, no less. Everyone's known about those two for years, but Dodgy Rog thought he was untouchable."

She tossed her blonde mane. "I've no time for Roger's ridiculous carry-on, but it's a bit sad that you can't be with whoever you want. I mean, who's it hurting? Obviously, Roger's forgotten that proximity to well-connected people doesn't mean you are one of them. In this country, it's only those lucky enough to be at the top of the pecking order who can get away with almost anything. It's a case of different rules for different people."

Blaise silently contemplated Dora's words; they brought back Maude's warnings about "getting above herself." If she did take the job, she vowed to remember what her new friend had said— and her own place in the scheme of British life.

"Gosh, Blaise, I've been prattling on again, when you obviously have such a lot on your mind," Dora said. "I promise we'll talk everything over, only it will have to be later—we're almost at Mary's shop."

Blaise looked around. She'd been so preoccupied that she'd scarcely noticed they'd been walking beside a busy thoroughfare. Girls with long hair, black stockings, and knee-high boots swung their way past the usual butchers, grocers, and bakers interspersed with smart coffee bars and fascinating little shops selling books, antiques, or art supplies.

"The King's Road is the place to be if you're over all that middle-aged, middle-class respectability we've been stuck with for so long," Dora said. "I mean, no offense, Blaise, you look very smart in that pencil skirt and grown-up jacket, but wouldn't you like to dress in something a bit younger?" Dora did a quick little skip. "England's been stuffy and tired for too long. Honestly, it's 1960! Life should be more about young people like you and me."

"You and me?" Blaise puzzled. "But I'm strictly working class and you obviously come from the other extreme. I'm not even sure my parents would know what a finishing school is, let alone understand all those unspoken rules that seem to govern society—at least, over here."

"That might be the way things are now, but I think pretty soon it's not going to matter. Talent and energy, being creative— that's what's going to count. Speaking of which, here we are."

Bazaar looked from the outside as if it had once been a typical London house, although the iron railings that would have stood between it and the footpath had been removed, creating a courtyard effect at the front, while the usual row of windows had been replaced by a wide expanse of glass.

"Wow!" Blaise stared at the window display. The two shop mannequins, with their long legs and high cheekbones, were unlike any she'd seen before. Dressed in tiny suits made of traditional tweed, each was holding a long fishing rod that stretched across the window. Most extraordinary of all, the ends of their lines dipped into a glass bowl in which swam a pair of live goldfish.

"If your friend's designs are half as original as what she puts in her window, they must be incredible," Blaise said.

"There's nothing like them in London or, I'm willing to bet, anywhere else." Dora pointed toward the door. "Let's go in."

To Blaise's surprise, Mary Quant was not at all intimidating. She was in her mid-twenties, small and friendly, and a bundle of energy, dressed in a bright red dress with a white collar and a very short hemline. She threw her arms around Dora, singing out, "Hello, hello!" before stepping away and asking, "Who's this you've brought with you?"

"Blaise Hill, a colleague from Australia," Dora said. "We're sort of sharing the interview."

Blaise smiled. "I love your window."

"Mad, isn't it? At least it won't end up like our last one." Mary giggled. "My husband, Alexander, and I decided it would be a brilliant idea to dress up a mannequin in a gorgeous gray flannel outfit and arrange her so it looked like she was taking a lobster out for a walk on a leash. We spent ages scrubbing out a giant lobster shell, but obviously not long enough, because by the next morning the whole place smelled to high heaven!"

Blaise burst out laughing.

"I know, wasn't it ridiculous? I can't imagine what possessed us," Mary said. "Anyway, now that you're here, why don't you take a look around? And while you're at it, try on anything you want."

Blaise hadn't felt this out of place since the day she'd first appeared on *The Clarion*'s fifth floor, clad in her old pleated skirt and sad little blouse. Suddenly, she couldn't wait to tear off her conservative garb.

As if she could read Blaise's mind, Mary said, "When I first set up Bazaar, I thought, why should a young bird wear the same styles as her mother? At first we sold clothes and accessories that other people designed. There were some lovely things, but I soon discovered I couldn't find enough that I liked, so I started making my own. Of course, I was still at art school then."

Mary began pulling a selection of little skirts, knitted tops, and dresses from the racks. "I was so poor," she confided, "that each day I had to make certain I sold everything I'd made the night before just to be able go back to Harrods and buy more material. Luckily, everything flew out of the door. Alexander and I knew so little about the business side of things, we didn't even realize that designers could buy fabrics at wholesale prices!"

"Where do you get your amazing ideas?"

"These days it's more a case of bottom up than top down."

"What does that mean?"

"It means that style is being set by girls wearing inexpensive clothes like these in fun clubs and bars and in the High Streets. They either buy them from me, or sew them up themselves. I love our customers, they don't care about status symbols. These girls will go for anything as long as it's new and different. Speaking of which, I think you should put this one on first."

Blaise changed in a hurry, reappearing moments later in a short, bright blue sleeveless dress with a round neckline edged in red. It was so exciting to feel young and carefree that she shook her hair out of its chignon and shimmied across the store while Dora and Mary whistled and clapped.

She stopped, a little embarrassed, when in the middle of this raucous reception, a young, shaggy-haired man with a couple of cameras slung around his neck wandered in.

"Ah, my favorite photographer has arrived!" Dora cried. "Hi, David." She gestured toward Mary and Blaise. "I need some pictures of Mary showing clothes to this stunning young thing. Just snap away—you know what I like."

While Blaise appeared in one adorable dress after another and Dora peppered Mary with questions, the photographer took dozens of shots in rapid succession.

"All done," he announced then turned to Blaise. "You're not a model, are you?"

Blaise laughed. "Not on your life. I'm a reporter."

The photographer's stylishly rumpled appearance was as far from the immaculate elegance of Cecil Beaton as could be imagined.

"My name's David Bailey," he said, handing her a card. "If you change your mind, let me know. A girl with your face and your legs has plenty of potential."

Blaise shook her head. "I can tell you right now, I'm sticking with newspapers."

As the photographer strolled off in the direction of a large black motorcycle, Dora said, "I think we have everything we need for a nice little feature. Now, what are you buying?"

Blaise hadn't intended to purchase a thing, but found it impossible to resist the blue and red dress and another in gray flannel with several rows of black stitching around the hemline. What had come over her? First she seemed to have taken up late-night drinking and dancing in shady places and now she was buying clothes she couldn't imagine ever wearing—certainly not if she accepted Gifford's job.

Blaise smiled to herself. She could just imagine Her Majesty's reaction if *The Advocate*'s new royal correspondent dared to turn up at the Palace in one of Mary's skimpy creations. But the dresses were surprisingly cheap, and anyway, weren't travelers supposed to return with a few souvenirs? She could even take home something special for Ivy to wear. That is, if she did go home. She still hadn't made a decision.

They had just left Bazaar when Dora announced, "The Markham Arms is just next door. I don't know about you, but I'm starving."

It was a busy pub and, with its creaking dark wood and leather-topped barstools, gave the appearance of being traditional, although the stream of people coming in and out were mainly young and bohemian-looking. Most of the boys wore their hair long like David Bailey, and if the girls weren't sporting little black skirts and loose jerseys, they were dressed in the same gray flannel or bright block-color dresses that Mary Quant designed.

"What we need is a couple of half-pints of bitter and a ploughman's lunch," Dora said. "That's basically a hunk of bread, a slab of cheddar cheese, a couple of pickles, and a dollop of chutney. The servings are quite big, though, so we could share if you like."

Blaise realized she was hungry, too. Her dinner with Charlie seemed a long time ago and the day had been packed with one unexpected event after another. Her mouth watered when the laden plate appeared on their table. She was tearing off a chunk of crusty bread when Dora said, "Now, what's all this about you being offered a permanent spot as the royal correspondent?"

Blaise frowned. "I'm pretty confused about whether to take it or not. What do you think?"

"Don't be silly! That's not the sort of job you pass up," Dora said. "Plus, we can be chums. That party I told you about, for my flatmate? It's because she's tying the knot next Saturday, so there's a room going at my place from the end of the week—if you want it, that is." She scribbled some details down on her paper serviette. "Here's my address."

Her hazel eyes danced. "There are hardly any women working on Fleet Street," she said, "and most of them are old battleaxes who've had to struggle for so long among all those bloody men that it's hardened their hearts just as much as their faces. It would be fabulous to have someone of my own age to share everything with. You must say yes."

"Hey, you're going too fast again!" Blaise smiled. "I wasn't expecting anything like this to happen. Right now, I'm completely torn."

"It sounds to me as if you've left someone special behind."

"You're right, but it's not the sort of person you're probably thinking about. I've a younger sister, Ivy, who's been really sick with polio. My mum's devoted to her, but there are so many other ways she depends on me. It's hard to explain, but I've always felt Ivy was my responsibility." Her throat suddenly dry, Blaise gulped down a mouthful of the bitter.

"I think you're on the wrong track," Dora said. "Surely you're underestimating Ivy. If she's anything like my sister, she'd want the best for you. And you don't have to stay here forever. Only, the next few years in London will be amazing—I can just feel it in the air."

She leaned forward, bubbling with enthusiasm. "Life will be taking off in all sorts of new directions, and you could be part of it. I bet you'd have the opportunity to cover much more than royalty. There's going to be new fashion, new art, new music, and"—her voice took on a more sober tone—"before long, I think there'll be a new government."

That was curious, Blaise reflected. In her own way, Dora had just expressed a very similar view to Johnny Norton.

"Did you ever read the Mary Poppins books when you were young?"

"What?" Blaise felt disoriented by Dora's abrupt change of subject. "Of course I did—P.L. Travers is an Australian author, you know."

"I had no idea," Dora said. "Well, don't you remember the part about the wind changing? That's what's happening right now. You may not have been blown onto Cherry Tree Lane, but you've landed on Fleet Street, which has its own sort of magic."

She patted Blaise on the shoulder. "You know what I think. But you have to make up your own mind."

# CHAPTER TWENTY-SEVEN

Blaise rang Charlie Ashton as soon as she returned to the flat. "How are you feeling?" he asked. "Not too under the weather?"

"Quite honestly, I'm exhausted. All I want to do is crawl under the covers."

"With me?"

"Don't be ridiculous," she giggled. Somehow, Charlie was able to make outrageous remarks without causing offense. "Actually, something unexpected has turned up." She paused. "I need a bit of time to myself to think about it."

"Nothing awful, I hope?"

"Not at all. It's just that it looks as if I could be staying in London longer than I'd thought. There's lots to sort through, so, I'm sorry, dinner tonight is out."

"Wouldn't you rather eat chateaubriand with me than egg on toast all alone in that oversized flat?" Charlie asked.

"Even that delectable prospect couldn't tempt me." She yawned. "Let's leave it for now."

Blaise filled the marble bathroom's vast tub with steaming water, then poured in some of the rose-scented oil. As she sank into the warm, fragrant liquid, she felt herself begin to unwind. After a blissful fifteen minutes, she put on a fluffy white bathrobe, turned off all but one of the lights in the sitting room and switched the radio on. The music from *Swan Lake*, the ballet she'd seen in Sydney, was playing quietly on the BBC. *Perfect*, she thought as Tchaikovsky's romantic score floated through the air. Now, all she needed was that egg on toast. Ever since Charlie had mentioned it, she could think of nothing she'd rather eat.

She'd just located a frying pan when the doorbell rang. Blaise felt a prickle of annoyance. There was such a thing as persistence, but Charlie was taking it too far.

She flung the door open, her eyes fiery.

Adam Rule stood before her. His chiseled features and dark hair were as striking as ever, although his smile revealed that same hint of unexpected vulnerability she'd glimpsed before.

Her breath caught in her throat.

"Blaise, I wanted to see you . . ." He was uncharacteristically awkward. "Look, I can tell it's a bad time. I should leave you alone."

Blaise made an effort to collect herself. "You don't have to go. It's just—I wasn't expecting anyone," she said with feigned nonchalance. "You might have noticed I'm not exactly dressed for company." She colored, aware that his eyes had dropped to her robe. "As you're here, though, you might as well come in."

Blaise wasn't tired anymore. She felt exhilarated. As Adam followed her into the sitting room, the sound of the lush music, the scent of roses on her skin, the feel of the bathrobe brushing against her bare legs—all acquired a heightened intensity.

"A drink?" she asked. Adam's presence seemed to fill the dimly lit room, making her heart race. She needed to steady herself.

"Thank you," he said. "I'll sort myself out." There was a slight tightness in his jaw, a hesitation in his mellow voice. He walked over to an antique sideboard on which stood crystal glasses and decanters, then poured himself a brandy. "Can I get something for you?" he asked.

She nodded. "I'll have the same."

Blaise knew that, having barely eaten all day, the alcohol would go straight to her head. She didn't care.

They sat down at opposite ends of a wine-colored velvet sofa. Adam ran his fingers through his hair, stared down at his glass, glanced up at her. She was certain she could see attraction in his eyes, could feel that invisible silken thread that connected them begin to tighten. Yet he didn't make a move toward her.

A moment of silence passed. He picked up his brandy, drank, but still maintained his distance.

Blaise couldn't bear the tension spiraling through the room a second longer. There were too many unspoken words that needed saying. "Adam," she began, more boldly than she felt. "What's going on? After Palm Beach I was so confused. You *hurt* me."

"I'm sorry," he said. His voice was low, his expression veiled.

She tried again. "I have to know: do you have any feelings for me at all? If not"—she looked away—"I'd rather we didn't meet again. I don't think I could bear it."

Blaise gulped some of her brandy, hoping the potent spirit would still her nerves. Instead it reminded her of the taste of Adam's lips when he'd kissed her in the boathouse. "I know I was rash, stupid really, calling you the way I did, but—"

He broke in. "Blaise, listen to me." At last he drew closer. "You have hardly been out of my thoughts. But that night at the beach—it was all wrong."

"Was it? Was it *really*?" Her temper flared. "I knew what *I* wanted," she said, her face hot. "It seems you didn't."

Adam looked exasperated. "There are things I've done I'm not proud of. I wanted to show you I was capable of something a little nobler than my past behavior. Then, just maybe, you'd cut me some slack when you heard any less than flattering remarks about me."

"There have been a couple," Blaise admitted.

"I'm not surprised. When I said you deserved a better man than me, I meant it."

"I don't care about other people's opinions!" Blaise protested.

She swallowed another mouthful of her drink. This exchange was heading in completely the wrong direction. "Look, why don't we draw a line," she said, "forget whatever did or didn't happen in the past? We could be just two people who met each other on a park bench or a bus and, well, take it from there."

"Life's not as simple as that."

"It can be."

Very deliberately, she took Adam's glass from him and put it on the coffee table next to her own. He touched her cheek. "The past is never over," he said.

Aching with doubt, Blaise wondered if this encounter would turn out to be another misguided catastrophe.

Then he reached for her. His mouth met her mouth, their lips parted, and she no longer needed him to explain anything.

As they kissed, deeper and deeper, he brushed the tips of his fingers along the line of her jaw, down her neck and then to the narrow space between her breasts. "I've been dreaming about you," he said. He drew back the collar of her robe and kissed one shoulder. "But this is so much better."

Blaise felt the sash around her waist coming undone, the robe dropping to the sofa. Every one of her senses sang.

Adam stood up, his breath ragged. His gaze traveled from her face down to her full breasts and back again. "You're even more beautiful than I remember," he said.

She let out a small cry of surprise as he scooped her up in his arms, carried her into the next room and set her down gently on the bed. "Don't move an inch," he insisted, before quickly taking off his clothes. She had never seen a naked man before. He'd called her beautiful, but she thought his taut, muscled body was beautiful, too.

Adam lay so close to her she could smell the brandy on his breath and a trace of soap on his skin mixed with something musky and masculine.

"You won't change your mind this time, will you?" she said.

The way he looked at her made Blaise's heart skip a beat.

"Hell, no."

At first, he was achingly tender. He caressed her face, each limb, and the smooth plane of her stomach with immense care, as if she were an object so rare and precious that he feared breaking her. But his fingers kept drifting back to her breasts, grazing her nipples, taunting them until she moaned helplessly.

As she pressed herself against him she could tell he shared the yearning that had enveloped her. "Slowly," he whispered. "I'm not finished with you yet."

He left a trail of faint kisses, soft as butterfly wings, starting at the base of her throat before gradually moving toward her belly. Blaise shivered with pleasure as he turned his attention to a more hidden place, licking and teasing until a sweetness swept through her, overlaid by a luscious sensation that soon became feverish.

Then Adam's broad chest was above her breasts, his hips were against her hips and the lock of hair she remembered had fallen across his forehead. "You have no idea how much I've wanted you," he murmured, gazing into her clear blue eyes. As he melded his body with hers, she felt an intense wave of desire that a moment of sharp pain only intensified.

All that mattered was their being together, being one, touching and kissing and moving, gently at first and then more and more powerfully. It was like flying and dancing and drowning and, finally, as if she existed at the very center of a savage storm, until Adam gasped and she was gasping, too, and calling his name.

Her breathing had slowed, but she remained in his arms, sensing that he was as reluctant as she was to bring to a close something that had transported them both so exquisitely.

When at last they separated he kissed her softly and stroked her tangled hair. The moonlight that streamed through the window high above Cadogan Square had turned his eyes into two silvered pools. "Blaise," he said in his wonderful low voice. "I know this was your first time, but, God, I hope it was good for you." He turned toward her. "Because I've never felt like this before."

"It was very, very good," she said dreamily. Blaise was as light-headed as she'd been when the airplane that brought her to London first soared high in the sky, remaking her understanding of the world below. Being with Adam had changed her. But perhaps she had changed him, too.

"I'm used to staying wary, keeping my emotions under lock and key," Adam said quietly. "I've learned it's safer that way."

Blaise waited, sensing how hard it was for Adam to disclose his feelings.

"The first couple of times I came across you I was intrigued. Later, I freely admit I was incredibly attracted." He smiled. "To tell you the truth, when I saw you at the Hotel Australia last year, I wished like hell I'd never arranged that interview with Alexandra's lady-in-waiting. All I can remember is desperately wanting to kiss you."

"But you did keep in touch; you gave me all those tips."

"I told myself I was still paying you back for helping Joe." He gave her a quick grin. "If I'm honest, I just wanted to hear your voice on the other end of the phone."

Adam cupped her delicate face in his hands. "I guess what I'm trying to say is that I knew you were special right from the start, but I wasn't about to risk becoming involved. Even without the Ryan business, that was enough to make me keep my distance." He gave her a long, slow kiss. "Yet here we are," he said softly, "and I seem to have given up all my best intentions."

She had always wanted him. Discovering he had felt just as drawn to her was intensely moving. Yet for so long something, some hidden wound, had caused him to turn away. "Adam, what made you like this?" she whispered.

"It's a long, long story," he said. "Let's keep it for another day."

They nestled side by side beneath the soft, feather-filled quilt, with Adam's chest pressed against the curve of her back. Just as her drowsy eyes closed, Blaise felt him reach across and take her hand. The last thing she remembered was the pressure of his fingers, still clasping her own as if she were a lifeline and he was afraid to let go.

"I have some good news for you," Blaise said the following morning as, naked, she walked from the bathroom into the bedroom. "I would have mentioned it as soon as we woke up, but you insisted on distracting me."

Adam wore only a towel wrapped around his waist. "I've something to tell you, too," he said with a delighted smile. "But if you keep wandering around like that I might be forced to distract you again."

He didn't take his eyes away from her as she began to dress. First, she slipped into a pair of white silky pants, then into a suspender belt. Next, she eased on her stockings, stepped into a skirt and put on a pair of high heels. She was still hooking up her low-cut lace bra when he said, "I think that's where you should stop."

"But I'm only half dressed," she protested.

"I know. You may not be aware, but I'm an excellent mathematician. By my calculation, that additional fifty per cent you're planning to add should be reduced immediately. I believe subtraction would be the best solution to the problem."

Adam kissed her on the mouth, before moving on to the swell of her breasts. "I really should help you take all these unnecessary things off." He slid down a bra strap. "Starting with this."

"I wish I could stay." Blaise sighed. "But I can't be late, not today."

"Why, what's going on?"

"It's what I've been trying to tell you," she said as, ignoring her protests, he slipped off the other strap. "I've been offered an opportunity that's beyond my wildest dreams. The newspaper has asked me to take on the job of royal correspondent permanently. I'm going to accept as soon as I see the editor this morning." She could barely contain her excitement. "It means I'll be living here in London, near you."

"No!" Adam looked horrified.

"What's the matter?" Blaise said, taken aback. "I thought you'd be pleased." She had an awful feeling in the pit of her stomach.

"Blaise, when I arrived at your door last night, I wasn't even sure you'd let me in." Adam sat down heavily on the edge of the bed. "All I knew was I couldn't bear the thought of you being on one side of the world and me on another. I wanted to tell you that I'd transferred the majority of my business interests to Australia . . . but, pretty soon, talking about my financial arrangements didn't seem so important."

"Well, can't you simply run everything from here?" Blaise said as she grabbed a striped cotton shirt from the wardrobe and began doing it up. A few minutes earlier her mind had been filled with sunlit visions of a romantic future. Now she felt as if a black rain cloud had descended upon her.

"If only I could." Adam groaned. "There's a huge mining deal I've been working on; I've sunk most of my funds into it. The entire enterprise is an enormous gamble. I've never been one to shy away from playing the odds, but if it's got any hope of coming off I have to conduct the negotiations personally."

Blaise's spirits plummeted even further. "When do you take off?"

"I fly out this afternoon. My house is closed up so I've been staying for a couple of nights in a rented flat. I'd imagined you would be following soon afterward."

"This is the worst timing!" she said, shaking her head. "I can't quite believe it." Blaise tried a tentative smile. "But at least once the deal is done, you'll be back in, what—a few weeks? I'll miss you desperately, but at least it's not so long to wait."

"Not a chance. I need three months to make sure the enterprise is running smoothly. This is a high-stakes business, and if I'm not on site, it could go off the rails very fast."

"Three months!"

"I know." Adam looked as miserable as she felt. "I'll leave you the number at the flat I've been renting. Maybe we'll have time for a chat before I set off for the airport."

"I don't want to say goodbye over the telephone. It's better if we do it now."

He kissed her sweetly and slowly.

"I'm so sorry, but I really have to go," Blaise said in a small voice. "Which means, once I walk out the door, I won't see you until August."

Adam held her in his arms for the last time. "Sadly, that's right."

Blaise raised her eyes to his. "Well, at least promise me one thing."

"Yes?"

"Don't stay a minute longer than you have to."

# CHAPTER TWENTY-EIGHT

After hearing a faint "Enter," Blaise walked into Gifford's office.

The man immediately succumbed to a coughing attack. This time his narrow shoulders shook as he was racked by spasms. He'd acquired a yellowish pallor and looked far worse than when she had seen him only twenty-four hours earlier.

"I can return later if this isn't a good time," she said.

"It's as good as any," he wheezed.

"It's just that I didn't want to hold anyone up. I've made up my mind."

"And?" The poor man looked completely drained.

"I accept. Please go ahead and cable Mr. McInerney. I'd also appreciate it if you could tell him I'm very grateful."

"Well, at least that's settled," Gifford said, clearing his throat. "Miss Hill, welcome to Fleet Street."

Back at her desk, Blaise's thoughts became chaotic. In the space of one day her life had completely changed. Her mind whirled as she dwelled on Adam and their passionate lovemaking. She remembered how tender he'd been, taking everything slowly, treating her with infinite care. A tingle ran through her as she recalled the way that, later, they'd both become more abandoned.

It was so unfair. Not only had they shared a blissful experience but, just as importantly, Adam had also finally begun to reveal a little of himself, all on the very night before he left the country. She bit her bottom lip. Despite his passionate declarations, she already caught herself wondering if, when he was so far away, he'd maintain his trust or even his interest in her. They'd spent so little time together, whereas in the long months ahead he'd be sure to come across plenty of women who'd be only too happy to provide a man like him with their undivided attention.

No, Adam *was* a better man than that. His loyalty to the Blacketts proved it; he would never betray her. All the same, she thought gloomily, three months would feel like an eternity.

She fetched herself her third cup of coffee that morning, returned to her desk and did her best to refocus her thoughts. At least her new job would provide plenty of distraction.

Blaise flipped through her trusty guidebook. At eight million, London's population dwarfed that of Sydney's, which was only a quarter the size. It was a city graced with public squares and classical monuments, palatial hotels and marble temples of commerce, grand law courts and bustling docks. It also boasted a cluster of lavishly stocked emporiums such as Harrods and Harvey Nichols, a host of gilded theaters, vast cathedrals, museums filled with treasures, and the Houses of Parliament, in addition to that seat of royal power which also happened to be among the few sites she had actually visited—Buckingham Palace.

Somehow she had to make sense of this complex world, most particularly the unique role that the queen and the royal family played in it. She had so much to learn, so much to discover. What if she stumbled and fell by the wayside?

After two nights now with barely any sleep, Blaise was running purely on caffeine and nervous energy. She had to send a cable to her parents, but even this was challenging. Finally, she settled on something that wouldn't alarm them.

*LONDON STAY EXTENDED STOP SENDING LET-TER STOP LOVE BLAISE*

It would be far easier to explain about her unexpected job opportunity in a letter than in a telegram. A telephone call couldn't even be considered—the cost would be prohibitive.

Still agitated, Blaise drummed her fingers on her desk. The next thing she had to do was tell Dora about her decision. Then she realized that she didn't actually know where Dora worked—it wasn't in the newsroom with the rest of the editorial staff.

She waved Colin over. "Where are the reporters who work for the Women's Section?"

"You mean the girls down the hall?" He tugged at his cowlick. "Just go out the main door, turn left, and walk all the way down the corridor."

Blaise shook her head. Here in the great city of London, *The Advocate*'s version of the "ladies of the fifth floor" was the even more modest sounding "girls down the hall." It seemed that, no matter which side of the world you were on, female reporters were destined to remain in quarantine.

"I'm thrilled you've taken the job," Dora said, giving her a hug. "And does that mean you can come and share the flat?"

"If you'll have me. I'd love to drop in after work tomorrow and have a look."

"What's wrong with tonight?"

Blaise hesitated. "I think I need another night in. There's been a lot going on."

"Okay, tomorrow then."

Blaise looked around the Women's Section for the first time. "Don't tell me that the journalists here also spend their time in the pub," she said. "Where is everyone?"

"To tell you the truth, we're hopelessly understaffed," Dora said. "There's only me, a part-time stylist, and a sub. We don't even have our own editor, and the section's desperately in need of at least one more reporter. The trouble is no one takes women's news stories seriously."

"Tell me about it," Blaise said with a sympathetic smile. "All the same, *The Clarry* has more staff on its Women's Pages than you do here, and we're a paper with a much smaller circulation." She glanced at the clock on the wall. "Well, I'd better be off. I've a heap of research planned for today, but first I have to see Norton about a girl who came in off the street with a wild story."

"Not that pretty thing I saw in reception yesterday?"

"That's the one. It's unlikely that what she's said adds up to anything, but you never know. Anyway, I'll tell the chief and leave it up to him."

Norton crossed his arms. "What are you doing bringing me a story like this?"

"It would be big news—if it's true," Blaise shrugged. "What do you think?"

"What I think is that it's time you heard a few home truths." Norton scrabbled through the piles of paper on his desk before locating a crumpled packet of Lucky Strikes. "Even if what this Keeler girl says checks out, which it might—it wouldn't be the first bastard in the royal family's history—the story won't ever get a run. At least not in this paper."

"Not if it turned out to be a massive scoop?"

Norton lit a cigarette and inhaled hungrily. "Ah, we journalists like to pretend that we write without fear or favor, that no one dictates which stories we run and which ones we let disappear into the ether. The fact is Sir Ernest gets to call the shots about what's in and what's out of his papers. He won't print something that would harm his beloved royal family. So you tell this girl, nothing doing."

He leaned back in his chair, exposing a wide expanse of shirt front that strained across his belly. "By the way, Mr. Gifford just phoned. I'm pleased I'll be seeing a good-looking girl sitting in the newsroom at last."

Blaise glared at Norton.

"Simmer down," he said. "I was just about to say I got some good reports about your work from Ed."

"Ed? Who's Ed?"

Norton had a glint in his eye. "You don't think Roger Croft was discovered doing the rumba by accident, do you? This is a great newspaper office—we can track anyone down." He blew out a series of hazy smoke rings. "Edgar McInerney has been trying to find a way of getting you over here for a while—said you needed to broaden your experience. I knew Croft was an inveterate liar, so . . . all we had to do was wait until he shot himself in the foot, so to speak."

Blaise raised her eyebrows. She wondered what other behind-the-scenes maneuvers took place in Sir Ernest's organization that she knew nothing about.

# CHAPTER TWENTY-NINE

Blaise sat opposite Christine Keeler in a poky coffee shop that displayed slices of unnaturally yellow iced cake in its window. The place was frankly depressing, but Christine had seemed so desperate when they'd last met that she couldn't face turning her down over the telephone.

"I'll be honest with you, they're not going to run it," she said, stirring a cup of grayish liquid that might once have come into contact with something resembling coffee.

Christine's small pointed chin jutted forward. "But you don't understand, I really need the money. And anyway, it's all true, I can prove it."

She groped in her handbag. "When I was on the way to the loo I decided to have a look in Tony's bedroom. I knew that he and the princess were getting married, so . . . I thought I might be able to pick up a souvenir, even if it was just one of her hairpins. Only I came away with something else—it's this letter."

Blaise choked on her coffee. "Wait a minute!" she spluttered. "You mean the man you've been talking about is Antony Armstrong-Jones?"

Christine nodded. "Yes, Tony's the royal, or near enough, anyway. The letter's from a bird called Camilla Fry." She placed a pale gray envelope on the table. "It's just like I said. This Fry woman is having a baby in a few weeks' time, and she's one hundred per cent sure it's Tony's."

Camilla Fry was the wife of Armstrong-Jones's would-be best man. The story was turning out to be even more extraordinary than Blaise had thought. A quick scan of the letter confirmed exactly what Christine had said. At the bottom of the page, in a different hand, were scrawled the words: *Darling C, I agree, the timing's not the best, but at least we can count on J to do the right thing. All the same, make sure you burn this letter, won't you? Love T.*

The handwriting could be easily checked by an expert, but it certainly didn't look like a forgery. Blaise recollected Cecil's acerbic commentary at Buckingham Palace. He had mentioned Camilla Fry's "roving eye" and, now that she came to think about it, the expression on his face when he'd remarked, "I believe they're *both* extremely fond of Tony," had been particularly arch. At the time she'd paid little attention, but now she realized that by the sound of it, Armstrong-Jones's relationship with the Frys was of a highly irregular nature.

It was a sensational story, all right, though of the most salacious type imaginable. Blaise was relieved Norton had turned it down flat. She would have hated to be associated with publishing something that was guaranteed to create an enormous scandal at the expense not only of the Frys, but also of Camilla's as yet unborn, innocent infant. Saddest of all, it would be Margaret, the blameless new bride, who would undoubtedly suffer the deepest and most public humiliation.

"Christine, do you realize how the princess would feel if, less than a month after she married Tony before millions of people, a newspaper announced that her husband had just become the father of another woman's illegitimate child?"

"I've had a baby myself," Christine said in her flat little voice. "Only it was too early. He died after six days." She shrugged. "To tell you the truth, I was lucky I didn't have one before. When I was living with Mum in a bloody railway carriage my stepdad and his mates wouldn't leave me alone."

For the first time, Blaise realized how damaged Christine was. It was asking too much to expect her to display much empathy for a princess, after the traumas she'd endured. "I'm very sorry," she said.

"Yeah well, it happens. But the thing is if you don't give me the money, I'll have to go to the *Mirror*. They like stories like this."

"I'll give you the money *not* to tell anyone—how about that?" The words seemed to have leapt from Blaise's mouth entirely of their own accord.

"It's all the same to me."

"So, do we have a deal?"

"Seems a bit weird but, if that's what you want, sure. Just give me the two hundred quid, I'll hand over the letter and that will be that. It's not that I want to get anyone into trouble but," she shrugged again, "I don't see why these people make out they're better than us. A girl like me who just wants a bit of fun out of life . . ." She had a quaver in her voice. "Well, let's say we always seem to end up losing out."

"That sounds really tough," Blaise said gently.

Christine pasted an over-bright smile on her face. "Once I've become a real model, maybe everything will work out."

Blaise walked away from this dispiriting scene, berating herself for making such a reckless bargain. A scandal like this would be hideous for any ordinary woman, but Margaret was far from that; she inhabited a fame-fueled, rarefied stratosphere where even the tiniest incident was avidly reported by the world's press. The feeding frenzy would be unprecedented. But where was she going to find the two hundred pounds she needed to make the entire awful mess disappear?

Blaise left *The Advocate* in a hurry. There was just one person she could turn to, yet as she sat on the crowded Tube, heading for Knightsbridge, she tried desperately hard to come up with an alternative. She hated the thought that, after their wondrous night together, the first thing she'd be doing would be asking Adam for money—that is, *if* she could contact him. He'd said he'd leave her the phone number of the place where he'd been staying, but as she'd told him she didn't want it he probably hadn't bothered. Anyway, by now he'd be on his way to the airport.

Blaise shuddered. She could hardly go to Mr. Gifford or Johnny Norton. *The Advocate* might not carry negative stories about the royal family, but paying money—and such a lot of money at that—to kill off a piece was another matter entirely. She'd had absolutely no authority to make her impulsive offer.

As soon as Blaise was inside the flat she started searching for Adam's phone number. There wasn't a note next to the bed, in the study, or the sitting room. Other than the usual pair of silver candlesticks, there was nothing on the dining room table.

"Thank God," she exclaimed when she walked into the kitchen and saw a piece of paper propped up against the fruit bowl. *I will be counting the days*, it said, above Adam's name. In the lower right-hand corner he'd scrawled a phone number next to the words *I know you're not keen on the idea, but if you happen to come home early, try to call anyway. I'd love to hear the sound of your voice one last time.*

She flew back to the study and picked up the phone. Maybe there was a chance Adam hadn't left yet.

Blaise felt faint with relief when she heard him answer. "You're still here!" she exclaimed. "Do you have time to meet me at my place?"

"I was just going to ring you," he said. "My flight's been delayed, something about bad weather over the subcontinent. I'll get my things together and—"

Blaise broke in. "Adam, this is urgent. I have a problem."

"Give me twenty minutes."

When Adam arrived he immediately folded Blaise into his arms. "Nothing's happened to you, has it?" He tilted her chin up, a concerned look in his eyes.

"Not to me, no," Blaise said. "But something dreadful might happen to Princess Margaret. In fact, it would be diabolical for the entire royal family."

She sat down, exhausted, and rapidly explained the situation.

"You're right—it's horrendous. Bloody Tony, how could he?" Frowning, Adam walked over to the bow window and looked down.

"That was quick thinking though, darling," he said, turning back to her, "offering the Keeler girl what she wanted. It's the only way to make certain a story doesn't run. The technique's kept me out of the newspapers very effectively."

"Except I don't have the money."

"You know that's not a problem. I'll pay," Adam said. "The real problem is that the next time she's out of cash she's likely to take her story to another paper."

"Christine said she wouldn't. Anyway, she won't have the letter."

"If she goes to the *Mirror* it could still be enough to start some wild rumors. The paper is run by Lord Rothermere's nephew, Cecil King—a total bastard. He fills his rag with sordid trash other newspapers wouldn't dream of running."

Adam's face had grown hard. "Blaise, you must tell Keeler that if her actions lead to one word about this business being published, she will be charged with theft. Then give her this." He took out his wallet and handed her four hundred pounds.

"But this is twice what she asked for!" Blaise objected.

"From the sounds of it, the girl's had a tough life. At least it might help her get back on her feet."

Blaise blinked. Adam continued to surprise her.

He looked at his watch, frowning. "As for Princess Margaret, the public might focus on the holidays in the Caribbean or the glamorous charity events, but the truth is, she's a great deal more vulnerable than you might think. Just imagine what it was like when her doomed romance with Peter Townsend was dissected on the front pages of the world's newspapers day after day. And she adores Tony—there's no telling what she might do if this scandal comes out."

"When you put it like that," Blaise said, "I suppose four hundred pounds is not so very much to save someone's sanity—maybe even their life." She looked at him, her head to one side. "You do have an extraordinary knack of making problems vanish."

"It's how I've survived," he muttered. For a moment, his eyes reminded Blaise of storm clouds.

This was one of the most revealing comments Adam had made. If circumstances had been different, she could have seized the moment and questioned him about what it was he'd been so anxious to bury. But her last precious minutes with him were slipping away.

"So, I give Christine the money, she hands over the evidence, and then I burn it," she said. "End of story."

"Not quite. This kind of situation is like a slowly ticking time bomb. One way or another, it will inevitably go off, although let's hope it won't be for a very long time."

"I've got a ticking time bomb of my own," Blaise blurted out.

"What, that Ryan business? It's sorted. Put it out of your mind."

"That's easier said than done," Blaise retorted. Ryan's death still weighed on her conscience—perhaps it always would. Lately, she'd also found herself wondering exactly how his gold watch had ended up on the wrist of a murdered hitman.

"Sorry," she said. "I'm upset."

"Then let me reassure you, darling. There's nothing to worry about." Adam poured himself a brandy and soda. "Do you want a drink?"

Blaise shook her head.

"Right now," he said as he sat down in an armchair, "my principal concern is that the queen isn't blindsided. Girls like Keeler are easily manipulated and, from what you say, she'd like nothing more than to become a celebrity. That letter has to go to Her Majesty."

"What do you think the queen would do with the information?"

"Most likely keep it to herself. She's a great deal more worldly than you might think—has had to be, married to Philip. The last thing she will want is to cause her sister pain by ruining her marriage. You never know, despite everything, it might still turn out to be a success."

"I hate to mention it," Blaise said promptly, "but there's a flaw in your plan. I might be a royal correspondent, but I can't exactly march up to Buckingham Palace and knock on the front door. I'm a commoner, after all."

Adam swallowed the last of his drink. "I did a good turn for her long-term aide, Martin Charteris, once—what it was doesn't matter, but it does provide me with a certain access." He stretched out his hand. "Give me the letter and I'll ensure Martin receives it in the strictest confidence. He knows all about keeping secrets. He'll pass it on to Her Majesty, and then it will be her decision as to what she does with it."

Blaise was startled. Adam had certainly spread around a lot of favors, with at least some of them in very surprising places. She couldn't imagine how he'd come to know so many important people, but right now it was just one more question that would have to wait.

"What about Norton, the paper's chief of staff—he's aware of the story," she said.

"I suspect Johnny Norton is a royalist at heart, otherwise he wouldn't have worked for Sir Ernest for all these years. I'm betting he's a great deal more interested in discovering something that will damage the Conservative Party."

Adam seemed to have an answer for everything.

He walked back to the bow window and looked down. "The car's arrived. My bags are in the boot, so we'll be heading straight for the airport." He sighed. "Where's the phone?"

"In the study."

"I'll ring Martin right now and ask him to send one of his flunkies over to collect the letter."

Adam returned after only a few minutes.

"So this really is goodbye," Blaise said miserably. She picked up the napkin with Dora's address on it and handed it to him.

"Here, take this. A friend's asked me to room with her—at least you'll know where I'm likely to be."

"I still can't believe I'm leaving the one woman I've spent my nights dreaming about," he said with a groan.

He gave her a final passionate kiss before striding toward the door. "I'll see you in three months' time," he said. Then he walked away.

Blaise wandered forlornly into the sitting room and collapsed onto the sofa. They had been as intimate as a man and a woman could be, yet in so many ways Adam remained a mystery. She still didn't know if he had any criminal connections; it was the last thing she'd wanted to bring up the night before, and now it was too late. She'd done exactly what she had promised herself she wouldn't do—given in to her attraction instead of first building a relationship. Perhaps she'd ruined everything.

"Don't be such a self-indulgent idiot. He said he couldn't bear to be without you," she whispered, hoping that saying the words out loud would make her feel more certain of his return. It was her own insecurity—born of poverty and the countless forms of knock-backs, put-downs, catcalls, and jeers she and every other woman she knew put up with every day—that had driven her to think the very worst of Adam.

But a different voice, silent this time although harder and harsher, came spiraling up from that tough, Enmore part of her. It told her that Adam Rule was capable of anything.

# CHAPTER THIRTY

Blaise sucked in her breath. While checking her diary, she'd suddenly remembered the white envelope she'd picked up a couple of days earlier from her pigeon hole in Editorial's reception. She had hastily cast it aside somewhere on her crowded desk, but where was it now, and what if she'd missed an important royal event?

Ever since Adam's departure two weeks earlier she'd been edgy. He might have brushed off her concerns about the murder, but she couldn't rid herself of a nagging fear that eventually her part would be discovered. This morning she'd been so preoccupied she had almost collided with a mustachioed man wearing a brown trilby hat when she'd rushed out of the Sloane Gardens flats. Then, after she'd arrived at work, still distracted, one of the subs had chewed her out for misspelling the name of a royal duke, the sort of embarrassing error even the rawest cadet shouldn't make. He'd growled and said she'd better pull herself together.

Having finally spotted a white corner poking out from beneath a pile of press releases, Blaise seized the missing piece of correspondence. She noticed idly that, although the envelope bore her name, it hadn't been stamped. Still, that wasn't so unusual. Invitations were often delivered to her at *The Advocate* by hand.

Blaise quickly tore it open, but instead of the embossed card she'd expected, there was a sheet of paper on which was typed a single line.

*HOW DID IT FEEL WHEN YOU HELD THE KNIFE IN YOUR HAND?*

Blaise took a sharp breath, her eyes wide with alarm. The "Ryan business," as Adam called it, hadn't been sorted at all. Somebody knew her secret.

She sat for a minute, thinking, then read the note once again. It made no sense. How could anyone in London know about Paddy Ryan? And why would they send a message like this, anyway? Blackmail was the only motive she could think of, although surely anyone who knew her would be aware she had no money. Unless it was an attempt to get at Adam—through her. But that couldn't be right, because no one was aware of their relationship. She certainly hadn't told a soul and she doubted Adam had. If anyone played his cards close to his chest, it was that man. The only person who'd brought up the possibility was Charlie Ashton, but she'd ruled him out immediately.

Charlie! She'd slipped up there as well, neglecting to call him back when he'd already rung several times. Blaise screwed the bit of paper into a ball. Nobody suspected her—she had Adam's word. Anyone could write a stupid note like this. That ridiculous line about holding a knife was straight out of the pages of pulp fiction. The letter must be some juvenile prank by one of the newsmen. Maybe some hack thought it was hilarious that a former police rounds ringer who specialized in crime had ended up as a royal correspondent.

She was on the verge of tossing the letter into the bin when, on an impulse, she smoothed out the crumpled page and put it into her handbag. It was nothing, a joke, that was all. But if she received any other idiotic messages, she'd try to work out who'd been responsible and then confront him. She was growing tired of "putting a lid on it," despite her dad's warnings.

A fortnight had passed and there'd been no follow-up to the annoying note. Wrapping her trench coat around her as she trudged down Fleet Street, Blaise decided that even though it had prompted a return of that old disturbing dream, the one where a dead body rose from a sandy beach, life was looking up. This was more than she could say for the weather; June might be summer in England but what with a spate of icy rain and blustery winds, it was worse than a Sydney winter.

"Hill!" a voice called out from across Fleet Street. It was George, a good sub she'd become friendly with.

Fortunately, most of the ogling seemed to be over and done with. Pretty soon, she hoped, the novelty of having a woman in their midst would wear off and everyone in the newsroom would regard her, like George did, as just another reporter.

"Have you heard anything?" he said when he caught up with her.

Of all the myriad bits of news that flew through the air in this part of London, there was just one matter Blaise was certain he was asking about. She could imagine it, wraith-like, drifting across editorial floors and down rickety stairways, zigzagging through El Vino's, the Stab, and the Mucky Duck, up Cheshire Court and down Hanging Sword Alley. It would have started as a whisper that had turned into gossip, then firmed up as a rumor before eventually achieving the solid form of a fact. *The Advocate*'s long-standing editor, Mr. Max Gifford, OBE, ex-Harrow, ex-Cambridge, was retiring due to ill health. So far, however, nobody knew who was replacing him.

At ten thirty a.m. the answer swept through the newsroom. Edgar McInerney, formerly of the leading Sydney newspaper *The Clarion*, had been appointed. Blaise sat back in her chair, smiling delightedly. The prospect of working for a man she both knew personally and respected was the first really good thing to have happened to her since Adam left. So far, she'd been disappointed to receive only a postcard from him with two scrawled words: *Missing you.*

At eleven Bernard Glyn, the foreign editor, reported he'd just seen McInerney walk into *The Advocate*'s headquarters. He also mentioned that the bespectacled Australian was not wearing the city dress favored by London's editors. General speculation among the reporters followed as to whether this oddity meant the man—an Antipodean, after all—simply didn't know the form, or if it signaled his intention to stamp his own style on the paper.

At eleven thirty, Blaise saw McInerney for herself when, with Norton at his side, he walked into the newsroom wearing an ordinary blue suit. She noted that, perhaps as a concession to local sensibilities, his shoes had been polished.

"Good morning, gentlemen," Norton barked. "I'd like to introduce our new editor, Mr. Edgar McInerney. A few of you might have come across him, some time ago now, when he was this paper's chief of staff and I was a political correspondent. Hill worked for him in Australia, of course," he added as an afterthought.

"Mr. McInerney is a newspaperman through and through. He's broken more stories than you've had hot dinners, so just in case any of you lot think he'll be an easygoing, wet-behind-the-ears bloke from the colonies, you've got another think coming."

More than two hundred faces stared at the two men.

"Thank you, Mr. Norton," McInerney said. "I would like to begin by wishing my distinguished predecessor, Max Gifford, much improved health and a happy retirement." He paused. "No doubt you'll find my approach a little different from his. I'm what you'd call a hands-on type and a pretty blunt speaker.

"*The Advocate* is an outstanding publication. Naturally, I'm extremely proud to have been appointed the new editor. But, putting that aside for a moment, no doubt you're all wondering what is it I want from you, its staff. Not much, other than to give this newspaper your very best.

"By that you might think I'm talking about devoting one hundred per cent of your energies to *The Advocate*. Well, I'm not. I want you to consider what 'going above and beyond the call of duty' means—and then go off and damn well do that."

He gave a brief smile. "During the next week or two, I'll be looking forward to meeting every one of you. Mr. Norton here will continue as chief of staff—you won't find a better one, certainly not on Fleet Street. Even so, it doesn't matter who you are, my door is always open if there's something you think might require my particular attention."

An unusual quiet had descended on the editorial floor.

"Now, find me some stories—real, breaking news that our readers can't get anywhere else. That's all for now, gentlemen."

The section editors, the reporters, the subs, and even the copy boys broke into spontaneous applause. It was the only time, Blaise thought, McInerney looked in the least bit uncomfortable.

It wasn't until late in the afternoon that a new memorandum was distributed. First, it revealed that Mr. Thomas Trent had been appointed the new editor of their Sydney-based sister paper, *The Clarion*. Blaise was thrilled for Tommy. He'd been so kind and generous to her when she was just starting out. He was also an outstanding journalist and deserved the promotion.

But the next paragraph contained the more astonishing information. It stated that, as recent publishing trends had indicated the Women's Section of *The Advocate* required significant expansion, Mrs. Marguerite Hawthorn, editor, and Miss Harriet Lawrence, reporter, would be joining the newspaper in due course.

Blaise immediately dashed down the corridor, where she found Dora wearing her black turtleneck sweater with a startling hot pink skirt.

"Isn't it fabulous news?" Dora said with a smile as wide as Blaise's own. "I don't know Mrs. Hawthorn but you and Harriet seem to think she's the bee's knees, so she must be good. Think of all the extra pages we'll have, the fashions we can cover, the interviews!"

Blaise wrinkled her forehead. "I know that Harriet has been dying to get over here, but I'm surprised that Marguerite is coming, too."

Dora lowered her voice. "I've heard a rumor that she and Mr. McInerney share something more than a working relationship."

Blaise burst out laughing. The very idea was preposterous. But then, the more she thought about it, the more likely it seemed. First of all, she had never heard any mention of a Mr. Hawthorn— if he'd ever existed, he clearly wasn't around anymore. Perhaps more importantly, both Hawthorn and McInerney were consummate professionals, dedicated to their work. Despite their sharply contrasting styles—especially in matters of dress—maybe this had drawn them together. Of course, the rumor could be just one more example of the notorious unreliability of newspaper gossip, but still . . .

Blaise's musing was interrupted by Colin. "Miss Hill? I thought I might find you in here," he said. "You're wanted down in the darkroom." Colin scratched his nose. "Apparently there's some sort of muddle about the photos that were taken this morning at the Duke of Edinburgh's reception for World War I veterans. They've been mixed up with the pictures from the other event you covered—was it the Queen Mother's tea for war widows? Something like that, anyway."

Blaise rolled her eyes. "It should be blindingly obvious which are which—not to mention who is who. But all right, I'll go downstairs and see what's going on."

A red light shone outside the darkroom, which meant the photography boys were developing film. She knocked on the door so they'd know she was waiting outside.

"Hill, is that you?" she heard a voice yell from within. "If it is, come in right away."

Blaise was surprised. No one went inside the darkroom when the light was on; it was an ironclad rule.

For a moment she hesitated, then the same voice shouted, "Well? Don't keep us waiting." Blaise pushed the door open. Things seemed to be done differently around here.

It was difficult to see in the dim interior, with its weird, blood-colored lighting that made the place look like an outpost of hell. She pushed her way past various pieces of equipment then stood looking up uncertainly at the line strung across the room.

Newly developed black and white photographs, attached by pegs, were drying like washing—perhaps these were the shots they'd wanted her to look at.

"Guys?" she said, peering through the red gloom.

Suddenly, a rough hand came from behind and covered her mouth. At the same time, a chunky man sprang forward and grabbed her around the waist. She was sandwiched between the two of them.

"Ready for a treat, darlin'?" the one who had his hand over her mouth hooted.

"A little slap and tickle, isn't that's what you young girls like?" said the other man, who gave her a squeeze. "I've heard Aussie girls are always up for it."

It was when she heard their burst of drunken laughter that her fear disappeared. This might be simply another stupid prank, but she wasn't going to give these deadbeats the satisfaction of thinking they'd scared her. Within seconds she'd bitten down hard on the first man's hand while ramming her knee between the legs of the second. Both let go suddenly, roaring with pain.

Blaise took to her heels and fled.

She was breathing hard, could feel the adrenaline still coursing through her, as she ran back up the stairs to the newsroom. Had they really thought she'd burst into tears like some sort of cream puff? There wasn't anyone who'd grown up where she had who didn't know how to fight dirty. She'd come across far tougher types than these blokes, ever since she was a little kid.

Blaise marched over to the chief of staff's glass-fronted office, wrenched open the door and slammed it behind her.

"You don't look your usual cheerful self, Hill," he said drily, through a cloud of cigarette smoke.

Blaise set out exactly what the men had done.

"Any injuries sustained?"

"Not by me."

"Well, I can't see as you have much cause for complaint," Norton said.

"I don't believe this! Those jerks were all over me. Aren't you giving them the sack?"

"Hill, settle down. Surely you've realized by now that boys will be boys—especially when they've had a few. Don't worry, I'll find out who was working and tell them to pull their heads in, as you Aussies say."

"So that's all?" Blaise protested. "What am *I* supposed to do?"

"You're supposed to go back to your desk and write whatever news you can dredge up about our blessed royal family," he said. "Oh, and this time make sure you get the bloody spelling right."

Blaise stood her ground, glaring.

Norton rose to his feet, folded his arms across his bulging stomach and growled, "Now, Hill!"

So much for things looking up, Blaise thought as she stalked out of the chief of staff's office. And so much for any hope that women were treated differently on Fleet Street than on a Sydney newspaper.

# CHAPTER THIRTY-ONE

Dora held up a flimsy blue aerogram. "Sorry, I forgot. This came for you yesterday."

Blaise had moved in to Dora's pretty Chelsea flat, with its pink and white striped sofas and porcelain pots of matching petunias, in early May, nearly a month earlier. Number 6A, 18 Sloane Gardens belonged to Dora's parents, who spent most of their time in Monte Carlo. "It's some sort of income tax thing," she'd said airily.

When Blaise had left Sir Ernest's Knightsbridge abode she'd felt utterly bereft. Although she'd been looking forward to rooming with Dora, it had meant severing her last remaining link with Adam. At first, in the still, dark hours of the night, it was thrilling to conjure up memories of their passionate lovemaking. But as one lonely day followed another, their fervent encounter had begun to seem more like the sort of tale a Scheherazade might tell—intensely felt, terribly romantic, but increasingly unreal.

"Let me see," Dora said, putting on her round owl glasses as she peered at the flap on the back. "It's from a Mr. Adam Rule— now, why does that name ring a bell?" She frowned. "Wait a second, I think my big sister Edwina knew him . . ."

"Dora, you're such a sticky beak."

"A *what*?"

Blaise laughed. "It's what we call a person who sticks their nose into someone else's business."

"But you will tell me about Adam, won't you?" Dora said, handing the aerogram over.

Blaise blinked back a sudden tear. "Honestly, I wouldn't know where to begin."

Ignoring Dora's look of concern, Blaise retreated into her bedroom. The curtains were made of green and white chintz, as was the bedspread, and on one wall hung a small watercolor of Winchester Cathedral. Over by the window sat a cane settee, upholstered in white linen and liberally strewn with green velvet cushions. It was the perfect place to read Adam's letter.

After the first paragraph Blaise's stomach began to flutter. Adam's description of what he longed to do with her once he returned filled her with a sudden, intense longing.

She lifted her eyes from the page and stared down onto the street. The sight of a uniformed maid walking briskly toward one of London's bright red post boxes; a man in a trilby stepping out of a black taxi cab; even the rounded vowels of the voices below floating up through the open window—all these things reminded her of just how far apart she and Adam were.

Any trace of the thrill she'd felt had evaporated by the time she turned her attention back to his aerogram.

*After more trouble than I'd anticipated, the deal eventually went through. The problem is I'm now stuck in the far west of Queensland (where it's hot as Hades), trying to make sure that this vast copper mine is being worked properly. I'm writing to you in Cloncurry, which at least has a postal service, but please don't worry if you don't hear from me. At best, Cloncurry is a long day's drive away.*

Blaise couldn't imagine how it was that Adam, so urbane in his handmade suits and custom shoes, had a clue about mining. But then there was so much she didn't know about him.

*I hope you will visit this extraordinary place one day. The earth is a rich red and dotted with clumps of greenish-gray spinifex. There are also deep gorges where you can find waterholes and plenty of wildlife—mostly gray wallabies, red kangaroos, and dingoes that look like yellow dogs in the bright light. Then there are the flocks of pink Major Mitchell's cockatoos that take off without warning, soaring across a sky that is bigger and bluer than anything you'll ever see in the city—certainly not in London, anyway.*

*At night there are so many stars it's hard to look away. That's why there's nothing I like better than dragging my sleeping bag outside in the cool of the evening and staring up at the Southern Cross. I think I saw a comet the other night, but I might just have imagined it. It's easy for your mind to play tricks on you after you've been in the desert for long enough.*

*Usually, I'm so exhausted from working at the mine that I fall asleep pretty quickly. But if I'm especially lucky, the next day I remember dreaming about a remarkable, blue-eyed woman.*

*Adam*

Blaise sighed. It was a lovely letter, but she didn't even have an address where she could write back. Adam was rapidly becoming an intangible ghost.

As a faint breeze rustled the leaves in the cypress trees, Blaise gazed across the manicured lawn at the crowds of people standing between the rear wing of Buckingham Palace and a sparkling ornamental lake. "Isn't this too wonderful?" she said.

Harriet giggled. "Remember how I taught you to curtsy that day in the park? I never imagined we'd find ourselves attending a Royal Garden Party together."

When the official invitation, issued by the Lord Chamberlain, had arrived at *The Advocate* with "*and guest*" written next to her name, Blaise had immediately asked Dora.

"Thank you, but no," she'd said, making a face. "Now that debutantes are no longer presented at Court, the queen's started inviting us to her garden parties instead. Quite honestly, I've seen enough oversized hats to last me a lifetime. Take someone who would really appreciate it."

"Like who?"

"Harriet is due to fly in next week—you should ask her if she'd like to go."

Standing beside Harriet this day, Blaise realized she was the perfect choice—Harriet was in her element.

Blaise tapped her friend on the shoulder. "Look at the Duchess of Argyll," she said. "Doesn't she look wonderful in that Hardy Amies cream silk coat and matching hat? The pale yellow roses pinned to its crown are terribly elegant—I think I recognize Freddie Fox's handiwork."

"Goodness, you're so knowledgeable about the finer things in life these days," Harriet said with a grin.

"Hardly." Blaise laughed. "If you hadn't run me through the dos and don'ts of Garden Party etiquette last night I'd probably have turned up here and disgraced myself."

"Nonsense. And by the way, you look every bit as chic as the duchess. I adore the way you've added that flat grosgrain bow to the front of your hat, and that navy and white spotted dress is perfect on you, even if it is on loan from Dora. You've never looked better." She peered at Blaise from beneath her dark lashes. "Which is the reason I'm wondering why you don't seem to be dating any eligible men—or, when it comes to that, any men at all."

"I did meet a guy, a real sweetheart. We had a fantastic night out, but someone else entered the picture and things became complicated. Then, he left the country and . . ."

As if on cue, Charlie Ashton, wearing a gray three-piece morning suit and a striped tie, came bounding toward her.

"Hmmm, looks as if one of your mystery suitors is coming your way," Harriet said.

"Do you mind if you leave me for five minutes? I'm planning on putting him off."

"If you insist." Harriet smiled. "I'll go and amuse myself by counting the number of ladies wearing pastel chiffon frocks."

Charlie appeared at her side just as Harriet strolled off. "Hello, remember me?" he said, beaming.

"Don't be silly, of course I do."

"Really? I was beginning to think I'd been quite forgotten," he added, a little less exuberantly, "especially as you haven't returned my calls. I've not blotted my copybook again, have I? If so, I can't imagine how."

"No, nothing like that." Embarrassed, Blaise looked away. She really should have phoned Charlie back. "I've just been so tied up," she said apologetically, "what with one thing and another."

"Tell me, is it really a thing or another chap that's proved so distracting?"

Blaise attempted a light-hearted laugh. "Definitely a thing. Loads of them, in fact—my new job, for a start. Then there was moving into a friend's flat. Actually, one of the girls I'm sharing with is here today, but she's gone off to look at dresses and hats." Blaise scanned the sea of people. She shouldn't have sent Harriet away; Charlie's questions were making her uncomfortable. "My friend Dora was keeping a room free for her parents so that whenever they visited from Monte Carlo they'd have somewhere to stay, but it turns out that the Major and Mrs. Fraser-Barclay-Hughes would far rather check in to Claridge's."

Charlie seemed not to notice Blaise was ill at ease. "Ah, you must mean Pandora. I'm an old chum of her sister, Edwina, but I think she's living in New York now." He shook his head. "She's a clever girl, though awfully . . ."

"What?"

"Fanciful. Had rather a wild imagination, as I recall—I believe it runs in the family. And who's Harriet?"

"Oh, she's a journalist, too," Blaise said. "She and Dora went to finishing school together in Switzerland."

"Sounds like a very cozy little trio," Charlie said. "But you can't spend all your time with your girlfriends. Why not enjoy some of the delights of the London season with me? Royal Ascot is on this week. Then there's boating at Henley and the tennis at Wimbledon, that sort of thing."

She would have loved to go to all these events—if only Adam

had been the one asking her. "I'm sorry," she said, "but I don't want to become involved. I'm just too busy." She'd had a great time with Charlie, but ever since she and Adam had spent their magical night together Blaise had been reluctant to date anyone. The fact that the two men had obviously had a serious misunderstanding only made her more diffident.

"Who said anything about getting involved? I thought we were friends." Charlie looked genuinely upset. "Why can't we just be pals and have a good time? I know, let's go back to the 400 Club on Friday night."

Blaise felt a stab of guilt. Charlie had danced attention on her, but she'd simply dropped him without any explanation. And a night out with such an amusing, uncomplicated man did have appeal, especially as he'd made it clear he wasn't after romance. There wasn't much point staying in, moping about someone who might as well be a figment of her imagination.

"All right, friends it is—and that sounds lovely," she said.

"I promise you won't regret changing your mind."

Blaise decided that the way Charlie's smile made the corners of his eyes crease was really quite appealing. "Are you still employing Andy?" she asked. Now she was a permanent member of staff, she had access only to *The Advocate*'s regular pool drivers to take her to assignments. It was ages since she'd seen the cheery chauffeur.

"I am. The man's been quite a find."

"Then pick me up at 18 Sloane Gardens at, say, nine o'clock."

As she spoke, she caught sight of a hat with red poppies bobbing toward her. "Here's my friend," she said, waving in Harriet's direction. "Which reminds me, I'd better start doing my job. See you soon."

"There goes a chap who looks pleased as Punch," Harriet remarked as Charlie disappeared into a cluster of tailcoats and floral frocks. "Who is he?"

"Oh, that's just Charlie. We're only friends."

"Are you sure he feels the same way?"

Before Blaise had a moment to tell Harriet she'd grasped entirely the wrong end of the stick, she felt, as much as saw, a ripple pass through the crowd. There was a general turning of heads and taking up of positions at the appearance of the queen, glowing in a blush-pink hat and coat, by the side of the Duke of Edinburgh on the terrace in front of the Palace's circular Bow Room.

It was exactly four p.m. Blaise watched as the crowd stilled, adopting a uniformly erect posture as a military band struck up "God Save the Queen." Next, the royal couple moved onto the lawn, guarded by Beefeaters wearing scarlet coats, red stockings, red rosettes on their shoes, white Elizabethan-style ruffs, and flat black hats. The men herded the milling guests into several ragged rows before, without exchanging a word, the queen and the duke parted ways and each began walking down the lanes. After a dozen or so steps, a favored individual was selected by a courtier and duly presented to either His Royal Highness or Her Majesty.

"Come on, Harriet," Blaise said. "We have special tickets to the Royal Tea Tent, where, I'm told there will be only 120 guests. Let's wait there until the queen and the duke arrive. We'll have a much better view of them."

"Golly, how did you score that sort of entrée?"

Blaise shrugged. "Must be something to do with Sir Ernest being so thick with the Windsors."

Inside the tent, white and gold teacups imprinted with the monarch's initials were arranged on long trestle tables covered with crisp damask cloths. Milling guests eyed a tempting array of tiny chocolate eclairs, Victoria sponge cakes and other mouthwatering treats.

Blaise was sizing up a strawberry tart when the queen and Prince Philip entered the tent. Sidling closer to the royal couple, she heard Her Majesty ask one elderly dowager, "Have you come far, Lady McIver?" After a brief response, the queen said, "From Inverness? What a long way." A remarkably similar exchange was repeated as various worthies were introduced.

Blaise was just thinking that the queen must have decided

this was a suitably bland question appropriate to almost every individual when, to her astonishment, Her Majesty's attendant, a man with close-cropped red hair and a thick moustache, stopped in front of her. "Your name?" he muttered in a Scottish accent. Feeling dazed, she told him.

"May I introduce Miss Blaise Hill, Ma'am," he said stiffly.

Blaise's mind went blank. The curtsy she had practiced so diligently failed to materialize. Then, in a panic, instead of waiting for the queen to address her first as protocol demanded, to her horror she heard her own voice babbling away. Her self-control seemed to have vanished. Could she really have gushed, "I'm thrilled to meet you?" Had she actually asked how Her Majesty was coping with her new baby, Prince Andrew?

The queen looked bemused. Eyebrows were raised. Blaise whirled around, her cheeks on fire. More than anything, she wanted to escape from this embarrassing situation. Then she heard a collective intake of breath. She had turned her back on Her Majesty, another unpardonable offense.

Blaise slunk behind an oversized display of palm fronds and peonies. It was now oddly quiet. Her bizarre conduct had reduced the Royal Tea Tent's inhabitants to a state of appalled silence, broken only when she heard the queen remark, "I believe it's time for an egg and cress sandwich."

Blaise hung her head. For weeks now, she'd been kidding herself. A girl like her might be equipped to deal with a couple of inebriated photographers, but she was way out of her depth in this rarefied milieu.

She was close to tears when she felt a hand on her elbow. Half expecting it would be one of the Beefeaters, intent on ejecting her from the Palace grounds, she looked up to see a man with a high, domed forehead who was wearing a pristine morning suit. "So this is where you've hidden yourself," he observed primly. "Dear me, you do seem to have made a bit of a mess of things. I thought you might appreciate some advice on the correct way to respond to Her Majesty."

"I'm sorry," Blaise said despondently. "It's just that I became overwhelmed and forgot everything."

"Protocol exists for a reason, Miss—"

"Hill, Blaise Hill."

"Good Lord!" The man stared at her. "I'm Martin Charteris," he said with a marked change in demeanor, "and it is I who should be apologizing." He seemed to have turned into another being entirely. "Sometimes we old hands forget that it's easy to become overawed when one is presented to Her Majesty for the first time."

Charteris drew Blaise further behind the palms. Lowering his voice, he said, "Miss Hill, you were invited here today for a reason. The Queen is very grateful for the service you rendered to her sister. I might add, she has also commented about the much improved standard of reporting since you became *The Advocate*'s royal correspondent."

Blaise began to feel a little better. "So I'm not going to be sent to the Tower?" she asked with a touch of her usual spirit.

"Certainly not," Charteris said with a chuckle. "But, returning to that other matter," he added in a more serious tone, "I'm sure you would understand that your quick-witted intervention on behalf of Princess Margaret cannot be publicly acknowledged. Nevertheless, Her Majesty believes herself to be in your debt."

"Surely not, Mr. Ch-Charteris," Blaise stuttered.

"In that regard," he continued smoothly, "I have been instructed to provide you with this." He gave her a small card, blank except for a handwritten telephone number. "Keep it somewhere very safe. The number is known to just a handful of trusted individuals and is to be used only when you find yourself in great need."

Despite the warm weather, Blaise shivered. She'd had that awful dream again only a couple of nights before; it had stirred up all her old anxiety. Perhaps, as the alarming note had suggested, there *was* someone who knew she'd been present at a murder.

Maybe the urbane Charteris, practiced secret-keeper and deft burier of scandals, had in reality been issuing her with a warning.

Blaise straightened her hat. She was letting her imagination get the better of her.

Charteris steered her back into the middle of the tent. "Don't worry," he assured her. "As I have the honor of being the queen's assistant private secretary," he smiled, "my friendly attitude toward you will be quite enough to show everyone that all is forgiven."

He shook Blaise's hand with what seemed genuine warmth, although she suspected it would be impossible to divine what this wily courtier's real feelings were about her or, for that matter, anyone else.

"It has been a pleasure, Miss Hill," he declared in a loud voice before excusing himself in order to greet the New Zealand High Commissioner.

Suddenly, Harriet was by her side. "Where on earth have you been?" she said. "Some sort of commotion broke out behind me while I was waiting for the world's largest teapot to be filled. By the time I finally had a cup of Earl Gray in my hand, you'd vanished."

"I was receiving a private briefing from a Palace official about . . . constitutional procedure," Blaise said quickly.

"Well, I certainly hope that was more interesting than it sounds." Harriet rolled her eyes. "If you ask me, I think it's time we explored the queen's gardens—I believe they're enchanting. Unless you'd like a scone first?"

As Blaise shook her head, she discreetly slipped the card from Martin Charteris into her handbag. Somehow, instead of providing comfort, his gesture had made her feel nervous. He hadn't said she should telephone *if* she found herself in great need, but *when*. No doubt he meant nothing by it, though it left her with the uncomfortable feeling that, at some unspecified time in the future, she might need rescuing.

# CHAPTER THIRTY-TWO

Harriet snapped her fingers in front of Blaise's eyes. "Hey, come back from wherever you are," she said. "I was asking how you felt about Charlie Ashton."

"Harriet, I thought we were here to look at Turner's paintings." Blaise smiled. "You know, elevate the mind, that sort of thing."

It was a midsummer Sunday, but slate-gray rain had been falling steadily since early that morning. A visit to the Tate Gallery had been her idea; as Ivy was mad about the seascapes of J.M.W. Turner, Blaise had decided that if her sister couldn't see these tempestuous masterpieces for herself, at least she'd be able to pass on her impressions in a letter. Ivy had written only last week, demanding more details about London's museums and famous works of art. It wasn't right. Ivy was the gifted, artistic member of the family. She should be the one standing here, thrilled by these luminous depictions of stormy skies and turbulent seas.

Blaise's wave of guilt only added to her dejection. Since Adam's letter, she hadn't received a line from him. By now she'd had weeks to turn over their relationship—or whatever it was—in her increasingly troubled mind. Lately, she'd even begun to wonder if she had made an enormous mistake. Maude had always insisted that her daughters must not, under any circumstances, sleep with a man until they were safely married. "Just you remember, people might think they're so modern these days, going on about space rockets and what have you," she'd warned the girls, "but a fellow will still drop you flat if you give him what he wants without putting a ring on your finger first. That's one thing that won't ever change, not in a hundred years." She had folded her arms with grim certainty. "Not even if some idiot flies to the moon."

Blaise hadn't said anything to Maude, but she'd never agreed with this advice. Unlike her poor mum, she was a modern woman with a profession, forging ahead on her own terms. She'd conducted her personal life—such as it was, she thought wryly—in the same way. It had been Blaise herself who'd made it abundantly clear to Adam that she wanted to make love to him. Why shouldn't a woman have desires too?

But perhaps she'd made a wild miscalculation. There were enough girls in her neighborhood who'd acquired questionable reputations. The local boys used to snicker and call them "tarts"—or worse. Is that what she'd become? Just another tart, an easy one-night stand? Maybe Maude *was* right, and beneath even Adam's suave exterior he was in reality no different from most other men, taking his pleasure where he found it before moving on. God knows, she'd offered herself up on a plate.

For all she knew, he wasn't even at the wretched mine but in Sydney right now, devoting his time and attention to other women. She could write to Joe, ask him if he'd seen anything of Adam Rule. But considering that course only made her squirm. It was so underhanded and, even worse, humiliating.

Blaise took a breath. At least she never had to worry about anything like that with Charlie. Their friendship had remained, as he'd promised, blissfully uncomplicated. "Why do you want to know about him?" Blaise asked Harriet.

"Because you've been out with Charlie quite a bit but you don't show any signs of that 'swept away' look a girl has when she's keen on a man. In fact"—Harriet narrowed her eyes—"I'd say you're pining for someone else entirely."

"Don't be silly," Blaise retorted.

"Well then, why are you always rushing to see what's in the post?"

"I'm just hoping for a letter from home."

"Nobody looks that disappointed when they don't hear from their mum and dad."

Blaise blushed.

"Ha! I knew I was right," Harriet said. "Dora and I had a talk about it the other night. She thinks you might be interested in someone called Adam Rule. Only, you've never said a word about him to either of us. What's going on?"

Blaise had held back from telling the girls about her relationship with Adam, partly due to its connection with the Ryan debacle but for another reason too. She and Adam had spent no more than a few hours together and yet she had slept with him. What would Dora and Harriet think of her behavior? She didn't want them to see her as some sort of tramp—but right now, she needed help.

"Actually, I'm really glad you've brought Adam up," she said. "I thought I could work things out by myself, but I'm completely confused about everything."

Harriet smiled sympathetically. "Sounds like it's just as well we're meeting Dora downstairs for lunch. I can't think of a better spot for a heart to heart."

Blaise had never seen a room like the Rex Whistler Restaurant. Every wall was covered by the artist's otherworldly murals. Painted mainly in deep blues and greens, they conjured up a mythical landscape replete with sylvan glades, rivers and mountains, classical statuary, a miniature hunting party, tiny towns, and even a number of little men intent on exploring their fairytale surroundings by way of minute bicycles.

"What's its name?" Blaise asked, gazing over the top of her menu at the extraordinary work.

"*An Expedition in Search of . . .* something or other," Dora said. "I can't remember exactly. But I do know that in the 1920s, when the restaurant first opened, it was called 'the most amusing room in Europe.' Can't you just imagine all the Bright Young Things in their beaded shifts and cloche hats pouring in?"

"That's enough for now about frocks, or art." Harriet smiled. "Blaise wants to have a little chat."

While her friends were determining what to order, Blaise quickly decided on which details it was safe to include in an account of her and Adam's . . . *liaison* was perhaps the best way to put it, and which must definitely be left out. In the end, she said she'd met him through an old family friend, which was more or less correct.

"Right from the start, he seemed to have this knack of anticipating just when I needed help with tricky situations. And he turned out to have a surprising range of contacts. I'm sure the interview he arranged with his friend, who just happened to be Princess Alexandra's lady-in-waiting, was solely responsible for landing me this job here in London."

"So it was Adam Rule who persuaded her to talk to you. I wondered how you managed to swing that," Harriet said.

"Yes, but there was always more to it." Blaise hesitated. "You'll think this is the most hopelessly romantic cliché, but from the moment we met I felt drawn to him by a sort of . . ."

"A sort of what?" Dora prompted.

"An irresistible force." She held up her hands. "I know, I know, even I think it sounds ridiculous."

Blaise sat back in her chair. It was a relief to finally reveal her feelings. "Adam is the most intriguing man I've ever come across. Incredibly attractive, rather complicated, too, but I think he's also damaged somehow. And he's really good to the people he cares about, no matter whether they're at the top of the tree or just struggling." *From the queen's sister to Joe Blackett*, she reflected. There couldn't be two individuals who were further apart.

Blaise drank a little wine. "Nothing much happened between us for ages." The boathouse encounter was far too difficult to talk about. "Then I saw him at the royal ball. We danced and, the way he looked at me . . . it's hard to explain, but I began wondering if Adam might feel the same way I did. A few days later he turned up at the Knightsbridge flat and"—she looked around, making certain that she couldn't be overheard—"he stayed the night."

"You mean . . . ?"

"Yes." Blaise was whispering now. "It was my first time."

"And how was it?" This came from Harriet.

"Perfect."

Her friends exchanged a look.

"Have I shocked you?" she asked anxiously.

Dora giggled. "Darling, what exactly did you think Harriet and I were up to with that French ski instructor? It wasn't all downhill racing. We both had a huge crush on Frédéric," she said, "and secretly daydreamt about him all the time. That is, until we compared notes one Sunday morning and discovered he'd had his wicked way with each of us on consecutive Saturday afternoons. We were meant to be receiving private lessons—which, when you look at it, I suppose we were," she said archly. "So, no, we're not shocked, not at all."

Harriet gave Blaise a serious look. "Only this isn't just a crush for you, is it?" she said softly.

Blaise shook her head. "It might have been at first. But not now. The problem is, after that night, he had to return to Australia, and since then I've only had one letter and the odd postcard. I know he's meant to be stuck at a remote mine in the Queensland desert until sometime in August, but still . . . I keep doubting him."

"August is still a couple of weeks away," Harriet said. "I don't see why you're so worked up—unless you have reason to believe he's not trustworthy."

Blaise's stomach churned. Could she trust a man who never spoke about his past, someone she barely knew, who was far better informed about drug dealers and hitmen than any respectable businessman had a right to be? She didn't know what to say.

Suddenly, Dora looked up. "Do you remember me telling you that Adam Rule knew my big sister Edwina?"

Blaise sat forward. "Yes, I do."

"Well, since we started this chat, I've remembered something about it. I was eavesdropping on Edwina years ago—you know how kids lurk around, hoping to hear stuff they're not meant to— and she mentioned him. He was in real trouble about something—

and it involved none other than your good chum Charlie Ashton. Won't that make things awfully difficult when Adam returns?"

Blaise pushed her barely touched poached salmon to one side. "Charlie and I are just friends. I'm sure whatever happened between him and Adam was all a misunderstanding. Maybe I can help patch things up between the two of them."

"If that's what you think, you're being naive," Harriet said. "You might be tough and smart and talented but, I'm sorry, that doesn't mean you have a clue about men. You admitted yourself," she said in a gentler tone, "you're not exactly experienced."

"Well, I'm not so witless I wouldn't notice if Charlie was coming on to me. The most he's ever managed is a goodnight kiss on the cheek."

Harriet waved her protests away. "Perhaps he's just playing a long game. He is a politician, after all. Beneath that hale and hearty, cheerful old Charlie routine, he must be at least a bit devious."

The trio suspended their conversation while a waiter removed their plates.

Dora picked up the bill. "Tell you what," she said after a quick perusal, "I'll ask Edwina. She's an academic, an anthropologist, actually, studies lost tribes and whatever. Right now, she's somewhere in the middle of the Amazon rainforest, but eventually she'll return to New York. I'm going to write to her the minute I'm back at the flat. Seems to me it would be a good idea to discover exactly what this blow-up with Charlie was about."

"And in the meantime," Harriet frowned, "maybe you shouldn't spend quite so much time with the Honorable Mr. Ashton."

"Perhaps you're right," Blaise said, hoping to put an end to the conversation. Her friends might have the benefit of their finishing school sophistication. No doubt they knew a great deal more about men than she did. But not only had she been exposed to a horrific death they couldn't possibly imagine, she'd begun wondering whether the man she adored might have played a part in the murderous revenge that had followed. If there was anyone they should be concerned about, it was Adam.

# CHAPTER THIRTY-THREE

Blaise wandered along the Chelsea Embankment beside the slow-moving River Thames, determined to come to a decision.

Since June, only one more pale blue aerogram, postmarked Cloncurry, had landed on the doormat of the Sloane Gardens flat. She'd been dismayed to learn that, following a string of problems, Adam's return would now be delayed until mid-September. Then she'd caught her breath when he'd detailed, in a couple of romantic lines, the memories he dwelled upon while lying beneath the stars in the red desert at night.

Blaise sighed. All she and Adam had were memories, and not many of them. Yet as a faint breeze softly ruffled her hair, the sense of him, the feel of his touch and the sound of his voice haunted her. She missed him terribly.

That was why she'd ended up seeing so much of Charlie. He provided such wonderful, undemanding distraction. Although they'd never returned to the Flamingo, he had taken her back to the 400 Club, to a new play in the West End, the opening of an exhibition at the Royal Academy, a Mayfair dinner party and a cocktail reception at the American Embassy attended by some of Britain's most fascinating people. They'd even had a spectacular meal at a swish restaurant called Mirabelle two nights earlier to celebrate Charlie becoming the Assistant Minister of War to the recently promoted John Profumo. She'd relished these exciting new experiences and, true to his word, Charlie had continued to keep everything between them light and amusing. There might not have been any daring young photographers, designers, or writers in his circle, but that just made spending time with Harriet and Dora's more bohemian mates all the more fun.

As Sir Ernest was ensconced in his Cap Ferrat villa enjoying a long recuperation, Charlie had continued to engage Andy to drive him to whatever unofficial event they'd happened to be attending. Whenever Andy collected her en route to picking up Charlie, he was his usual, cheery self. She had even managed to blur what it amused her to think of as the class distinction between the two of them, so much so that they'd taken to greeting each other with "Hello, me old china" as a private joke.

"Seeing as you're asking, Miss," he'd told her one evening when she'd pressed him to share more rhyming slang, "'dog and bone' is a phone, 'bees and honey' is money and—here's a good one—'pork pies' are lies. Only the expressions are shortened, see, so if someone's fibbing we just let it be known that the bloke's telling porkies." Then he'd added, half to himself, "In my line of work, you overhear quite a few of 'em."

Oddly, whenever Charlie joined her in the Jaguar, Andy immediately became silent and formal. She'd even caught him watching them in his driving mirror with a frown on his face that made him look more like a concerned father than a middle-aged chauffeur who'd been hired for the night. Well, he needn't worry, she'd told herself. Charlie never took a single liberty. Either he was simply not attracted to her, or he'd made up his mind to concentrate on his political career and wanted no distractions.

Deep in thought, Blaise watched the gray-blue river drift by. All the same, she had a problem, and it was entirely of her own making. It had first come to her attention after Charlie had introduced her to a supremely elegant woman in her late twenties over martinis at the American Ambassador's party. "Meet Bronwen Pugh," Charlie had said. "You two will get on famously—she's the muse of that French designer chappie Pierre Balmain."

The willowy mannequin was engaged to the much older Lord Astor, but it was her fascinating description of life as a high-fashion model in Paris that captivated Blaise, especially once she discovered that Bronwen had crossed paths with Dior's Australian favorite, Grace Woods, the same vibrant beauty Blaise herself had seen gliding down the catwalk back in Sydney.

Charlie had been right. They formed an immediate bond, so much so that Bronwen interrupted a vigorous discussion between the two men concerning the likelihood of Britain entering the Common Market. "Bill, darling," she said to her fiancé, "once we're married, I absolutely insist that you invite Charlie and his lovely girlfriend to visit us at Cliveden."

*Girlfriend.* That word, and all the assumptions that lay behind it, worried her.

Then, during the following week, Charlie had shown Blaise around the Palace of Westminster. Parliament hadn't been sitting, but she'd been able to view the grand House of Lords with its red leather benches and great gilded throne, on which the queen sat in her royal regalia during the Opening of Parliament. Next they'd visited the less elaborate House of Commons.

"What are those for?" she'd asked, pointing at the floor. Running parallel to both the Government and Opposition's front benches were a pair of red stripes that stood out in vivid contrast to the green carpet.

"The space between each stripe is just a little more than the width of two swords," Charlie explained with a grin, "and woe betide any member who doesn't keep to his side. It's where the expression 'crossing the line' comes from—there's meant to be only verbal combat inside these walls."

Blaise nodded. It was easy to picture Charlie rising to his feet and commanding the House's attention armed only with his good-humored persuasion.

They were in the Members' Lobby, examining the bronze statues of former leaders, when the prime minister himself stopped and greeted Charlie warmly. After Charlie introduced Blaise, they exchanged a few pleasantries, before Macmillan observed, "You know, Miss Hill, there's no telling how far Mr. Ashton can go, although, of course, it's much more difficult for a single man." He then turned his attention to Charlie. "You should do something to remedy that, young man." His tone was jocular, but Blaise couldn't help noticing that, as he'd spoken, he'd glanced in her direction.

Once the prime minister was out of sight, Charlie quickly reassured her. "Hope that didn't bother you. Harold's getting on; must be the old boy's idea of a joke."

Macmillan's remark had been the final straw, the reason she was here now, gazing at a barge quietly chugging down the Thames. If only she had listened to her friends' advice and not spent so much time with Charlie. Adam's return might still be a month away, but if even the prime minister of Great Britain was jumping to the wrong conclusion, then she had no time to waste.

They were sitting at a small table in the art deco American Bar at the Savoy Hotel, yet despite the two whiskies Charlie had drunk in rapid succession, he did not look at all happy.

"Why worry what other people might think about something that isn't any of their business?" he said testily.

Blaise flared with annoyance. "You of all people should know how gossip is spread—and the problems it can lead to." She pursed her mouth. "Everyone has the idea we're practically engaged!"

"Who cares? We know we're only friends, and that's all that matters." Charlie put his glass down on the table abruptly.

"It's still best if we spend some time apart."

"Well, I don't agree."

If Blaise hadn't known Charlie better, she could have sworn that a look of scorn passed across his face. "I would have thought you'd want to talk this over properly. Instead, you've chosen to ambush me, and I'm already late for a meeting with the chief whip."

Blaise felt awful. Charlie had been a good mate, sweet and considerate, and now she was walking away. No wonder he was peeved—but she had no alternative. She was just about to say goodbye when his usual amiability returned, catching her by surprise. "Before we part," he said fondly, "I want you to know I think the world of you, Blaise."

Charlie's heartfelt declaration made her feel even worse. She didn't want to put an end to their friendship—but she couldn't risk damaging her already tenuous relationship with Adam.

He was turning to leave when he hesitated. "If you need me," he said with a sad smile, "you know where to find me."

Blaise thought she'd never endured such a dull Monday. The only royal engagement she'd been assigned was the Duke of Edinburgh's attendance that afternoon at a display of knot tying and tent pitching by a group of Boy Scouts who excelled at such tasks. *Poor Prince Philip*, Blaise thought. Then again, he was an outdoorsy type—perhaps he liked that sort of thing.

She stared out of a soot-smeared window then idly straightened up a stack of press clippings one of the copy boys had dumped on her desk. She wasn't sleeping well, would toss and turn for hours as she dwelled on Adam. She seemed to feel permanently tired, which was probably the reason she'd been so nervy lately. Once or twice she'd imagined she was being followed by the same man with the trilby hat and moustache she'd bumped into in Sloane Gardens. Only last night she thought she'd seen him out of the corner of her eye, before he melted away. Blaise told herself a good night's sleep was all she needed.

She had at last adjusted to London. By now, she'd memorized the map of the Tube, as well as the exact location of each one of the city's significant landmarks, from Tower Bridge to Big Ben. She had even begun to tolerate the occasional baked sausage wrapped in batter, that peculiar English delicacy known as Toad in the Hole, although nothing had so far induced her to try jellied eels, the famous East End dish Andy swore by.

There had been no more mishaps at royal functions, her copy was well received and she hadn't experienced any further problems with drunken colleagues. In fact, the two wretched photographers who'd given her so much trouble had long since taken her aside and offered her their abject apologies—which she'd reluctantly accepted—before buying her a drink at the Cheshire

Cheese. She couldn't imagine what Norton had eventually said to them, but whatever it was, they'd seemed genuinely sorry about the darkroom incident. The pair, whose names she had discovered were Mike and Ben, now went out of their way to be as helpful as possible.

Yet Blaise was restless. She tapped her foot, stared at the pile of clippings, then looked balefully at her typewriter. Finally, she jumped up and walked briskly out of the newsroom. A chat with the "girls down the hall" would buck her up.

She found Harriet peering from beneath her newly cut fringe at some of David Bailey's latest black and white images.

"Who's that beautiful model?" she asked, pointing to a photo of a wide-eyed girl with superb bone structure.

"Her name's Jean Shrimpton. Bailey spotted her while she was posing for a Kellogg's Corn Flakes ad, of all things. He says she'll be the face of the '60s."

"It must be fabulous to be out there, discovering new talent," Blaise said wistfully. "Once you've attended your first Trooping the Color at Horse Guards Parade or been to Westminster for the Opening of Parliament, I have the feeling royal rounds are likely to become incredibly repetitive."

She picked up the photograph and took a closer look at the cute, mattress-ticking dress Shrimpton was wearing. "Although I don't think I'll ever become as passionate about fashion as you and Dora, I have become genuinely interested. But then you know what most of the royal ladies go in for."

"God, yes," Dora chimed in. "Stiff, formal clothes for official engagements, or suitably long tweed skirts and headscarfs on their country estates."

"Exactly. It's a long way from Mary Quant."

"Why don't you write something for the Women's Section?" Harriet asked. "Marguerite said only the other day that she missed your flair."

"Did she really?" A moment later, Blaise was knocking on Marguerite's door.

"This *is* fortuitous," Marguerite said in her familiar drawl as she uncapped her Montblanc pen. "We haven't spent nearly enough time together since I arrived in London."

Blaise noted that sitting on her desk was a vase containing full-blown, creamy roses—she felt certain *The Advocate*'s premises had never been graced by floral arrangements before the arrival of the Women's Section's stylish new editor.

"There's something I'd like to run that would be perfect for you." Marguerite made a note on the pristine writing pad in front of her. "I know you do have a penchant for *news*," she said with unmissable emphasis. "It's about this furor that's broken out at Christian Dior—their clients were up in arms after the last show and now their designer has been conveniently called up by the French army to go off and fight in the war with Algeria. I hear there's been some secret maneuvering behind it all. Can you come up with six hundred words by tomorrow afternoon?"

Feeling a welcome burst of energy, Blaise rushed back to her desk, eager to start work. The story she'd been assigned concerned the fallout from the controversial "Beat" collection designed by Yves Saint Laurent, the man who'd been chosen to lead Christian Dior after its founder's untimely death. Blaise and her friends were mad about his cutting-edge creations, but Dior's increasingly conservative clientele had been outraged. Following several phone calls to Paris, two of Marguerite's sources had put forward the theory that none other than Dior's financial backer, the textile magnate Marcel Boussac, had orchestrated Saint Laurent's conscription. What would become of the fragile young man, they had asked, and who would now helm the famous couture house?

It was a joy to research and write an article that, for once, didn't mention a single top hat or tiara. In fact, her spirits were so improved that, later that day, Blaise even found the Scouts' demonstration of the correct way to tie bowline, double-hitch, and figure-eight knots mildly entertaining.

The following afternoon she was perched on a chair in the Women's Section.

"I do admire Saint Laurent for taking his inspiration from the street," Blaise said to Dora, who was checking her copy. "It was an incredibly radical step for a couturier, especially one designing for such a renowned fashion house. But I can't imagine that rich Frenchwomen are ever going to buy black crocodile-skin jackets, even if they are lined with mink."

"You'll see," Dora insisted. "Yves is far too talented to be ignored. One day, those same snooty Parisiennes will be clamoring for everything he creates."

She picked up Blaise's copy. "This is really good. You've a way of zeroing in on the important points but without sacrificing the story's entertainment value. It will be just Marguerite's cup of tea—or should I say, glass of Veuve Clicquot."

Blaise returned to her desk in a mood of pleasant self-congratulation, although by the time she'd finished writing up her article on that morning's official opening by the Duke of Kent of a new gin distillery, of all places, she was gritting her teeth. She'd soon go mad if she didn't have something more substantial to cover. Producing the odd article for the Women's Section was all very well, but there'd be no hope of future advancement if she couldn't work on at least the occasional hard news story.

As Blaise looked around for a boy to ferry her copy over to the subs' desk, an idea came to her. Tommy Trent—how often she'd been inspired by his advice—had told her that if she couldn't slip through the cracks in the brick walls that barred her progress, she'd have to batter them down. The truth was, she'd always been a "nothing ventured, nothing gained" kind of girl. It had worked out well with Marguerite. Tomorrow morning she would simply approach Johnny Norton about the issue. Then she paused. Hadn't the editor himself declared on his first day at *The Advocate* that his door was always open?

Blaise made up her mind. She'd go straight to the top.

# CHAPTER THIRTY-FOUR

"Come in, Hill. What is it you want to see me about?" McInerney said, looking up from his desk. "Last time we spoke you seemed pretty pleased with your new job."

"I don't want to quit or anything like that," she reassured him. She'd thought overnight about what she should say.

"Glad to hear it, Hill." McInerney put on his horn-rimmed spectacles then shuffled through an untidy pile of paper until he found what he was looking for. "Yes, I made a note. Sir Ernest likes your reports. The Palace is happy and even I've been surprised at how quickly you've taken to royal rounds. So what's bothering you?"

"It's just that—you know I've always wanted to take a crack at hard news, something I can really get my teeth into."

McInerney scratched his head. "Good idea," he said.

Blaise was taken aback. Such rapid consent hadn't figured in her imaginary script. Maybe the editor had noticed the piece she'd written for Marguerite in today's paper. She'd tried for something that was not just about Saint Laurent's frocks but had a real news angle. Or perhaps Marguerite herself had put in a good word—if the rumors were true, she and McInerney were pretty tight these days.

"I didn't think I'd ever be saying this to a girl, but I suppose times are changing and, God knows, you've proved you can deliver the goods on at least one notable occasion," the editor said. "Mind you, I don't want any surprises like your last little trick with—what did we end up calling it? Yes, the 'Bondi Beach Body.'"

He removed his glasses, leaving them perched on top of volume one of the *Shorter Oxford English Dictionary*. "This is the deal: neither Norton nor I will assign you to a story. You're on your own, Hill, understand? But if you bring in something worthwhile—and by that I mean a real scoop—then I'll see what I can do."

Blaise had spent the past hour trying to think of a way to unearth a hard news story so compelling that she couldn't help but be taken seriously. On the one hand, the solution to her problem was blindingly obvious. On the other, it would mean asking Charlie for an enormous favor. That thought made her feel decidedly uncomfortable. She wrestled with this dilemma for a further five minutes, before telling herself *Needs must*. This could be the only chance she'd ever have of making McInerney sit up and take notice. She immediately dialed the private number of Great Britain's Assistant Minister for War.

"Ashton."

"Charlie, it's me. Blaise," she said.

"Blaise, I'm so happy to hear from you."

Encouraged by his affectionate tone, she ploughed on. "You told me at the Savoy I could call on you if I needed anything."

"I'm a man of my word, Blaise."

She swiftly explained what McInerney had said. "So you see," she added, "what I'm after is something that will make a real impact." Blaise paused. "I realize it's a lot to ask, but do you know of anything that could help me out?"

"As a matter of fact, your timing is excellent," Charlie said in a much friendlier manner than she'd expected. "Do you remember how to find my ministerial rooms?"

"Yes." Blaise's heart beat a little quicker. This could be her lucky day.

"Unfortunately, I won't be in, but I'll tell my secretary you have permission to pick up a document from my private office by four o'clock. You will find two different folders sitting on my desk." He went on to explain which one she'd require. "And Blaise," he added, "don't tell a soul where you found it."

"Goes without saying." She paused. "Like to give me a hint as to what I'm likely to discover?

"The specifications for the advanced missile system Britain is purchasing from the USA. The information is embargoed until tomorrow morning, which means you'll be a day ahead of everyone else. Will that do?"

"Charlie, that's fantastic! You must know that every reporter on Fleet Street's been after those details. I can't tell you how much I appreciate this."

"Blaise," he said gently. "That's what friends are for."

The next day, Blaise rose early, dressed in a hurry and rushed down to the news booth in front of Sloane Square station. "Steady on, pet," the surprised vendor muttered when she threw a few coins in his general direction. She grabbed a copy of *The Advocate* and—there it was: her story, splashed across the newspaper's front page. Quickly, she scanned the racks of publications. Not another paper had a word about the Macmillan government's new military hardware. She'd scored a scoop, and on Fleet Street.

Blaise danced her way inside the station and onto the platform. By the time she entered the newsroom, she found herself whistling an old Elvis tune. She'd delivered exactly the type of story McInerney had demanded. It didn't matter a jot that all too soon she'd be stuck covering yet another reception for a foreign leader, this one held by the queen in honor of President Kwame Nkrumah of the brand-new Republic of Ghana. Her professional prospects had not merely brightened; they positively gleamed.

Not many journalists were in editorial that early in the morning, but, all the same, she couldn't help noticing an eerie silence as she walked down the aisle toward her desk at the back of the room. She caught Gerald Hanger, the paper's grizzled industrial reporter, giving her a particularly sour look. Then he pointed at her. With the rest of his fingers balled into a tight fist, his hand resembled a gun.

*Old school*, she thought. The man obviously didn't approve of women covering a subject like defense. Well, he was just going to have to get used to it. With a front-page story to her credit, nothing was going to hold her back.

Half an hour later she was familiarizing herself with both the pronunciation of the Ghanaian president's name and his revolutionary past, when Colin ran over and told her she was wanted by Mr. McInerney.

Blaise felt a warm glow. She'd been anticipating this summons since the moment she'd come in.

"*Hill!*" McInerney glowered at her. "Do you have any idea what you've done?"

Blaise noticed that Norton was also in the office. Sitting sprawled in a chair, he looked equally furious.

"What's the problem?" Baffled, she looked from one to the other. "I uncovered a fantastic story before anyone else—I thought that was what you wanted."

McInerney thumped his desk. "I'll tell you what the problem is. The official specifications for the new missiles were released by the Ministry for Defense early this morning, and your figures are all wrong. You've made *The Advocate* a bloody laughingstock—and on my watch!"

"Who was your source?" Norton growled.

"I can't say, but it was someone at the very top." Blaise's head was spinning. She wouldn't betray Charlie, but she couldn't comprehend what the hell had gone wrong.

McInerney looked at Norton, who shook his head. At that, the editor stood up, strode across his room and flung open the door. "Get out, Hill," he said angrily. "Go back and do the job that you're meant to, covering garden parties and bloody scouting jamborees. That's all you're fit for."

It took every bit of self-control she possessed not to burst into tears straightaway. Only once she'd reached the safety of the ladies' toilets did Blaise start to cry. Somewhere along the line a colossal mistake had been made. But whose fault was it?

After ten minutes she managed to compose herself. She splashed water on her face, brushed her hair, and freshened up her lipstick before returning to her desk, determined to ring Charlie. One way or another, she had to salvage her career.

He didn't answer her calls. Finally, having left a string of messages, she departed for the Ghanaian reception, although that hardly provided any respite from her misery. Blaise was forced to endure the withering stares of every other correspondent present.

Returning to *The Advocate* to write up the event only provided fresh horrors. By this time, the newsroom was filled with reporters, which meant she was forced to pass by a horde of men as each one of them clenched a hand and silently pointed at her with one extended finger. The lot of them had followed damned Gerry Hanger's example. It was like being confronted by row upon row of firing squads.

That night, Blaise rang Charlie again as soon as she reached the sanctuary of the flat. To her relief, this time he picked up immediately.

"I don't understand," she wailed. "I took the sheet from the blue file on your desk, just like you told me to."

"I said it was in the red," Charlie said quietly. "The blue file contained estimates that were completely out of date."

"But I was sure you said the blue." How could she muddle something so important?

"I'm sorry, Blaise." Charlie spoke in the gentlest possible tone. "You made a mistake."

After a mournful goodbye, Blaise slowly put the receiver back onto its cradle. It wasn't a complete disaster. At least she still had a job. However, as newspaper gossip inevitably circled the globe at something approximating the speed of light, she'd now ruined whatever chance she might once have had of being assigned to hard news, not only on Fleet Street but also back in Australia. As far as her career was concerned, she would never rise any higher. Every path would be blocked, every door would slam firmly in her face.

It had taken only a moment's inattention to lose everything she had fought for.

By noon on Friday, Blaise was sure she'd never felt more wretched in her life. She scanned the newsroom listlessly. Joining some of the reporters who'd started heading off for their favorite lunchtime pubs might cheer her up, but although the gun-pointing stunt had been dropped, they wouldn't let her live down her front-page blunder that easily. She was in no mood to put up with the inevitable jokes told at her expense. The day before, Dora and Harriet had brought her a small bunch of blue hyacinths and a box of peppermint creams from the exclusive Mayfair chocolatier Charbonnel et Walker, but they weren't around today. Both girls were out on a shoot, which meant she'd have no one to keep her company while she ate a lonely lunch at the same sad little cafe where she'd met Christine Keeler.

To her surprise, she'd received support from an unexpected quarter. When she'd arrived at work that morning, Mike and Ben had actually clapped her on the back in a genuinely companionable manner. Ben had said, "It was a beauty, all right, but you're not the first to screw up." Mike had added, "And you sure as hell won't be the last. You'll see, they'll give you another crack at news."

Blaise knew the men were trying to be kind; maybe they even believed what they'd said. Yet one simple fact had escaped them. If you were a woman, there were no second chances.

Her wretched phone started ringing again. She already had

a stack of messages, but she wasn't in the mood for dealing with any of them.

"Yes!" she snapped.

"How are you bearing up?" Charlie asked sympathetically.

Blaise slumped forward. "Considering I've ruined my career and seriously embarrassed the paper, about as well as can be expected."

"Maybe I can help. The least I can do for a friend who's hit a rough patch is come up with a bit of distraction. How about driving down to the Cotswolds with me after work," he said, "and staying at Beech Hall for the weekend? It's a glorious place, guaranteed to take your mind off your troubles."

"Charlie, that's very generous, but no thank you." Adam was due back the following weekend; other than her recent disaster, it was all she thought about. She didn't want anything else to go wrong.

As if he'd read her mind, Charlie said, "Father will be up in Scotland, but there'll be plenty of others coming down so you've no need to worry about giving anyone the wrong impression. You could relax and have a bit of fun."

"Sorry, the answer's still no."

"Blaise, I broke a serious government embargo just to help you," he said, sounding hurt. "I hope you're not blaming me for what happened."

Blaise winced. She'd been thinking only about her own misfortune whereas, after bundling him out of her life, Charlie had still been prepared to take a huge personal risk, purely for her benefit. He was the kindest man she had ever met; the least she could do was agree to visit his family home.

Suddenly, the combination of open space, a dear friend, and blissful tranquility was hugely appealing. But a weekend was too long.

"Blame you?" she said. "Not at all. I mucked things up all by myself. Only I'd rather catch the train there tomorrow—and I'll have to be back in London the following day."

As she put the phone down, Blaise felt the first tiny chink of optimism break through her gloom. Twenty-four worry-free hours spent in the English countryside would act as a circuit breaker, reviving her spirits and clearing her mind. By the time Adam returned, she'd be a new woman.

# CHAPTER THIRTY-FIVE

The moment the chugging train left London's grubby outskirts behind, Blaise's heart felt a little lighter. By the time she encountered the Cotswolds' gentle, rolling landscape with its quaint picture-book villages, lush meadows, and flocks of cotton-wool sheep, a welcome feeling of peace had descended upon her. Yes, there'd been a barb of alarm when she'd first taken her seat in the carriage. Then she reminded herself that she'd only be at Beech Hall for a day and a night.

She closed her eyes and thought about Adam, picturing the special smile he had that revealed a glimpse of his troubled soul. After he'd left for Australia she'd allowed all sorts of crazy suspicions to creep into her mind, but once she was in his arms again, there would be no more doubts. Just recalling their one night together was enough to make a sudden heat coil through her body. They would finally have the chance to talk about where he'd come from and what it was in his past that he was so reluctant to disclose. She was in love with Adam. Perhaps if she loved him enough she could make him whole again.

Blaise caught sight of Charlie's mop of blond hair as he waited outside Bath Spa railway station. He strode toward her, calling out "Wonderful, you've arrived!" then gave her a warm hug.

Charlie stowed her carryall in the boot of an old Bentley. "Hop in," he said, opening the door. "Before we set off for the house, I'll take you for a spin around Bath."

With its honeyed stone buildings glowing in the late morning sun, the town was a revelation. Blaise marveled at the elegant crescents of eighteenth-century Georgian residences, the charming public squares and streets that had been laid out with precision. "It's enchanting," she said, her eyes sparkling. "I feel as if we've just driven through the pages of a book by Jane Austen, *Persuasion* perhaps, or *Northanger Abbey.*"

As they drove past signs pointing the way to the River Avon, the Roman Baths, and the Assembly Rooms she mused, "I'd love to come back one day and explore Bath properly."

Charlie glanced at her. "You know I'd be happy to take you."

Blaise smiled back at him. She was lucky he'd been a part of her life. It was such a shame that, once Adam returned, their friendship would most likely wither away. If only she could bring about a reconciliation—

Charlie broke into her thoughts. "You're rather quiet," he said after they'd been driving for half an hour.

"It's been a tough week."

"Well, we're not far away. Just around this bend and . . . here we are," he announced as they passed between old stone gateposts topped by rearing griffins. "We're on the Bennington estate now—nine hundred acres of forest and prime farmland."

They were driving along a narrow road lined with ancient oaks when Blaise exclaimed, "That must be the loveliest house I've ever seen!" Beech Hall was a three-story, classically inspired mansion built in the same warm, golden stone as the buildings in Bath. A profusion of yellow roses curled over its portico and, in the forecourt, sprays of water danced in an urn-shaped bowl mounted on a mossy plinth.

"The manor dates from the 1780s," Charlie said proudly. "We've had a few modern innovations put in since then, thank God, although the beech wood it was named after still stands in the southeastern corner of the estate."

Blaise walked through the front door into a large foyer with a black and white checkerboard floor and soaring walls on which hung oil paintings she assumed depicted Charlie's ancestors. One picture in particular, oddly familiar, of a beautiful girl with dark hair drawn back from her face and light, watchful eyes, captured her attention. Perhaps she'd seen something by the same artist in one of Marguerite's art books.

She was about to ask Charlie who the portrait depicted when a bustling woman appeared from a door at the rear.

"Ah, Mrs. Coote, how nice to see you again." He turned to Blaise. "I'll leave you in our housekeeper's excellent care and give you a chance to get settled."

The gray-haired little woman whisked Blaise upstairs to a room painted pastel blue. In pride of place stood a four-poster bed with a filmy white canopy draped overhead, looking as if it belonged in a fairy tale. Blaise's first thought was how much Ivy would have loved it. She had always adored anything that had a touch of glamour and magic. Blaise smiled to herself. So far, all that was missing was a spare duke.

"The other guests have already left for a day's shooting, Miss Hill," the housekeeper said, "but a light luncheon can easily be provided for you and Mr. Charles in the drawing room. Unless you would prefer me to pack you a picnic?" she asked.

"What a splendid idea, Mrs. Coote." Charlie poked his head around the door. "My friend here is in great need of fresh air."

They left the house via a side gate, with Charlie leading the way. "I'll take you to one of my favorite spots—it's by the lake. I played there all the time when I was small, sailing toy boats and that kind of thing. Then later, when I decided to run for parliament, I used to practice my speeches in front of squawking ducks and geese."

Blaise laughed as she imagined the scene.

"It proved to be excellent preparation for addressing the House of Commons," he said with a chuckle.

The pair strolled across verdant lawns until they reached a large weeping willow that grew at the water's edge. "This is the place," Charlie said as he unfolded a tartan rug. Blaise laid out the contents of the picnic basket: a pile of thinly sliced smoked salmon sandwiches, some ripe plums, two pieces of fruitcake, and a chilled bottle of white wine.

Everything was perfect—the lake with its reflections of wispy clouds drifting across a washed blue sky, the gentle baaing sound of sheep floating toward her from a nearby meadow, the balmy September weather—yet Blaise couldn't relax. The mention of Charlie's boyhood had brought her thoughts back to Adam. This would be her last opportunity before he returned to ask Charlie why they'd fallen out. If she knew what lay behind their animosity, she'd have a much better chance of smoothing things over between the two of them.

They'd munched their way through several sandwiches and had nearly finished the wine before Blaise seized her chance. "You know how you were talking about your childhood just then," she said in as casual a manner as she could manage.

"Mmm?"

"Well, the first time we met you told me you'd practically grown up with Adam Rule. I was wondering how that came about—and why you're on such bad terms now."

Charlie flung down his napkin and threw the remains of the plum he'd been eating into the lake. She'd never seen him like this before; he was acting like a child having a tantrum.

"You *do* know Adam, don't you?" he said petulantly. "I can tell by the tone of your voice—it's the way people speak when they want to disguise their interest. If there's one thing I've learned to recognize in politics, it's when people are trying to hide the truth. I've always suspected there was something between you two."

"You're overreacting, Charlie," Blaise retorted. "Just because you don't want to have anything to do with the man doesn't mean I can't see him." She took a deep breath and attempted to rein in her temper. "I wasn't lying when I said I hardly knew Adam. I did see him a couple of times before he flew back to Australia, but I don't have any idea about where he's from or, for that matter, much of anything else. Honestly, Charlie, what's it to you?"

"Oh, my poor little Blaise." He sighed, a world-weary expression on his face. "It's time you learned the truth about Adam Rule."

"Fire away," Blaise responded with a touch of defiance. She didn't appreciate being patronized, not by anyone, and certainly not by Charlie, especially while they sat in the grounds of his privileged family's enormous estate.

"Adam Rule is quite simply the most self-serving, manipulative man I've ever come across," Charlie said.

Blaise flushed. "That's a vicious remark." Her vivid eyes flashed in the sunlight. "I don't understand why you'd say such horrible things!" She realized she was shouting.

"He lies and lies and no one can tell—that's why. Adam is totally without scruples." Charlie stood up and held out his hand. "Let me help you up."

"I don't need your help," she said tartly.

"I wouldn't be too sure about that." There was an expression of pity on his face Blaise didn't appreciate.

She struggled to her feet.

"We can collect the picnic things later," Charlie said in a more conciliatory manner. "It might be easier if I explain everything while we take a walk."

Blaise marched silently next to him along a path that wound its way around the edge of the lake. "Perhaps it's in the genes," he said at last.

"What the hell does that mean?"

"Just listen, Blaise, and I swear I'll reveal the whole story. But before I do, remember I'm only telling you this because I don't want to see another girl ruined."

Blaise swallowed hard.

"It was not until after a terrible tragedy occurred that my father took me into his confidence. I suppose he was searching for the reasons Adam became what he is. I'll start at the beginning, and then you can make up your own mind."

She glanced warily at Charlie. "All right."

"Father's first cousin, Emilia, was a wild girl, prone to sudden passions," he began. "Even so, you can imagine how shocked the family was when it turned out she was pregnant. Even worse, it seemed that the culprit was Albert Rule, an itinerant stonemason who'd been employed to repair a statue in the rose garden. At least, that was the story—I'm not sure she knew who the real father was." Charlie broke off. "I'm warning you, this is not a pretty tale."

"I'm a big girl," Blaise said, pressing her lips together with irritation. She couldn't see how an old scandal had any bearing on his disagreement with Adam.

"Despite her condition, Emilia flatly refused to marry this Rule fellow, but Father said if she didn't he'd cut her off without a penny. Both of her parents were dead, you see. My Great Uncle had perished in the Boer War and his wife died soon afterward. Emilia was only eighteen so, as her legal guardian, Father had absolute control."

"I gather the marriage went ahead then." Blaise thought Charlie's tale was beginning to sound like a Regency novel.

"The local vicar obliged one afternoon. Afterward, Father told Emilia that now she was respectably wed she need never live with the child's supposed father but could reside with him and Mother in Beech Hall. It was 1931; I was born just a few weeks later. I suppose he imagined we'd grow up in the nursery together, almost like twin brothers. That wasn't to be. Emilia remained only long enough to recover from giving birth—to Adam."

"You're second cousins then?" Blaise hadn't expected that. She couldn't imagine two men who were less alike.

"Yes, worse luck. But one night, while Father was staying up in London at his club, Emilia ran off. She took her young maid with her, and the two of them—plus Adam, of course—boarded a ship for Australia."

For the first time Blaise felt she was beginning to understand Adam's reticence to speak about his past. It was only natural he'd be reluctant to delve into these painful events. "Where did Emilia go?" she asked.

"Ended up as a barmaid in a rough and ready mining town called Mount Isa. Hell of a place—right in the middle of the outback."

As Charlie spoke, it seemed to Blaise as if another brushstroke had been added to her sketchy picture of Adam. He'd grown up surrounded by people who'd spent their lives gouging metal from the ground. No wonder he felt at home around a mine.

"I'll grant you, Adam's mother might have been, let's say, unconventional," she said, "but I don't see why her choices should have turned you against him."

Charlie sighed. "Believe me, I'll get to that."

Blaise stumbled, her legs suddenly unsteady. "Do you think we could rest for a bit over there?" she said, pointing toward a small white pavilion by the shore.

"You mean the Temple of Venus." Charlie smiled briefly when he saw her perplexed expression. "Father's little indulgence," he said. "I suppose that's why it's called a folly."

Blaise sat on a wicker chair while Charlie took another. Her stomach in knots, she waited tensely for him to continue. She felt she should be hearing these revelations from Adam, not Charlie. Everything was unfolding in the wrong way.

"Father inherited the title along with Beech Hall when he was a boy. With two elder sisters, and what with Emilia being an orphaned only child, he was the sole surviving Ashton male. He took his role of protector-in-chief of this family of ladies very seriously."

"Then he must have been beside himself when Emilia disappeared," Blaise said, adjusting a canvas cushion behind her head. She wished that Charlie would get to the point.

"He tried everything to find her, with no luck. Years later, long after he'd given up hope, he received a letter from a firm of Australian solicitors informing him that she had died of tuberculosis."

Charlie's brown eyes became very dark. "My mother passed away when I was only two years old—she'd contracted a fever in Spain while traveling with Father's sisters. When he learned Emilia had died, it must have brought back Mother's loss. I still remember how grief-stricken Father was when I returned to Beech Hall from my prep school for the summer holidays. Perhaps that was why he was so delighted at the prospect of seeing her son."

"Adam." Blaise's pulse quickened.

"That's right. He brought him to England—can you imagine? My father took this rough little Australian from the back of beyond, pulled various strings, and parachuted him into Eton College, where I also happened to be starting my first year of studies—we'd both turned thirteen by then. I'll never forget it. He arrived at Beech Hall looking like a street urchin and within weeks he was off to Britain's most elite boarding school in a tailcoat and a wing collar."

"That must have been a shock." Blaise's heart went out to Adam. She couldn't imagine what it would be like to lose your mother, then be uprooted from the only home you'd ever known, before being trussed up like a turkey and inserted into a rarefied institution catering exclusively to the sons of the British upper class. So far, all she'd gleaned was that Adam had been a blameless child who'd endured more than his share of trauma and upheaval, which meant Charlie was holding back his trump card. She felt a mounting dread.

"How did he cope with Eton?" she asked, now less keen to hurry Charlie on.

"Oh, he made some friends; I think I mentioned Tony. But mostly he was viewed as very much the untamed colonial—not without justification, mind you—so he received a fair amount of bullying. I stood up for him, of course; he was my cousin." Charlie shrugged. "But Adam was his own worst enemy. Too proud, you see, and too ready to lash out. He was always getting into fights. There are ways of doing things at Eton he didn't like, and he didn't hesitate to make his feelings known."

"What things?"

"Well . . . fagging, for example."

Blaise's eyes widened. "What the hell is that?"

"I know, it sounds a bit odd, but fagging's been practiced at Eton, and every other school like it, for hundreds of years. At the beginning of the first term, each senior boy chooses a new little chap he likes the look of. Adam was one of the first to be picked—he was good-looking even then. The junior boy is expected to perform jobs like, I don't know, clean the senior boy's shoes, wake him up in time for classes, and so on. Then, depending on the senior's boy's, ah . . . inclinations, there might also be some after-dark shenanigans. Except, Adam wasn't known for his cooperation."

"Little wonder. Poor Adam."

"We were all in the same boat," Charlie said sharply.

He ran his fingers through his corn-colored hair. "Even though Adam wasn't easy, I kept trying to do my best for him, smooth his way, hose down trouble. Not just at school, either, but when we both went up to Cambridge. However, that was where he crossed a line no decent man could tolerate."

Blaise swallowed nervously. Finally, they had arrived at the heart of the matter. She sensed that Charlie had been saving this speech up for a long time.

"It happened nearly a decade ago," he said, staring at the clusters of mauve waterlilies floating on the surface of the lake. "I was terribly in love with a girl named Olivia Riordan, whom I hoped to marry after I'd completed my studies. One afternoon—I remember it was a freezing cold day—I was looking for a textbook and realized I'd probably left it in Adam's room. I barged in, the way we always did and"—he hesitated—"that's when I saw the two of them in his bed. Olivia was struggling and screaming with terror but Adam had pinned her down. I yelled, threw punches." Charlie lowered his gaze. "I was too late. The worst had already happened."

Blaise felt ill.

"To ruin an innocent girl, the girl I wanted to marry, and in such a violent way . . ." Charlie raised his voice angrily. "Adam might have been my cousin, but nothing on this earth could excuse his behavior. I went straight to the college authorities. He was a brilliant mathematician, on his way to a First. Instead, he was sent down in disgrace."

"And Olivia?" Blaise asked, fearing the answer.

"The poor girl was hysterical, so incoherent no one could get any sense out of her. Lord and Lady Riordan took Olivia with them to their country estate, where she barely left her bedroom."

"What did you do?" she asked in a small voice.

"I drove down to the manor a few days later to tell Olivia that I loved her and wanted to take care of her," Charlie said grimly. "After I rang the doorbell, a maid let me in—she told me Lord and Lady Riordan were attending a function in the village and would not return until late that afternoon. I was desperate to see Olivia, but the maid said the household staff were under strict instructions not to admit anyone." His voice quavered. "I never saw Olivia again."

Blaise wished she could cover her ears and block out this horrible story. But she had to know the outcome. "What happened?" she asked, forcing the words out.

Charlie put his head in his hands. "That night I learned that Olivia was dead. Her bedroom was on the second floor; it had these big windows, you see. Even today . . ." He faltered. "I'm not sure whether she meant to throw herself out, or whether her trauma led to a terrible accident. But what I do know," he said, looking straight at Blaise, "is that the responsibility for this tragedy lies with just one man."

# CHAPTER THIRTY-SIX

She wanted to scream at Charlie, to accuse him of lying, to fly at him with her fists. She could not. The words Adam had spoken at the boathouse were seared into her memory. *I've more than enough on my conscience as it is.* Later, he'd claimed his reluctance to make love was because he wanted to show her he was capable of "something a little nobler" than his past behavior. She saw it now: his excuses were as good as an admission of guilt.

Blaise gasped for air, yet Charlie was still too wrapped up in his account to notice her distress.

"Adam denied everything, of course, tried to lie his way out of it," he said. "But he was still that wild boy from the ends of the earth, with a dead mother who'd chosen to shame herself and no father—none he'd ever known, at any rate. Who was going to take his word over mine?"

"So that was why Adam went back to Australia," Blaise said dully.

"Fled, you mean." Charlie scowled. "Father engaged a private detective, tried to discover what he was up to. It turned out Adam had begun secretly laundering large sums of money on behalf of an illegal enterprise. He bought property and invested in the stock market—all for a gang run by a family called Ryan."

The Ryans. Here was the reason Adam knew so much about them, how it was he'd been able to make problems disappear. But if Adam was tied up with the Ryans, then why did he cover up her and Joe's involvement in Paddy's death? Unless he had an ulterior motive. Perhaps steering the blame toward their rivals' henchman suited him. It would have delivered a far bigger fish to Theo Ryan than a couple of kids. Had pure self-interest driven Adam? Maybe he'd coldly calculated the entire plan. Blaise's cheeks burned. She'd provided herself as a nice little bonus.

"My father was determined that Adam's disgrace wouldn't end up tainting my life," Charlie went on, "so he did everything within his power to hush up the scandal. Cambridge certainly didn't want word getting out, and neither did Olivia's parents. The entire incident was buried, just like the information about Adam's activities in Australia. As a result, the world at large has no idea of the man's utter criminality."

Blaise thought she might faint. She gripped the sides of her chair as she recalled her ridiculous daydream on the train, the way she'd imagined she'd wave a magic wand and everything would be sweetness and light. But wasn't the real reason she'd never made more of an effort to delve into Adam's past that deep down she'd always been wary of what she would find?

When she'd learned that the police assumed Artelli's killing had been payback for Paddy Ryan's death, she'd been so relieved she was in the clear, and so grateful to Adam for giving her the details that led to her front-page story, that she'd chosen to ignore the mysterious way these twinned events had been put in place. She'd been drawn in by Adam's compelling manner, attracted by his looks: his broad shoulders, the shock of black hair, the silver-shilling eyes. Even now, even after Charlie's revelations, she felt stirred by the memory of his naked body, the power of his desire. She hated herself for her weakness, her naïveté, and her stupid, lovesick blindness.

"Are you up to walking back?" Charlie asked with a look of concern.

Blaise nodded.

"I'm very sorry—I can see I've shocked you," he said. "Unfortunately, the only way I could protect you was to share the whole, sordid story." His lip curled. "Talking about Adam hasn't been exactly pleasant for me, either."

But Charlie seemed unable to stop. "To be fair," he said, taking her arm, "when it comes to making money, Adam has a brilliant touch—a combination of rat cunning, his facility for maths, of course, and the willingness to take big risks. Right from the start, he was clever enough to make certain his own funds were invested in legitimate businesses. Then he began to forge connections, to give big donations to political parties, to draw people into his web by doing them special favors. No doubt he now considers himself untouchable. He's not, of course. Everyone has their Achilles' heel."

Blaise was so distracted by Charlie's disclosures she hadn't noticed they'd returned to the willow tree.

He gathered up the remains of their picnic then turned toward her. "There's just one more thing I have to say before we go back up to the house," he said gravely, "and that will be the end of it."

Blaise shuddered. Charlie's words were like blows; she didn't think she could bear any more.

"Rule can turn on the charm," he said, "although you probably already know that. Plus he's had the good fortune to inherit Emilia's looks."

Blaise realized that the beautiful woman whose portrait she'd seen earlier must have been Adam's mother.

"Unfortunately, she also passed on her bent for promiscuity." A look of disgust settled on Charlie's even features. "I suppose that's why his relationships with women have never consisted of anything but one careless conquest after another. That detective I told you about, out in Australia? He was in touch only recently, told me that right to this day Adam's still bedding one gullible girl after another. It's tragic, really. The man had so much to offer, but he couldn't escape his mother's legacy."

Charlie shook his head. "He's always believed he could have any woman he wanted. But Olivia was in love with me." His voice broke. "She wouldn't give him the time of day. I don't think he could stand it."

Her worst fears about Adam had been realized. No, that wasn't right. The truth was a thousand times worse than she'd ever imagined.

Blaise bit her lip so hard she tasted blood. She didn't want Charlie to see how distressed she was; the poor man was already struggling with his own grief. Only now did she fully comprehend that, contrary to Adam's claims, she'd never meant anything to him. All she had ever been was one more—what had Charlie called it?—careless conquest.

She was furious with herself. Adam had expressed just the right passionate sentiments, claimed he couldn't stop thinking about her, said how special she was—all of it calculated to ensnare her. Just because she had grown up in a hard-scrabble place and spent a few years working on newspapers, she'd assumed she was worldly wise. When it came to men, however, she'd acted like the inexperienced, innocent fool she really was.

All that concern Adam had expressed about Princess Margaret's welfare had been a sham. He'd simply used her—and Blaise— to add to the favors he was owed. Adam obviously counted on the fact that, should he ever find himself in danger of being called to account, those people he'd helped, even the royal family itself, would mount a rescue mission rather than take the risk of him exposing their deepest secrets. It wasn't blackmail, not quite, but it came very close.

Charlie introduced Blaise to his other guests when they reached the house. She did her best to act naturally as they had tea in the sitting room, to smile and answer their polite questions about Australia and how she was finding life in London, but the strain of pretending that all was well was close to intolerable.

By nightfall, Blaise was drained. When she tried to dress for dinner, her hands shook so much she couldn't zip up her frock. She sat on the edge of the bed, her head whirling with one anguished thought after another. Adam's unspeakable treatment of Olivia Riordan, his criminal activities, the way he exploited everyone he came across and, perhaps most devastating of all, his casual betrayal of her with other women . . . Groaning, she doubled over with pain.

She barely noticed the knock on her door. "Sorry to disturb, Miss, but everyone's waiting." Mrs. Coote walked into the room then stopped abruptly. "Oh dear, you don't look a bit well," she said.

Blaise looked up, smiling weakly. "Please give Charlie my apologies. I have a dreadful migraine." She couldn't face a formal four-course meal with a dozen new people. Her refreshing day in the country had turned into a nightmare.

After making an attempt to consume a little of the toast and broth Mrs. Coote sent up shortly afterward, Blaise felt so wretched she turned off her light.

Time passed. She smoothed her pillow, rearranged her quilt, but still she couldn't sleep. Each time she dozed off, the image of a terrified girl by an open window appeared, like an endless loop of film from a horror movie. Yet she was exhausted; she thought she'd never been so tired in her life.

Blaise woke with a jolt. Someone was holding her hand. A man's voice was saying, "Don't worry, I'm here now." But it was the wrong voice, the wrong man. She opened her eyes and saw Charlie standing beside her in the dim light.

"There, there," he said soothingly as he switched on a lamp. "You were shouting something—it sounded like 'Don't!'"

"I must have been dreaming about . . ." She blinked, trying to focus. "Never mind."

To her dismay, Charlie sat next to her and started stroking her bare arm. She shifted away.

"I've shared so much with you today," he said tenderly. "The worst family secrets imaginable. But there's one thing I didn't say." He paused. "I'm in love with you, Blaise."

Blaise was so astonished, she wondered if she was still dreaming. "But you've never said anything even vaguely romantic before! We've seen each other countless times and you haven't even tried to kiss me—at least, not properly."

Charlie moved closer. "That's because I never felt sure of you. I always sensed there was someone between us, that you were secretly in love with another man. Knowing him as I do, I suspected it might be Adam."

"I . . . I don't know what to say." Blaise felt overwhelmed. She'd already had too many shocks for one day.

"There's no need for words, my darling," he said. "Let me show you how I feel."

Blaise was sure he didn't mean to tear her nightgown when he took her in his arms, yet somehow his fingers became caught up in its wispy straps and they gave way.

"God, I'm sorry!" Charlie looked mortified. "I'm such a clumsy idiot. But"—his eyes rested momentarily on her exposed breasts—"you really are lovely."

She pushed him away. "It might be different with the debs in your circle," Blaise said primly, pulling the crisp cotton top sheet up to her neck, "but where I come from a girl doesn't entertain a man in her bed until he's put a ring on her finger." Inwardly she cringed: parroting her mother's words was the height of hypocrisy.

"Darling, please forgive me, I got carried away." Charlie looked so flustered and embarrassed Blaise felt sorry for him. "But you know how much I respect you," he said earnestly. "I don't suppose that makes a difference?"

"Not to me."

"Marry me, then." He smiled delightedly. "I can't believe that all the time we were seeing each other you never realized I was wild about you. Here's an idea: we could announce our engagement tomorrow."

"Charlie!" His proposal was so unlikely and so bumbling that for the first time in days she felt like laughing.

All the same, what other girl—particularly one from her background—wouldn't jump at the chance to become engaged to such a lovable man who was not only a member of the British parliament but also set to inherit a title and nine hundred acres? But she didn't care about honors or titles or a large bank account. Right at that moment, all she wanted was an end to these volcanic upheavals: the disaster at work, the wrenching truth about Adam, the shock of Charlie's proposal.

"I can't make a decision like that now," she said, still clutching the sheet with both hands. "For one thing, we've never had that sort of relationship. Isn't it usual to have a romance with a man before you become his fiancée?"

"Nothing I'd like more," Charlie said happily. "So you're not saying no?"

"I need more time."

"At least that gives me hope." He wrinkled his forehead. "Though you wouldn't happen to have a date in mind, would you?"

Blaise said the first thing that came into her head. "Twelve months from today." She wanted Charlie to go, to bring this endless day to a close. And a year seemed a long way away.

"I'd rather it was sooner," he said ruefully. "Darling Blaise, all I want is to take care of you, to cherish and protect you in the way you deserve. If I could, I'd move heaven and earth for you." Charlie kissed her chastely on the forehead, switched off the lamp and said goodnight.

Blaise breathed a sigh of relief. She knew she should be flattered by his unexpected proposal, but as she lay in the four-poster bed surrounded by darkness and the haunting sounds of the night, she felt no elation but only despair. Adam had broken her heart.

# CHAPTER THIRTY-SEVEN

The next three days passed in a blur of misery and exhaustion. Blaise dragged herself to the royal engagements she was obliged to attend, wrote up her stories mechanically, then went home and curled up on one of the pink and white sofas. Dora and Harriet tried to discover what was wrong, but she revealed only that Adam would soon be out of her life forever—and that Charlie Ashton had proposed.

"Please don't ask me any questions, at least not until I've had it out with Adam," Blaise begged.

On Thursday, after she received another of Ivy's letters, Blaise felt a little better. The wonderful thing about her sister was her unquenchable spirit. Blaise missed her pluck, her defiance of every limitation, especially now when she felt so wretched.

As usual, Ivy had peppered her letter with queries about palaces, princesses, and paintings. What Blaise hadn't expected to find was the carefully folded drawing that had been enclosed. It showed an old lady sitting at a tram stop with her string bag full of shopping. Ivy had captured the woman's aura of weary resignation perfectly.

After revealing that she'd started attending art classes at the local technical college, she had written about the improvement of her bad leg. *Thanks to you, I really think that one day, maybe quite soon, I won't even need my horrible caliper.*

By the time Blaise arrived at the letter's final paragraph she felt the first sliver of happiness she'd had since the horrendous day at Beech Hall. *I've been seeing a fair bit of Ned Williams lately,* Ivy had begun. *He might not live in a castle, but I still think he's the nicest boy I've ever met.* She'd then explained that Ned was being groomed to take on Tommy Trent's old position as *The Clarry*'s political roundsman.

Blaise smiled. She'd noticed the way Ned had gravitated toward Ivy during their long-ago backyard party in Fotheringham Street. As far as boyfriends were concerned, she couldn't think of a better candidate for her sister than bright, gentle Ned.

The next day, the pleasure brought about by Ivy's cheerful letter had evaporated. As Blaise contemplated Adam's impending return, a dark, jittery mood settled upon her. There was nothing for it. The only way to shear her connection to this dangerous man was to cauterize her heart with a dose of cold, hard reality. Blaise made herself recall his sins, over and over.

Although she'd been expecting a telegram, she still felt a jolt of alarm when it arrived later that afternoon. Trembling, she read the brief message.

*MEET ME SUNDAY BY PIANO RITZ HOTEL ELEVEN AM STOP ADAM*

"Not bad news I hope, Miss?" the delivery boy asked.

Blaise stared at the words on the buff piece of paper. "Yes and no."

Saturday crawled by far too slowly, although, strangely, as night fell the day seemed to have passed absurdly fast. To her shame, the prospect of seeing Adam was thrilling, even though she dreaded the next morning's confrontation.

A part of her—a part Blaise had done her best to suppress— taunted her during the night. She loved him still. It was like a sickness, this affliction. What did it say about her, that she could feel this way about a man who was so contemptible?

By Sunday, her anxiety threatened to derail her. After brushing her chestnut hair, which she now wore loose so it swung around her shoulders, Blaise put on a pair of black tights, a new pinstripe dress from Mary Quant with a white collar and cuffs, and a pair of flat black suede shoes. She peered into her bedroom mirror and saw she looked tired and strained, but she could do nothing about it other than add a touch of extra mascara and a little color to her pale face. Despite her careful preparations, by the time she arrived at the famous hotel, her stomach was churning. *Breathe*, she told herself.

She'd sworn she would confront Adam, make a few short, sharp remarks and walk away. Not in the Ritz, though, not in front of the hotel's superior staff and select guests. It would be better if she said what she had to say somewhere out in the open, far away from prying eyes. Fortunately, Green Park was nearby.

Months ago, it had intrigued Blaise to read in her now-tattered guidebook that the reason this urban retreat contained only meadows and trees was because when philandering Charles II was caught picking its choicest blooms for his current mistress, his furious wife, Queen Catherine, had ordered that every flowerbed be uprooted. The story might be apocryphal, but it now seemed to add to Green Park's suitability as a place to address other, infinitely more serious forms of betrayal.

Blaise strode into the hotel, determined to resist her attraction to Adam. Yet as soon as she caught sight of him by the piano, saw how his labors had left him leaner and harder, with a deep tan that only emphasized his unusual eyes and generous mouth, she felt her resolve begin to weaken.

His face broke into a wonderful smile as he walked quickly toward her. "Blaise, it's so good to see you," he said, kissing her cheek. "It's all I can do not to wrap my arms around you immediately."

Blaise felt the same way. "I'm not sure those ladies would approve," she said, struggling to maintain her reserve. She inclined her head toward a gilded lounge where matrons wearing hats and strings of pearls were occupying themselves with the Ritz's famous scones and pots of its Royal Blend tea.

"And that, darling," Adam said with a grin, "is exactly the reason why I have reserved a suite with a bottle of Bollinger waiting on ice. Shall we go up?"

Forcing herself to adopt an even tone, Blaise observed, "I recall you once recommended we should take things slowly."

"I must have been mad," Adam said with a look that made her heart race.

"All the same," she persisted. "Why don't we have a stroll in the park while we become reacquainted?"

He raised his eyebrows but said only, "Fine, if that's what you'd like."

She allowed him to take her hand as he led her out of the lavish hotel lobby and into the street. The park was only a few yards away.

As they entered this calmer world of sweeping lawns and ancient trees, she pointed to the left. "Let's head for that bench, the one behind all the foliage."

"Perfect," he said as they sat down. "Not a respectable teadrinker in sight."

Then Adam's arms were around her, his lips were on hers and Blaise was crushed against him. This was the moment she'd dreamt about for months. Every nerve ending danced. Resisting his embrace was agonizing, yet she forced herself not to respond.

Adam sat back, his expression cool. "So, when were you planning on telling me what's been going on? Because you're sure as hell not the same woman I said goodbye to in May."

Blaise couldn't contain herself any longer. Ashamed by her desire to seize Adam's hand and fly back to his suite, terrified that her rebellious feelings might prevent her from what she knew she must say, she turned on him.

"What's been *going on*, as you put it, is that I've found out all about you," she hissed. "Do you remember when I said that the past didn't matter? That was because I couldn't imagine you would turn out to be a brutal criminal. Treating me like a casual plaything while you spent your time with other women is something men—men like you, anyway—do all the time. But to attack an innocent girl, to terrify her so much that she took her own life . . . I don't know how you can bear to have that on your conscience."

"It strikes me," Adam said, clenching his jaw, "Charles Ashton's been busy spreading his poison. I never pretended I was perfect and, yes, I've known more than a few girls in the past—and some bad people. But Ashton is the most accomplished liar and the most dangerous person I've ever come across."

"He says the same about you, Adam," Blaise retorted. "But when you took off for Australia Charlie showed me nothing but kindness. He never once tried to take advantage."

"There are more ways of taking advantage of a woman than you could possibly imagine," Adam said, his voice icy.

"Yes, and you'd know all about them, wouldn't you?" She felt so hurt that all she wanted to do was to wound Adam as deeply as he had wounded her. "For your information," she said, "Charles Ashton wants to marry me—and I'm going to accept his proposal."

Blaise saw Adam flinch. Good, at least that had hit home.

"Ashton doesn't care about you," he said bitterly. "Can't you see? He's using you as a weapon against me."

Blaise leapt to her feet, her eyes blazing. She would not allow Adam another opportunity to humiliate her. "I suppose you think a tart from Enmore isn't good enough to be the future Lady Bennington. If you believe the only reason he's proposed is to get back at you, then you must have an even more inflated ego than I imagined." She dropped her voice. "Charlie loves me."

"This is madness." Adam seized her arm but she shook him off.

"Madness is when a girl is so traumatized by being raped that she throws herself out of a window. You're a monster, Adam. Don't write, don't phone, and don't ever come near me again." She was shaking with emotion.

He stood looking at her with his mouth set, his eyes turned steely and cold. "For God's sake, listen to me, Blaise. Don't—"

Blaise whirled around and bolted across the park. If she heard another word, if she stayed one more minute with Adam, she'd be lost. There was no way in hell she'd ever again give in to her attraction.

She was running hard, faster and faster, dodging startled nurse-maids with prams, curious tourists in deckchairs, yelping dogs and their owners. Only by moving swiftly enough, by putting as much distance as possible between herself and Adam, would she escape from the spell cast by this dangerous silver-eyed man. She ran until she had crossed the Mall's red surface, passed sprawl-ing Buckingham Palace, and entered the leafy surroundings of St. James's Park. Then she tore along the grass beside the narrow lake that led toward Horse Guards Parade. She could see herself there back in June, happily watching the spectacular Trooping the Color on the queen's birthday with the rest of the press pack. That was when she'd still had foolish dreams of a future spent with Adam, a future that now lay in ruins.

Blaise ran until she couldn't run anymore, until her lungs burned and her well of furious energy was exhausted. At last she collapsed on the ground beneath a thicket of plane trees, panting, shaking, sobbing.

Time passed. Blaise sat up, wiped her eyes and pushed back her hair. Above her, thick clouds had gathered in the sky. She was calm now, her muscles had ceased throbbing and her pulse no longer raced. But no matter how long she waited, or how hard she tried, she could not quell the terrible ache lodged under her ribs, deep within her heart.

The next day, the weather turned. As Blaise trudged down Fleet Street, relentless autumn rain poured from a low-hanging canopy of gray. She hung up her dripping raincoat and umbrella in the newspaper's cloakroom, squelched her way to her desk in sodden shoes, and collapsed into her chair. Her encounter with Adam had been so devastating she wasn't sure how she'd make it through the day.

Then she saw it—a white envelope with her name typed on the outside. *Don't let this be another horrible prank,* she thought. Not today, not when her world had become so bleak. As she read the single sentence, her hand flew to her mouth.

O'ROURKE HAS A WITNESS.

This wasn't something she could pass off as a joke; the Enmore murder had come back to haunt her. But if the superintendent had a witness, why hadn't he acted on it? And what could the letter-writer be after? She still hadn't received a request for money or, for that matter, anything else.

It was true, from time to time she'd sensed she was being watched, thought she'd seen the same man appear with unusual regularity—the one with the moustache and the brown trilby hat. He'd been at the Tube station, in her street, even outside her flat. Blaise shrugged her shoulders. The fellow probably lived locally; she was jumping at shadows. But if this mysterious figure *was* stalking her, then what did he want?

A wave of cold fear swept through her. A world that had once seemed solid and straightforward had turned into a confusing miasma filled with blind alleys and wrong turns. She'd left for London with such high hopes, but now her life was spinning out of control. First she'd embarked upon a disastrous affair with Adam, then she'd made a hideous professional error, and now someone she didn't know with a motive she couldn't fathom was bent on doing her harm. There was no one who could make her feel safe—except Charlie. Why had she never appreciated him properly? She didn't love him—at least, not yet. But he had sworn to cherish and protect her. In a dangerous, shifting realm, only he provided certainty.

PART THREE

*Queen*

# CHAPTER THIRTY-EIGHT

## June 3, 1961

"Are you happy?"

Blaise was shopping with Harriet in the King's Road when her friend's words pulled her up.

"What sort of question is that? You know what my life is like. There's the newsroom, where I've become more or less accepted. The royal rounds still have their moments, though it doesn't look like I'll get much further. It was hard enough being a woman," she said gloomily, "without me ruining everything last year."

She smiled for the first time. "Nicest of all, though, there's you and Dora, the best friends a girl could ever have. Which only leaves—"

"Charlie," Harriet said, finishing her sentence.

"Well, yes. He's a big part of my life, too. He's expecting to announce our engagement in September."

Although she'd never formally accepted his proposal, as the months had passed and their relationship had deepened, they'd come to share an understanding. Charlie was not just an adorable boyfriend, he was an outstanding man. When she'd written to Ivy about his sudden proposal, swearing her to secrecy, her sister had sent a letter straight back saying, "Are you mad? Marry him!" But for some inexplicable reason, she still wasn't over Adam. It must be because he was her first love, she thought sadly. Well, she'd certainly made a big mistake there.

Harriet put down the patent leather handbag she'd been examining. "It's just that it seems to me you've lost your usual—actually, here's a good French expression for you—your usual *joie de vivre*."

"And that would mean?" Harriet had set out to teach her a smattering of French phrases—she'd said Marguerite Hawthorn had insisted it was essential to her continuing education and, anyway, it was fun.

"Your usual full-throttle enjoyment of life."

"I guess we all have our ups and downs." Blaise wasn't in the mood for any more introspection. "Speaking of enjoyment, you know that Her Majesty is holding a banquet at Buckingham Palace in honor of dreamy President Kennedy and the gorgeous Jackie?"

"Of course. Everyone in the Women's Section has been watching their European tour on television with bated breath, wondering what Mrs. Kennedy is going to wear next. Personally, I think it would be impossible to outdo that ivory Givenchy she wore for the French government's dinner at Versailles—old President de Gaulle looked positively smitten. I wonder what dress she'll choose when she dines at Buckingham Palace."

"As it happens, you'll receive a firsthand report," Blaise said with a note of triumph, "because I've just discovered that *The Advocate*'s royal correspondent is the only reporter who's been invited."

"Don't tell me!"

"I believe the big boss pulled a few strings." Blaise felt her mood rise as she contemplated this landmark evening. It was on assignments like these when she still had the urge to pinch herself. "The problem is," she continued, "the dinner is less than a week away. I'm sure Mrs. Kennedy has her wardrobe well and truly sorted, but what on earth am *I* going to wear?"

As Blaise snuggled up against the green cushions of her settee on the night after the dinner, she thought how lucky she'd been that

Harriet had pulled a few strings of her own. Her clever friend had promised a new Italian couturier named Valentino that she would both feature a dress from his first collection in the Women's Section and ensure that the same gown was worn to the high-profile Kennedy dinner. The designer had been delighted at the prospect of this priceless publicity, and the dress was so beautiful that Blaise was certain she'd caught Jackie herself eyeing it enviously.

It was one of those rare, happy situations when everyone was thrilled with the outcome. Blaise's only disappointment was that the heavenly fitted gown of pale pink shantung was already lying wrapped in clouds of white tissue paper inside a large box waiting to wing its way back to Rome on board an Alitalia flight.

Ah well, what was it the girls said in situations like this? *C'est la vie.*

Blaise sighed. She hadn't seen any sign of Adam since their fiery encounter. She'd half expected—no, half hoped—that he would try to contact her, but she'd heard nothing. It had been nine months now, but she'd begun to doubt the pain he'd caused her would ever cease.

Her heart had felt as if it might leap from her chest when she thought she'd spotted him striding ahead of her on Bond Street a few months earlier and, more recently, in the vicinity of Whitehall. There'd been something about the set of the man's shoulders and the way his dark hair fell. She'd had to discipline herself not to call out, to run up and touch his arm. Afterward, she'd been miserable.

Try as she might, she could not forget him. Lately, she'd even begun to wonder if Charlie really had the right story; perhaps events hadn't unfolded in quite the same way as he'd understood them. She had let her temper get the better of her when what she should have done was give Adam at least a chance to put his side forward.

Blaise sat up so abruptly that the cushions cascaded onto the floorboards. What a little idiot she was. She simply had to recall Adam's own words about his guilty conscience to know that imagining he was innocent was nothing but a case of wishful thinking. And hadn't he himself said she deserved a better man? Well, that man was definitely Charlie.

Blaise frowned. What she should be doing was finishing the letter to Ivy she'd started before submerging herself in this pointless reverie. She found her pen and paper, picked up the cushions and settled back on the settee.

*Jackie looked stunning at the banquet in a sleek silk gown from Chez Ninon, an upmarket New York boutique that makes amazing copies of European designer gowns—in this case, one of Givenchy's—at a fraction of the price of the original. Unfortunately, the queen was not at her best in fussy Norman Hartnell blue tulle.*

*But the real drama concerned the guest list. The Palace's protocol department won't have a bar of divorcees, but Jackie insisted her sister, Princess Lee Radziwill, be included along with Lee's husband, Prince Stanislaw, despite the fact that she's on her second marriage—and he's on his third!*

*Anyhow, I believe the queen got her own back by declining Mrs. Kennedy's request to include either our fun-loving Princess Margaret (still madly in love with Tony, by the way) or the elegant Princess Marina. Do you know who was invited instead? As many Commonwealth Ministers of Agriculture as could be rounded up. Needless to say, Jackie did not look amused!*

Her expression thoughtful, Blaise stopped writing and put down the letter. Charlie had been at the dinner, but rather than seated near her lowly position was close to the Secretary of State for War, John Profumo. They were due to conduct top-secret talks with President Kennedy and various US State Department officials the next day, but the serious looks on their faces had indicated that discussions were already underway.

Charlie had confided in her that there'd been a bruising encounter in Vienna between President Kennedy and the Rus-

sian leader, Mr. Khrushchev, only two days before. Now both
the United States and the British governments were increasingly worried about just one thing: the Soviets' determination
to claim East Berlin. "I'm so lucky I can talk about these matters
to you, Blaise," he'd said, "knowing you won't say a word to
anyone."

Now that she knew Charlie better, she'd come to realize just
what a fascinating man he was, with an agile mind attuned to all
the complications of the Cold War world. Everyone spoke about
him as a rising star of the Conservative Party, and she could see
why. It made her lingering preoccupation with Adam Rule even
more perplexing.

It was exciting and flattering to be trusted with sensitive information by a man in Charlie's position—not that she wasn't
regularly tempted to pass on the odd tip to one of the reporters.
But Charlie had always said how relieved he was that Blaise ad-
hered to the same high principles he did: she wouldn't dream of
destroying his faith in her. If he ever discovered her secret involvement with a backstreet murder, she thought with her spirits
sinking, he would never forgive her.

At least one person at *The Advocate* knew far more about the
current state of international affairs than Charlie imagined. Bernard Glyn, the foreign editor, was a distinguished correspondent
who'd lived all over the world and had taken a shine to Blaise.
He'd told her the Americans had deep fears about a matter Charlie hadn't even mentioned.

"Since MI6's esteemed Berlin operative, George Blake, was
charged last month with betraying dozens of his fellow agents and
divulging a raft of secrets to the KGB, the Americans have been
more obsessed than ever with how many double agents might still
be infesting Her Majesty's Secret Service or, for that matter, the
UK government," he'd said. "They're wary of sharing any really
top-level intelligence with us for fear of where it will end up.

"You see," Glyn had added after a long puff on his Cuban
cigar, which only deepened the furrows already scoring his pon-

derous cheeks, "I have it on the best authority that, despite Blake's arrest, the leaks to the Soviets haven't dried up."

Blaise sucked the top of her pen. What a coup it would be for the reporter who unearthed that story.

"You're a perfect picture, Blaise." Charlie gazed at her happily. "See how much nicer it is to wear proper clothes instead of those Mary-something dresses your friends encourage you to go around in?"

Blaise smiled. Charlie could be awfully conservative, but then, Royal Ascot did have strict rules concerning ladies' wear. He'd come with her to Harrods and personally selected an outfit: a mint green, below-the-knee dress with a matching jacket, off-white shoes, gloves and handbag, and a large hat sporting an arrangement of white silk roses and leaves. Blaise had considered the look on the matronly side, but Charlie had loved it, insisting he'd pay for everything.

"Are you sure?" she'd asked.

"Think of it as an early birthday present, darling," he had answered. "And, while I'm at it, I'd better give you this as well." He'd then presented her with a deep-red box embossed in gold with the words "House of Garrard." Inside, nestled on a bed of white satin, was a string of glistening pearls.

"Charlie!" Blaise had been shocked.

It was an extremely expensive gift, but, all the same, as she stood by Ascot's famous track in her new clothes, with the pearls sitting sedately around her neck, she wondered if Charlie would eventually expunge everything about her that didn't match his image of the next Lady Bennington. Blaise supposed it was only natural he'd want her to fit into his life, although sometimes she had the sense that, little by little, the person she'd once been was fading from sight.

She checked her wristwatch. In only ten minutes it would be two o'clock, the precise time when the daily procession of open carriages bearing members of the royal family would begin. Charlie had just started explaining that the queen's landau would be pulled by four matching gray steeds from the Royal Mews, all handpicked and named personally by the sovereign, when she heard a throaty female voice with a foreign accent saying, "Mr. Ashton, what a pleasant surprise."

She turned around to see a slender, dark-haired woman wearing a navy silk dress and a black pillbox hat.

Blaise detected an expression she couldn't quite identify in Charlie's eyes.

"I don't believe you have met Miss Alexia Voldova," he said to her smoothly.

The woman gave Blaise a look that was cool and appraising. They shook hands and said how do you do. Charlie made a remark about the likelihood of rain, and then they parted ways.

"Who was that?" Blaise was intrigued, as much by the woman's appearance as by Charlie's reaction. She wondered if perhaps she was an old girlfriend.

"Alexia?" he said with an indifference she found unconvincing. "I believe she's an interpreter at the Soviet Embassy. The ambassador must have brought her along today to help him out while he hobnobs with British society. We were introduced at some diplomatic do."

"She's very beautiful."

Charlie shrugged. "I suppose so, if you like foreign types. But she's not nearly as pretty as you." He pointed at the first pair of horses with their red-coated riders and, behind them, a more distant blur of fuchsia pink. "Darling, do you see? That looks like Her Majesty."

"So it does." Blaise slipped her arm through his. Charlie had obviously decided to put an end to the subject of Miss Voldova. But then, she thought with a sharp pang of guilt, everyone had their secrets.

# CHAPTER THIRTY-NINE

## *July*

Blaise pushed open the door at Sloane Gardens. Her shoulders slumped. The girls were both out with their latest boyfriends and the usually cheerful flat seemed lifeless and bleak. She was wearing the sophisticated black dress she knew Charlie liked and had even had her hair put up during her lunch hour in a style he'd once admired, but it had all been wasted.

She wandered into the kitchen, blushing as she recalled the embarrassment she'd just endured. Having spent all that time, not to mention money, on her appearance, she had presented herself at the Dorchester only to sit alone at a table in its exclusive dining room, becoming increasingly cross while she'd waited for Charlie—who never surfaced.

Blaise sighed. After half an hour spent nursing a gin and tonic she had paid her bill and left, slinking past the restaurant's thin-lipped maître d' while feeling like a prize dunce. Worst of all, now she didn't know whether to be angry with Charlie or with herself. He did have an irksome habit of canceling dates at the last moment, usually blaming some political blowup or other, but he'd never just left her waiting for him before.

As Blaise poured herself a glass of water, she had the disconcerting feeling that tonight had, in reality, been her own fault. The week before, she'd gone to the theater, expecting to meet Charlie in the foyer. When he'd failed to appear, she'd managed to find a phone in the ladies' powder room and call him, but he'd told her she had the wrong date. "Oh no," she'd said out loud.

Feeling depressed, she put a couple of slices of bread in the toaster. After the theater episode, Charlie had laughed and said he'd never known anyone who was so disorganized. Since then, she'd begun questioning everything she did, compulsively checking her diary to make sure she didn't make any errors either in her social life or at work. Yet tonight, somehow, she had blundered again.

As Blaise spread a scrape from her last precious jar of Vegemite onto the toast, she puzzled over the reason for her mistakes. Sure, she'd had a major setback at work, and those anonymous letters kept her on edge, but no matter what had happened before in her life, she'd always been disciplined and confident. These days, she barely recognized herself.

"Why aren't you wearing the platinum heart with the sapphires I gave you, the one that was Mother's?" Charlie asked when they arrived at the ornate gates of the Astor estate. "You know how much it means to me."

As he'd not mentioned the pendant during their trip from London, she'd hoped he hadn't noticed it was missing. "I'm so sorry, I seem to have misplaced it." Blaise unconsciously touched the front of her dress, feeling the empty space where the pendant should have been sitting. She wasn't terribly fond of it—sapphires seemed such a cold stone to decorate a heart—but as it was one of the few, and certainly most precious of the mementos Charlie had been left by his mother, he'd be terribly upset if she'd lost it. "I was sure it was tucked safely into my handbag," she said, "but when I looked, it wasn't there."

"Honestly, darling, you're becoming vaguer and vaguer. I really can't imagine how you manage at work. I've been saying for ages that job is too stressful. Do try to keep your wits about you tonight, won't you? I mean this is Cliveden—you'll need to be on top of your game."

Blaise wondered if the evening's formal dinner would prove

to be a trial. Since her marriage the previous October at a registry office in Hampstead, Bronwen Pugh had become the third Lady Astor, but just a month earlier, over tea at the upmarket grocers Fortnum & Mason, she'd confessed that, although she adored Bill, life at Cliveden had not been the blissful experience she'd imagined.

"I'm living in the lap of luxury," she'd said, stirring her cup of orange pekoe, "with a huge staff, but I'm well aware most of them look down on me for not being an aristocrat. Then there's my lady's maid—"

"Your own maid? Surely that's a treat."

"Hardly." Bronwen grimaced. "I mean, if there's one thing I know about, it's clothes, but the woman insists on laying out exactly what she thinks is appropriate for me to wear every single day. I've simply no choice in the matter, and it's even worse now I'm in the family way."

She picked up a shortbread biscuit, thought better of it, and put it back on its plate. "Last week, I had the cheek to stroll into the kitchen and look at what was inside the fridge. That caused such a furor the chef handed in his notice. To make matters worse," she added quietly, "Bill insisted that I apologize."

Blaise had felt so sorry for Bronwen that when her friend invited her to "a huge weekend that's coming up" she had immediately agreed to attend. In any case, she'd been intrigued by Cliveden's reputation, not only for luxury—thanks to the vast fortune of Astor's American forebears—but also as a long-standing center of power and political plotting. Anything might happen during a weekend at the famous residence.

"Crumbs!" Blaise exclaimed as Charlie drove the Bentley down a broad avenue densely lined with flourishing lime trees. Rearing before her was a great three-story Italianate mansion, resplendent with arches and clusters of columns. Flanked on each side by two long, low-lying wings, Cliveden was built on a vast scale that made Beech Hall look like a modest country cottage in comparison.

After passing an oversized marble fountain consisting of a great shell from which aggressive jets of water arced over chubby Cupids and erotic female figures, they drew up at the entrance. Inside, Blaise found herself in a baronial-style hall with flagstones underfoot and tapestries on the walls. She couldn't help smiling at the absurd appearance of several freshly polished suits of armor standing like stage props in the corners of the room.

"It's a little theatrical, don't you think?" she whispered. Before Charlie could answer, she heard Bronwen's voice floating down from above.

"I'm so glad you're both here," she said as she glided down the stairs. Despite being five months pregnant, in her slim black pants and relaxed cream silk blouse she looked as elegant and as slender as ever. "You must come through and look at the parterre straightaway. It's quite magical."

Bronwen had not exaggerated. Beneath the elevated stone terrace at the rear of the house stretched several acres of vibrant green lawns in which eight interlocking rows of huge, wedge-shaped flowerbeds had been created. Their gorgeous display of late summer blooms scented the warm air with a heady fragrance. Just like everything else at Cliveden, Blaise thought, the enormous garden had been designed to impress.

"You can see the Thames through the trees." Bronwen gestured toward the right. "The scenery is terribly pretty by the river, but if you're planning on walking, I have to warn you it's 172 steps down—and then you have to haul yourself back up. There's a sweet little Tyrolean-style cottage you might like to look at, although it's currently occupied by a rather unusual chap. He's a good friend of Bill's called Stephen Ward," she added.

Blaise was trying to remember where she'd heard that name when Bronwen took her arm. "I'd love to show you up to your room," she said, "but I'd better leave it to the housekeeper. I don't want to prompt any more staff to hand in their notice, especially not during this weekend."

Blaise had dressed carefully for the night's formal dinner party, aware of how much her appearance mattered to Charlie. When he met her outside the door of her suite and exclaimed, "Darling, you could be a duchess," she breathed a sigh of relief. Then she remembered that had been exactly the same compliment Henry Higgins had paid Eliza Doolittle. She'd asked Charlie to take her to Drury Lane to see *My Fair Lady* because she'd wanted to see Cecil Beaton's sublime costumes, particularly those in the celebrated black and white Ascot scene. But it was Eliza's transformation from a cockney guttersnipe to an elegant lady—at least on the outside—that had made the strongest impression.

She was a bit of an Eliza herself, though she wasn't certain she wanted Charlie to play Professor Higgins. It was one thing to receive instructions on what to wear from Mrs. Hawthorn—that went with the job. But it felt a bit different when it came from your boyfriend, no matter how generous he was.

*What an ungrateful beast you are, Blaise Hill*, she told herself. She should be thrilled that the man in her life showered her with wonderful gifts.

Once again, Charlie had insisted on buying her outfit, a beautiful deep-blue gown. Though a little sedate for her taste, it had the decided advantage of making the most of her cornflower-colored eyes. If only she had been able to find that pendant. Charlie asked about it again on the way in to dinner, leaving her feeling even more unnerved about its disappearance. He was too sensitive to her feelings to chastise her, but she could feel his disappointment.

At least his good spirits returned quickly. It was the first time Charlie had been honored by one of the Astors' highly sought-after invitations, and as they entered the dining room she could tell by the way his eyes lit up that even he was impressed. With its decorative gilding featuring tiny pheasants, hares, and hunting dogs in addition to a veritable host of swags and curlicues, the effect was of yet more jaw-dropping splendor.

"Pretty, isn't it?" Bronwen smiled. "The paneling came from the hunting chateau where Louis XV installed his mistress, Madame de Pompadour. Oh, if these walls could only speak!"

Dinner unfolded in a manner every bit as grand as the decor. Outside Buckingham Palace, Blaise had never seen so many uniformed staff serve one delicious course after another. The guests were all much older than she was and terribly important, although to her surprise she realized that she'd grown so used to working in close proximity to the royal family that to be in this distinguished company felt almost normal.

The president of Pakistan, Field Marshal Ayub Khan, was guest of honor. Blaise had heard speculation among the reporters about his upcoming talks with President Kennedy concerning, among other topics, the shooting down by the Soviets of a US spy plane that had taken off from a secret base in Pakistan. How fascinating it would be to write about world events, she thought with a sting of disappointment, instead of the style of hat the Duchess of Kent was likely to wear to Wimbledon.

The Profumos were the only couple Blaise had met before. Despite his wife's presence, she was sure that when Jack greeted her he'd held her hand—and her gaze—a moment or two longer than she would have expected.

Because of the hot summer night the French doors to the terrace were wide open, allowing for floodlit views of the fabulous gardens. From time to time a perfumed breeze rustled the dining room's yellow silk curtains, but it was still so warm inside Blaise wished her dress's unforgiving lines had not demanded that she wear a corset. She shifted uncomfortably on her brocade-covered chair. How on earth the men were coping in their dinner suits was hard to imagine.

Thankfully, when the remnants of the last strawberry soufflé had been removed from the table, Bill Astor rose to his feet, asking, "Who's coming outside for a stroll in the grounds? We've a new statue of a boy riding a dolphin, and you might like to see the swimming pool."

"Darling, come on ahead with us," Charlie said to Blaise. Taking her arm, he led her across Cliveden's wide gravel forecourt just behind Bill and Jack Profumo. After arriving at a weathered stone enclosure, Astor opened a gate in the wall, then waved the three of them through into the secluded pool area.

"Cripes." Blaise giggled.

Charlie gave her a cautionary look.

Profumo laughed. "What *do* we have here?" he said delightedly.

A pair of curvaceous young women were frolicking in the water with three men, and the floodlights made it plain that one of the girls wasn't wearing the top of her skimpy bikini. To Blaise's surprise, she realized that the half-naked nymph was Christine Keeler, the same girl she'd paid for the story about Armstrong-Jones's illegitimate child. She certainly turned up in some unexpected places.

"Well, well," Charlie murmured to Blaise. "It seems Stephen Ward has brought his usual mixed bunch up from the cottage for a dip." Now she remembered where she'd heard Ward's name. He was the medical man Christine said she'd been living with.

A moment later, Bronwen and the rest of the guests ambled in, smiling archly at the uninhibited scene. Blaise was quite sure the others considered themselves far too sophisticated to exhibit any shock; anyway, Cliveden had a name for tolerating racy behavior. Bronwen, however, looked less than impressed. "Come on, everyone," she called out with strained gaiety. "It's time we went back to the house for some cognac."

Bill Astor wandered over to the side of the pool. "Stephen, old boy," he said with a wink, "when you and your pals are decent, join us for a drink."

Charlie squeezed Blaise's hand as they turned away. "Did you see that fellow, splashing around in the deep end?" he said quietly.

"Heavily built, in his late thirties?"

Charlie nodded. "That's the one. He's a naval attaché at the Russian Embassy, a fellow called Yevgeny Ivanov."

"He must be familiar with Alexia Voldova, then."

"I really wouldn't know. What's important about Eugene— that's the name he goes by over here—is that he's not a naval attaché at all."

"You don't mean—"

"I do. He's a spy."

"If he's a spy, he's keeping unusual company."

"Isn't he just?" Charlie replied.

They were walking back to Chelsea after going to the cinema to see *The Guns of Navarone*. War movies weren't really Blaise's style, although the actors' performances had made it worthwhile.

"You know, it's remarkable that truly intelligent people can be so stupid," Charlie said.

"Are you thinking of that character played by Anthony Quinn? The one who had it in for Gregory Peck, I mean?"

"What? No, I was actually thinking about Jack Profumo. Strictly between you and me, he's begun an affair with—remember the rather common little brunette we encountered cavorting in the Astors' pool? Her name is Christine Keeler."

"Of course." Blaise fanned herself with her hand: it was another hot night. "But are you quite certain about Jack? Surely he wouldn't have an affair with Keeler."

"Jack *is* known to have a roving eye," Charlie remarked. The air was so close even he'd dispensed with his usual jacket and tie.

"But Profumo is a middle-aged man and she can't be more than nineteen."

"That's hardly the worst of it," Charlie added.

"What do you mean?"

"The worry is, young Miss Keeler seems to be over-friendly with Eugene Ivanov, our Soviet friend. In fact, the day after we saw the two of them at Cliveden, he drove her back to London. I read the report from MI5—as you'd imagine, they keep a close watch over him."

"But you don't know what happened between them." She glanced at the billboards as they walked past the Royal Court Theater; it had developed a reputation for controversial dramas.

Charlie shrugged. "I can imagine. The point is, true or not, if Jack's even suspected of sharing his latest floozy with a Russian agent, given the current political climate, there'll be hell to pay."

"I can hardly see Jack divulging state secrets to Christine Keeler," Blaise said. "First, why would he, of all people, think that was a suitable subject for pillow talk? Second, from what I know of her, Christine wouldn't be remotely interested! And third, even if Jack did such a wildly improbable thing, what with those funny cigarettes she smokes, I doubt she'd remember what he said."

"You sound very knowledgeable about the girl." Charlie looked surprised. "I thought that night at Cliveden was the first time you'd come across her."

Blaise explained that Christine had turned up at the paper with a story to sell.

"I see." He put a protective arm around her as they turned into Sloane Gardens. "I hate the way your job brings you into contact with such unsavory types. I worry about you."

Charlie's concern made her feel special, even if it was unnecessary. "I'm hardly likely to get into trouble when I spend most of my time trailing around after the royal family," she said reassuringly. "I'm fine."

"Well, Jack certainly isn't. I've heard Miss Keeler has already been the cause of more than a few ructions. Profumo told me only yesterday that the cabinet secretary questioned him about the nature of his relationship—'like a headmaster grilling a naughty schoolboy' was how he described it. Unsurprisingly, Jack chose to deny everything."

"Poor Valerie," Blaise said, "and Christine. Sounds as if she's out of her depth."

Charlie shrugged. "Good-time girls like that come and go. In six months or so, no one will even remember her name."

# CHAPTER FORTY

## August

It was a scene of sound and fury. The newsroom was humming, reporters' fingers were flying and copy boys running as smoke billowed from dozens of cigarettes.

"What's happened?" Blaise asked the foreign editor. The only reason she'd come in on a Saturday was so she'd have a story ready to be printed the following night for Monday morning's edition. As *The Advocate* didn't publish a Sunday paper, she had been expecting editorial to be nearly empty.

"The Soviets have made their move," Glyn said, ashing a cigar. Blaise noticed that he'd abandoned his normal starchy city dress and was wearing a tweed suit and tie—he must have rushed back to Fleet Street from the country.

"They've started building a wall that will sever East and West Berlin," he continued. "By tomorrow the two halves will be completely sealed off from one another. Looks like old Winston was right, after all. His 'iron curtain' has well and truly fallen." Glyn's phone started ringing. "That will be my man at the Foreign Office," he said, turning away.

Blaise wandered back to her typewriter and loaded it with blank copy paper. A year earlier she'd written a story concerning the sudden departure of a butler by the name of Mr. Cronin from Princess Margaret's quarters in Kensington Palace. Apparently, there'd been what was discreetly referred to as a "clash of opinion" with Mr. Armstrong-Jones, which had led to the butler immediately packing his bags and taking off for a rooming house.

Now here she was, twelve months later, reporting on the multi-million-pound renovations the princess and her husband had ordered for their lavish new home. Blaise slowly shook her head. While surrounded by journalists writing about the most significant development of the Cold War, she was still covering the Armstrong-Jones's domestic arrangements.

What an unusual household that must be, Blaise pondered. During Margaret and Tony's Caribbean honeymoon of the previous year, it had been noted in *The Advocate*'s Births, Deaths, and Marriages pages—otherwise known as Hatches, Matches, and Despatches—that Camilla Fry had delivered a baby girl called Polly on May 28. Tony Armstrong-Jones had been named as one of her godparents.

"You wouldn't read about it," Blaise muttered.

Charlie set out the stringent measures—a twelve-foot-high concrete barrier topped by barbed wire; search lights and sirens; towers manned by guards with machine guns—the communist east had imposed on Berlin. "By now, anyone who hasn't already crossed over to the west is going to be stuck where they are, quite possibly forever."

Due to the political developments, Blaise had scarcely seen Charlie for over a week, but he'd asked her to meet him at a local Italian restaurant for a quick meal of spaghetti with a bottle of chianti. Blaise stared at the pile of limp pasta congealing on her plate. The sauce had the same metallic flavor as a can of tomato soup. "I used to dream about reporting on world events," she said.

"But you have your royal round. I imagine that's been jolly. Or perhaps you're beginning to find it's a strain." He smiled sympathetically.

"It's all right. Anyway, since my last effort to get somewhere ended so badly, it's unlikely the editor will give me another chance at covering hard news." She looked up. "What do you think, Charlie—should I keep trying?"

"Don't exceed your own limitations, that's my advice." He drank some more wine. "I'm sorry to say it, but I do worry about your state of mind. Remember how you turned up at the Dorchester on entirely the wrong night?"

"But I was sure you told me to meet you on Tuesday at eight o'clock. I wrote it down," Blaise protested.

Charlie frowned. "Darling, it's not the first time you've made a mistake. I'm concerned that this job of yours has become too much for a highly strung girl like you. To be frank, I'm relieved that once we are married, you will leave it all behind."

"But—"

"There are no buts about it," he said gently. "You know married women don't work, not in the circles I move in anyway. Valerie Profumo and Bronwen Astor gave up their careers for the men they loved and they were at the very top of their professions. I'd be humiliated if you didn't do the same. And God knows what it would do to my political career—the prime pinister would take it very badly. I'm sorry, but you do see the problems it would cause for me, don't you?"

Blaise didn't reply. Maybe it was just because she hadn't come anywhere near these women's stellar achievements that she felt she had to at least make an attempt to forge ahead. Hadn't she told McInerney, on the very first day she'd marched into his office, that she'd never let a man stand in her way? That feisty girl would have been shocked by this conversation.

"I've been thinking," he said. "If you hand in your notice now, we can announce our engagement straightaway. Why delay any longer?" he added. "After that, we should marry as soon as possible." He smiled widely. "I really can't bear all this waiting to make you my wife; every time I set eyes on you I want you more."

Blaise pushed her plate away. "But you did say a year."

She wished Charlie would drop the subject. The existence of those frightening notes in their white envelopes was a permanent reminder that she'd never said a word to him about her murky past. How could she marry Charlie with that on her conscience? Not only would she be deceiving him, but if her secret was revealed it would ruin his political career a great deal faster than keeping her newspaper job would.

"That's still an entire month away," he said, looking a little aggrieved. "And a year was your idea, not mine. I haven't demanded anything from you that you haven't been willing to do, have I? I've been living like a monk."

She went to say something, but Charlie held his hands up. "I'm not complaining. That was what I agreed. But I would be terribly disappointed if I were to discover that you're the kind of girl who leads a man on, takes every advantage a chap gives her, like lovely pieces of jewelry and pretty dresses, enjoying weekends at stately homes with Britain's top people thrown in, all the time promising she'll give herself to him once she has a ring on her finger—but then, at the last moment, reveals she has no intention of getting married."

He topped up his glass. "Fortunately for me, however"—he gazed at her lovingly—"you're not a bit like that. You're a girl in a million."

Blaise's stomach tightened. Wasn't she guilty of leading Charlie on, when, despite all she now knew about him, during the still dark hours of the night she still wanted Adam? She'd tried to put a clamp on her feelings, pushed Adam out of her mind. The man was despicable, morally bankrupt. But to her despair, at unguarded moments she caught herself longing for him. Not only that, she'd continued to play the sexual innocent with poor Charlie when in reality she was anything but.

Blaise felt a wave of nausea. She'd be breaking Charlie's trust if she backed out now, especially after he'd been so devoted to her. She might not adore him with the passionate intensity she'd felt for Adam, but she admired Charlie and everything he stood for; the love she felt for him was based on affection and respect. He'd vowed to cherish and protect her, and that's exactly what he'd done. Wasn't that the best, the safest basis for a happy marriage?

"Excuse me," she said. "I think there's something wrong with my spaghetti."

She rushed to the ladies' room, leaned over a toilet bowl, and was violently ill.

Blaise surveyed the pack of energetic dogs leaping around the grassed yard as the sound of their yelping resonated inside her head. *Be grateful for small mercies*, she told herself. At least it was pleasant to be sitting in the sunshine, out in the country, instead of either cooped up in the newsroom or stuck attending another stuffy reception.

She and a staff photographer had been taken by one of *The Advocate*'s drivers out to Whitehall, an establishment which had nothing to do with the British government but was instead a modest farm located in Surrey. Its owner had declared he was "Britain's leading breeder of prize-winning corgis," in a small display advertisement located toward the back of the newspaper.

As it was September, royal news was thin on the ground. The queen and the Duke of Edinburgh, with their three children, had retired to their castle in the Scottish Highlands, where they'd been entertaining a stream of titled relatives. Even Princess Margaret, who could usually be depended upon for a good story, had made only rare public appearances of late, as her first child was due to be born in November. Blaise wondered if the royal baby would ever discover he or she had an older sister.

"There's nothing to write about," Blaise complained that morning to the news editor, a man called Keith, who came from the Midlands. "Balmoral Castle's strictly off limits."

"Och, lassie," Keith had said in an execrable Scottish accent. "Surely you can find something. Go for a human interest angle, a piece that will put a smile on the readers' faces."

That's when she'd remembered the Whitehall advertisement— it was the word "corgis" that had caught her eye. As the queen's passion for the breed was legendary, Blaise had suggested it might do for a color story. "Just the ticket," Keith had said, but now, as the canine cacophony continued, Blaise grew less certain it had been a good idea.

"Her Majesty dotes on these little fellows, bless her," Whitehall's owner, a retired army sergeant called Ronnie Carruthers yelled over the din. He and Blaise were sitting at a small table drinking from glasses of his own, homemade lemonade. "Well, not these actual dogs, you understand. They're not as lucky as her lot."

"How's that?" Blaise had discovered Carruthers required little encouragement.

"For one thing, there's a special corgi room in Buckingham Palace, where they sleep in elevated wicker baskets lined with Egyptian cotton sheets, no less," he said, impressed. "And their food's prepared by a gourmet chef. Fillet steak, freshly caught rabbit, chicken breast—makes you drool, doesn't it?"

Blaise agreed that it did. "What would you say are corgis' main characteristics?" she asked, taking another sip of lemonade. It might still be the morning, but she caught herself thinking she could do with a decent splash of gin in it.

"Oh, that's an easy one," Carruthers said. "Just look at this lot. They're a bit noisy, I admit," he said with a laugh, "but they're friendly little chaps, loyal and very smart."

Blaise smiled as the dogs raced about on the lawn, wagging their stumpy tails with excitement while the photographer snapped away. She could see why the queen had become attached to them—in such a highly ordered life, being surrounded by these playful creatures must offer pleasant respite. "Any problems?" she asked, turning a page in her notebook.

"They can get a bit nippy," Carruthers admitted. "It's common knowledge among us breeders that Her Majesty's favorite dog, Susan, bit the royal clock winder a while back. To make matters worse," he said with a confiding air, "a few months later another of the corgis got stuck into a policeman who was on guard duty at Buckingham Palace. Now there's talk that the entire pack of little beggars have taken a strong dislike to the Balmoral postman."

"That must keep him on his toes," Blaise said, attempting to keep a straight face.

The photographer signaled that he was finished, so Blaise said goodbye to Carruthers and his corgis. They were nice dogs, she reflected during her journey back to London, but if this was the kind of story she was destined to cover for the rest of her career, leaving work might not be such a calamity.

That night, Charlie came around to the Sloane Gardens flat when Blaise had finished work. "I need to go back to the House," he said, "but I just had to see you."

"That's sweet." Blaise smiled. "While you're here, do you want a drink?"

"Since we're alone for once, I'd rather kiss you."

At first, Blaise had shied away from any more intimate behavior, telling herself she didn't want to make another mistake. But Charlie had said how demoralized she made him feel so often that one day when he'd begun fondling her breasts she had simply stopped pulling his hands away. Over time their intimacy had slowly increased, but the thrill Blaise was expecting had failed to materialize.

It wasn't that she didn't enjoy cuddling Charlie. He was a bit like an oversized teddy bear with an affectionate nature that was definitely endearing. And there was no doubt he appealed to plenty of women; she'd seen how they fluttered around him, batting their eyelashes and carrying on. With his attractive coloring and balanced features, Charlie was a nice-looking man by anyone's standards; he was great fun, generous, and cared terribly about her welfare. She mentally ticked off his attributes, even while they continued to kiss on the sofa. But for some inexplicable reason, her body simply didn't respond to his. Blaise was beginning to think there must be something wrong with her.

"Come on, darling," he murmured, "just relax a little."

"The girls will be home soon," she said, breaking away.

Charlie rolled his eyes. "Ah yes, Perfect Pandora and Heroic Harriet, always turning up at the wrong moment."

"Don't be like that," Blaise said, bristling. "They're my best friends."

"Isn't it time you moved out, found a nice little place of your own?" His tawny eyes were filled with concern.

"I could never afford it."

Blaise was astonished when Charlie offered to cover the costs. "I don't fancy being a kept woman," she laughed.

He looked offended. "I'm only thinking of what's best for you. I always do."

"Yes, I know. But I don't see what the problem is."

"That's because you have no idea how to judge people's character. Need I mention Adam Rule?"

Blaise felt a sudden spear of pain.

"I suppose when it comes down to it," Charlie said, changing tack, "I'm just keen to have you all to myself."

As if on cue, her friends burst through the door, laughing and chatting. When they saw Charlie, they immediately became more subdued.

"Girls," he said, acknowledging them with a polite nod. "I was just on my way out."

He gave Blaise a meaningful look. "Think about my idea, won't you?" he said before he disappeared, striding into the night with a jaunty whistle.

"Mmm, if I'm not wrong you're carrying fish and chips in that newspaper." Blaise sniffed the delicious aroma that had suddenly filled the room.

Dora smiled. "Want some?"

"If there's enough to go around."

"Don't worry about me," Harriet said breezily. "I'm going straight out again. Jean-François has promised to help me practice my irregular verbs." She went off to her room, reappearing a few minutes later with fresh lipstick and a different dress, then twirled out of the front door.

After fetching some plates and cutlery, Blaise joined Dora at their tiny dining room table. "Yum. Salt and vinegar—could there be a better combination?" she said as she munched on a chip. "Although Charlie would consider this sort of food terribly working class."

"I don't know why you care so much about his opinion. It's not like you," Dora complained. "And if Harriet were here instead of out with that French jazz musician, she'd say the same."

*Not this again*, Blaise thought. Her friends had never warmed to Charlie, whose only fault was being too conservative for their avant-garde tastes. Admittedly, his outlook might be on the traditional side, but what was so wrong with that?

"While we're on the subject," Dora continued, "I've been thinking about Charlie's mysterious disappearances. And then there's the way he doesn't turn up when he's meant to."

"Politics is unpredictable." Blaise shrugged. "And sometimes I screw up."

"Then what about the time he was supposed to be at that ministerial conference in Brighton, only you swore you'd seen him crossing Oxford Street?" Dora leaned forward. "Haven't you ever wondered if he's hiding something?"

Blaise stared at her friend. Dora must be overwrought. Charlie had said her family was fanciful; now it seemed her imagination had gone into overdrive.

"You're being ridiculous," Blaise said, putting her knife and fork down with a clatter. "One of the things I love most about Charlie is that he's so open. He tells me everything, even the latest gossip from Westminster."

"But Blaise—"

"Don't say another word," she warned.

Dora had never had a steady boyfriend the whole time Blaise had known her. Now the thought crossed her mind that perhaps she was envious of their relationship.

"Okay, let's forget it." Dora gave Blaise a conciliatory smile. "You know me—I've always gone for more bohemian types. Speaking of which, we haven't been to the Markham together for ages. Why don't we pop in right now? We might find Mary and Alexander and a few of their mad mates." She peered out the window, frowning. "That is, if it doesn't rain. It looks a bit threatening."

Blaise jumped up. "I'll bring my umbrella," she said, relieved that Dora was off on a new tangent. "Then we'll be ready for anything."

Saturday's walk along the Chelsea Embankment was not as peaceful as Blaise had hoped. The further she ambled, past the gray-blue Thames on one side and the fashionable houses of Cheyne Walk on the other, the more distressed she became. If only Charlie and her friends could get on. Poor Charlie was jealous of how close she was to Dora and Harriet, while they failed to appreciate his good old-fashioned values. The whole situation was maddening.

To make matters worse, another of those alarming letters had appeared on her desk only a few days earlier. Its message might have been vague, merely stating TIME'S NEARLY UP, but it had made her so anxious that it kept her awake at night.

Blaise forced her thoughts back to Charlie and the issue of her own flat. If he wanted somewhere they could be alone, he could simply invite her to his place, yet he always had an excuse: his charlady was off sick, the plumbers were needed, the walls were being repainted . . . In the end, she'd decided that a man with such a public life must simply like having his own private retreat. Now, she began to wonder if Dora was right. Maybe he really was hiding something.

As she watched a flock of starlings wheel across the sky, she had a flash of insight. Like so many other men, Jack Profumo and the rest of them, the truth must be that Charlie had a mistress. She dropped her gaze to the river, upset and depressed. If he was having an affair, it was all her own fault. She still craved the touch of the one man she had banished from her life. Now, because of this insane weakness for Adam, she'd driven Charlie into the arms of another woman.

After hurrying away from a glamorous fund-raising dinner for the National Gallery attended by Princess Alexandra, Blaise went straight to Charlie's office at the Palace of Westminster. He'd suggested that they meet there for a nightcap following a late sitting in the House of Commons.

This would be the perfect opportunity to approach him in a calm, sensible way, she thought as she put her head around the mahogany door. If there was something going on between Charlie and another woman, she had to know. She didn't think she could face being let down again.

After greeting each other with a kiss they both had a whisky, even though Blaise had never developed a taste for the drink. She could tell by his expansive manner, however, that Charlie himself had already downed several.

"You're so lovely, Blaise," he said, having taken a seat behind his enormous desk, "with your big blue eyes and cute little nose and your gorgeous figure. Everyone says so. Why don't you come and sit on my lap so I can appreciate you properly? You know, indulge me in a little 'boss seduces the secretary' fantasy?"

She was half inclined to do so. It would make Charlie happy; she might even enjoy it. But she took one of the brown leather visitor chairs instead. "I need to talk to you," she said.

Once she started, she poured out everything, detailing a string of instances when Charlie had done or said something that had led to misgivings. "So I began wondering"—suddenly, she felt far less certain—"if perhaps you might be, um, involved with someone else."

Charlie looked appalled. "How could you think such a thing? You know I'm not that kind of man—unlike others I could mention."

Blaise shrank back in her chair.

"Wait a minute, now I see what's been going on." Charlie frowned. "This is all Pandora's and that Chinese girl's doing, isn't it? I tried to warn you about those two before! Girls like that go around sowing doubt because they're incapable of appreciating a decent man who only wants to do the right thing by a young woman."

He walked over to Blaise, took her hands in his, and raised her to her feet. "I'm not foolish. I know you don't love me, at least not the way I love you," he said unhappily. "But can't you see? You're so terribly vulnerable, Blaise, and I'm the one person who can make sure you will always be safe. You need me."

He'd blamed Dora and Harriet. He'd declared his love for her. He'd even offered her his enduring protection. But he had not denied having a mistress.

She shrugged Charlie off and rushed out of the room.

# CHAPTER FORTY-ONE

Blaise removed her navy blue high heels as soon as she came home from work, threw her matching handbag on a chair, and collapsed onto a sofa. So much for that calm talk. Last night's discussion had gone completely off the rails. These days, she didn't seem to get anything right.

She sat forward abruptly, her hands balled into fists. *Damn Adam Rule.* If it wasn't for him, she might have been more trusting. She might even desire Charlie in the way she would like to. Now, she'd wounded him badly. And if by some chance he had strayed, well, hadn't he selflessly gone along for nearly a year adhering to the conditions she'd imposed on their relationship? He was a man, after all, not a medieval saint.

Sighing, she picked up a copy of British *Vogue* from the coffee table. A little light relief was in order. She flipped over one page after the other, but couldn't settle. Her mind kept darting back to Charlie's final, troubling words. He was right. She did need him. Somewhere along the line, what with the violent deaths of two criminals and everything else that had happened since, she'd become badly unmoored. Well, no longer. Charlie was a wonderful man. Straight after dinner, she'd call him, apologize for her outburst and ask him to meet her tomorrow night for a drink at the Savoy.

She could picture it clearly. She'd have her hair done and put on the little black dress she'd worn on their first date. They'd order champagne, she would look into his warm brown eyes, and then she would say, "I don't want to wait a minute longer. Let's announce our engagement right away."

If anything ever surfaced about her involvement with Ryan's murder, hadn't Charlie promised to move heaven and earth for her? And he wasn't just protective; he was kind and generous. Once they were married, she'd be able to help her family. Charlie knew all about Ivy; he'd probably even fly her to London for their wedding if she asked him. Her career would be over, of course—she couldn't pretend that didn't hurt. But if all she had to look forward to were stories like the one about Ronnie Carruthers and his blessed corgis, would that really matter so much?

Blaise let out a sharp, bitter laugh. When she'd started at the newspaper she'd had dreams of making it big. Now she could see she'd been kidding herself. The dice were loaded against women and there was not a thing she could do about it.

The sound of a key turning in the lock made her brighten; one of the girls must be back. A few seconds later Dora came into the room wearing a pair of knee-high boots and a dazzling lemon-yellow shift. "I have something to show you," she announced, a little out of breath.

"You haven't been shopping again, have you?" Blaise said with a smile.

Dora looked serious. "Nothing like that. I've received a letter from Edwina."

Blaise sat up so quickly the magazine went flying. "Have you taken a look?"

"I have." Dora handed her the piece of pale gray, lined airmail paper covered with neat script. "But you'd better read it for yourself."

Blaise's hand shook as she quickly scanned the letter. First there was a paragraph of general chitchat, followed by something about Edwina's work in the Amazon. Then a single line leapt from the page.

*Olivia Riordan was perfectly lucid when she told me it was Charlie Ashton who attacked her, not Adam Rule.*

"No!" The letter fell from her grip. "No, no, no!" she cried.

The room spun. She could barely breathe. Clenching her hands, she tried desperately to pull herself together, to concentrate.

"Blaise, are you okay?" Dora said anxiously.

Blaise was too numb to speak. Picking up the letter from the floor, she forced herself to keep reading.

> *Olivia swore me to secrecy. She was petrified of what Charlie might do if she ever told the truth, so she simply refused to say a word to anyone else about his assault.*
>
> *I'm certain he did enter her bedroom on the day her parents were out. That shy little maid of the Riordans couldn't have been more than fifteen—she would never have stood up to him. When Charlie walked into Olivia's room, the poor girl must have been so desperate to escape that she jumped out of her window. But I wouldn't put it past Charlie to have pushed her.*

Was it possible? Could it be that the man she had trusted above all others was capable of such deceit, such horror? And, if the unthinkable were true, how could she have blindly placed her faith in him? Blaise moaned. Hugging herself, she began to rock backward and forward.

Dora sat down next to her. "Come on, let's talk this through."

But Blaise still couldn't speak. Wrenching sobs racked her body. She cried for Olivia Riordan and she cried for herself.

"I'm so ashamed," she said at last, her eyes bleary. "I was only too ready to believe the very worst of Adam, just because I thought he had a wild past, he knew a few shady characters and he'd said some strange things I couldn't figure out. That was all it took!"

She rubbed her temples distractedly. "I thought if Charlie told me something, well . . . there's no one more respectable than a titled member of the British parliament—it had to be true. He always seemed so transparent."

Blaise dropped her hands to her lap. "When it came to politics, he didn't hesitate to confide in me," she said staring down. "I felt so damned proud that little Blaise Hill had the trust of this important man. Yet all the time he was lying and lying about what mattered most."

Dora patted Blaise on the shoulder. "Don't be so hard on yourself. You didn't know London, you started a new job and you were thrown into a completely different world. It's no wonder you were taken in by Charlie: he fooled everyone."

"Except you."

Dora gave a slight shrug. "Maybe I picked up a feeling from Edwina. It must have stayed with me."

Blaise lifted her head with a jerk. "I'm a newspaper reporter, for God's sake. I should have known better, had my wits about me, been smarter, something!" she raged. "But, stupid bloody working-class girl that I was, I fell for every tired old myth about the nobility actually being nobler than the rest of us."

Blaise looked at Dora with dismay. "Charlie made me feel I owed him everything, but he was the one who kept giving me expensive gifts I never asked for, taking me to exclusive places, insisting I couldn't manage without him."

Dora took Blaise's hand. "Remember how we saw that old black and white movie called *Gaslight* on TV the other night?"

"What?" It took a moment for Blaise to follow Dora's latest tangent. "Oh, I see what you're getting at. You're saying Charlie is like Ingrid Bergman's awful husband, the one who kept on making the lights in their apartment flicker, only he denied it, so in the end she thought she was going mad."

"Well, isn't he?"

"I kept muddling things." Blaise frowned. "Charlie said I was hopeless."

"Hopeless, my foot!" Dora exclaimed. "He's been purposely chipping away at your confidence all along, making sure you thought you were in the wrong places at the wrong times. And what about the missile story you wrote last year that you came to grief over?"

"But that was entirely my own fault. I mixed up two different files." Blaise hated it when anyone brought up this disaster.

"Really?" Dora said. "You have one of the sharpest minds of anyone I know. It's completely out of character for you to make a mistake like that—I think Charlie orchestrated the whole debacle."

Blaise's hand flew to her mouth. "Bloody hell!"

She sank back against the sofa. "I'm really sorry that I started acting like a pill, but things changed slowly and sort of insidiously. It was a bit like the old story about the frog in the water that boiled so gradually he never realized it was killing him."

Blaise shuddered. "Now I look back, I can see there were dozens of ploys. Charlie tried to control the clothes I wore and the people I saw—he even wanted to separate me from you and Harriet. All the time he was manipulating me so cleverly that, in the end, I didn't know who I was anymore." Her voice dropped to a miserable whisper. "And, worst of all, I've lost Adam forever."

Blaise's agony was raw. Charlie might have supplied her with a string of vicious lies about Adam, just when she was at her most vulnerable, but she alone had destroyed the precious bond they had shared. Because of the furious tongue-lashing she'd doled out, any feelings Adam might once have had for her would have been replaced by something far darker and uglier. If only she'd been more worldly and less insecure. If only she'd kept her temper in check. If only, if only.

Blaise looked up to see Dora heading back from the kitchen with a glass of water. "Thanks," she said, gulping it down. While Dora perched on a chair opposite, Blaise glanced back at the letter. "That's odd." She frowned. "This has taken a long time to arrive from New York."

Dora shifted uncomfortably. "I've actually had it for two weeks."

"*Two weeks!* How could you keep something so important from me?" Blaise made no attempt to keep the hurt from her voice.

"I'm truly sorry," Dora said. "I was going to show you on that night we had fish and chips. But when I started expressing my doubts about Charlie, you stood up for him so passionately that I honestly wasn't sure you'd believe a secondhand account like Edwina's."

A cloud of dismay settled upon Blaise. She'd dismissed Dora as overly imaginative, whereas she was the one who'd been immersed in a world of delusion.

"I thought that only hard, up-to-date evidence would convince you," Dora continued. "Trust me, I now have something that shows Charlie is light years away from the knight in shining armor he's made himself out to be."

Blaise jumped when she heard the front door slam.

"Harriet? We're in the sitting room," Dora called out, before turning back. "I'd better warn you, she won't be alone."

"Dora, please," Blaise begged. "Right now I can't cope with other people." Her head was beginning to ache. "I'm sorry, but I'm going to crawl into bed."

"Wait," Dora insisted. Harriet appeared a moment later, closely followed by the dapper figure of Cecil Beaton, and Andy, still wearing his chauffeur's uniform.

Blaise was bewildered. Surely Dora must have known that she'd want to nurse her grief in private.

"Hello, me old china," Andy said gently, drawing his eyebrows together as he took in Blaise's red, swollen eyes. "Thought a bit of fortification might be needed." He set down some beer on the coffee table.

"Good evening, my dear. Sorry to catch you unawares." Beaton kissed her on the cheek. "And perhaps these will help." He held up a bottle of Beaujolais and a large manila envelope.

"What's going on?" Blaise said. "I don't understand."

"Hang on." Harriet fetched glasses and poured drinks. "Okay, let's all sit down."

Dora crossed her long legs and began. "After I received Edwina's letter, I was worried sick, so I told Harriet we had to do something quickly."

Harriet's shiny black hair swung forward as she nodded. "I

suggested we ask Andy if he could help, given he's been driving Charlie around. Andy, shall I keep going?"

"Might as well," he said, looking uncomfortable.

"Andy told us Charlie had asked to be taken to some unusual places, including a small house tucked away in a side street in Bloomsbury. He also disclosed that he'd heard Charlie telling you 'porkies,' either about where he was going or where he'd been."

Andy chipped in. "I was in a state about it, too. Chauffeurs don't tell tales—at least, not if they want to keep working. Only, I've always had a soft spot for you, Miss. I had a fair idea Mr. Ashton was carrying on behind your back, so when these young ladies approached me I—pardon my language—spilled me guts."

He crossed his arms, scowling. "Once, when I picked Mr. Ashton up from the Flamingo, he had a dark-haired woman with him; said she was with a diplomatic mission. At the time, I told myself it was none of my business, but he wasn't exactly conducting himself as if it was a professional relationship, if you get my drift."

"So, let me get this straight," Blaise interjected. "You're saying you discovered Charlie has a mistress? I admit I've been pretty slow on the uptake, but even I had finally worked that out."

Curious, she turned to Cecil. "What is your part in all this?"

He gave her a wry look. "Despite our history, it's quite impossible to remain cross with a girl like Pandora. When she asked me if I would discreetly take a picture of whoever it was Charlie was seeing, I agreed instantly. All I had to do was to find out from Andy when and where the couple were likely to turn up. In the end, it was very easy. I simply loitered behind a hedge while I snapped them going into that funny little house in Bloomsbury."

Cecil sipped from his glass of Beaujolais. "The thing is, I was never convinced by Charlie Ashton's innocent act. If you remember, Blaise, I was even dubious about that so-called accident when he spilled his drink down your back at Her Majesty's ball. And anyway," he winked, "I've never been averse to a little mischief."

Blaise's thoughts began to whirr. Tommy Trent had once told

her she'd be a decent reporter when, after merely spotting two people together, she'd know who they were and have a good idea of what they were up to. A picture was beginning to form in her mind. All she needed was one remaining piece of the puzzle.

"Cecil," she said, "I think it's time I saw one of your photographs."

He slid a sharp black and white print out of the manila envelope.

Blaise felt a rush of adrenaline as she stared at the shot. "Of course," she murmured.

"Don't tell me you know who she is?" Harriet asked.

"Oh yes," Blaise answered slowly. "This woman"—she held up the image of a dark-eyed brunette—"is Alexia Voldova."

Andy whistled. "So that's who Mr. Ashton was all over in the back seat of the Jag."

"I think there's more to it than that. You see," Blaise continued, "Miss Voldova is employed by the Soviet Union."

"Oh my God!" Dora's eyes opened wide.

"Exactly," Blaise said. "It looks to me as if the Honorable Charles Ashton may well have been busy betraying queen and country. The Russians are desperate to know if the USA is going to supply West Germany with nuclear warheads, and he is one of the very few people in the United Kingdom with access to that intelligence."

She thought back to her conversation with the foreign editor. Hadn't Glyn told her that, despite the recent arrest of a high-level spy, the flow of top-secret information from Britain to the Soviet Union had never ceased?

Blaise looked at her friends. "I believe Charlie is a traitor," she said. "Now all I have to do is prove it."

# CHAPTER FORTY-TWO

The next morning, Blaise knocked on Johnny Norton's door.

"How are you, Hill?" he said.

"Well as can be expected."

"It's probably about time we had a chat." Norton scratched an ear.

"I'm glad you think so," Blaise said. "Because I never repaid you for that beer you shouted me in the Stab. How about we meet there at noon—drinks are on me. Unless you'd prefer somewhere else?"

"The Stab'll do," he said. "Now, why is it I have the feeling there's something you want to get off your chest?" He slapped a meaty thigh and laughed suggestively as Blaise left his room, her teeth on edge.

At exactly five past twelve she was sitting in a dim corner of the Stab's gloomy bar, nursing a glass of beer with her back to the room. Norton sat opposite with a foaming pint in his hand and the obligatory packet of crisps on the table.

"You know, Hill, your work is good—far better than Croft's who, for all his deficiencies, had a great deal more experience than you have." He took a large gulp of his drink. "I've always wondered what went wrong with that front-pager you wrote." He looked genuinely puzzled. "Just seemed a bit out of character."

When Blaise remained silent, Norton shrugged. "Okay, if that's the way you want it. Well then, why exactly are we sitting here in this cozy little spot? I'm not kidding myself you're after my scintillating conversation."

Blaise took out one of the photographs that didn't include Charlie from the manila envelope. "Does she mean anything to you?"

Norton looked blank.

Blaise told him the woman's name, adding, "Voldova is an interpreter at the Soviet Embassy."

Norton immediately seized the print. "Well, well," he said, stroking his chin. "It's all beginning to make sense."

"What is?"

"Funnily enough, only yesterday a little bird mentioned her to me." He gave a snort of disgust. "Now I've seen what she looks like, our great British security service strikes me as even more than usually myopic, especially considering the Russkies' fondness for honey traps." Norton looked up. "You know what those are, don't you?"

Blaise shook her head.

"It's when they prime some good-looking woman to inveigle her way into a man's bed, the sort of man who has access to secrets he might want to trade, either for a price or else to avoid blackmail—sometimes both."

Blaise narrowed her eyes. "So who's your little bird?"

"Facts of life, Hill." Norton pursed his mouth. "Every major paper on Fleet Street has an in-house spy MI5 inserts on the sly. Only I happen to have a good working relationship with our bloke."

"You mean there's a man on this newspaper who's associated with the British secret service?" Suddenly warm, Blaise loosened her new Liberty scarf.

"Oh dear, oh dear, you *have* led a sheltered life. Wake up and smell the roses, Hill," Norton said. "Those hardened reporters who've had a string of postings in the world's biggest trouble spots—they know more about what's really happening on the ground than any local chappie from MI5. They've an instinct for trouble and their sources are rock solid."

He paused to cram a handful of crisps into his mouth. "I think our man was merely fishing, seeing if I'd react to her name. It didn't sound to me as if he had anything concrete on her."

Bernard Glyn, Blaise thought.

"Which makes me wonder why my old newsman's nose is telling me you've stumbled onto something." Norton eyed Blaise thoughtfully. "So, let me make myself perfectly clear. Right now, I don't have a clue what you might or might not have found out about this Russian woman and I'm not asking you to tell me." He bared his discolored teeth in what might have been a smile.

"Of course, you'd need to bring us hard, incontrovertible evidence—and by that I mean pictures of a meeting, the details of where it took place, the time, and the date, plus anything else you can come up with. In other words, enough to build a water-tight case."

He leaned across the table. "But if you can tie Alexia Voldova to a highly placed employee of the British government, I can promise you one thing. As far as I'm concerned, you'll be able to cover whatever you bloody well like."

Norton took a gulp of his beer, then wiped his mouth on the back of his hand. "Perhaps that toff MP boyfriend you've been knocking around with can give you a lead. Ashton, isn't it? He must have a fair idea of who's who and what's what."

"I imagine he does," Blaise said.

She walked away from the Stab possessed by a grim determination. Charlie had driven a young woman to her death and lost Blaise the love of her life. But now she had the opportunity to expose his treachery—and to resurrect her career. With Adam gone forever, she reflected bitterly, her job was all she had left.

"Can you see them?" Blaise whispered. She and Cecil were standing in the deep shadows cast by a tall stand of azalea bushes. There was no one else around: presumably, few people came this way unless it was spring, when the plants would be covered with vivid blooms.

"He's just sat down on a bench," Cecil replied in an undertone as he peered through the telephoto lens of his camera. Andy had phoned earlier to say that Charlie had expressed a wish to be dropped near the Isabella Plantation, a dense woodland setting in Richmond Park. "Said he needed some air," Andy had muttered.

Cecil had agreed to continue his undercover work when they were at the Chelsea flat. "During the war, the Ministry of Information commissioned me to document the Blitz. Shooting pictures of debutantes is all very well," he said, glancing at Dora, who smiled and rolled her eyes, "but I've been rather missing those daring forays."

It was very quiet. The shrubs rustled faintly as small creatures, squirrels perhaps, scurried about in the undergrowth. Several deer had just passed, the sound of their hoofs muffled by fallen leaves and damp grass, when Blaise heard Cecil murmur, "She's here."

As he began shooting one frame of film after another, Blaise looked through the binoculars she'd borrowed from the sports desk. There could be nothing quite as satisfying as spying on spies, she thought, as Voldova, wearing a black belted dress with a white scarf over her hair, sat down on the opposite end of Charlie's bench. She gave no sign of recognizing him.

Blaise blinked, trying to improve her vision. Cecil's powerful lens would greatly magnify the details, producing sharp, accurate images. But the binoculars were still strong enough for her to see that resting innocently between Charlie and Voldova was last Wednesday's copy of *The Advocate*. Blaise felt a surge of excitement as Voldova casually reached into her bag, brought out an identical issue, and placed it on top of its twin.

After a few more minutes, each took one of the papers and walked away in opposite directions. Blaise lowered the binoculars, satisfied. Anyone who wasn't focusing as hard as she had been would have missed it. But she'd seen the pair swap their copies of the newspapers.

Blaise sat next to Cecil, her pent up energy pumping, as he drove sedately away from Richmond Park in his black Mini Minor. She was desperate for him to put his foot down hard on the accelerator, but this wasn't the time to be attracting attention. Once Cecil reached his studio, he placed the film in a canister, raised an eyebrow and said, "Good luck, my dear. I'd take you to Fleet Street myself, but I'm expecting the next Duchess of Marlborough in half an hour." Blaise thanked him swiftly, ran to the nearest cross street, and hailed a cab.

As soon as she arrived at *The Advocate* building, she sprinted up the stairs to the photographic department, praying that Ben and Mike had been rostered on. She needed help, and that pair owed her a favor.

"Thank the Lord," she muttered when she saw the red light outside the darkroom was turned off. Blaise burst through the door, panting. "Boys," she said breathlessly, "am I glad to see you."

Startled, Ben and Mike looked up quickly.

"I've some film here that needs to be developed straightaway," she explained. "Only, please don't tell anyone about it. This is something I need to keep seriously quiet."

The two men exchanged a look. "Right you are," Ben said, tapping the side of his nose.

Mike nodded in agreement, adding, "But you'll have to nip outside."

Blaise paced up and down outside the darkroom, waiting impatiently. Finally, Mike stuck his head around the door.

"The prints aren't dry yet, but you can come and have a look."

Blaise hurried over to the row of glossy black and white pictures dangling from the line overhead in the strange ruby light. The first shot showed Charlie and Voldova sitting on the bench, the newspapers lying innocently between them. Blaise frowned. The photo hinted at a covert meeting between a Member of the British Parliament and an employee of the Soviet Embassy, but it wasn't proof that a single item of classified information had passed between them.

She scrutinized every print, feeling increasingly downcast. There might be sufficient evidence to incriminate Charlie, but there wasn't enough proof to condemn him.

"Anything strike you about that first shot?" Ben asked.

Blaise looked again. A strip of white with some black marks ran along the edge of one of the newspapers.

"Now, take a gander at this last picture," he said, fishing a dripping photograph out of a tray of developing fluid. "I blew it up."

It took just a glance at the enlarged print to see that the stripe was in reality an inch or so of paper that was protruding from a copy of *The Advocate*. Only the tops of the block letters printed across it were visible, but it wasn't hard to determine what they said. Next to the seal of the United Kingdom were two unmissable words: TOP SECRET.

Blaise looked from Ben to Mike. "Thank you," she said steadily, though her pulse was racing. "I reckon we've nailed the bastard."

# CHAPTER FORTY-THREE

The mail was still lying fanned out on the doormat when Blaise returned home the following night. She shuffled through the small pile, saw a letter postmarked Paris for Harriet, another for Dora from Monte Carlo, a flyer for a Cliff Richard concert and, last of all, an airmailed letter from Australia. The hand wasn't familiar, so she flipped over the envelope, which was large and bulky, to check the name on the back. To her surprise, *A. Black-ett* was written in sprawling letters. It was from Joe's mother, Agnes.

Blaise gulped. Perhaps Joe had suffered some sort of break-down, or maybe he'd confessed. If so, he must have left her out of it, otherwise a couple of bobbies would have turned up at her door already.

She tore open the letter, only to find a couple of scrawled pages together with another sealed envelope addressed in a different, neater hand. Blaise caught her breath. Written on the front of the smaller envelope was the name *Adam Rule*.

Agnes's own letter was brief.

*Dear Blaise,*

*I'm sending this to you as young Ivy told me you were mixed up with a man by the name of Charles Ashton. I don't know if he ever told you about Adam's mother, Emilia, but if he did, whatever he said would have been a pack of lies. That won't be his fault, mind you, although there's plenty that is. Even Adam doesn't know the truth about his mum. But I do.*

*You see, I was Emilia's maid. I stayed with her when she fled from England and all the time she lived in Mount Isa. When Adam was just a wee chap, we used to take it in turns working shifts at the pub, so as he would always have someone to look after him. Before she passed away, Emilia asked me to give him a letter she'd written, but she made me swear I wouldn't do it until Adam had reached his thirtieth birthday.*

*That should fall around about the time you receive this. I would have given the letter to Adam myself, but he disappeared into the desert for ages and now I'm not sure where he is. Joe said, seeing as you were the smartest person he knew, if anyone would be able to find him, you could—that's if he's gone back to London, of course.*

*Please try to track him down and hand the enclosed envelope to him personally. Joe reckons he heard Adam mention Eaton Square once, but I haven't a clue if he lives there or not.*

*My only other request—and this one's for Adam—is that he makes sure you read the letter, too. Adam is the best man I know, makes deposits into my bank as regular as clockwork. We couldn't get by without him, what with Pete's weakness for the horses.*

*I've always been very fond of you, Blaise, and I'm grateful for the way you've stood by our Joe. You're a strong girl and you're loyal, just like your mother. See you don't get yourself into any trouble.*

*Sincerely,*
*Agnes Blackett*

The letter was astonishing. She'd never dreamt that Joe's mother had been Emilia's maid; only now did she understand what had bound Adam to the Blacketts. But there was obviously a great deal more that had yet to be revealed. Adam had always seemed wreathed in mystery—now it appeared even he didn't know the secrets that lay buried in his mother's past.

Blaise swallowed hard. As she had no idea where Adam was, she couldn't help him and she couldn't help Agnes. She couldn't even help herself.

"I've heard from Charlie," Blaise said when she joined Dora and Harriet for lunch the next day. The girls were eating sandwiches amid the clouds of white hydrangeas growing in Middle Temple Gardens, a verdant haunt not far from Fleet Street and the nearby Inns of Court.

"What did he want?" Dora asked as a pair of robed and be-wigged barristers strolled by. "It sounded like he was pretty upset when you met up in his office."

Blaise removed a dampish salad roll from a brown paper bag. "Because I made a big song and dance about how he never invites me to his place, he's organized a dinner for two from Harrods Food Hall with caviar and champagne at his flat tonight."

She felt as if a fog had lifted. Now she knew the truth about Charlie, her old resolve was back. Never again would he get the better of her. "Charlie's been expecting to announce our engagement any day. I suppose since I brought up the mistress business, he's afraid I'll call the whole thing off." Blaise crushed the paper bag she was holding into a tight little sphere. "He's just up to his old tricks again, trying to manipulate me by going over the top."

"But surely you're not turning up?" Harriet asked. "It could be dangerous."

"Harriet's right," Dora insisted. "Just phone up and say you and Charlie are over."

Blaise stuck out her chin. "No way. I'm going to face him."

She took a moment to steady herself when she arrived at Charlie's flat. As he'd be expecting her to appear thrilled by his invitation, she tried to arrange her face into a suitably grateful expression.

Blaise knocked on the door. Charlie opened it, smiling when he saw her dressed in a slim black skirt with the pearls and a soft black silk blouse he'd given her. "You look lovely, darling," he said approvingly.

The flat was strangely anonymous. The walls were white, the rugs on the polished floorboards were dark red, and the furniture, although expensive, appeared as if it had been bought as a job lot. With its heavy drapes and bland collection of etchings, it seemed more like a hotel room than someone's home, a place designed to hide rather than reveal anything about its owner's identity.

Charlie went to kiss her on the mouth but Blaise turned her head, so his lips landed on her cheek instead. Frowning, he said, "I hope this isn't about the other night. The only reason I was upset was because of the awful things you suggested. It's a terrible feeling when the woman you adore starts accusing you of God knows what."

What a relief it was to be immune to Charlie's emotional blackmail. Rather than making her feel guilty, his twisted words now had the opposite effect. She felt stronger and more confident than she had in a long while.

He walked over to the round dining room table, took an open bottle of champagne from the ice bucket and poured out two glasses. "Never mind, I'm sure you won't do it again." Handing Blaise a glass, he said smoothly, "Here's to our future together."

The gleeful expression on Charlie's face was intolerable. "You're joking," Blaise erupted. "I wouldn't marry you under any circumstances."

Charlie looked thunderstruck. He pulled up a chair and sat down, saying, "What on earth is the matter now?"

"For a start, I know all about Alexia Voldova."

"Well, what do you expect?" he said, having quickly recovered his aplomb. "A man has needs, and you won't let me make love to you before we're married. This way I don't have to bother you."

It was her fault again. Charlie was nothing if not consistent, Blaise thought grimly.

"Anyway," he continued with a condescending smile, "a mistress is the usual thing among men in my set. I'm prepared to give her up once we're married—so you see, Blaise, you have nothing to worry about."

Blaise laughed contemptuously. "Do you honestly think I care about who you've been sleeping with? You're a traitor, Charlie, that's all I'm interested in. As a matter of fact, I have enough proof to hang you out to dry—there are photographs of you passing documents to your little Soviet friend, just for starters."

Charlie gave three slow claps. "Well done—I didn't think you had it in you. But I can't see a single picture, so . . ." He shrugged.

"They're in a very secure place." Blaise had personally watched on as, with McInerney's permission, Norton locked the negatives in the editor's safe.

Charlie's nonchalant manner was disconcerting. Why was he sitting there calmly sipping champagne with a smirk on his face? There was nothing for it but to plough on. "You lied about Adam, too," she said. "It was you who raped Olivia Riordan. You might even be guilty of something even worse."

She put her hands on her hips. "Everyone supported your version of events because you were the heir to the Bennington title, and who was Adam? The son of a fallen woman, a runaway bride. He was thrown out of Cambridge, abandoned by your father, and banished from Beech Hall. Adam had to live with the knowledge that Olivia's parents blamed him, and him alone, for their precious child's death. He paid a heavy price for your offense—and you know something? So did I."

Charlie didn't try to contradict her. He merely continued to lounge in his chair, as if immensely bored.

Blaise boiled with anger and frustration. "You set out to wreck my career," she spat. "I can't believe it never occurred to me that you switched the folders. So it's ironic, don't you agree, that now you've handed me the scoop of a lifetime. I have every intention of exposing your dalliance with a Russian spy—as well as your treasonous behavior—right on the front page of *The Advocate.*"

As soon as the words left her mouth, Blaise realized Charlie's unnerving silence had made her reckless. She should never have revealed her plans.

Whirling round, she rushed toward the door, but Charlie was already ahead of her. In one rapid move he turned the key in the lock and shoved it into a pocket. "You little trollop," he sneered, pushing her up against a wall.

Finally, the mask had dropped. The famously charming Charles Ashton had been replaced by a cold and ruthless man.

His face was only inches away from her own. "Are you actually so deluded that you think a man like me couldn't do better for himself than a tramp who's grown up in a bloody Sydney gutter?"

Charlie had the same look of scorn she thought she'd seen pass briefly across his face a year earlier, when she'd tried to end their relationship at the Savoy bar. "You're just a piece of dirt people like me wipe off their feet," he said.

Blaise flinched. She'd not expected Charlie would be this vicious.

"Remember the ball for Princess Margaret?" he jeered. "I saw the way that bloody leech watched you, long before you even knew he was in the room. I couldn't believe it—Adam Rule, in love. Never thought he was capable."

Blaise couldn't suppress a moment of elation. *Adam had been in love with her.* If even Charlie was convinced, it must have been true. Then a dark mood immediately descended. She'd made it so easy for Charlie to tear her away.

"You really hate him, don't you?" she said. "Want to tell me why?"

The look on Charlie's face reminded her of a furious child. "I couldn't stand the way Father doted on Rule, insisting he be treated the same way as me, when I was his only son—and who was he? Nothing but a distant relation who turned up like a thief in the night and stole his way into *my* life, *my* home, *my* world."

Dropping his hands, Charlie turned away and sat back down at the table. "When you were wandering around with Cecil Beaton, I followed Adam down a corridor. That's when I told him I'd already reserved the little whore he'd been eyeing all night. The bugger took a swing at me."

Blaise colored. "You bastard."

Charlie rubbed his cheek at the place where his bruise had bloomed. "I think you'll find there's only one bastard in this lamentable tale. I never believed that story about Rule's father being a stonemason. I'll bet Emilia shagged half the estate workers."

He picked up the champagne bottle and refilled his glass. "It wasn't hard to tell you had feelings for Adam, too; it was written all over your face. But I had a lucky break when the fool took off for Australia."

Blaise went to speak but couldn't. She remembered how lonely she had felt, the way she'd begun to doubt Adam.

"That's when it occurred to me there was a way to not only crush my bloody cousin, but also to ensure he wouldn't try to reveal the truth about that stupid Olivia Riordan." Charlie looked at her coolly. "I knew that if I married you, there'd be no chance of him ruining my political career. He'd never disclose what really happened if he thought it would sweep you up in a scandal. Anyway, who would believe him? It would be merely a case of the past repeating itself."

Blaise glared. "You're utterly unscrupulous."

"That's rich, coming from you." He laughed.

"What the hell do you mean?"

He folded his arms, an unbearably smug look on his face. "It occurred to me that I might not be the only one who has something to hide."

She froze. "I have no idea what you're talking about."

Charlie let her wait, taking his time while he drank more champagne. "I assumed that with your pathetic background, you might be guilty of a transgression or two yourself. And, as you're aware, I know the value of a good private detective."

Blaise's thoughts flew to the trilby-wearing figure she'd kept coming across, the shadowy presence she'd glimpsed in doorways and at street corners. "You had me followed, didn't you?"

"From the beginning." He nodded. "When I heard Rule had spent the night in Sir Ernest's flat, I knew that meant you'd let him into your bed. Not really as pure as the driven snow yourself, are you?"

A malicious smile spread across his face. "Naturally, I didn't confine my investigations to London. I had Father's man in Australia thoroughly examine your past."

Blaise took a sharp breath. Charlie looked unnervingly sure of himself.

"I'll put this very simply. If you try to expose me, Blaise, I'll make sure that the police know you murdered a man in cold blood."

She struggled not to show her fear. "This is crazy. I've never murdered anyone!"

"Blaise, you have no idea just how crazy life can be." His voice dripped with patronizing self-assurance. "My man turned up a witness—it's amazing what you can discover if you spread enough financial inducements around. So far I've kept things calm by supplying him with cash, but I can let him off the leash any time I choose."

"Those anonymous letters—"

"Unsettled you, did they?" Charlie laughed, pleased with himself.

"There's a boy by the name of Joe Blackett," he added. "For some reason, Rule is close to his family. I believe young Joe's in the frame as well. This witness is prepared to swear on the Bible that he saw the two of you engaged in an illegal narcotics deal. Things got out of hand, and five minutes later there's a man called Paddy Ryan lying dead on the ground. Oh, and you were the one holding the bloody knife in your hand. I only need to say the word, and the fellow will make a sworn statement."

Blaise sat down slowly on a nearby chair. All the fight had left her.

"Luckily," Charlie continued, "you're a beautiful woman. Sexy, too." He looked her up and down. "That night at Beech Hall I caught quite a good look at what you have to offer."

"I'm never going to sleep with you," Blaise said between gritted teeth.

"What are you talking about?" he leered. "There is such a thing as conjugal rights. Once we're married, you'll please me whenever I feel like it."

Blaise flushed. "You heard what I said. There's no way I'll be marrying you!"

"You have no alternative." He crossed the room and hauled Blaise to her feet. "At least as Adam's already had you, I won't have to break you in," he murmured while gripping her shoulders. "As a matter of fact . . ." He slowly ran the fingers of one hand down the front of her blouse. "I've been wondering if he's taught you any interesting tricks. I'm broad-minded, you know. You could try them out on me."

"God, you're a pig," Blaise hissed.

"Hear me out," he said in the same silky tone. "Remember, if you marry me, I can make all your unpleasant past disappear. And you'll never have to work again—as you well know, I wouldn't hear of it. Naturally, I'll pay for your frocks and so on, as long as they meet with my approval, but you won't have any money of your own."

Charlie stepped back, crossing his arms in front of himself. "So, what's it to be, eh? The future Lady Bennington, wife of a distinguished man who could well rise to the very top—or a piece of trash doing life in prison? I can't see how you'll be able to help dear little Ivy then, let alone your penniless parents. Of course," he said with a show of benevolence, "if you marry me, I'd be prepared to be generous." He paused for a moment, allowing his words to sink in. "However you look at it," he said, "the choice doesn't seem very difficult."

Blaise stared at Charlie in disbelief. She had to hand it to him. He was supremely gifted: a brilliant, scheming double-dealer who'd placed her in an impossible position. There was no way out now. The walls were closing in.

"You're the most devious human being I've ever come across," she whispered.

Charlie looked as if she'd given him a compliment.

"All that gossip about your so-called friend Jack Profumo spilling classified information to Eugene Ivanov via Christine Keeler, the girlfriend they supposedly shared. None of it's true, is it? It's you who's been spreading the rumors. And the joke is, you're the one who's been passing secrets straight to the Russians by means of your own mistress."

"Jack's in my way." Charlie shrugged. "This is my opportunity to forge a fast track to the top. If the scandal's big enough, Macmillan will resign. Alec Douglas-Home might be next in line, but he doesn't have what it takes. Then it will be a case of, 'Cometh the hour, cometh the man.' As for the Russians, they do pay terribly well," he said with a self-satisfied smirk. "How do you think I've managed to hold on to the Bennington estate?"

Charlie grasped Blaise's face with one hand while dangling the front door key in front of her eyes.

"I'm letting you go now, my sweet, but remember, I won't hesitate to send that witness out to do his worst if you breathe a word of what's just passed between us. So you see, I'd think very hard before you show those photos to either your newspaper or to the police. In fact, you'd better give all the prints and the negatives to me so I can burn them. There's a good girl, as soon as you can."

She felt his grip tighten. "And don't go running off to Adam Rule, will you? Because I'll know if you do. I'm putting on an extra man or two to follow you."

Blaise's shoulders slumped. Charlie had thought of everything.

"If you make any contact with him, I'll not only expose you and your pal Joe—I'll also make sure Adam is accused of money laundering on behalf of the Ryan gang. Frankly," he said, "I don't know how he's been able to get away with it for so long.

"Even better, according to my Australian detective friend questions are being asked about a gangster's body that turned up at Bondi Beach. With any luck, Adam will be charged with that too. Just think," he jeered, "you could both end up spending the rest of your days in a cell."

Charlie released her so abruptly that she staggered. "What a long chat we've been having," he said, glancing at the grandfather clock in the corner. "It's just as well we've aired all this now, though, as I've organized a little surprise party for you tomorrow night at the 400 Club. It starts at eight-thirty. Come early though, won't you, Blaise? I'll be announcing our engagement on the dot of nine."

Blaise knew he was searching for a reaction, wanted to see a look of desperation on her face. She steeled herself, determined not to give him that satisfaction.

"There's just one last thing," he said casually. "If you don't show up, the deal's off. The consequences will be unpleasant, but"—he paused—"you'll only have yourself to blame." He grinned malevolently. "On second thoughts, maybe it would be wiser if I kept you here until the party. You could entertain me overnight."

Blaise was terrified. She desperately needed to escape from Charlie's flat. But first she'd have to come up with a strategy, one that would at least buy her the next twenty-four hours, even if right now she could see no way out of his horrific trap. She took a deep breath, tried to think. Charlie wanted a victory. Well, she'd let him know he'd won.

"Don't worry, I'll be there." She allowed herself to look beaten.

"Good. I had a feeling a girl like you would appreciate the benefits of my proposal." Charlie looked unbearably pleased with himself.

"But there is one thing that's puzzling me," Blaise said, frowning. "If you have the means to send Adam to prison, why don't you do something about it straightaway?"

Charlie shook his head. "You still don't understand, do you? It's because you, my dear little Blaise, are Adam's Achilles' heel, the one small chink in his emotional armor."

Blaise felt a new wave of dismay.

"I'd far rather Adam be out in the world," Charlie crowed, "suffering each time he sees a picture of us in the paper, runs into us somewhere or—just imagine it—learns of the successful delivery of our first child. The mere fact he will know that I alone possess the woman he loves will bring me endless satisfaction, while for Adam it will be a living hell."

He smiled. "As a matter of fact, I'm thinking of sending Mr. Rule a wedding invitation."

# CHAPTER FORTY-FOUR

Finally, she was home, cocooned in the safety of the Sloane Gardens flat. Blaise brushed wordlessly past her friends, rushed into her bedroom, and flung herself onto the bed.

Charlie had lured her into a frightening maze. No matter how often she turned over the situation in her mind, testing theories, spinning half a dozen strategies as a juggler might whirl plates, she could not discover a way out. Every plan she devised plunged to the ground and crashed.

After a restless night of dreams filled with dread and despair, Blaise heard the doorbell ring. Praying it would not be Charlie, come to gloat over their impending engagement, she was surprised to discover it was another delivery boy, who left her with a telegram.

Blaise felt the faintest rise of her spirits. The only other telegram she'd received here at the flat had been from Adam. She told herself there was no way in the world the cable could be from him, yet she couldn't quite extinguish the thought that, just perhaps, he'd decided to make contact, and at the very moment when she needed him most. She eagerly ripped open the envelope and scanned the brief message.

A scream tore from her lips. Then she crumpled to the floor.

"Blaise, what's happened?" Dora ran into the hall with Harriet following closely behind her.

Harriet helped Blaise to her feet. Dora scooped up the telegram and read it aloud.

*IVY IN HOSPITAL STOP SERIOUS STOP LETTER*
*COMING DAD*

Blaise broke down, sobbing. Despite the horror of the last twenty-four hours, nothing compared to this blow.

"You can't wait for a letter to arrive," Dora insisted, immediately taking charge. "Do your parents have a telephone?"

Blaise nodded.

"Good. You're coming inside and sitting down. Then you can write down their number and I'll dial International."

"No," Blaise said weakly. "It will cost a fortune. I couldn't afford it."

"That's what parents are for, at least, one's whose tax problems are so bad they're required to live in Monte Carlo," Dora said firmly.

"And while Dora's doing that, I'll fix you a cup of sweet milky tea." Harriet made for the kitchen. "I'd better bring you some gin while I'm at it."

Somehow, Dora managed to make the tricky connection to Australia via the international telephone operator with relative ease. As Blaise held the receiver up to her ear, she heard her father's dear, familiar voice echoing from half a world away for the first time in more than a year.

"Blaisey, is it really you?" he said. "Gee, we've missed you." Then he told her about Ivy. Having convinced herself that the exercises she'd been doing for such a long time had greatly improved her leg, she'd taken off her brace and attempted to cross Fotheringham Street alone and unaided. "All she wanted was to be like everyone else," Harry said. "A car was coming down the road and . . ."

"No, I can't bear it," Blaise whispered.

There was a silence filled by ghostly fizzes and crackles.

"By the good grace of God, Ivy wasn't hit." Just for a moment, her father sounded perfectly clear. "But as she staggered out of the way she lost her balance. The poor girl fell, struck her head on the curb, and has been unconscious ever since. She looks bad, Blaisey."

The deteriorating connection could not disguise Harry's fear. "She'll need months of round-the-clock care, but it's not covered by the government like the polio was, and we don't have the money to put Ivy in a decent place." His voice broke. "We've been through too much to lose her now."

"Don't worry, Dad," Blaise said, gripping the receiver, her knuckles white. "I'll get the money."

She was shaking when she put the phone down.

"If you can't afford an overseas phone call, how will you do that?" Harriet asked with alarm.

"By marrying Charlie." A single tear trickled down her cheek. "He'll pay for Ivy's treatment, I'm sure of it. There's nothing that will appeal to his vanity more than a big show of generosity—plus it will strengthen the hold he already has over me."

Harriet looked puzzled. "What hold?"

In a rush, Blaise told her friends the whole story—about her and Joe, and how a gangster had met with his death on a long-ago night in a quiet Enmore street. She bowed her head, avoided looking at their faces.

Dora spoke up immediately. "I'll stand by you, whatever happens."

"Me too," Harriet said.

Blaise was deeply touched by her friends' loyalty, but they couldn't help her. For the rest of her life she would be nothing but Charlie's kept creature. He held a sword of Damocles above her head, suspended by the finest of threads.

Blaise shivered. She would never, ever be free of him.

"Thank you both," she said, hugging Harriet and Dora by turn. "What you've said means the world to me. But right now I'm heading in to work. It's quiet when it's this early, and I've a lot of thinking to do."

The bitter irony, Blaise reflected as she stepped into the Tube, was that Charlie's traitorous activities had provided her with the story of a lifetime. It would have made her name—every newspaper in the world would have been chasing Blaise Hill. But, to her profound regret, this international scoop would never see the light of day.

A split second later, she felt only shame. This issue was infinitely more important than the future of her career. Countless lives would be at risk if Charlie continued to leak secret information to the Soviets. Relations between Great Britain and the United States would be irreparably damaged, allowing Khrushchev and the nuclear-armed Soviet Union to become ever more powerful. Surely it would then be only a matter of time before the USSR conquered West Berlin.

What was it Tommy Trent had told her way back in Brown's cafe? *Once you start looking the other way, you might as well give up the newspaper game.*

In her heart, Blaise knew he was right, yet if she revealed anything at all about Charlie's treason, the consequences not only for herself but also for those she loved most would be devastating. Trent might have insisted "without integrity, you're nothing," but she was in an impossible position.

Those moral principles Trent had espoused with such fervor had been overtaken by the gravest personal risk. This situation was no longer about a reporter uncovering a story, no matter how far-reaching its significance. Blaise herself had become an integral part of that story. It was all very well to talk about "crossing the line." But what happened when the line between observer and observed, formerly so defined, became blurred, distorted, bent out of shape?

She couldn't protect herself, but if only she could slip away unseen by Charlie's watchers and somehow locate Adam, she'd throw herself on his mercy and beg him for the money for Ivy. Next, she'd warn him about the likelihood of trouble. Maybe she would even have a chance to say how much she loved him. And wasn't there the slimmest possibility that together they might be able to think of a way to foil Charlie?

She left her seat on the Tube and walked toward the exit, weighed down by renewed despair. She had to stop this pointless speculation. Why would Adam help her? She'd called the man a monster, then deserted him for Charlie, all without giving him the chance to explain himself. "Face it, Hill, you've well and truly burnt your bridges," she murmured despondently as she began to trudge along Fleet Street. In any case, she had no idea where Adam lived. Agnes's letter had mentioned a vague recollection of Joe's, something about Eaton Square, but as clues went that was next to useless. Unless . . .

As Blaise arrived at *The Advocate*, she had a sudden inspiration.

"Can't keep away from me, Hill?" Johnny Norton said when she stuck her head around his door. "What are you after so early in the morning?"

Blaise took a seat. "This time I really need your help."

"I'm listening."

"Do you remember, ages ago, when we were talking about Roger Croft's high jinks in Portofino, you said *The Advocate* could find anyone?"

Norton shrugged. "So what?"

"Well, I desperately need to find someone. It's a matter of life and death—and it could lead to that Voldova scoop we've been talking about."

"Stories about national security are always tricky." Norton groped through the debris on his desk for a crumpled packet of cigarettes. "If the government slaps a D-notice on us, we won't be able to publish a bloody word." He lit up. "What the hell, it's worth a punt. Who are you looking for, where was his last address, and what does he look like?"

Blaise told him what she knew.

"Rule . . . that name rings a bell. Financier type, isn't he? Bit of a mystery man, as I recall." He blew out a cloud of smoke then coughed raucously. "How long do we have?"

"I'll need the information no later than four o'clock today if I'm to have any hope of putting a plan in place."

He frowned. "It'll be tight."

Once she was back in the newsroom, the minutes ticked by slowly. An hour passed, and then another. More and more reporters trickled in, but Blaise received no word from Norton. Eventually, she was obliged to attend a royal reception for the British Women's Institute hosted by the Queen Mother. Blaise tried to focus on Her Majesty's frock (lavender floral) and her remarks (lengthy), but found it impossible to keep her mind on the task. Finally, having consulted her wristwatch so often she'd begun to attract disapproving glances, she slipped away from Kensington Palace, hailed a passing taxi and returned to *The Advocate*.

Blaise ran to her desk, hoping she'd see a message from the chief of staff. Still nothing. In sheer frustration, she strode down the corridor. "I've asked Norton to help me find Adam," she told Harriet and Dora. "If he'll see me, and it's a big if, I'm praying he can help. At least I'll be able to warn him about Charlie's intentions."

"I thought you said Norton was a hideous oaf," Harriet said.

"He is, though I suspect that buried deep beneath that ghastly exterior beats a carefully hidden heart of gold."

Blaise began playing nervously with a lighter that had been left on the desk, clicking its flame on and off. Suddenly, she threw it down. "God, I'm such an idiot! I was forgetting that, even if Norton does track down an address, Charlie is having me watched. The minute he knows I've gone to see Adam, he'll do everything in his power—and he does have a great deal of power—to see we're charged with murder. He'll destroy us both."

"Ever fancied being a blonde?" Dora asked.

"Are you quite mad? I can't believe you're talking about hairstyles at a time like this!" Blaise snapped.

"Calm down," Dora said. "You don't want Marguerite bearing down on us, wondering why we're all in a tizz. The thing is, I've had an idea. There's a long blonde wig in the fashion cupboard I can easily trim up a bit. You could put that on, as well as this." She pointed to her own short red shift. "Then all you have to do is wear my owl glasses and, *voila!* You're no longer Blaise Hill, royal correspondent, but Pandora Fraser-Barclay-Hughes, Women's Section reporter."

"You're brilliant!" Blaise felt a tiny glimmer of hope. "But it's already past three thirty p.m., and I still don't know where Adam lives."

She returned to her desk, promising herself she wouldn't check the time again until she had finished writing her report on the Queen Mother's reception. Only then did she look up. The bold black hands of the newsroom clock were positioned at exactly four o'clock.

Blaise slumped forward, her head in her hands. Now, only a miracle would provide her with the possibility of escape.

It arrived at exactly four-twenty in the hands of Colin the copy boy. "Mr. Norton said to give you this right away," he said breathlessly.

Scrawled on a piece of paper was an address in Eaton Square.

Blaise planted a quick kiss on the astonished Colin's cheek then made a hurried return to the Women's Section. "I've got it!" she cried.

"Well, what are you waiting for?" Dora was already grappling with her zip. "In five minutes' time, you will have the singular pleasure of being me."

# CHAPTER FORTY-FIVE

Waiting for a cab on Fleet Street was agony, and when one of the creaking black vehicles did eventually pull up, Blaise was obliged to smartly elbow out of the way another reporter who'd tried to leap in front of her. Breathing hard, she sat hunched in the back seat as the cab jostled with traffic past the Savoy, inched around busy Trafalgar Square with its statues of lions and Nelson's Column, and crept through Admiralty Arch. "Hurry!" she urged the driver. By the time the cab started trundling along the Mall, dodging the tourist buses that circled the Victoria Memorial, turned right past Buckingham Palace, and climbed sluggishly up crowded Constitution Hill, her nails were digging into the palms of her hands.

Only when the excruciating trip ended and she'd finally arrived at the address in Eaton Square did Blaise realize she had no idea what she would say to Adam. But then, what did it really matter, considering he would be sure to slam the door the moment he saw her?

Flustered and horribly ill at ease, Blaise stood beneath the portico of the white four-story townhouse, trying to still her nerves. Grasping the brass door knocker, she forced herself to do no more than tap politely. Somewhere inside she thought she could hear the faint strains of Tchaikovsky being played on a gramophone, yet she received no response. Abandoning all restraint, she hammered furiously on Adam's door. Still, no one came.

"Damn, damn, damn!" It hadn't occurred to her that he might simply be out or away, that fate would decree their stars would fail to align.

Crushed, she was turning to go when the door swung open. It was Adam, his dark hair tousled, his white cotton shirt hanging undone. The thought struck her that he might have just wrested himself away from a woman. She stared at him, her blue eyes filled with anguish. He looked at her, obviously shaken, but she couldn't read his expression.

"Blaise? What the hell are . . ." He frowned. "You'd better come inside."

Blaise was so overcome that she couldn't say a word as she followed him into an elegant sitting room with a white marble fireplace and contemporary paintings on the walls.

"I apologize for my appearance," he said stiffly. "I've only just returned from Australia and—"

"No, I'm the one who looks strange." Blaise pulled off her wig and glasses.

"And you're here . . . why, exactly?"

Adam's unyielding reserve was devastating. She'd rather walk barefoot over broken glass than endure this cool formality. "Adam, please," she begged. "Be angry with me. Yell, scream, swear at me. I deserve it. But don't act as if we never meant anything to each other."

She saw something flicker in his eyes.

"I am so very sorry," she said in a rush. "You were right. Charlie Ashton poisoned me against you with his lies. I've only just discovered the truth, but now I'm in terrible trouble."

Adam gestured toward a sofa covered in black suede. "Sit down and tell me what you have to say," he said evenly.

Her voice trembled as she gave the briefest version of events she could, finishing with Ivy's horrific accident. Adam stayed leaning against the neo-classical mantelpiece, his eyes never straying from her face.

Blaise stood up when she finished. "That's it, the whole awful story," she said shakily. She felt immensely sad. Seeing Adam again only reminded her of the brief happiness she'd shared with him. Now she knew there was no hope. Everything that had once been whole and perfect was destined to remain shattered.

"Look, you probably want me to leave," she said, her head down. "There's no reason why you should help, let alone forgive me. But, before I do, I want you to know"—she raised her despairing eyes to his—"that I have never, ever stopped loving you."

"Blaise." Adam's voice broke as he said her name. A moment later he had crossed the room, she was folded in his arms and he was kissing her tenderly.

"I wish to God I'd known what was going on," he said, stroking her hair. "I was too damned proud and in too much pain. When you said you were marrying Charlie my world collapsed, I felt so abandoned and so deeply betrayed. I'd experienced it all before; every one of my defenses kicked in. I should have gone after you, forced you to listen to me."

He groaned. "Instead, I took off for Queensland and headed to the mine. I pretty much worked night and day, and tried not to feel anything. I wasn't very successful." His eyes misted. "I thought I'd go mad, thinking about you."

As Adam held her tightly, the heartache Blaise had carried with her for so long was replaced by a sweet euphoria. Yet even this was tinged with fear. Because of Charlie's devious scheming, she was perilously close to losing Adam all over again.

"My wretched temper didn't help," Blaise said softly. "But mostly, I was in way over my head. I thought I was worldly, but I didn't understand anything."

"You're far from the first person to be taken in by Charlie Ashton." Adam's mouth narrowed to a firm line.

"And now he has power over both of us."

"I wouldn't be so sure of that. There are people in this country with infinitely more authority than Charlie."

Blaise was at a loss. "Who do you mean?"

"Surely you haven't forgotten. Martin Charteris told me himself he'd given you a special, private telephone number."

"I memorized it straightaway." She shrugged. "Faces, names, numbers . . . it's what reporters do. But how could a Palace courtier possibly help with a situation like this?"

"He can relay the treachery you've uncovered to someone who may well assist a great deal. Remember, behind all that royal pomp and pageantry you report on every day lies a source of very real power."

He took her hand. "You must ring Martin, darling—it's the only way out of this nightmare—but not from here. This is a matter of national security, and from what you've told me, I can't guarantee my line isn't tapped."

He quickly laid out a set of directions. "I hate to send you off alone, but I can't risk Charlie's watchers recognizing me. Which means you'd better disguise yourself again." He handed her Dora's glasses and the blonde wig. "I couldn't bear it if anything happened to you."

Blaise followed Adam to his back door. "Be careful," he said.

With her pulse beating quickly, she turned right into Eaton Mews. Forcing herself not to run, she walked briskly past a long row of garages that would once have held horses and carriages until she reached the next intersection. On the left-hand corner of the street stood one of London's famous red telephone booths.

Blaise looked around quickly. To her dismay, she saw a suspicious-looking man in a gray raincoat loitering nearby, a woman with her hair in an untidy bun who seemed engaged in nothing better than guarding a trolley of shopping, and a lanky boy doing something or other to the bell on his green bicycle. Any one of them could have been in Charlie's employ. She would simply have to risk it. Attempting to appear as if she hadn't a care in the world, Blaise opened the door of the booth, dropped some change into a silver slot, and called the number she'd been handed at the Queen's Garden Party.

She took a deep breath. The phone rang once, twice, three times before, to her immense relief, she heard a voice say, "Charteris."

"It's Blaise Hill."

"Miss Hill." His diction was crisp and precise. "As you have rung this number, I'm assuming you wish to alert me to some kind of trouble."

"Dire trouble." Blaise rapidly informed him of the evidence proving that the Honorable Charles Ashton, Assistant Minister for War, was betraying Great Britain. "Mr. Charteris," she added, "I'm sorry, but if immense damage is to be prevented, the matter needs to be dealt with urgently."

"Her Majesty will be advised immediately. I can assure you, the appropriate quarter will be warned. And Miss Hill . . ."

"Yes?"

"I am grateful for your continued service to the Crown."

The meeting they were summoned to at number 10 Downing Street was brief. Apart from her and Adam, only Harold Macmillan and the heavy-browed director general of MI5, Sir Roger Hollis, were present. Blaise recounted her story once again, then drew Cecil's pictures out of her briefcase before spreading them over the prime minister's desk.

Macmillan's demeanor was that of a tired man grappling with events he could no longer either control or comprehend. He began by stressing that he very much hoped "this appalling Ashton affair" would never become known to the public.

"There's a Russian about to defect, name of Anatoliy Golitsyn," he said. "He's offered to identify a number of British double agents and Kim Philby may well be among them—the very man I personally cleared in the House of Commons!"

He began to knead his temples. "I'm spending my nights worrying about how many more of the buggers are out there."

The prime minister topped up his whisky from a cut-glass decanter. "If that wasn't sufficient cause for alarm," he said gloomily, "I also have the damned uncomfortable feeling that, sooner or later, this Profumo business is going to blow up."

Macmillan picked up the prints with a look of distaste. "Fortunately, Sir Roger has assured me that MI5 is well equipped to take care of Charles Ashton." He looked at Hollis, who nodded briefly. "I have instructed him to handle the situation swiftly and, above all, with discretion."

Macmillan rose to his feet. "Miss Hill, Mr. Rule, I'm going to leave you in Sir Roger's capable hands." He picked up a sheaf of papers. "And by the way, as far as I'm concerned, this meeting never happened."

At precisely ten minutes past eight, Blaise walked into the 400 Club wearing both a significant amount of Shalimar perfume and a tightly swathed emerald green cocktail dress held up by only the narrowest of straps. Her hair was piled loosely on top of her head, she had on her tallest stilettos and her mouth was a luscious-pink pout.

Charlie leaned against the bar in a private section roped off with red cord, sipping a whisky. "So you've come," he said, smirking. "I rather thought you would." His gaze swept over the curves of her figure. "And what a delectable sight you are."

Blaise hid her revulsion. It had struck her that Charlie also possessed an Achilles' heel—he was enchanted by his own clever-ness. Tonight, she would play to his overwhelming conceit.

"I have to hand it to you, Charlie, you have me in a corner," she said. "Although, as you pointed out, being the next Lady Ben-nington will have its compensations."

"I'm glad you've come to your senses." Charlie preened.

"You frightened me with that talk about prison, though."

"It's always an option."

Blaise could see how much he was relishing the prospect of her forever dancing to his tune. She gave him an uncertain smile. "I decided I'd better do something to persuade you that wouldn't be a good idea."

"What did you have in mind?" His eyes darted toward her.

"I reserved the Director's Suite. I'm going up there now, be-fore the guests start to arrive here at the bar. I know we won't have long, but if you come up a few minutes after me, well, as you've already pointed out, I'm not exactly a vestal virgin." She paused, letting the moment stretch. "Let's just say I'll do everything I can to please you."

"Christ, Blaise, I knew that good girl act was a masquerade," Charlie said delightedly.

She gave him a wicked smile. "You have no idea just how bad I can be."

Blaise had to wait for only two and a half minutes before she heard a knock on the door. Charlie was really incredibly vain, she thought. No wonder the Soviets found it so easy to set him up in a honey trap—and how satisfying to be using exactly the same tactics against him.

"Do hurry, Charlie," she urged him. "I've a surprise waiting."

He burst in, already panting, then stopped in his tracks.

"Evening, Charles," Adam said from a chair in the corner.

"Mr. Ashton." Sir Roger's acknowledgment was delivered from a chesterfield sofa.

"What the hell is going on?" Charlie blustered. "You two," he turned toward Blaise and Adam, "are finished. And as for you, Hollis, I'll have your hide for this trick. Don't you worry—the PM will hear all about it."

"Actually, Mr. Ashton," Hollis said, unperturbed, "it was Mr. Macmillan who insisted I attend this little gathering. Do sit down." He indicated a seat. "We're going to have a chat."

Glowering, Charlie flung himself into the chair drawn up opposite.

"Now, there's no need to worry about your guests. The club's manager has been informed that you've been called away on urgent political business. He'll sort everything out."

"What is it you want?" Charlie said coldly. He might be trying to maintain his authority, but his jiggling foot told Blaise he was rattled.

"Surprisingly little, under the circumstances." Hollis made a show of consulting his notebook. "Mr. Ashton, we know all about your corrupt arrangement with Miss Voldova. There's plenty of photographic proof"—he indicated several prints set out on the coffee table in front of him—"of a very high quality."

Charlie went to speak, but Hollis held up his hand.

"This is what the PM has requested. You will resign immediately from Parliament, claiming a previously undiagnosed medical condition—I'd be as vague as possible if I were you." He drank from a glass of iced water. "Then all you need do is retire to the country and try to live a quiet, decent life."

Blaise was disgusted. So this was how outrageous criminal acts committed by one of their own were dealt with by the British establishment. Men like Charlie received the merest tap on the wrist before they were permitted to fade respectably into the background with their reputations intact.

"Naturally," Hollis continued, "in addition to an extensive interrogation, MI5 will keep you under indefinite surveillance. The security service will know who you're meeting, when, where, and much else besides."

Charlie swore under his breath.

"Frankly, you should be delighted you're getting off so lightly. Of course," Hollis said as he gathered up the pictures, "if you don't do the right thing, the PM, MI5, and, indeed, Special Branch will adopt a very different attitude. As you would be aware, the penalties for treason are quite harsh in this country. Do we understand each other, Mr. Ashton?"

Charlie's face was ashen. "Perfectly," he said.

"Very well. Sign this. It's your letter of resignation to the prime minister." Hollis handed over a pen.

Blaise watched as Charlie signed his name without hesitation.

"Mr. Ashton," Hollis continued, "outside this door are two MI5 officers named Heath and Rivers. They will immediately escort you out of these premises and into a waiting car. Miss Hill and Mr. Rule will follow behind."

"Why on earth is that?" Charlie protested.

"Unfinished business, I believe."

"Well, at least tell me where I'm going."

"I'm sorry—I thought I'd made that clear. You will be taken straight to Beech Hall."

There was a pleading note in Charlie's voice Blaise had never heard before. "Please, you must let me telephone my father. If we arrive in the middle of the night the poor man will think it's an invasion."

Hollis passed him the phone. "Make it brief."

The call was answered quickly. "Father?" Charlie said. "That's right, it's me. Look, I realize it's late, but I'm afraid I need to come home straightaway—and I won't be alone."

# CHAPTER FORTY-SIX

Andy was parked behind the 400 Club, outside the small theatrical agency where Blaise had asked him to wait with the Jaguar. Once she and Adam were inside the car, she quickly introduced the two men then gave Andy a brief rundown of the night's events.

"Well, me old china," he said, "it looks like you got what you wanted."

"I hope so." Blaise frowned. She wondered if everything had proceeded just a little too smoothly. Charlie still had the ammunition he needed to make a great deal of trouble.

"You look exhausted," Adam said, his voice low and warm. "We have a good two hours or so before we reach Beech Hall. Why not make the most of it and rest?"

Blaise pulled off her high heels, groped in her bag and then slipped on her favorite suede flats before settling back. The Jaguar's leather seats were as soft as they were comfortable, and the thought of resting her weary head on Adam's shoulder was immensely appealing . . . but not yet. One more task lay ahead.

She reopened her bag. "Agnes Blackett said I was to give you this," she said, handing over the eighteen-year-old letter she'd been keeping for him.

Switching on the overhead light, Blaise added, "And she insisted that I read it, too."

It was nearing midnight when Blaise caught sight of Beech Hall. Without the sun's rays warming the stone walls, its formerly welcoming appearance had been transformed into something more menacing. Even the yellow roses had become sinister and cloying.

The MI5 car that had brought Charlie was waiting when the Jaguar pulled up by the fountain which someone—a gardener most likely—had turned off, so that it stood looking parched and neglected. Andy and Rivers both opted to stay with their vehicles. The others walked into the house.

"Hello!" Charlie called out loudly as soon as they entered the hall. "I'm here!"

A few minutes later Mrs. Coote appeared. Her cardigan had been fastened with the wrong buttons and there was a solitary overlooked roller still caught up in her gray hair. Frowning, she led Blaise and Adam, Heath, who was tall and sported an American-style crew cut, and a disgruntled-looking Charlie into the drawing room.

Lord Bennington, resplendent in a plush burgundy smoking jacket, was in front of the fireplace, nursing a neat whisky. He turned round abruptly. "Charlie, my boy, this is a welcome surp—" He stopped, a look of bewilderment on his face. "I don't understand. What the blazes is Adam doing here? And these others, who are they?"

The clink of glassware broke the silence that followed as Mrs. Coote returned to the room with a tray bearing tumblers and a decanter of whisky. "I thought your guests might appreciate a nightcap, my lord." She set down the tray on a table. "If you require nothing more, I'll retire for the night."

Heath cleared his throat. After informing Lord Bennington that he worked for MI5, he set out the reasons for Charlie's sudden resignation and subsequent banishment with a detached, clinical precision.

Bennington sat down heavily in an armchair. "Son?" he asked unsteadily. "Is he telling the truth?"

"I have nothing to add," was all Charlie said. He'd taken up his father's place by the fire, where he stood with his arms crossed and a surly expression on his face.

Bennington threw back the rest of his whisky, then poured himself another. "Nothing?" he said disbelievingly. "Nothing at all?"

Charlie shook his head.

"However, I do." Adam spoke for the first time. He held out Emilia's letter.

Bennington paled.

"I see you recognize the hand," Adam said coldly. "My mother wrote to me shortly before she died, but I received her letter only this evening. It's taken a long time, but at least now I know what really went on at Beech Hall—and the true identity of my father."

"I knew it wasn't that stonemason," Charlie burst out. "The woman was a slut."

"Shut up, Charlie. You know nothing about this," Bennington shouted. "Emilia was an angel."

Blaise took one of a pair of club chairs located in a dim corner. She felt wretched for Adam, dismayed there was nothing she could do to help him. But this was family business, the airing of private secrets and sorrow.

Adam's icy tone only made his anger more palpable. "That didn't stop you forcing yourself on her, did it? Your own cousin, the ward you'd sworn to protect."

Bennington crumpled, his body folding in upon itself as a moan escaped from his lips.

Adam turned toward Charlie. "You were right about one thing," he said with a bitter smile. "That stonemason story was pure fantasy. Our father—ironic isn't it, to think we are actually brothers—paid a tradesman named George Rule to go through a sham marriage."

"You're lying!" Charlie spluttered.

Bennington looked up, his expression somber. "It's true."

"You ruined my mother's life," Adam said scathingly.

"I offered her a home," Bennington cried. "I wanted to take care of her—and you."

Adam looked at his father with contempt. "What, you actually expected Emilia to dwell happily under the same roof as the man who raped her? Or did you think how convenient it would be to keep her close at hand, so you could continue your assaults whenever the urge took you?"

Blaise had never seen Adam's eyes as hard. There was no indication of the turmoil she had witnessed when he'd first read Emilia's letter on the way to Beech Hall. He'd been shocked then, assailed by grief for his mother. Blaise had held him in her arms as he shook with emotion.

"Because of you, this 'angel' you talk about felt safe only after she'd escaped far beyond your reach. Christ almighty"—for a moment, Adam's control faltered—"my mother was still in her teens when she fled. Can you even begin to imagine what sort of life she led? No wonder she died when I was still a child."

"You returned to me," Bennington murmured.

Adam made no attempt to hide his disgust. "What you mean is, you had me shipped over to England. Then you spent years trying to make a proper English gentleman out of me, and nearly succeeded, too, until it all went horribly wrong."

"At Cambridge."

"That's right." Adam paused. "Because Charlie is exactly like you: a degenerate coward who raped a defenseless girl, then compounded his crime by blaming it on an innocent man."

Bennington choked on his whisky. "What?! Charlie, is that right? Was it really you?"

Charlie shrugged.

"My God. So . . . so you mean, all along, Adam was telling the truth?" Bennington said slowly, staring into his empty glass.

Even though watching on from the corner, Blaise could see how shaken the man was.

Adam sat down on a sofa. "But you refused to listen." For the first time his face reflected the depth of his pain. "I still remember the day you threw me out of Beech Hall. I swore I'd never return."

Blaise fought back her tears. After all he had endured, it was little wonder Adam had been so closed and wary, so reluctant to speak about his past. Then she'd made everything infinitely worse by wrongly accusing him and deserting him herself. She'd acted in exactly the same reprehensible way as his father had done.

Bennington poured himself a fresh glass of whisky with a trembling hand. "I loved Emilia, desired her to the point of obsession. One night, I went for a stroll and came upon her, alone in the Temple of Venus. I . . . I couldn't help myself."

Charlie clutched at his chest as if suddenly winded.

Bennington sighed. "When you reappeared, Adam, looking so like your mother, it felt like a chance to make up for what I'd done. I was determined you'd receive all the advantages Charlie enjoyed. After all, you were also my son."

"But that didn't go further than paying for Eton and Cambridge, did it?" Adam's eyes darkened to a pewter shade. "At the time I needed you the most, you turned your back on me."

Bennington's voice dropped. "You're right. The college authorities, Olivia's parents—they all followed my lead," he said in an agonized tone, "and I didn't lift a finger to help you." He shook his head. "You'd been conceived in violence: I thought it had poisoned you. But all along it was Charlie who'd inherited my perverse nature. Can you ever forgive me?" He searched Adam's strained face, waiting tensely for an answer.

But Adam didn't reply.

# CHAPTER FORTY-SEVEN

"Look here, Heath," Charlie muttered. "I need to use the lavatory. That is, if you'll permit me to visit the WC in my own home." Now that he was in Beech Hall, a touch of his old bravado was back on show.

Heath was as cool as ever. "I will accompany you, sir," he said, "and wait outside the door."

"Good Lord, it's like having Nanny on duty all over again."

"Even so." Heath followed Charlie out of the room.

Lord Bennington seemed oblivious to everyone. Wrapped up in his own thoughts, he gazed at the fire, a distant expression in his eyes. Adam had taken the club chair next to Blaise. She held his hand as he spoke to her quietly.

Suddenly, Heath burst into the room. "That bloody man has escaped!" he shouted. "Quick, is there another means to get out of the downstairs cloakroom? The window's far too small for a grown man to crawl through."

Bennington looked up with a start. "There's a panel at the back of the airing cupboard," he said. "It connects with a tunnel that comes out in the coach house. My grandfather put it in when—"

But Heath was already moving. "Rule!" he called over his shoulder. "Show me the way. You know the layout of this place."

Adam raced ahead, leading Heath and Blaise across the hall, down a corridor and on through a door into a rear courtyard.

The three of them pounded across the flagstones toward the shadowy coach house, only to see a powerful black Mercedes roaring out of its open doors. "Shit!" Heath exclaimed. "All hell will break loose if that bastard gets away."

He'd barely finished speaking when Andy arrived with a screech of the Jaguar's brakes. "I heard the commotion," he said. "Thought you could do with a ride."

"Get in," Adam told Heath. "He's taken the lane the estate's workers use, but there's a shortcut through those trees on the right. If we're quick, we might be able to head him off before he reaches the open road." The pair hurled themselves into the car, immediately followed by Blaise who slammed the door shut.

"You're not leaving me behind!" she said, ignoring Adam's thunderous expression.

Andy immediately took off for the wood, tires squealing. The heavy car bumped over stones and clods of earth, its headlights illuminating the spreading branches of the beech trees hanging low overhead.

"Faster!" Heath cried. Andy accelerated. With its engine straining, the Jaguar hit a stretch of gravel, lost traction, and was suddenly airborne—just as it reached the junction with the service lane.

It happened too quickly to allow for more than a split second of horror. One moment Blaise could feel the Jaguar flying forward, the next there was a juddering crash as it rammed into the side of the speeding Mercedes.

Blaise blinked. She couldn't have blacked out for more than a minute, but it must have been long enough for Charlie to crawl out of the smashed Mercedes, for now she could see him on the lane up ahead, running for his life despite a pronounced limp.

With the three men only just beginning to stir, there was no time to wait. Blaise heaved the crumpled door open and scrambled out. She would run Charlie down if it was the last thing she did. It was unlikely she could stop him entirely—with his height and weight he could easily overpower her—but if she could just slow his escape until the others caught up there was still a good chance he'd end up facing a British court.

Anger made her swift. Breathing heavily, Blaise picked up a fist-size rock as she flew down the lane. She was gaining on Charlie, could hear his uneven footsteps smack the ground and glimpse his crop of blond hair, nearly white in the moonlight. Minutes later, she was upon him.

"Charlie!" she screamed. He staggered, the shock of her sudden appearance throwing him momentarily off balance. Blaise grabbed hold of one of his flailing arms. Then she slammed the rock as hard as she could against his chin.

Blood began pouring from a jagged wound, leaving a trail of red, ragged patches down the front of his shirt. "You bitch," he grunted. He tried to shake her off, but Blaise clung on, terrier-like, and swung at him again.

She was taken by surprise when Charlie hooked his free arm around her throat. Blaise dropped the rock and tried to pull away, but his hold was so tight that just taking her next breath was a struggle. Her heart pounded wildly as he yanked a revolver out of his waistband and held it to her head.

"Put it down, Ashton," Rivers said as he emerged from the wood. The nuggety man was pointing his revolver straight at them.

Charlie bared his teeth in a snarl. "Wouldn't you say I have the upper hand?" he called out. "I'll happily shoot this tramp if you try anything. Drop your weapon, now!"

Rivers' gun landed on the ground with a thud.

"I see you left your car parked across the exit. That was kind of you," Charlie crowed. "Throw your keys to me, there's a good chap, or I'll shoot the girl."

He kept his gun trained on Blaise while he picked up the keys, quickly stowed them in his jacket, and resumed his choking hold.

"Blaise is going to drive me away." He prodded her with the steel muzzle. "If you try to stop me, I won't hesitate to put a bullet in her head. And don't think some kind of misplaced sentiment will get in my way. She's a nothing, always will be."

Blaise could feel the cold tip of the gun boring into her skull. Gasping for air, she knew her strength was beginning to ebb. Charlie had always wanted to dominate her. Now, his power was complete.

"Blaise!" She saw Adam in the distance running toward her, his face contorted by fear. Heath was next to him, a pistol in his outstretched hand.

"Get rid of that," Charlie yelled, jerking his head toward Heath, "and Rule, don't try to play the hero, will you? I've already told your friend here that I'm more than happy to kill your little whore."

Blaise could see Adam's eyes flash as he stopped, his fists clench.

"Both of you, do what he says," Rivers warned.

As the men stood by helplessly, Blaise felt Charlie begin to drag her backward, using her body to shield his. His hold was suffocating, his gun was still slammed up against her temple, and there was no possibility of a rescue. He'd trapped her again, only this time he had murder, not marriage on his mind.

Rage swept through her. She'd rather die than let Charlie use her to get safely away. He might think she was a nothing, but she'd show him exactly what Blaise Hill was capable of. Furious, she jammed her elbow into Charlie's ribs as hard as she could

There was a deafening crack as a bullet whizzed past her head. The force of her jab had made Charlie lurch back, skewing his aim and loosening his hold on her throat. But he still had the gun in his hand and she couldn't depend on a second chance. Quickly twisting around, she lashed out at him with the same vicious streetfighter's kick she'd last used in *The Advocate*'s darkroom.

Then the world exploded. Her ears filled with a great roar as she plummeted into a vast, silent black ocean.

Blaise was conscious of strong arms holding her, of a blanket around her shoulders, the scent of brandy in the air. At first she thought she was at the boathouse with Adam. But she couldn't smell the salt spray, couldn't hear the restless movement of the waves slapping against the sand. It was the crackle and hiss of the fire that told her she was at Beech Hall.

Her eyes fluttered open. Adam leaned over her, the skin across his cheekbones stretched tight and his brow lined by worry. "Thank God," he said.

"Help me to sit up," Blaise whispered, her throat swollen. She clutched at the blanket, not because she was cold but because she felt numb and disorientated. "What . . ." She tried again. "What happened? It sounded like the end of the world. Then nothing."

"I thought I'd lost you." Adam's smooth voice cracked with emotion. "I should have remembered what a fighter you are." He attempted to smile while gently tucking a strand of her hair behind her ear. "I'm not surprised you fainted, though. Charlie very nearly throttled you."

"It's hard to swallow," she rasped.

"This might help." Adam poured some sweetened tea into a mug and passed it to her.

Blaise took a sip. "Tell me the rest of it."

"Thankfully, while Andy was in the Jaguar guarding the driveway during our little chat inside the house, Rivers was staking out the estate's service exit. That's how he came to be waiting in the beech wood when Charlie tried to make his escape."

"Where's Charlie now?" Blaise asked huskily as the two MI5 men walked into the room.

"If you recall, you attacked him," Heath said drily. "He started firing but the shots went wide—not exactly surprising, after that kick you gave the man. It provided my colleague"—he turned to Rivers—"with just enough time to recover his gun and deal with the situation."

"Deal with the situation—what does that mean?" Blaise felt faint.

"Charles Ashton is dead."

Charlie, dead. He'd always been larger than life, with a deceptive ebullience that had drawn nearly everyone into his web.

Blaise forced down some more tea. She'd come so close to being his wife.

"Sir Roger has been informed," Heath continued, running his hand over his spiky hair. "All the necessary arrangements are in place."

He explained that two ambulances, one for Charlie and another for the driver of the Mercedes, had just departed, while a tow truck was taking Andy and the badly damaged Jaguar back to London.

"So Charlie had help," Blaise said, surprised. "Was this driver badly hurt?"

"Seems all right," Rivers spoke for the first time, "other than concussion and some fractured ribs." He frowned. "Although there is one unusual thing. It was a woman. Dark-haired, good-looking."

Blaise glanced at Adam. "Voldova," she said.

"We had a feeling Ashton might try something," Rivers added, "after Sir Roger told us about the phone call he made from the 400 Club. The look on his Lordship's face when he saw Charlie walk into the drawing room was enough to confirm our suspicions."

"Ashton had rung his Soviet handler." Heath was speaking again. "When he said he needed to 'come home straightaway' he wasn't referring to Beech Hall. He meant Mother Russia."

"How can you be so sure?" Blaise asked.

"The false passport and the one-way ticket to Moscow in the Mercedes' glove compartment didn't leave much room for doubt."

"Did you find anything else?"

"Just one other item," Rivers said. "Curious, really. It was a sapphire-studded pendant in the shape of a heart."

# CHAPTER FORTY-EIGHT

The slender ray of sunshine streaming through the narrow space that separated the two damask curtains played across Blaise's face. She was lying beneath a gossamer canopy with one of Adam's arms still wrapped around her. Somewhere outside in the grounds of Beech Hall, a robin was warbling. Despite the terrible events of the previous night, she'd enjoyed the deepest sleep she'd had for months. Blaise felt a pleasurable ripple of anticipation. The combination of her narrow escape from Charlie's deadly embrace and Adam's heady presence was exhilarating. On a day like this, anything was possible.

"Good morning, beautiful," she heard Adam say. He leaned across and pinched her upper arm.

"Ouch!"

"Sorry, darling," he said with a grin, "but I had to make sure you were real. For a moment there I thought I was back in the desert and you were a hallucination."

"Well, don't keep checking." Blaise wrinkled her nose. "Otherwise I'll be black and blue." She stretched, yawning. "Yesterday was without a doubt the longest day of my life."

"I hope you're feeling better," Adam said. His light-hearted expression failed to erase the concern in his eyes. "MI5 might have been impressed by the fight you put up—so was I, by the way—but I was still terrified at the thought of what that lunatic might do."

Blaise's eyes clouded. "I just wish I'd worked things out much earlier. Maybe then this nightmare would never have happened."

Adam stroked her cheek. "You couldn't possibly have known what sort of man Charlie was. I should have forced you to let me explain."

Blaise sighed. "I hate to say it, but I wouldn't have paid any attention. Charlie knew exactly how to manipulate me."

She took Adam's hand. "Thank God I finally woke up to him, even though I nearly lost everything—including you—in the process."

"Last night I wanted to talk about my feelings for you," Adam said with a smile. "I remember that's what you asked me to do back at the Knightsbridge flat. But you fell asleep before I had a chance to say that I missed you horribly every single day we were apart. And, just in case you're wondering," he said in his mellow voice, "once I'd held you in my arms there was no one else. I only wanted you. I still can't believe I'm actually lying next to the woman who has been occupying my dreams."

"Well, don't go pinching me again," Blaise said, making a face.

"Actually, I have quite a different plan." He began kissing her neck. "Now that I've established you're flesh and blood . . ."

"Not here," Blaise whispered. "Not in this place."

"Then I think we should leave for Eaton Square straightaway."

"I'm afraid I can't do that either. I've some work to deal with first."

Blaise went to the wardrobe and slipped on Adam's shirt before sitting down on the edge of the bed. She picked up the phone on the table beside her and immediately dialed Johnny Norton's direct number.

"Chief of Staff," he answered gruffly.

"It's Hill. You know that story about Voldova and a British traitor we've been talking about?" Despite her fizzing excitement, Blaise tried to keep her voice steady.

"Are you saying you've got something for me?"

"I am, and the scandal's even bigger than we thought. It's going to rock the government, just like you said—and it's ours exclusively for the next twenty-four hours." Blaise paused. "Do you have anyone reliable who can take it down?"

"Yeah, me."

"Don't tell me you still remember how to do shorthand." She stifled a giggle.

"That's enough lip, Hill. Just give it to me, will you?"

She began dictating the story: "The Honorable Charles Ashton, Assistant Minister for War, died last night while attempting to flee to Moscow after MI5 agents discovered he was a Soviet spy—"

"Jesus!" Norton exclaimed. "I wasn't expecting your bloody boyfriend would turn out to be the mole. Go on."

"In a dramatic shootout, Mr. Ashton was killed in the grounds of Beech Hall, the Cotswolds estate belonging to his father, Lord Bennington . . ."

Although Blaise hadn't made a single note, she dictated the entire story effortlessly.

"This is sensational, Hill," Norton exclaimed. "Every newspaperman on Fleet Street will be wondering how the hell we've got hold of a scoop like this. The House of Commons will be in an uproar and the Yanks will be beside themselves—not to mention the PM. It'll be the beginning of the end for Macmillan." Blaise could hear him smacking his lips with satisfaction.

"There's more," she said. "During his escape, Ashton held me hostage with a gun to my head."

"*What?*"

Blaise could imagine Norton's gleeful smile, the way his buttons would be straining across his belly as he leaned forward eagerly over his notebook.

"Well, give it to me," he said. "We'll run that separately, stick 'An eyewitness account by our on-the-spot reporter' at the top of it."

Blaise rattled the piece off. Then she said, "Will I be getting a byline on both stories?"

She listened as Norton sucked on a cigarette. "Christ, I'm

happy to put your name on the flipping crossword if you keep delivering news like this."

"Sounds good," she said, frowning with concentration. "Maybe you could get someone onto the PM's office for a quote. It's worth doing a recap on Burgess and Maclean's escape to Russia, too, with a bit about Macmillan's questionable defense of Kim Philby. From all accounts, Philby's been in bed with the Russians for years."

"Yeah, yeah, you don't need to tell me how to do my job, Hill," Norton growled. "By the way, what did your new pals at MI5 say about the pictures?"

"We can't run anything that shows secrets being passed, though the rest are all right. Sorry if I'm stepping out of line again, but—"

"But bloody what?" Blaise could tell Norton was in a hurry to get her stories typed up and sent to the subs.

"I'd tell Ben and Mike to get into the darkroom and develop some more prints as soon as they can. A couple of undercover blokes who call themselves Heath and Rivers will be in to collect all the negatives before the end of the morning. And Norton?"

"What now, Hill?"

"I'll give you a number where you can reach me."

"And that would be because . . . ?"

"I won't be in for a couple of days."

# CHAPTER FORTY-NINE

Blaise barely noticed the landscape she was passing through. She had a hazy impression of green and gold farmland and scattered townships, of traveling down highways and crossing bridges, but she was aware only of how much she longed to be alone with Adam. It was maddening to be so near to him and yet still be constrained by the official MI5 limousine with its official MI5 driver.

One look at Adam told her he felt the same way. She covered his hand with her own and mouthed the word, "Soon."

When the car eventually pulled up in Eaton Square they exchanged a quick glance. Blaise stepped out first and Adam followed rapidly. A moment later they were inside his front door.

"At last," he said, holding her tightly as he buried his face in her hair. "Blaise . . ."

"Yes?" Her stomach fluttered.

"I'm taking you upstairs."

By the time they reached the bedroom they were already half undressed. Adam had unzipped Blaise's green frock while kissing her hungrily. She'd unbuttoned most of his shirt and undone his trousers. Both kicked off their shoes. Blaise slipped out of her lacy briefs. Then Adam drew her down onto a deep-blue Persian rug.

There was no languorous stroking or unhurried caressing. They had yearned for each other for too long. Blaise was swiftly engulfed by Adam's passion, far more intense, wilder and deeper than before, until he gripped her, shuddering, and she felt a heady rush of sensation.

Then Adam kissed her again and again, cradling her in his

arms as their breathing slowed. "I'm sorry, darling. I hope I wasn't too, um, eager," he said, looking endearingly bashful.

"Couldn't you tell I wasn't objecting?" Blaise smiled. "Although I have to admit," she rubbed one of her shoulders, "I've had enough of being on this rug. Let's take a shower."

They stood facing each other beneath the jets of cascading water. He was gentle now. Hands slick with soap, he glided the tips of his fingers along her collar bones and over her breasts. "I cannot tell you how inviting you look," he said. "You should spend much more time naked, preferably dripping wet."

Blaise reached up and lathered Adam's tapered back, then slid her hands across the well-defined muscles on his chest and down his lean torso. "Seems like it's time for us to dry off and try out an actual bed," she murmured.

Languid and warm, they stretched out on the cool linen sheets. "You know, I've always thought you were remarkable." Adam kissed the hollow at the base of her neck. "I just didn't realize *how* remarkable."

"So, worth waiting for, then?" Blaise asked, propping herself up on one elbow. "I mean, despite my terrible temper, which I'm sorry to say, you've seen in full flight."

"Come here," Adam said with a grin. "Perhaps I should make sure about that."

Now, they made love slowly and sweetly, each intent on delighting the other until Adam said, "Blaise, what you're doing to me right now is almost unbearably wonderful, but I don't want to rush things again."

She paid no attention.

"Fair warning, darling." He groaned. "If you don't stop I can't be held responsible for my actions."

"All right, you win," Blaise said with a pout. "I won't do a thing."

A delicious tension coiled within her as Adam's lips found her tender nipples and his hands began to caress the soft inner sides of her thighs. When his fingers drifted toward that most exquisitely sensitive part of her, she shivered with pleasure. "This was a very good idea," she whispered.

And then neither of them wanted to delay any longer. Adam was taking his weight on his elbows and kissing her; she was grasping his broad shoulders and wrapping her legs around his hips. Yet, even as they moved in a thrilling rhythm, still he controlled his desire until the moment came when she cried out and together they were consumed by a fierce joy.

They didn't leave the house that day. Adam brought up chilled Bollinger from the kitchen then went back for dark chocolate truffles, figs, and purple grapes. They ate and drank, exchanged stories and shared confidences. Blaise told Adam about her family, shedding tears when she spoke about Ivy. He described his mother and a childhood spent surrounded by the red Queensland desert.

They spent hours discovering each other's bodies, Adam delighting in Blaise's soft curves and smooth planes, Blaise tracing the outline of his shoulders and the hard contours of his chest.

Night had fallen when Adam reached for her hand. "I'm a little concerned you might think I'm only interested in keeping you in bed for as long as possible." He smiled.

"Now, what would have given me that impression?" Blaise said, her blue eyes impish.

Adam became serious. "I'm crazy about your mind and your spirit. Plus you have this knack of demolishing every emotional barricade I've ever had. Both of us have grown up in rough places. We've learned to live, even excel in new worlds, but do you think—"

She interrupted him with a kiss. "Let's talk later," she whispered. "And this time, *I'm* in charge."

There it was, propped up against the coffee pot. As Blaise devoured the breakfast of fresh orange juice, toast, and scrambled eggs Adam had whipped up, she stared at the front page of *The Advocate*. Finally, a scoop she hadn't been forced to sneak into the paper under someone else's name, a scoop in which not a single fact could be disputed. After all her setbacks and crushing disappointments, she'd actually done it. Blaise swore to herself that, no matter where life took her, she would never again let anyone undermine her.

Charlie Ashton might have been protected by privilege and social position, he might have blinded everyone with his charm and cleverness, but she, Blaise Hill, from a place he'd described as "a bloody Sydney gutter," had been the one to publicly unmask and shame him, and in the best way she knew—through the pages of a newspaper. No doubt there'd be others who would follow in his treacherous footsteps, but if she could take Charlie down then no one was untouchable.

Adam poured them both some coffee. "Just as well I took the phone off the hook," he said, buttering a piece of toast. "It's impossible to make a good breakfast when there are constant interruptions from hordes of people, every one of them insisting they speak to *The Advocate*'s new ace reporter."

"You would make some lucky boss a wonderful secretary." Blaise grinned.

"Well, I'm certainly getting in some practice. So far you've had invitations to appear on the BBC, speak on the radio and, at last count, there've been job offers from at least three other newspapers. Even the American television networks have been ringing." He sipped some coffee. "All this attention being paid to my beautiful, clever girl makes me feel even luckier that I have you all to myself—at least for the next twenty-four hours."

Adam leaned across the table and kissed away the crumbs at the corners of her mouth. "Speaking of which, I've been thinking about how you might like to spend the day. Does looking at a few paintings then a late lunch at Claridge's sound good to you?"

"Ordinarily, I'd say it sounded perfect. Except, after so much drama, what I'd really like most is to swing by my flat, throw on some jeans and go for a long walk in a park. We'd better not make it Green Park, though—that seems to have an unfortunate effect on me."

"Have you ever been to Kew Gardens?" Adam asked.

"Not yet."

"Right then, that's settled. You'll love it."

By the time they had admired the ten Chinese roofs of the soaring Great Pagoda, inhaled the fragrance of the sprawling rose beds and then wandered through the vast glass-domed Palm House with its rainforest set amid humid clusters of orchids and ferns, Blaise was dragging her feet.

"Gosh," she said, rubbing her eyes, "I'm suddenly incredibly tired."

Adam kissed her just beneath her left ear. "I can't say I'm surprised."

After propping themselves up against the cracked trunk of an oak tree, they gulped some of the water and ate the apples they'd brought with them. "I'm glad we've stopped," Adam said. "There are things I need to explain to you."

"The Ryans?"

He nodded.

"I was wondering when you might tell me about them." She looked up at the pale, clear sky and waited.

"I'm not excusing myself," he began. "But I was only twenty when I was flung out of Cambridge—which I'd loved—and sent packing by my father. I was penniless, hostile, and bitterly resentful."

A sharp breeze had begun to blow, its chill the first hint of winter.

"Once I'd worked my passage back to Australia, all I wanted to do was lash out at the world, and make enough money so I'd never be dependent on anyone," he said, glancing at Blaise.

"Funnily enough, I met Theo Ryan because I'd tracked Agnes down. She was about the only person in my life I trusted by then, even though I hadn't seen her since I was a boy. After she'd filled me up with her homemade meat pies, Joe's dad invited me out for a beer."

He paused while a couple of children ran by chasing a ball. "Pete Blackett's always been fond of a drink and he's mad for the horses. He knew Theo was dabbling in SP bookmaking and was down at the pub taking bets." Adam shrugged. "Theo was looking for someone with a knack for numbers. Turned out we were a match made in heaven.

"He was good to me, taught me a lot about the way the world works, not that he didn't slap me down when he thought I needed it. I suppose he became the father I'd never had."

Blaise hugged her knees to her chest. It was cold now, but she didn't want Adam to stop.

"Theo figured out pretty quickly that he wasn't fully exploiting my talents. By the time I was twenty-one, I was handling most of the Ryan family's considerable cash flow."

"And now?" Blaise asked, trying not to reveal her anxiety.

"I'm not proud that I spent over three years of my life enriching a criminal enterprise," Adam said. "But I promise you, every business I've been involved in since then has been strictly legitimate."

Blaise felt as if a mist was clearing. At last she knew what Adam had really meant when he'd referred to his less than noble past.

"Actually, it was Agnes who straightened me out," he continued, smiling for the first time since he'd started his account. "In the end, I found myself on the receiving end of a major dressing-down. The worst part was when she said that my mother, who'd gone through hell on my behalf, would have been ashamed of me. That's when I knew I had to get away."

"What happened next?" Blaise prompted.

"I went to see Theo the day after, said I wanted out. He knew I'd never say a word about him or the rest of the family's activities because if I did, their payback would be ugly. But that wasn't the only reason I kept quiet."

Adam rubbed his chin thoughtfully. "Even though Theo is as crooked as they come, his relationship with me was always completely honest. I know it sounds strange, but I respected him."

Stretching, Adam set his back more firmly against the trunk of the oak. "After Paddy died, I called in to see Theo and pay my respects. The man was beside himself, as you'd expect. Right from the start he was convinced that the Tomassis were responsible for his brother's death. And, of course, he was well aware their favorite assassin was that scum Donny Artelli. Theo Ryan had Donny in his sights all along."

Adam's jaw tightened. "I never told Theo that his assumption was correct, but I freely admit I didn't encourage him to look elsewhere. How could I?"

Blaise steeled herself. She feared she was about to learn that Adam had done more than merely stay silent. "So Donny's murder . . ."

"Was fortuitous."

Blaise gave him a sharp look. That explanation wasn't nearly good enough for a decent reporter, not even for one who was desperately in love. "He was found wearing Paddy's gold watch, Adam," she said stiffly. "How do you explain that?"

He reached for the bottle and swallowed some more water. "While Superintendent O'Rourke's been on the take from the Ryans for years, Frank Tomassi's inside man was a sergeant at Newtown, the police station handling the investigation. I heard that this sergeant waited a couple of years until the case was declared cold, then lifted the watch from the evidence room and personally handed it to Frank. He probably figured he'd land himself a nice little bonus by delivering a valuable trophy. Donny was all too happy to take the credit for Paddy's murder, so Frank passed the watch on to him as a reward for services rendered. After that, well, events took their course."

Adam gazed into the distance. "The moment Donny Artelli started flashing around Paddy's gold watch, he might as well have signed his own death warrant."

"But how do you know this?" Blaise shivered. Hearing Adam speak in such a familiar way about Sydney's underworld was unnerving.

"You're not the only one who's ever cultivated mates in the police force," he said.

A shower of golden leaves floated down from the oak tree.

"I wish that was end of the story," Blaise muttered. The weight of her awful suspicions about Adam might have been lifted, but a sickening apprehension now settled upon her.

"When I first came to Eaton Square I told you Charlie's man in Australia had come up with a witness. That's why he had such a stranglehold over me." She'd fixed her eyes on a distant grove of trees that were beginning to display the vibrant crimson and orange of their autumn livery. "Whoever it is must still be out there."

Adam shook his head. "I don't believe a word of it. Ryan's men were all over the neighborhood after Paddy died, same as O'Rourke's officers. If someone really saw you or Joe, it would have come out at the time."

"Well then, how did Charlie find out what happened?"

"Look at the facts," Adam said. "There are only five people who know what went on that night. You and I have never spoken to anyone, and I would bet my life Agnes hasn't. Joe's always been too terrified, so we're left with the most obvious source—Pete Blackett. Most likely, he was sounding off after one too many in the pub and gave some garbled version to Charlie's man. Pete's always tended to cry in his beer during a spell of drinking. I can just imagine him going on about being a rotten father, and how his boy was in big trouble."

A spike of fear made Blaise flinch.

"Don't worry," Adam said, his voice low and reassuring. "With Charlie gone, there'll be no money coming this hired investigator's way. He hasn't any incentive to spill what he heard and, anyway, he'd have realized that Pete loves his son. Drunk or sober, if it came to a police inquiry, he'd never give Joe away. All Charlie's man has is pub talk that's strictly hearsay."

"I hope you're right," Blaise murmured.

"Trust me, O'Rourke won't take this any further. He's wrapped up the case and both he and his paymaster, Theo Ryan, have the result they wanted. It's over."

Blaise sighed deeply. After so many sleepless nights and days filled with worry, it seemed that the trauma and fear were finally behind her. She felt as light and as free as the oak leaves dancing in the breeze.

Adam hugged her to him, rubbing her back. "You're cold. Shall we go home?"

"In a few minutes." She took a breath. "There's something else we haven't talked about."

"Yes?"

"What happens next—to us, I mean?" Her stomach turned over when she saw Adam shrug. She desperately wanted to know how he felt, to have everything out in the open once and for all. But perhaps the timing was wrong. Maybe they'd already delved too deeply into troubling subjects.

"The mine is up and running, there's an excellent man I've left in charge and the whole enterprise is making a fortune. I'm looking at other mines in Australia, but there are investment opportunities here in the UK, too," Adam said.

That answer told her nothing.

"The truth is, though," he said softly, as the pale afternoon light reflected in his eyes, "what matters to me most is being with you. This past year, when I thought I'd never see you again, was close to intolerable. I guess what I'm trying to say is—I'm hopelessly in love with you."

Blaise realized she'd been holding her breath. Very slowly, she exhaled.

Adam leaned over and gently smoothed back her hair. "Going by the number of phone calls you've already had this morning, I'd say right now you're Fleet Street's most in-demand reporter. But quite frankly, I'll live wherever you want, whether it's here, in Australia—or Timbuktu." He put his arm around her. "I'll gladly marry you, Blaise, if that's what it takes, but if the idea doesn't appeal, well—hell, just stay with me anyway."

*Marry.* He'd said it so casually, dropped the word into a sentence as if it held no significance. Perhaps, after the wedded pretence imposed on his mother, it didn't mean much to him—but the world at large wouldn't feel the same way. Blaise frowned. This conversation would have to be set aside for another day.

"There's only one thing I'm certain of right now," she said. "I'll never be happy anywhere until I know that Ivy is all right." She stood up, brushing blades of grass from her jeans.

"Well, that makes for an easy decision," Adam said as they began to follow the path leading back to the main gates. "If you're able to organize some leave from the paper, we'll fly to Australia. Once we're in Sydney, I'll make sure Ivy is looked after by a top neurologist and receives all the therapy she needs. I've been supporting one of our leading hospitals for a while now—thought I might as well do something useful with my money."

Blaise threw her arms around Adam. "That's the best news ever! I can't imagine how to thank you."

"Really?" he said with a captivating smile. "I have a few ideas."

# CHAPTER FIFTY

*Sydney, March 1962*

Blaise sipped champagne with Adam by her side, her cornflower-blue eyes sparkling in the dappled sunlight as she took in the spirited scene, which, six months earlier, she'd have never thought possible. It had been her father's idea to hold the engagement party "right in the middle of Fotheringham Street," despite the backdrop of ramshackle houses and straggling trees.

When a passing cloud cast a momentary shadow, Blaise reached for Adam's hand. Shuddering, she recalled those first few harrowing days after they'd returned to Australia. Ivy had hovered between life and death. Seeing her sister lying so still and white had been even worse than when she'd been trapped in the iron lung with polio. Blaise had been overwhelmed by the fear that Ivy would never regain consciousness. But then there'd been the joyous milestones that had followed. Her sister opening her dark eyes for the first time, whispering her first words, taking her first faltering steps.

Harry had muttered shakily, "She's come back to us." Blaise and Maude had clung to each other, tears streaming down their cheeks. Since then, thanks to Ivy's fierce determination and the expert help Adam had arranged, she was almost back to her usual vivacious self. A slight hesitation in her speech was the only remaining evidence of the ordeal she had suffered.

"I know you feel bad about the stuff that's happened to me," she'd said haltingly to Blaise just before finally leaving the hospital. "But none of it was your fault. In any case, the way I look at it, I've given death the slip twice. Maybe three times, if you count the day we went for a dip at Nielsen Park," she added with a touch of her old cheek. "That must make me the luckiest girl alive."

Only then did Blaise realize that Ivy had never been a victim. Her sister was triumphant. She had won and won again, despite battling with the gravest circumstances. When Blaise had left her bedside that day she'd felt one more burden lift. Ivy herself had banished her guilt. It was a precious gift.

Once her sister had returned home, Ned had wasted no time. He'd dropped onto one knee, proposed, and been accepted immediately, although the pair had decided to postpone an announcement until Ivy was well enough to throw herself wholeheartedly into a party. At last that day had arrived, and everyone they knew had turned up to celebrate.

Rallied by old Mr. Crawford from the boarding house on the corner, that morning the neighbors had made a concerted effort to rid Fotheringham Street of its moldering rubbish. A small brigade of housewives had then swept it clean before their husbands set up roadblocks made from greengrocer's crates. Next, the families had heaved out their own furniture, so that weary revelers had chairs to sit on and heaped platters of food could be placed on a variety of kitchen tables. Blaise had helped set out the feast, which included Agnes Blackett's meat pies and Jean's lamingtons as well as the less familiar spicy salads and sweet pastries from the new Lebanese family across the way.

Now, beneath a bright cobalt sky and the red and yellow bunting Joe and Ned had strung up between Fotheringham Street's off-kilter telegraph poles, the party was in full swing. Blaise smiled as she saw Ivy, unselfconscious despite her metal caliper, moving from one group of friends to another as she laughed and chatted. She looked gorgeous, clad in the short red velvet Mary Quant dress Dora and Harriet had dispatched from London.

"It's our engagement present!" they'd squealed down the phone during another overseas call funded by the unsuspecting Major Fraser-Barclay-Hughes.

Blaise's heart soared. It was hard to believe that Ivy was the same girl who had spent so much of her short life in a hospital. Perhaps almost as miraculous, just a fortnight earlier Blaise had managed to entice her mother into the Exclusive Fashions floor of Sydney's leading department store. She looked around and spotted Maude standing beside a spindly bottlebrush tree while talking to Jean with an unusual degree of animation. Clad in peach silk chiffon and a matching straw hat, she would not have looked out of place at a royal garden party.

Adam squeezed Blaise's hand. "How are you feeling?"

"On cloud nine."

"Good. So you won't mind if I leave you for a moment and have a word with your boss? I'm interested to hear what McInerney thinks of the Labor Party's election chances."

"Go right ahead. As a matter of fact, someone I know is headed this way."

Edgar McInerney had arrived in Sydney the previous week, having been dispatched by Sir Ernest to report on his Australian operations. Somewhat curiously, Blaise reflected, it had also been deemed necessary for Marguerite Hawthorn to accompany him during this review.

Wearing a striking tangerine frock with a flared skirt and a black leather belt, she greeted Blaise with an arch expression on her face. "So," she observed, "I see you did have your eye on that handsome young man after all." Marguerite tilted her coiffed blonde head in Adam's direction. "By the way, did you ever uncover his mysterious past?"

"I did, actually."

Marguerite inserted a lit cigarette into her ebony holder and drew back. "I imagine that had its challenges."

"Did I hear you mention something about uncovering a mystery, Hill?" McInerney asked as he and Adam joined them. "Because the last thing Norton and I discussed before I left London was a new job for you. It's time your sleuthing abilities were more fully utilized."

"What did you have in mind?" Blaise smoothed her vivid blue, off-the-shoulder dress. She had learned from past experience not to try to guess what McInerney might say next.

He took off his horn-rimmed spectacles and slipped them into a coat pocket. "Something along the lines of a roving investigative reporter," he said. "I have a strong feeling there's at least one more big political scandal in the UK just waiting to break. I'm sure I don't have to tell you about the rumors concerning a second British politician—even more senior than Ashton—who's got himself mixed up with a Russian agent and an enticing young woman."

Blaise's eyes widened. A job like that would be the culmination of everything she'd hoped for. It was true, other newspapers had made tempting offers. But McInerney had taken a gamble on her, a sassy teenager from the wrong side of the tracks—and a girl at that. There was no way she'd let him down.

She glanced at Adam, wondering what he thought of McInerney's offer. Months had passed since their conversation in Kew Gardens, but what with the worry over Ivy, Adam flying around outback Australia scouting for new mines, and her own travel backward and forward from London, the future of their relationship had remained unresolved. The one thing she knew was that she didn't want to be any man's possession, not even if that man was Adam.

McInerney was still talking. "Anyway, turn it over in your mind. We can work out the details back in London." There were a dozen questions Blaise was dying to ask, but as Ned and Ivy had just wandered over she merely nodded her head.

Suddenly, the street was filled with a booming sound. "I should have known 'That's Amore' would be Tony Marcello's first choice of music," Ivy said with a giggle, straining to be heard above the noise pouring from Tony's enormous new speakers. "I can't believe that ridiculous track has ended up being our song."

Ned grinned. "Well, let's make the most of it." They moved away to a cleared area in the center of the street, where he held Ivy gently as he swayed her around.

"That's the most love-struck bloke I've ever seen," Harry announced before grabbing Maude, rounding up Ned's parents, and joining the happy couple.

Blaise turned to Adam. "Looks like it's our turn." As he took her in his arms, the lush music and the mood were so romantic it was all she could do not to reach up and kiss his lips. Then she found her arms were around his neck, she'd pulled him toward her and she was actually kissing him, right there in the middle of Fotheringham Street surrounded by everyone.

"If that's the effect he has on you, even I might have to start playing Dean Martin," Adam said, his face lit up by a delighted smile.

The mood altered abruptly after Ned called out, "Hey, Tony, how about spinning some of my discs?"

With the squeal of an electric guitar, dozens of guests started dancing energetically to the wild strains of Australia's own Johnny O'Keefe belting out "Shout." Soon, Ned and Ivy's friends and the Hill family's neighbors, Aunty Jean and the Marcellos' seven-year-old twins, the three Blacketts, Tommy Trent, and even Kev Kennedy, his bloodshot left eye wandering more wildly than ever since he'd downed numerous beers with his crime-writing mate Mike Morton, were whirling up and down the street in an ever-changing kaleidoscope of movement and color. Hats, jackets, coats, and ties were torn off and abandoned, along with any remaining inhibitions, as the rock and roll music of Chuck Berry, Buddy Holly, and Elvis Presley worked its magic.

The tempo underwent one more dramatic change when Tony sneaked in another of his own favorites and "Mambo Italiano" began playing. Suddenly, there was a flash of tangerine as Marguerite stalked forward with McInerney in tow and began a stylish Latin routine complete with expertly executed spins. The pair were quickly surrounded by a large circle of excited partygoers, stamping their feet as they clapped in time to the pulsating beat.

After a round of applause Blaise made her way over to Marguerite. "I see Adam is not the only one who's made a habit of keeping secrets," she said to her with a wink.

As the two women toasted each other with champagne, the magnificent waltz from *Swan Lake* began to float over the rundown neighborhood. It had been Blaise's only request. "Excuse me," she said. "I'm off to find my dancing partner."

Blaise sighed with pleasure as Adam began waltzing with her in the middle of Fotheringham Street with just as much ardor as he had in Buckingham Palace's ballroom. "I think you should know," he said, when the last dreamy notes faded, "that after this party is over I'm taking you for a drive."

Jean gave Blaise a quizzical look. "Adam's a fine man," she said. He had just left the two of them with a promise to return bearing slices of Gina Marcello's Italian chocolate cake and fresh glasses of the champagne he'd supplied.

"Yes, he is." Blaise had no intention of giving anything away. In any case, she had absolutely no idea what lay ahead for the two of them.

"Please don't take this the wrong way, Jean," she said, "but why didn't you ever marry?"

"I had my romances, don't you worry about that, but I always valued my independence too much," her godmother said tartly. "I like earning my own money, thank you very much, even if it's still nothing like what the blokes get. You're lucky to be paid the same wage as a man, but it only happens on the newspapers."

"Some of the politicians are talking about bringing in equal pay for all women."

Jean gave a snort of disgust. "Yes, and pigs might fly."

"You've turned out to be a bit of a dark horse," Blaise said. "Which makes me wonder—did Agnes Blackett ever tell you or Mum anything about Adam?"

"Oh yes, we knew the whole story, including the shameful way the boy was treated. Your mother and I were the only ones she's ever confided in."

Blaise was shocked. "So that's why Mum always went on about being wary of the rich and entitled." She understood her mother better now.

Jean nodded. "It's not surprising Adam took the odd wrong turn along the way. But look what he's made of himself. He's a credit to his mother—and to Agnes." She gave Blaise another look. "What's going on between you two, anyway?"

"Shhh." Blaise smiled. "I think Dad's about to say a few words."

Pete Blackett helped Harry up onto a greengrocer's crate standing right in front of 68 Fotheringham Street. Behind him, the shabby home's freshly painted yellow door glowed in the late afternoon sunlight. Harry squinted at the crowd as he waited for the exuberant guests to settle down.

"There's no need to introduce myself," he said when their noise had died away. "You all know me and my wife."

Maude gave a regal wave.

"And you also know why I'm standing up here, probably looking like a bit of a galah," he continued. "It's because Maude and I want to thank you for helping us celebrate Ivy and Ned's engagement."

There were cheers and the beating of hands upon tables.

"Once, a long time ago now, our eldest and I were talking about the only ways to climb out of Enmore. For those who don't know, that's via one of the four Ps. There's a pugilist, what you'd call a pro fighter, joining the police—though hopefully not like a few from round here—or else entering the priesthood. The problem was, none of them were any use to a girl."

"Good one, Harry," someone called out.

"And then," he continued, "last but not least, there's the press. Well, turns out that's the one that's come through for the Hill family. I'm pleased to say that not only is Ivy engaged to *The*

*Clarry*'s new crime reporter, clever young Ned, but she's also been offered a job on the same paper working as a sketch artist. Ivy will be drawing the crims and the legal men who turn up at the law courts, but she tells me she might just get to do the odd illustration for the Women's Pages."

Fotheringham Street rang with hearty applause, interspersed with cries of "Good luck, Ivy" and "Well done!"

"Wait on, you lot." Harry held up one hand as he smiled. "I haven't mentioned Blaisey yet. She's proved herself a real shooting star, covering the royal family, no less, as well as a big spy story over in London."

By now, Harry was beaming. "I couldn't be prouder of what our two girls have achieved. Which just goes to show that maybe Enmore—rough, tough, and rowdy as it is—wasn't such a bad place to grow up in, after all."

# CHAPTER FIFTY-ONE

It was nearly sunset when Blaise slipped into Adam's sleek car. "So, am I allowed to know where we're going?" she asked.

"I think you'll work it out pretty quickly."

As the city's thrusting office towers, the voluptuous curve of the harbor, and then the neat suburbs were left far behind, they passed into a more exotic landscape where slender eucalypts sheltered lush ferns and coiling vines. "Palm Beach," Blaise said. "I should have guessed."

Gazing at the foam-tipped breakers and shadowy headlands, she reflected upon the past two extraordinary years she'd spent in London. She was no longer just that feisty girl from Enmore: her innocence had been exchanged for something more complex.

"Buckingham Palace seems a very long way from dear old Fotheringham Street or, for that matter, this tropical paradise," she said.

"I'll never forget the moment I saw you in the queen's ballroom." Adam turned the steering wheel as he navigated the winding road. "I'd been preoccupied, kicking myself about the clumsy way I'd treated you, and suddenly, there you were, this ravishing woman—looking like the proverbial dream come true."

"I was a bit stunned myself, not that I had any intention of letting on." Blaise smiled. "One way or another, it was an eventful evening. Did you know that the Duchess of Buccleuch's emerald brooch disappeared?"

"I seem to remember reading an excellent report about it written by *The Advocate*'s royal correspondent," Adam said as he rounded a bend.

Blaise giggled. "I'm sure Cecil Beaton was hoping one of Armstrong-Jones's pals would be blamed. God knows, Tony has his faults, but Cecil was scalding."

"Your friend Mr. Beaton wasn't dubbed Malice in Wonderland for nothing," Adam said drily.

"But what do you think really happened?" Blaise asked. "Reporters don't like loose ends, you know."

A pensive expression passed across Adam's face. "Some secrets take a long time to be revealed," he said.

They continued in silence, both preoccupied by their thoughts.

"Hey!" Twisting abruptly, Blaise pointed over her shoulder. "Weren't we meant to turn off back there? You know, so we can walk on the beach."

"I finally had the house sorted out." Adam took one hand from the wheel and let it rest on her knee. "So, luckily for us, we don't need the boatshed."

Blaise removed his hand. "Oh, but we do."

"Why's that?"

"Because I can't think of anywhere else I'd rather be alone with you."

"Well in that case . . ." Adam swung the car around, returning to exactly the same place where he'd parked the first time they visited Palm Beach. As he opened Blaise's door, she inhaled the intoxicating tang of the sea.

Once again, they strolled barefoot on the cool sand, although instead of the sultry darkness Blaise remembered, the light from a full moon played on the water, scattering white fragments on the ripples of iridescent green.

Adam unlocked the door and Blaise followed him inside. He lit the oil lamp, then pushed the windows wide open.

"I see the brandy's still here, and the rug," she said. "A bit dusty, aren't they?"

Adam gave her a wry look. "I didn't have the heart to come back and take them away."

They sat down on the familiar corduroy couch. "Maybe we should have a drink to celebrate our return," he suggested.

"Not now." She didn't want anything to cloud her experience of Adam, of this place, of this night.

He took Blaise's face in his hands and brought it close to his own. "Well, as I'm determined to make up for the last visit, I should probably warn you . . ." He paused while he kissed her. "I might have to undress you again."

She ran her fingers through his dark hair. "You told me then that I deserved a better man, but you were wrong. There *is* no better man than you—not for me."

Adam looked into her eyes with his silvery gaze. "Ever since that day in Kew Gardens," he said in his beautiful voice, "I've been hoping you would give me an answer to my question. As you haven't, before I make passionate love to you—which this time I fully intend to do—I'm going to ask you once more. Do you think you might consider staying with me, on whatever terms you would like?"

"Well, that would depend on the length of our agreement." She smiled. "How long were you thinking?"

"Forever," he said.

Later, much later, as they lay entwined in each other's arms, Blaise listened to the music of the ocean. There was no roaring, no pounding, not now. The waves moved to a different rhythm, rolling forward as softly as breath, on and on and on.

# AUTHOR'S NOTE

Where does the spark that compels you to write a book come from? It might be something as ephemeral as a photograph in a newspaper, a brief conversation overheard on a bus, or an intriguing exchange taking place between strangers while you're waiting in line at the local cafe. But sometimes inspiration derives from the people you've known all your life.

By the end of my late father's days he had received two knighthoods from the queen, one from the pope, another from the president of the Philippines, and various other impressive accolades. Among his organizational feats, all conducted on an honorary basis, were numerous royal celebrations, a papal tour, a visit by a US president, and the opening of the Sydney Opera House. He was a regional newspaper publisher, a long-term member of the NSW state parliament, and wrote the distinguished tome *Australian Protocols and Procedure*. All this was achieved by a man from a poverty-stricken family, a man who had left school at the tender age of fourteen to work on Sydney's *Daily Telegraph*.

Growing up, I was enthralled by his exciting, sometimes hilarious and at times touching stories of both the world of journalism and the pre-gentrified, tough inner city. More recently, I began to reflect on how these experiences shaped his remarkable life. Then I found myself wondering: what if he had been born a girl? What vast challenges would that girl have faced, and who might she have become?

This was the starting point for *The Royal Correspondent*. The street that my heroine, Blaise Hill, grew up on was the street where Dad lived. The pranks that were played on her when she was a copy boy were played on him. Likewise, he was the recipient of much of the advice *The Clarry*'s reporters passed on. His own father—named Harry, just like Blaise's fictional dad—told him about "the four Ps."

I was drawn to the era of the early 1960s, as it was a time of tremendous change. In 1960, there was widespread shock when Princess Margaret married not merely a commoner—the first daughter of a king to do so in 400 years—but an unconventional photographer. In retrospect, this seems a particularly potent symbol of the upheavals to come, yet, at the time, Great Britain was a society still largely governed by deeply conservative pre-war, some would say Edwardian, ideas—as was Australia. Just a few years later, the Swinging Sixties were well and truly underway, miniskirts were all the rage, women began demanding greater equality and, thanks to the advent of the Pill, embraced sexual freedom. The traditional class structure was also challenged by the widespread impact of a dynamic group of rebellious young people—musicians, writers, artists, filmmakers, and designers—who dominated contemporary culture during this wildly experimental decade.

With its explosive combination of sex, drugs, class, and espionage, the Profumo Affair rocked Britain and even its far-flung former colony, Australia. This scandal, together with the defection of several upper-class British spies to the Soviet Union, prompted ever more Britons to question whether those at the top of society deserved the automatic respect they had previously commanded.

John Profumo was forced to resign from the office of Secretary of State for War, from Parliament and from the Privy Council in June 1963, when it was revealed he had lied to the House of Commons about his affair with Christine Keeler. This followed Keeler's sale to the Mirror Group—for two hundred pounds—of an incriminating letter Profumo had written to her. It was this transaction that provided the inspiration for the scene in which Keeler sells a scandalous letter to Blaise.

Profumo's liaison was never proved to have led to any breach of national security. He steadfastly maintained complete public silence on the subject while devoting himself to charity for the rest of his life. Christine Keeler, having served time in prison for perjury connected to separate circumstances, died in 2017 at the age of seventy-five. Contrary to Charlie Ashton's prediction, she has proved to be an enduring cultural icon, aided by recent on-screen depictions and an alluring photograph of her taken in 1963 by Lewis Morley, for which she posed while straddling a chair, seemingly naked.

I included other scenes in the book, ranging from the infamous Kennedy dinner at Buckingham Palace to that crucial Cold War event, the building of the Berlin Wall, in order to illuminate the tectonic social and political shifts taking place in the world at that time.

With the possible exception of the queen, the British royal family may no longer attract veneration. However, one only has to consider the huge success of television series *The Crown* and the countless news stories devoted to the unorthodox Duke and Duchess of Sussex alone, otherwise known as Prince Harry and Meghan Markle, to know that royal activities continue to intrigue millions of people around the world. Delving into a largely hidden 1960s realm of veiled power and influence led me to reflect upon just how much has changed.

In these days of rampant social media and tell-all exposés, I found it fascinating to look back on the way high-profile scandals could be kept hidden. For instance, although Antony Armstrong-Jones (later Lord Snowdon) was indeed the father of a child born three weeks after his marriage to Princess Margaret in 1960, he did not publicly acknowledge his parentage of Polly Fry until it was confirmed by DNA testing in 2004.

Other establishment secrets were also buried. My inspiration for the British government's plan to allow one of the book's characters to live on in respectable obscurity, despite having spied for the USSR, was Sir Anthony Blunt. In 1964, Blunt was offered complete immunity in return for his full confession. He was even permitted to continue in his prestigious role of Surveyor of the Queen's Pictures, until his unsavory past was eventually revealed in the British Parliament by Margaret Thatcher in 1979.

Certain aspects of the monarchy have remained unchanged

since the days of Queen Victoria. In 1867, the British constitutionalist Walter Bagehot famously wrote: "The Sovereign has three rights: the right to be consulted, the right to encourage, the right to warn." It is of course the third right that the queen utilizes to such effect in *The Royal Correspondent*. One can only speculate as to which issues she is warning Britain's current prime minister about.

The technique of "gaslighting" takes its name from a 1938 play and two later films. I have referred to the best known, the 1944 version starring Ingrid Bergman. This insidious form of emotional abuse slowly undermines victims, so that they question their lived reality, their judgment, and often their sanity. The US-based psychologist Dr. Elinor Greenberg contends that there are three main forms of gaslighting in romantic relationships: hiding objects, so that the victim doubts herself; changing something about the victim so that she loses self-esteem and begins to conform to the perpetrator's fantasy; and separating the victim from friends and family in order to heighten control. Gaslighting also entails misdirection, emotional blackmail, and outright lies, more often than not combined with a disarming degree of charm.

I thought it was important to show how a determined and highly manipulative man could undermine even an intelligent, spirited woman like Blaise, exploiting her isolation, inexperience, and insecurity. Sadly, the practice (which is not gender specific) continues to be widespread, not only in romantic but also in professional and, increasingly, political spheres.

On a lighter note, it was huge fun to delve into the world of late-1950s and early 1960s fashion. Both the Christian Dior and British Cotton Board parades took place at David Jones, attracting widespread publicity. The research I conducted for my last book, *The Paris Model*, provided some fabulous additional material regarding the 1957 Dior show in Australia. The fine exhibition held by the National Gallery of Victoria to mark the seventieth anniversary of the House of Dior's establishment was particularly helpful in this regard. That the great Dior's first and last collec tions were both shown in remote Australia seemed so unlikely and so special that I had to include them.

Mary Quant became an international fashion leader during the 1960s, and is widely credited with inventing the miniskirt. I visited the first Mary Quant retrospective exhibition, held in London's V&A Museum in 2019, and was struck by the freshness and originality of her designs. The descriptions of her extraordinary shop windows were inspired by her autobiography.

A host of other real events found their way into *The Royal Correspondent*. To name just a few: the famous Buccleuch emerald brooch did disappear on the night of Her Majesty's pre-wedding ball for Princess Margaret; Cecil Beaton, dubbed Malice in Wonderland by Jean Cocteau, was a distinguished wartime photographer (the queen herself recommended him to the Ministry of Information); and, tragically, there was a polio epidemic in Australia in 1956. Also, Yves Saint Laurent was conscripted into the French army in 1960. He lasted for only nineteen days before suffering a nervous breakdown. His own, legendary label was established the following year.

For the sake of the narrative, I was obliged to move back by a few months the announcement of the architect selected by the NSW government to design the Sydney Opera House. Likewise, the Soviet military attaché, Yvegeny Ivanov, was not among those frolicking in Cliveden's infamous swimming pool on the night John Profumo first set eyes on Christine Keeler, but took to the water with her on the following morning.

I awarded Ghana's first president, Kwame Nkrumah, a solo royal reception hosted by Her Majesty because Ghana was the first of Britain's African colonies to gain independence—another sign of the times.

Astonishingly, the ban on married women working for the Australian Public Service (which was vigorously supported by unions) continued until 1966.

During the period in which *The Royal Correspondent* is set, the official basic wage for women was an appalling 75 percent of the male wage. Journalism may have been an exception but, as Blaise discovers, in practice women were almost exclusively shunted into working only for the women's pages. This both hampered any chance of advancement and ensured female journalists were frequently on a lower pay grade than their male counterparts. Shockingly, an equal minimum wage, regardless of sex, was not legislated for all jobs until 1973, although, nearly five decades on, whether the gender pay gap has ever been adequately addressed remains doubtful.

The discriminatory White Australia Policy Harriet encountered was first legislated in 1901. Significant reforms took place in 1966, although it, too, was not formally abolished until 1973.

I was lucky to trail around after Dad when I was a child, visiting several smoky newsrooms in which journalists still pounded on typewriters, looking on as hot metal was set by printers and, of course, watching in awe while the huge presses spun out fresh newspapers. Those memories remain vivid, though over time they have become blended with my father's anecdotes so that I no longer know what I saw and what I was told. Fortunately, a number of highly experienced journalists, past and present, were able to assist regarding many common practices. However, as these varied from newspaper to newspaper, I selected the examples that best served Blaise's story.

It was a treat to walk in her shoes, first in Fotheringham Street, Enmore, and then in a variety of other locations in Sydney and London. Rest assured, if Blaise visited the ballroom at Buckingham Palace, watched ladies enjoying tea at the Ritz Hotel, wandered through Green Park, stood in the Kings Road in front of Mary Quant's first boutique, visited Westminster Abbey and the Houses of Parliament, or took in Bath and the Cotswolds, then I did too. This "on the ground" aspect of the research was such a pleasure that it was difficult to convince myself I was actually working! Becoming lost in books and newspaper accounts of the period plus conducting a wide range of interviews (credited in the acknowledgments) also proved as fascinating as it was useful.

When it came to Fleet Street, I was fortunate to receive an illuminating personal tour from the distinguished journalist, editor, and media executive Stephen Claypole. His vivid descriptions of the "Street of Shame" in its heyday, the buzz of London newsrooms, and the atmosphere of the many pubs patronized by the great newspapers' thousands of thirsty employees were invaluable.

I am indebted to the outstanding women who forged their way in journalism at the same time as my heroine. The darkroom scene, which was inspired by the experience of Jillian Rice, is but one example of the abuse and prejudice they routinely encountered. That so many went on to establish important careers is a testament to their grit, talent, and determination. This book is a tribute to those pioneering women and the many that have followed in their footsteps.

# ACKNOWLEDGMENTS

A huge thank-you to my publisher, Anna Valdinger, who embraced *The Royal Correspondent* with enthusiasm right from my very first, sketchy outline. She then continued to give the book her boundless expertise and unstinting support while contending with all the challenges of lockdowns and isolation. My thanks also go to Alex Craig for her invaluable structural edit and to Fiona Daniels for an insightful and inspiring copy edit, plus to Nicola Young for her scrupulous proofreading.

The HarperCollins team were, as always, a dream to work with: senior designer Hazel Lam created another stunning cover; senior editor Scott Forbes devoted careful attention to both text and production; and campaign manager Jo Munroe and all the account managers have been fabulous champions.

Special thanks to my agent, Catherine Drayton, for her wisdom and guidance and for making sure that my books find their way to readers around the world.

I am so fortunate that my father both shared stories with me and wrote an unpublished account of his colorful newspaper experiences. They have been extraordinarily vivid resources.

I am also grateful for the generosity of numerous outstanding journalists. All contributed stories ranging in nature from the hilarious to the downright shocking, plus a host of technical details. As describing their stellar careers would easily fill many pages, I have mentioned only those aspects that relate directly to this book.

Tony Delano, over ninety and as quick and witty as ever, worked as the Fleet Street–based correspondent for the now-defunct Melbourne newspaper *The Argus* during the late 1950s before joining London's *Daily Mirror*; Anne Woodham began her newspaper career in Sydney on the *Daily Telegraph*'s women's pages before relocating to the *London Evening News*; legendary editor Ita Buttrose was another graduate of the *Daily*

*Telegraph*'s women's pages; Robin Amadio, a long-time reporter of the social scene, also started at the *Daily Telegraph*; following a cadetship on the *Maitland Mercury*, Jillian Rice became one of the few female journalists to bypass the women's pages and work solely in the newsrooms of the *Daily Telegraph*, the *Mirror* (albeit as Women's Editor), and *The Australian*; Stephen Claypole was a journalist at the *London Evening News* and the *Daily Express* during the 1960s; David Dale provided memories of times past at the *Sydney Morning Herald* and of life as a foreign correspondent, plus kindly lent me his rare 1965 copy of *The Journalist's Craft* (edited by Lindsay Revill and Colin Roderick); and Susan Williams was formerly the women's editor at the *Daily Mirror*, and still writes a fine lead.

Among the fascinating books I relied on for material regarding the Royal Family were: *Princess Margaret: A Life of Contrasts* by Christopher Warwick; *The Wicked Wit of Princess Margaret* compiled by Karen Dolby; *Ma'am Darling* by Craig Brown; *Lady in Waiting: My Extraordinary Life in the Shadow of the Crown* by Anne Glenconner; and *Snowdon: The Biography* by Anne de Courcy. *An English Affair* by Richard Davenport-Hines provided a trove of information on the Profumo scandal and British life in the early 1960s.

The fashion scenes were helped greatly by: *In Vogue: Sixty Years of Celebrities and Fashion from British Vogue* by Georgina Howell; *Christian Dior: The Man Who Made the World Look New* by Marie-France Pochna; *Dior in Vogue* by Brigid Keenan; *Quant by Quant* by Mary Quant; and *Yves Saint Laurent: A Biography* by Alice Rawsthorn. Other particularly useful publications included: *The Sixties* by Arthur Marwick; *My Paper Chase: True Stories of Vanished Times* by Harold Evans; *Gossip: 1920–1970* by Andrew Barrow; *Buckingham Palace* by Pamela Hartshorne; *Toward the End of the Morning* by Michael Frayn; and "Fleet Street at Closing Time," an article first published on March 6, 1988, in the *Observer*.

A big shout-out to my early readers and great friends Jane de Teliga, Susan Williams, and Lyndel Harrison, together with my beautiful daughter-in-law, Anna Reoch. There are so many ways you helped make this a much better book—and provided me with endless encouragement.

My family, particularly my dear mother, Sybil, and my fabulous children, Bennett and Arabella, never failed to buoy me up throughout the writing process, as did my husband, Philip. He also remains my favorite man with whom to share tea at the Ritz.

Deepest appreciation goes to the enthusiastic booksellers who have given my books so much support. Despite the many challenges of operating in a pandemic, you have been wonderful!

Most important of all, many thanks to all my readers. I love seeing you at events—virtual and actual—and am incredibly grateful for your fantastic messages. It is a joy to share the lives of my characters with you.

Photograph by Juli Balla

Alexandra Joel is a former editor of the Australian edition of *Harper's Bazaar* and *Portfolio*, Australia's first magazine for working women. She has also contributed feature articles, interviews, and reviews to many national and metropolitan publications.

Her first novel, the bestselling *The Paris Model*, was published around the world, including in the United States, Canada, Germany, and Romania. Alexandra's memoir, *Rosetta: A Scandalous True Story* was optioned for the screen by a major US-owned production company. She is also the author of *Parade: The Story of Fashion in Australia* and *Best Dressed: 200 Years of Fashion in Australia*.

With an honors degree from the University of Sydney and a graduate diploma from the Australian College of Applied Psychology, she has been a practicing counselor and psychotherapist.

Alexandra has two children, lives in Sydney, and regularly visits London with her British-born husband.

To connect with Alexandra, visit:

AlexandraJoel.com

**f** @AlexandraJoelAuthor

**◉** @AlexandraJoelAuthor